I0542526

Two Roads East

Philip Montgomery

Copyright © 2012 Philip Montgomery

All rights reserved.

ISBN: 0987051717

ISBN-13: 9780987051714

All rights reserved. This publication (or any part of it) may not be reproduced or transmitted, copied, stored, distributed or otherwise made available by any person or entity, in any form (electronic, digital, optical, mechanical) or by any means (photocopying, recording, scanning or otherwise) without prior written permission from the publisher. The moral right of the author has been asserted.

Layout and map by Tango Media Pty Ltd, Sydney.

www.tworoadseast.com

This book is a work of fiction. The names, characters, places and events in this book are a product of the author's imagination or have been used fictitiously and are not to be construed as real. Any resemblance to real persons, living or dead, actual events, locale or organisations is purely coincidental.

Prologue

Think back to the year nineteen ninety seven. Think of a world without television, without mobile phones and the internet, where a telephone line to the outside world relies on luck and the goodwill of an operator. Think mountains and mists and ancient traditions, and a country just opening its doors to the world after centuries of isolation. You've thought of Bhutan in the 16th Year of the Fire Ox, and like Sophie Vella you may need a map to imagine this tiny Himalayan Kingdom when an unexpected journey beckons.

Astrologers would say that Sophie, a Washington human rights lawyer prone to big bold decisions, and Steve Andrews, an over-travelled, over-worked roads engineer who has lost the idea of home, 'had the moon and stars aligned for them'. After all, 1997 was auspiciously 'the year of overcoming difficult things'. And so, two different roads they took so long ago must join again.

In this adventure of love, lies and deceit, there is more than just long-ago lover's angst lurking in this last Shangri-La. A multi-million dollar fraud on the biggest international aid project in the country, Two Roads East, is blamed on Steve and if he can't prove his innocence the brutal Hangrila gaol will be his new home. But, after all this time, Sophie has other plans...

Contents

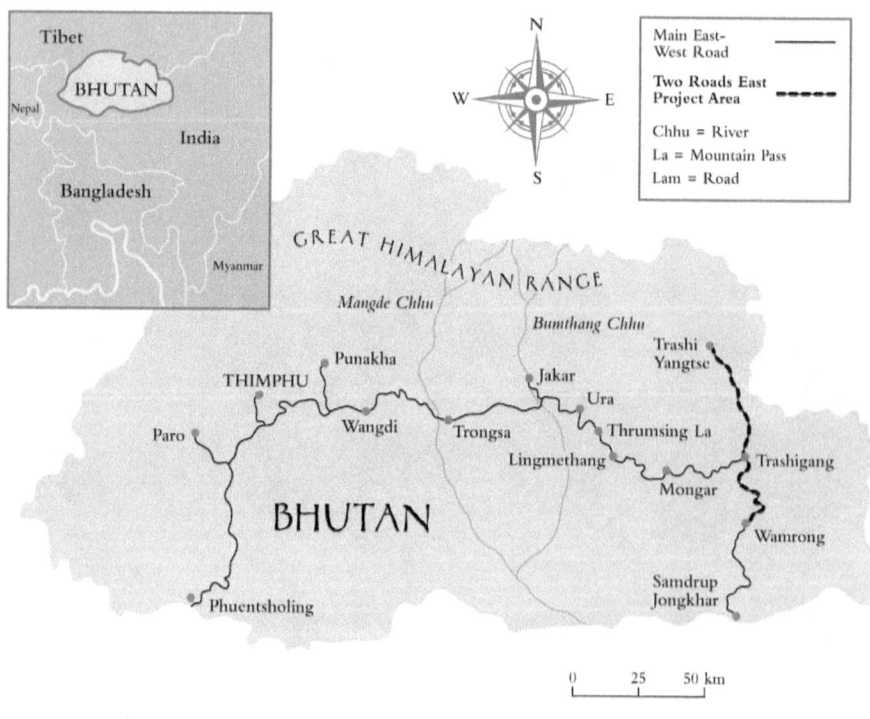

1: *The letter in his pocket*

TRANSARCO
Engineering for a developing world

8th September, 1997

Mr. Stephen Andrews
Roads and Bridges Division

<u>Re: What the hell is going on?</u>

Steve,

You're lucky I'm travelling and wasn't able to track you down by phone.

Have you been asleep at the wheel? I don't know what you've let happen over there, but the Bank's auditors have raided our Sydney office and are going through every project for the last ten years – Ellen tells me there's archive boxes stacked to the ceiling. All we're doing is answering their bloody questions. There's serious talk of a black-listing. Let me remind you what that means: our reputation, built over fifty years, in tatters; contracts cancelled; hundreds of jobs lost, including yours and mine; and stock-holders worldwide looking for someone to blame for their losses.

The Board's already asking for a scalp over this one and it won't be mine. I'll tell you this once only - fix TWO ROADS EAST, stay there until you do, or face me when you get back with your resignation signed. On second thoughts, mail your resignation from gaol.

No discussion, no excuses, just bloody fix it.

Terry Bradshaw
Vice President

2: *An unexpected journey*

On the wrong side of midnight, Sophie flung open her front door, dumped her bags, kicked off her shoes and ran to the answering machine. Thank god, the green light was blinking. Now, just let it be a message from Marie. An impatient finger hit the play button. Relief and anger mingled as music and laughter smothered the voice she wanted to hear. Finally, thank god again, she heard her daughter's voice. But, it sounded as though Marie was calling from a bar, her mood more defiant than apologetic.

Sophie turned on the lights and played the message again. Within moments she was shrieking, "How could she! How could she?" When it dawned that Marie hadn't left a phone number, that there was no right of reply, Sophie launched into a mad, one-sided rant at the answering machine and hit it with her fist when it wouldn't talk back. She sobbed, she shouted, she soul-searched and she slept on the lounge until the first jab of morning light reminded her that she was expected at work at eight.

Sophie showered and dressed, poured herself a cup of strong coffee and replayed Marie's message.

'Hey Mom, it's me. No need to worry, I'm fine, it was all a mix up, I was never missing, I just didn't tell anyone I was leaving. I guess you know by now I'm in Byron Bay; a small beachside town that's about as far east as Australia goes. It's a tourist spot, famous for its surfing, alternative culture and all that, but I'm sure you know that's not why I'm here. I've already tracked Steve down, and don't worry I haven't let on who I am. He's not here right now. He's in Asia somewhere, working, he'll be back in under a month and Mom it's crunch time; that's how long you have to find him and tell him about me, otherwise he's in for one heck of a shock when he gets home. I'll just walk up to him at the airport nearby here and introduce myself as the daughter he never knew he had. I know you don't want that Mom, and I know you'll never just call him, that you think this sort of tough news should be delivered in person. So do it Mom, it's time. He still works for that big multinational, TRANSARCO, that's a start and with all your contacts there in Washington it should be easy enough to find out where he is right now. I've gotta run, no hard feelings huh, this is what I had to do, it's my right and I've waited about eighteen years too long for it. Oh! Nearly forgot, I'm trying out for a job at the BeachFront Hotel tomorrow morning. After, I'll get a card for my cell phone and let you know a number you can call me on. Love you, Mom, byyee'.

With thoughts of blackmail screaming through her head, and already running late for work, she searched the highest shelf of her closet for a shoebox and retrieved a small tapestry covered photo album and a black travel journal all bound together with string. She placed the bundle in her briefcase and prepared herself for a day of big decisions.

At lunchtime in her fifth floor office she told her PA that she didn't want to be disturbed and closed her door. She undid a knot of string that hadn't been loosened for years and flicked through a few pages of the album, stopping at a photo taken in 1978. Centerpiece were two young lovers, in the background was a place she knew every acre of; the vineyards of her early life rolling in a summer haze to the horizon. She cast thoughts of what could have been aside and focused on Steven Andrews. Now she was desperate to know everything she could about him, just who was he nineteen years on from that perfectly captured day?

It took just one call to reveal that this engineer who specialized in building roads in far flung places was leaving China within days and was heading towards the Himalayan Kingdom of Bhutan where he would be working for two weeks. Was it possible for her to get from Washington to Bhutan before he left there? Possible! She had no choice now; her own impossible, head-strong daughter had seen to that. And yes, Marie was right about one thing, there are times in one's life when a telephone call just won't do - and this was one of them, she'd deliver her news to Steve face-to-face; however painful that might be. After an hour's research she decided that The Kingdom of Bhutan, this Last Shangri-La, had a certain mystique about it, appropriate even to the nature of her task.

An hour later she was on the phone to Mountain Adventures, New York. She'd already called three others that specialized in Himalayan adventure travel and they'd just laughed at the thought of arranging a trip to Bhutan inside of a week. But fourth time lucky, after she'd explained what she wanted to do the owner of Mountain Adventures sounded just as relieved as she was, 'A lucky day for both of us ma'am, we've had a late cancellation, an accident. One seat only, the tour's been booked out since June'. Perfect, Sophie thought until she compared Steve's itinerary with the details she'd jotted down from Mountain Adventures. They'd be on the same flight from Bangkok to Paro, and after nineteen years, a meeting in a crowded airplane was not part of her plan. She stifled a desperate urge to panic, noticed that Steve was booked into economy and picked up the telephone again to change her flight to business class — she'd avoid him, and then arrange a coincidental meeting within their first couple of days in Bhutan. Sophie hadn't worked out how this would come about, but the fine detail often came to her on the spot, she'd worry about that later.

All that was left to do now was to tell her boss Alex, who was also her ex-husband, that she was taking over a week's leave in less than a week's time. She expected him to explode in anger, but she was used to that. She'd manage it. Knowing him, he'd probably laugh when he heard that Marie had, without telling a soul, departed her gap-year Indonesian language studies in Bali to hop on a flight to Brisbane, then a bus to Byron Bay to wait out her father's return. Sophie didn't need reminding of how many times Alex had said to her to get over it, to tell Steve they had a daughter and to work it out from there. In his words, Sophie had chained herself to a problem and thrown away the key. Only she knew differently. How, when Marie was still very young, she'd swallowed her pride for her daughter's sake to make contact with Steve. How, when a letter to Steve was returned unopened, she'd called his parents' number, the only phone number she had for him, and how she'd been answered by Steve's brother Bill. How lost she'd felt when Bill had scoffed, 'Christ, not another one he's got up the duff. I don't know where he is now, last I heard he's shacked up with a journalist on the coast somewhere. If you want my advice, forget the bastard. We have.'

While she waited for Alex to call her back, she picked up her well worn journal to reconnect with three months she spent with Steve in 1978, backpacking through Central America. The encounter with her then twenty-year-old-self, she had to admit, was challenging. It left her in no doubt that her arguments with her own parents, and her impetuous decisions, mirrored her daughter's. And as much as she hated to admit it, Marie's extreme measures were perhaps a fitting response to her own extreme procrastination.

As the phone rang she closed the journal at a page she'd scrawled on the long way home from Costa Rica without the man she loved.

October 23rd, 1978

An hour out of San Jose, on my way home
...now, miles from the bus stop, the driver's been forced to take a detour off the highway ... only the dust that hurtles up behind me can block out what's happened.

I've taken the long way home - to put three months of heaven followed by thirty hours of hell into some rational form, to come up with possible answers.

But the idea of 'rationality' can't exist right now. The only idea that keeps slipping in and out of my mind is a quote I once read,

'The cruelest lies are told in silence.'

Was it a lie? I still don't know, but I do know that I don't do 'silence' well! I found that out yesterday when all my pleading, all my tears, only got me a ticket on this bus...and all that's left in the space between yesterday and today is two roads; the one I'm on North and the one Steve's on, South.

3: Welcome onboard Druk Air

Sophie sweltered as the small airplane sat motionless on the tarmac in Bangkok. She held Steve's itinerary and stared at the line she'd highlighted; he was in Seat 14B, in Economy. She pictured him sitting back there, comfortably unaware of who'd just joined him on the flight. Her smug thoughts were short-lived: the music stopped and the intercom crackled to life. "Druk Air apologizes for the delay. We're waiting for a passenger on a connecting flight from Beijing."

A passenger coming in from Beijing! Steve's been in China. She scanned his itinerary again and found Thursday, September 25, 1997. There it was, he was on the early Thai flight; the early flight that was now late. And she'd waited deliberately long to be last to board, now she was sitting in an aisle seat and he was going to pass within inches. What would she do if he recognized her?

She grabbed for her sunglasses, put them on and straightaway sweat stung her eyes. She dared not wipe them, and she waited. God it was hot! Why didn't they start the damn airconditioning?

Her eyes were riveted on the heat-soaked blacktop outside when she heard the airhostess speak to someone. She glanced up and saw a tall dark-haired man stooping to enter the cabin. She snatched Tuesday's *Washington Post* from her lap and buried her face in it. She listened hard and her heart raced. She heard the hostess's cheery welcome and as soon as he spoke she knew it was him. She held her breath and prayed. The hostess greeted Steve like a long-lost friend. They were standing right beside her, chatting about where he'd been and how long it was since his last trip to Bhutan. His voice hadn't changed. He moved and his hand almost touched her shoulder. Seconds passed, but it stretched to a lifetime until she overheard. "Fourteen B, your usual seat, is waiting for you, Mr. Steve." Still Sophie dared not breathe. She held the *Post* so close the newsprint was a blur. Then the hostess opened the curtain to the economy cabin and Steve moved through.

Sophie exhaled in a sigh and let her shoulders slump. With deliberate care, she lowered the newspaper and looked up and down the empty aisle. A Japanese businessman was staring at her behind black-rimmed spectacles so thick his eyes were pinpoints. She smiled. His mouth stayed a straight line. She waited until she heard the airplane engines roar and felt the air-conditioning kick in. Only then did she turn the pages of the newspaper she'd been avoiding. Amongst yet more tributes to a life cut short, she flicked past article after article on the on-going investigations into the car crash that had claimed the life of Princess Diana.

She found the 'Around Town' column that she'd been warned about on page 7, and what she started reading about herself was worse than she'd imagined it would be. 'Talk in the cor-ridors of the State Department has it that Sophie Vella, newly appointed...' And under the double column of gossip was the photograph that she'd hoped they'd lost: the caption stung just like it did the first time she read it. Sophie hardly noticed the airplane lift off and the disarray of the sprawling city below her was no match for the disarray in her head — which was filled with the telephone conversation she'd had with Marie, what was it, two days ago now. Sophie still couldn't believe how casual Marie was about the whole thing, she'd been more concerned about her new job waiting tables at some hotel by the beach, and how she was taking surfing lessons, than she was about the ticking time-bomb she'd lobbed through her moth-er's open window. And when she'd chided Marie about call-ing Steve's home, Marie's retort was immediate and cocksure; 'Mom, their house overlooks a headland, you can see it from the beach. I watched them for a few days to work out that there was no man around the house and that Steve's wife left for two or three hours at the same time each afternoon. I just waited for her to go out and the boys to come home from school and I rang pretending to be from Steve's travel company, just wanting to double-check on his travel plans. Huh, it was so easy, teenage boys are a giveaway if you know how to talk to them.' Even now, days after the event, Sophie choked on the thought that Marie had dared speak to her half-brother. At the time Sophie had been speechless, all she'd managed to say was, 'Please don't do it again,' but she'd be more forceful when she rang Marie next, from Bhutan.

Four hours out of Bangkok, in the last row of economy, Steve Andrew's deep reserve of patience was being strip-mined. Seated next to him, Farley Farrell's initial dread of small airplanes had turned to exuberance. Their flight had been smooth as silk and Farley had entertained it by telling Steve about home; all about home, about his life in and around Brooklyn. Steve had had no choice but to reciprocate, and to his dismay he'd found that Farley's curiosity for things Australian knew no limits. Also to his dismay he'd found that the strange Brooklyner beside him had an uncanny ability to loosen tongues. Unusually for him, Steve had been led to talk about his wife Miranda, her job, his job as a road engineer with TRANSARCO, their kids Ric and Tim and their home-life in and around Byron Bay overlooking the Pacific Ocean.

Farley commented innocently enough, "From what you've told me, you're away so much it's hard to believe that you keep it all together."

With Bradshaw's letter still fresh in his mind and rankling, Steve swallowed hard and said nothing. And that admission by silence opened up another line of questioning that Steve himself couldn't believe he was buying into. Why was he telling an almost perfect stranger about his work and marriage problems, about how hard it was on his boys and how he wasn't sure where it would all end?

Then Farley pointed to the work file in Steve's lap, the one he was meant to be reading but hadn't managed to open, and said, "Two Roads East...What's that?"

"It's the project I'm managing, it's funded by the South Asia Infrastructure Bank, or SAIB as it's known in the trade. That's why I come to Bhutan so often."

Farley said, "SAIB, gee, never heard of it," and before Steve knew it, he was telling Farley about how he got his start in the development business, his project staff in Bhutan including his driver, Karma, his Chief Engineer, Seattle-born and bred John Rawlinson and the project's junior engineer from Tasmania, Martin Pickel. That led to another line of questions about where was Tasmania. Steve responded by pointing out the window and saying, "Your first view of real mountains."

Up ahead, the Himalayas jutted like uneven saw-teeth into a vast arc of ink blue. Farley's face was pressed to the window as the Druk Air flight began its descent. The airplane, its wings held as high and white as a seagull's, started falling into billowing clouds: big angry-gray clouds that had been comfortably below them all the way from their stop in Calcutta. The intercom crackled to life.

"Huh, here comes the warning for the chilips," Steve said over the roar of the engines.

"What are chilips?" Farley murmured uncertainly.

"Us. Foreigners."

"We are thankfully having you onboard with us today..." the pilot's Indian–English accent cut-in crisp and clear. "If this is your first trip into Bhutan, the sides of the mountains may appear very close to the wingtips when we descend from the clouds. Please don't worry, this is quite normal for an approach to Paro airport."

The color started draining from Farley's face as he said, "Ohh! How close?"

"Very close," Steve replied with a frown. Then the intercom clicked off and Flight KB106 shuddered as it plunged deeper into swirling cloud. Steve noticed Farley's grip on his knees tighten, and he added, "Yeah, I reckon you could touch the trees if you were sitting on the wing."

Farley shot a nervous glance sideways, "You're kidding me?"

The airplane shook violently and its wings flapped. There was a moment of uncertain calm. Steve mouthed the words, "No...mate," while Farley steadied himself.

Outside it was as though the lights had been turned off. Then a downdraft hit like a hammer and they went into a free-fall. Farley groaned, "No! Ohhh! No!" while his hands searched feverishly for something solid to hold. He grabbed at the bare forearm on the armrest beside him. His fingers clenched, and held tight.

"What the bloody hell," Steve said as he tried to free himself.

But Farley's grip tightened as they dropped out under the cloud and the tree-clad mountainside was right there at the wingtip. "I'm..." Farley whimpered as Steve watched the Brooklyner's eyes close, his head swirl on a rubberneck and consciousness leave him like it was his last day. Farley lurched sideways. His head came to rest on Steve's shoulder and his iron grip went limp.

On the ground at Paro, Steve shook Farley's outstretched hand and wondered from the feebleness of it how long the other would stay standing. Farley, with pallor akin wet cement said, "It's been good talking with you, Steve. Sorry I umm, lost it back there."

The Australian smirked. "Forget it."

"No...I owe you lunch for that, ah, performance."

"Thanks, but don't bother, Farley. I'll get over it."

Farley insisted.

Steve Andrews resisted.

Farley insisted again, he was almost pleading.

"Okay, Farley." Steve, fearing another scene, relented, "you win, lunch tomorrow it is. Meet me at the Blue Poppy restaurant in Thimphu at half past twelve."

Farley, pleased and relieved, repeated the time and place and added, "I guess it's easy enough to find?"

Steve, not a man for ceremony, murmured, "Yeah, ask at your hotel. See you there." Then he watched Farley wobble across the tarmac toward his trekking group assembling outside the small arrivals terminal, seventy yards away. Steve felt putout, intruded upon. Farley's head had been in his lap before he'd been able to revive him. He shrugged and lifted his gaze. Prayer flags fluttered unconcerned on a rocky outcrop across the valley, and beyond, forested hills rose into cloud shrouded mountains. Behind him, a group of young monks off the airplane was being welcomed back by an even bigger group; suddenly the sounds and the feel and the laughter of this ancient mountain kingdom were as familiar as yesterday.

With the trekking party through immigration, no one else bothered to get into a line. One by one and in no particular order, names were called in Dzongkha or English, then passports were processed and stamped. While waiting, Steve's thoughts centered on the churning in his stomach and Bradshaw's letter. His knees were shaking but he reassured himself; Two Roads East had been going well enough, there'd been problems for sure, but projects and problems go hand-in-glove. There was nothing that would cause auditors to descend. Surely? And anyway, when had he ever trusted Bradshaw's view of the world?

More in the moment, would Karma be there to meet him? Just once, would his driver be on time? Karma had many good qualities, but punctuality wasn't one of them. All too often a landslide or some other natural catastrophe, such as a problem with one of his three wives, delayed him. In this event Karma would always contact a next of kin (of whom he had many), and Steve's transport needs would be taken care of by Karma's brother, one of his many brothers-in-law or a cousin — once, twice or even three times removed. Today, in the mood he was in, Steve wanted his own driver.

4: The Brooklyner

Sophie saw the Mountain Adventures' twelve-seat bus parked at the far end of the airport car park. Anna Dudinsky guided her group across and gathered them for a formal welcome and briefing: they'd look around Paro for the afternoon, stay overnight at the Thunder Dragon Inn and drive to Thimphu in the morning. She also introduced their Bhutanese guide and driver, Tashi. Sophie was standing off to one side and only half listening, the four married couples from Philadelphia were hanging on Anna's every word and the other member of the trekking party, the Brooklyner, was ashen faced and unsteadily propped against the side of the bus.

While Anna spoke, Sophie warily eyed her travel companions up and down. She'd be spending a week with these people, who were they? The Philadelphians looked like they'd be fun, but self-contained; clearly they weren't there to make new friends. Anna and Tashi would be busy organizing things, which left the man slumped against the bus. Her heart sunk, he didn't look like someone she'd choose to spend a week with. Was it the close-cropped, almost orange, hair? His hunched shoulders? Or was it the fake wraparound Oakleys? Whatever, he looked entirely misplaced. She hoped first impressions were wrong, took off her hat and sunglasses and walked toward the man who appeared barely able to stand.

She extended an open hand. "Hi, I'm Sophie Vella."

He turned ever so slowly and forced a sickly smile.

Sophie said, "Are you okay, Mr...?"

"Oh sorry," he swallowed hard and his Adam's apple bounced up, then down, "It's Farley."

They shook hands. Sophie's grip was firm, Farley's weak and wet. "You sure you're okay?"

"Sure." He straightened to almost her height and pulled his shoulders back. "I'm just a bit...umm..."

"Queasy," she said without thinking, then covered by adding, "Hey, no surprise. That was really something wasn't it, the landing here at Paro?"

Farley lowered his eyes. "Hmm, heck yeah."

Anna called them to board the bus. Sophie got on first and sat in the front row, the Philadelphians followed her and introduced themselves as they passed. Farley, like a doorman, waited to board until after Anna and Tashi. Sophie overheard him say, "no, please...ladies first". Anna was hiding a wry smile as business-like, she took the single seat up-front. Then Tashi settled himself behind the wheel. Sophie covered her mouth with her hand to hide a giggle as Farley looked around to make sure he was last and clumsily closed his hand in the sliding door. She saw him wince, pull his hand free and shake it as he muttered to himself.

"Mind if I sit here?" Farley said and slumped into the only spare seat. Sophie forced a smile. It was obvious that she and Farley would be doing a lot of sitting together, unless of course she fancied breaking into the close circle of married friends: four couples that had known each other since college days at Penn State, clearly decades ago.

Tashi let the glow-plugs warm. He hit the starter three times, then let the oil pressure build. They drove slowly along the narrow road adjacent to the runway. As the bus traveled north alongside the Paro River, Farley squeezed his sore hand between his knees and talked about Brooklyn, how this was his first trip abroad. Sophie nodded and said nothing as they crossed the river just under the Dzong; the massive fortress they'd soon learn about. When they pulled up outside the Snow Leopard restaurant, Farley was still talking double-time and she was only half-listening — her mind firmly fixed on what the next day or so might bring.

5: The King is learning golf

Outside customs was a melee of meetings and greetings. Steve made his way through the crowd, walked out of the terminal and looked around. He saw Karma perhaps fifty yards away, he was leaning back on the hood of the project's Landcruiser; feet and arms folded, nonchalantly on time. Steve thanked divine intervention then pushed a rusted and rickety luggage trolley across the broken surface of the car park. But, as the trolley wheels twisted and jumped and the uneven weight of his luggage pulled him off-course, Two Roads East had slipped from his mind. What he'd divulged to Farley, and now the welcoming crowd, disturbed him. Wives hugging husbands, children reuniting with parents, lovers embracing, friends greeting friends and monks greeting monks; it brought back too many memories. Memories of his homecoming just over a year ago. He'd been working in Cambodia for three months and the bitterness of his welcome home, the surprise that Miranda had in store for him, was still a pit in his stomach. From those thoughts, a dark cloud descended and settled on him like a lead balloon.

At twenty yards, Steve noticed Karma's ever-present smile, then that he'd washed the Landcruiser and worn his best gho; maroon tartan with as fine a weave as a driver's wage could buy. As Steve approached, Karma straightened his knee-length, kimono-style robe then leant over to pull up his long socks and check the polish on his leather shoes before saying, "Mr. Steve sir, good seeing you again." Karma guided the trolley the last few yards to the car.

Steve let him take the luggage, and mumbled, "Hi Karma."

"How was your flying this time?"

"Can't complain I guess." Steve said, "I was sitting next to the most unlikely trekker I've ever met, a guy called Farley. He was great for a laugh."

Karma beamed. Perfect white teeth shone under a neatly trimmed mustache, he repeated "Farley" a couple of times until he said it the way Steve had.

They started loading Steve's luggage. Karma grimaced and joked on feeling the weight of Steve's travel-worn black suitcase, "Oww, so heavy, Mr. Steve."

"Yeah," Steve said gruffly, "I've just come from six weeks in China. Most of that is paper, reports and stuff."

Karma's face lit up and his mustache twitched. Steve knew what he was thinking, that China would be something to talk about all the way to town. Karma, like most Bhutanese men, was not tall but stockily built and straight of back. His shiny black hair was cut short and his smooth brown face crinkled easily into a grin. Over the past few years, they'd already made the return trip to Trashigang eight times. That meant over three hundred hours together, driving the mountain roads and talking, sharing a joke or listening to music.

Karma pushed the rear doors of the station wagon shut. "We go, sir?"

Steve started to say something, stopped, then nodded and moved toward the passenger door. How many times had he asked Karma not to call him sir? At first he thought he'd break the habit, but he'd soon realized there was no connotation of subservience — besides it was a habit that would die hard — and Karma was a man of habit.

Steve remembered that first conversation well. "Karma, there's no need to call me sir, Steve will do."

"But sir, all the other foreigners…"

"Never mind them, just call me Steve."

Karma had given the idea deep thought. "Yes sir, Mr. Steve sir. I try."

Now Steve considered Karma a friend in an odd sort of way. Karma loved to talk, and if there was nothing to talk about, he could happily talk about nothing for hours. Years ago, on their first trip east, Karma had said that it was an auspicious sign when he discovered that he was ten years to the day, Steve's junior. He'd pronounced grandly, 'In Bhutan your birth-date means a lot, it shapes your destiny, there is no escaping it, Sir Steve.'

With Steve frowning and Karma grinning and waving hellos, they pulled out of the car park and turned east. There were thirty-three miles to drive, and though Steve knew they'd be the last of the airport traffic to arrive in Thimphu, he wasn't concerned, it was not a road to hurry on. Steve pushed back in his seat, stretched and groaned, he immediately felt jet-lagged. As one sharp corner merged into the next, the single width of blacktop climbed high above the valley floor. Over the revving of the big diesel motor, Karma asked about China; what was Steve doing there, was it like Bhutan? Steve would have preferred to sit in a gloomy silence, but he knew Karma wouldn't allow it. He sighed and then talked about his work on the Friendship Highway project. "It's been anything but friendly," Steve said too seriously for it to be a joke. "And no, China is nothing like Bhutan." Drawn out of his quiet introspection, Steve asked what had been happening in Bhutan since his last visit six months ago. Karma filled in the news as best he could: the season had been kind, Bhutan was a land of plenty at the moment; Monday was the Blessed Rainy Day holiday, it didn't rain; the king and his four queens were enjoying good health, an American had been in town teaching the king to play golf; there was talk about television coming to Bhutan some day and how the king was worried that it would erode Bhutan's unique culture, Karma added, "I reckon we are the only country in the world without television Mr. Steve"; some dacoits had been caught robbing a sacred chorten, the police took them in and…

Steve saw Karma's grip on the wheel tighten as he shifted down two gears and pulled into a steep right-hand bend. Karma sounded the horn; it was immediately answered two-fold by the blast of the twin air-horns fitted to the front of the Thimphu Express — the passenger bus that should have been at the airport a half-hour ago. Karma hit the brakes and yanked the wheel. Steve grabbed for the panic-bar. Gravel sprayed against the side of the Landcruiser as the bus passed within inches. Karma sat like a breathing statue. Finally he muttered, "He's late. Again!" White-knuckled, Steve looked over the side of a sheer cliff. The riverbank was directly below him, hundreds of feet down. Steve closed his eyes and shook his head. He decided to let his driver drive; he'd ask Karma later, what happened to the chorten thieving dacoits.

6: *After lunch at the Snow Leopard*

Sophie found the luncheon banquet at the Snow Leopard a spicy introduction to Bhutanese cuisine. While she and the Philadelphians tried every dish, each seemingly hotter than the last, they watched Farley pick at plain rice, lentils and yogurt. Red-faced, he explained that his appetite was better in the evenings. Over coffee, Sophie heard that he was a florist and worked in his mother's shop on Flatbush Avenue. That the two of them lived above it.

When it was Farley's turn to ask the questions, Sophie gave away as little as she could; she said she was a human-rights lawyer in the State Department, she worked on Latin American issues. Farley's wide-open eyes and the tilt of his head pleaded to know more, but Sophie changed the subject. She asked why he'd chosen to come to Bhutan.

Farley squirmed. Uneasy brown eyes looked right past her. His boyishly round face frowned. "Ah, I guess I needed a change." He stopped and thought, then continued, carefully phrasing each word. "And heck, I need *to* change. I went into Mountain Adventures and told them I wanted a real challenge, that I wanted to prove myself. The travel guy there didn't hesitate, he said, 'trekking in Bhutan'. I didn't know where Bhutan was, but I signed up on the spot."

After lunch, Anna suggested they look around Paro town for awhile and then meet up again at three. They headed off together with Farley in the lead and Sophie between Jim, a retired medical specialist, and his wife, Nancy. They walked around aimlessly, peered into every shop window and bought nothing. It didn't take long for Sophie to work out that Jim, a fine looking man with longish gray hair and a barrel chest, she'd get on with; and that Nancy, a fine looking woman with a mouthful of heavily worked-over teeth, she wouldn't.

Farley was unsettled, he said he'd never had foreign currency before and he wanted the experience of spending it. But Anna had said to them when they left the restaurant, 'Paro has some great handicraft shops, though better to buy at the end of our trip, otherwise you'll have to carry everything with you.' When Farley asked Sophie for her views on the matter, she shrugged and said, "I don't know, I'm not here for mementos of the carrying kind."

Nancy chipped in, "Oh, don't be a spoil-sport," and they crossed the street. Farley stopped and stared. There, sitting cross-legged on the footpath was an ancient woman weighing out chilies on a brass counter-balance. He knelt in front of the woman, "I've got to have that. How much you sell for?"

The old woman looked back at Farley with curious eyes and a toothless grin, she held up six fingers.

He said, "Six ngultrums, no more?"

The old lady nodded.

Sophie did a quick sum in her head, they'd just got over forty ngultrums to the dollar, there had to be something wrong. The Philadelphians gathered around to watch the cut and thrust of commerce on the street.

Farley held up a crisp ten-ngultrum note and passed it over. The old lady gave him a bundle of shiny red chilies. He looked down and laughed. "I want the balance, not the chilies." She handed him two coins and bowed her head. He pointed again at the shiny brass balance and counted out six ten ngultrum notes and handed them across. His gesture met no immediate response, then the old lady started weighing more chilies, the longest and fattest she had.

Farley turned to Sophie for advice. Impatiently, she shrugged and said. "Perhaps it's not for sale?"

"No!" Farley replied, "Everything's got a price."

Sophie frowned and knelt next to him. She began, "One..." and in clipped, dot point fashion gave three reasons why this wasn't going to work.

Farley's mouth dropped. "Oh! Of course. You're right, without the balance she hasn't got a business. And without a business..." He stuffed chilies into the pockets of his pants and shirt until overflowing and left the rest.

As they hurried back to the restaurant with Farley in the lead again, Sophie overheard Nancy say to Jim, "Poor Farley, did you hear the way she spoke to him?"

The bus was loaded and waiting for them, Sophie apologized to Anna for Farley and his chilies and wondered again at how she could get rid of him. Soon, they sat uneasily rigid as their bus snaked its way along a narrow road that led out of the valley.

As they gained height, Sophie saw that the smaller yellow fields of ripened mustard flower soon became a patchwork on the green and brown of the larger rice paddies around them. Then the ice-blue waters of the Paro Chhu, which she could see in the mountains to the north were confined to narrow gorges, spread out and meandered over the pebble covered riverbed. Willows lined the banks and cattle crossed in the shallows. The gentlest of breezes lifted the sound of rippling water and the air was cut with the fragrance of pine resin and juniper. She wasn't here for scenery, but Sophie found herself being drawn in.

While her mind was wandering and without warning, Tashi pulled up in the middle of the single lane blacktop. They all got out and looked upriver. Sophie saw a burnt-orange sun hung low and lazy over the mountains behind them, and before them was a steep-sided valley with a wide ribbon of quiet water running through it. On either side of the Paro Chhu, and stretching up to the forested hillsides, were the fertile colors of agriculture. At riverside, the Dzong rose white-walled and ancient above a covered footbridge that crossed the river. The cameras from Philadelphia whirred and clicked and superlatives built on each other until there was no better view, anywhere.

Sophie said nothing, she stood spellbound as the words of the others blurred to a murmur. She blinked and opened her eyes and it was still there; she wanted to say something, but to whom? Momentarily, her reason for being there was all but forgotten, she allowed herself to be taken in and away.

By now, several cars had lined up behind their bus. The other drivers, not being able to go around, just waited. In one of the cars, a boy of perhaps six caught Sophie's eye. He blushed and sank out of sight. His older sister called out the open window. "Hello Mista. Why you come here?" Sophie smiled in reply. Wasn't it obvious? She was just an ordinary tourist here for an extra-ordinary meeting.

7: Four clocks - Same time

In Thimphu, Karma pulled into the cobbled driveway leading up to the Zangbo Guesthouse. Before the motor died, Namgay flung the double-doors open. "We been expecting you, Mr. Steve," the manager announced proudly. "We hold our top room, just for you."

Steve forced a grin. "Well done Namgay! Any messages for me?"

"Yes sir, a fax letter from Australia and a message from the Minister for Roads. But messages can wait, first lunch...no?"

"No!" Steve put out his hand for the messages. He clenched the minister's note between his teeth and opened the fax to see who it was from. He glanced at a child's handwriting and a smiley round face drawn in the bottom right-hand corner. His ten-year old son, Tim, had written it. As Steve folded the page for later, he reflected on how Bhutan not only lagged the rest of the world with television, but with the internet and email as well: if Miranda and his twelve year-old son Ric could email him, then he might hear from them occasionally, as he had in China, but it was only Tim who'd bother to write and send a fax.

The three of them carried Steve's luggage into the reception area. It was dark with pretended formality. Steve glanced up at the four wall-mounted clocks behind Namgay's desk; despite their brass labels, London, Rome, New York and Thimphu, they all said two-thirty.

Steve finished his registration formalities and opened the note from the minister, Lyonpo Rinchen Dorji. He could feel Karma watching him as he read. Even so, his shoulders slumped and he said, "shit" under his breath. He looked up and saw Karma brace himself.

"The minister can't see me this afternoon," Steve said, without hiding his irritation. "He'll call in the morning and meet me sometime tomorrow." Steve ploughed his fingers through his hair. He grimaced. "Shit! I work six weeks straight and I can't get one bloody day without traveling or a meeting!"

Still Karma said nothing, his eyes were firmly fixed on the ground between his feet. Steve could see that Namgay was also avoiding eye contact, he made busy shuffling papers across the reception desk.

Steve summonsed attention from both of them and said, "Okay then, I'll take it easy this afternoon, here. Karma, I'll call you tomorrow, when I know what's happening."

"Yes sir, anything else?" He was clearly keen to leave.

"Yeah, I guess Rawlinson wants us to do his shopping as usual?"

Karma echoed tentatively, "Yes sir, the usual."

Steve squeezed his forehead with tense fingers, "Jeezas! And I've promised to have lunch with Farley tomorrow, too!"

"Farley? The least likely trekker?"

"Yeah. That one."

"Hmmm, I hope he's paying, sir." Karma didn't even wait for his joke to fall flat, he added quickly, "When we go east?"

"Saturday as usual."

Karma repeated "as usual", brought his heels together and stood at attention. He turned military-style and promptly left the way he'd entered.

The Zangbo Guesthouse was five stories high with no lift and stairs so steep they were like a fire escape. Once again Steve had the attic room – the Zangbo's top room was not Steve's choice, but Namgay wouldn't hear of it, he insisted, 'his top foreign guest would get the top room'. By the time Steve had checked in, agreed his plans with Karma, climbed the stairs and unpacked, then climbed back down to the restaurant, it was well past three p.m. The restaurant, recently renamed The Royalty Room, was empty. He took a table overlooking the town, ordered and glanced down at the hand-made paper envelope he was holding. It contained Tim's one-page fax, which he knew would be his only communication from home unless he made the call. And after the call he'd made from Beijing, the one that was answered curtly by a now familiar male voice, an adult voice, that wasn't without its problems either.

Hot and sour soup was served. It was hotter and sourer than usual. The first taste burned all the way down and got Steve thinking about burnt fingers. About how he got to be who he was, where he was. About the bid that started it all. He'd promised Miranda that this one would be different, that he had it all sorted, then at the last minute and without giving a reason, SAIB postponed the Two Roads East bidding process by three weeks which had caused Steve to cancel the family holiday he'd already booked and paid for. He worked the entire winter school holidays while Miranda did her best to keep Ric and Tim busy and to keep supporting a line of business that never seemed to deliver what it promised. In the middle of the bidding war, an urgent problem came up on his Friendship Highway project in China which meant that his orderly work-plan was abandoned for a mad scramble to the closing date. With three days to go even the most even-tempered and faithful of his team were starting to ask tough questions and doubt his ability to pull it off yet again. They were all working twenty hours a day when, with less than forty eight hours to the bid deadline, Josh Nichols, Steve's chosen team leader called up to casually announce that he was pulling out of the bid, that he'd been offered a project in Mindanao with an NGO whose team leader had had to resign in a hurry. Josh had assured Steve the NGO deal was so good that there was no point in trying to get him to change his mind. That was when Steve started the frantic search within TRANSARCO which located Rawlinson in Seattle. But Rawlinson, no beginner in the game, guessed the squeeze that Steve was in, no team leader and less than two days to go, and added ten percent to his already high fee rate for the privilege of helping Steve out. To add injury to insult, the air-conditioning unit in the **TRANSARCO** Sydney office caught fire the night before the bid was due to go out by courier at 8am the next morning. Within minutes the office was filled with acrid, orange-gray fumes that couldn't be gotten rid of because the windows didn't open. At that point even Steve's most loyal helpers deserted and he worked alone all night finishing, photo-copying and binding **TRANSARCO**'s bid documents. With a hacking cough and throat that felt like sandpaper, he staggered out the door at eight the next morning with an envelope for a courier who (without precedent) arrived over two hours late. Steve was then on tenterhooks for days waiting for confirmation that their bid had been delivered in time. By the time he arrived back home in Byron Bay he was so sick with a head cold and laryngitis that Miranda's patience was tested beyond breaking point. The consolation he had assured her would come when **TRANSARCO** won the bid. 'And you get to spend even more time away from the boys' she'd added bitterly before the door slammed.

Steve signaled for a drink as he opened the envelope and laid Tim's fax on the table in front of him. He stared at it blankly. Bijaya, the tiny young waitress and general helper around the guesthouse, put on some Bollywood music then brought three plates to the table in two busy hands. He glanced up and nodded, "kadinchhey."

Steve picked up Tim's letter again and read.

Dear Dad,

Ric says hi, so does mum. Ric and I have been surfing lots, the water is still cold and we're in our wet suits. We haven't caught a fish since you've been gone, but the new mountain bikes are fun. School is going okay but Ric says his new teacher gives too much homework. Ric also said to remind you about his 13th birthday party, can we still go camping like you said we would? Tim finished with a few lines about Clancy, their *black and white border collie, chasing a possum up a tree and said that mum would write later. He'd printed DAD under the smiley face and signed off, Luv from Mum, Ric and me.*

Steve let the letter drop. Bijaya served him coffee; cup in one hand, saucer in the other. He put his elbows on the table and his head in his hands and sighed. The township below him was already creeping into shadow, and as evening calm was settling over Thimphu, a storm was brewing in Steve's mind. He knew that Miranda wouldn't write. Occasionally she'd add a few lines to one of the kid's emails, but not to a fax, that'd be too personal. Losing Miranda still troubled him, but not near as much as what Ric had said to him the day before he left for China. He'd gotten both the boys up early to go fishing, and as they walked sleepy-eyed along the beach he'd tried to put a positive spin on things. "Eight weeks isn't long," he'd said, "I'll be home before you know it." Ric had only spoken his mind when he'd mumbled, "Dad, I don't care when you get home." Steve thought he'd misheard and joked, "What do you mean, Ric, I'm no longer your fishing mate?" Ric had looked up at him and didn't even try to hide his tears. "Dad, I can't think about when you'll get home, 'cause when you do, you'll just go again." With heads bent, the three of them had walked the length of the beach without another word. And how long had it been since Ric bothered to write anything other than a quick hello, goodbye, gotta go?

The four clocks in reception read four thirty when Steve made his first call home. The operator let it ring until Miranda's cheery "Hi, I can't take your call..." on the answering machine cut in. Steve muttered, "Huh, it's nine there, the boys have school tomorrow and they're not home yet. Okay, I'll try again in an hour," and handed the phone back to Namgay.

He was downstairs again at five forty and once again got the answering machine. This time he left a message, "Hi, me here, I thought I might have caught you all at home after ten on a school night, anyway, I'll send a fax and try to call tomorrow..." He handed the phone to Namgay and said, "Thanks, I'll be back soon to use the fax machine." Namgay knew when to keep his head down, he took the phone and grunted, "Yes, sir."

Back in his room, Steve started a letter home, and before the first line was written a now familiar churning was in his guts. How long did Miranda expect him to keep on pretending? Her last words on the matter still jangled in his head. "It's what's best for the boys, Steve. That's what's important. Not you, not me! The boys." He placed his palms flat on the desk and stared at the back of his hands. It seemed to him that Miranda's interests and those of the boys always aligned better than his own did. And the boys couldn't have an opinion, because they weren't to be told. And he went along with it because he could see no alternative just now, and 'just now' seemed to have stretched over a very long time.

His troubled line of thinking brought images of Miranda to the fore. What a fool he'd been. It was only a year ago that his eyes had been opened. He'd been away from home for three months. He'd flown overnight from Bangkok, then changed planes in Sydney after a five-hour wait. He hadn't slept for thirty hours when he came out of their local airport to a peck on the cheek and the news that Miranda wanted him to drive the forty or so minutes to Byron Bay. "Why?" he asked?

"Because I've got something important to tell you," she said. He later realized it was easier that way, easier on her. While he drove, she didn't have to face him as she pulled the carpet of his life out from under him. It still surprised him how calm Miranda had been as she explained that she was in love with someone else. Calm when she said that Steve was still a good man and a good father but that it was now another man, a man he knew, that she loved.

On guesthouse letterhead he hand-wrote,

Thimphu, Thursday, 25th

Dear Miranda, Ric and Tim.

Great to get your letter when I arrived. Sounds as though things at home are going just...

He stared at his own unsteady handwriting. He slowly screwed up the page and threw it at the trash bin. He walked to the window and rested his forehead against the cool glass. A minute later he sat down again and wrote,

Thimphu, Thursday night

Hi guys,

Arrived safely, but tired, it's been a long trip. The job in China was tough. The Friendship Highway wasn't that friendly. I tried to call a few times and you were all out, I'll try again tomorrow night.

He filled in the rest of the page with how glad he was to hear it was all going so well, how he missed them and how he was looking forward to getting home for Ric's birthday and to taking the boys and Clancy camping. He added the required something about mum deserving her week away when he got back, and signed off with love.

8: We are having the very best dictionary

When Namgay knocked on his door, Steve was still half-asleep. He checked his watch, it wasn't yet seven, unusually early for Namgay to be up and about. Namgay knocked again and called out with an unmistakable touch of urgency, "There's a note from the minister, sir." Steve threw back the covers, crossed the room, opened the door, thanked Namgay, closed the door again and then unfolded the page. He read;

> *Friday, September 26, 1997*
>
> *Dear Steven,*
>
> *Meet me at my offices at five p.m. sharp. Last week, SAIB's sybaritic banker, Dr. Narguli called in here on his way out to the project. He left me with a problem that has been the reason for the delay in, and will be the subject of, our meeting.*
>
> *Yours,*
>
> *Rinchen Dorji, PhD*

Steve read and reread the note. 'Sybaritic banker', the words eluded him. He cursed himself for not having packed a dictionary. The minister was well known for having a wide vocabulary that he used freely, almost every time Steve visited there was a relic of old English pulled out from under a carpet, seemingly just to confuse him. On Steve's last visit, the minister had referred to a 'lacuna' between promise and performance on one section of the road. At first Steve had envisioned something four-legged, the Bhutanese equivalent of a vicuna standing in the way of progress. Only later, when he'd had time to consult a

31

dictionary, did the minister's displeasure become clear. And not only was Narguli now a 'sybarite', his problem with Two Roads East was now the minister's as well. Steve's mind jumped back to Bradshaw's letter and his warnings about hordes of auditors. But the project was on budget and on schedule, wasn't it? Steve threw the minister's note at the desk, "Shit, Narguli and his bloody problems. What's he going to tell me now? The work's great, Andrews, but we've just realized that TRANSARCO has been working on the wrong roads for the past three years." Steve and Narguli had had their first disagreement the first time they met, and the status quo had prevailed on each and every subsequent occasion. As Country Program Manager for the bank, Narguli had overall control of the four SAIB projects in Bhutan. That meant Narguli answered to the minister and Steve answered to both of them. And while the minister didn't care much for hierarchy; the pecking order and his position in it was what drove Narguli's working life. It was as though being responsible for the smallest country in South Asia was a challenge to Narguli's ego; a challenge that he responded to by reminding all he met that he could have put his hand up for the Sri Lanka or Bangladesh posts, but chose Bhutan because it needed him most.

Steve glanced at his watch, thought ahead to his lunch with Farley, remembered that the duty-free shop closed at two on Fridays and decided to do his shopping for Rawlinson before lunch. He caught a glimpse of himself in the mirror behind the desk and knew immediately that the stress on his face couldn't leave the room: Buddhist Bhutan and angry chilips didn't mix. He breathed deeply and tried to summon some calm. It didn't come quickly. Was it something about Narguli? Perhaps just the mention of his name? Or was it Bradshaw's letter, and the possibility that his professional life was about to unravel even quicker than his home life?

Still on edge, Steve showered then dressed, went downstairs and asked Namgay to call Karma at home. Namgay let the phone ring and when it answered he handed it over to Steve who asked his ever-ready driver to be at the Zangbo by nine. Steve explained that they'd have to do their shopping first thing, that he had to meet Farley at half twelve and that the meeting with the minister wasn't until five. Karma said with a breathless hint of hesitation, "At nine, sir? I'm little busy this morning!" Steve knew exactly what Karma would be busy at, it happened every time he had to go east: Thimphu wife would be making the best of things before Karma left town again. Karma's ability to satisfy three women in three different parts of the country was legendary, but Steve knew that the legend came at a price. That price was timeliness. Steve answered sharply, "Yes, nine," then went to the Royalty Room for breakfast.

At nine fifteen, while waiting at reception for Karma, Steve asked Namgay if he knew what a 'sybarite' was. Namgay replied confidently, "Ahh, yes, the sybarites. They're a religious group, sir. They're mainly in India. In the south." Steve was only half-convinced, nevertheless he thanked Namgay profusely and decided to call Rawlinson. Steve knew there was a risk in that, that Rawlinson might add to his shopping-list, but there was an equal risk that Karma wouldn't make it until ten, there may not be time later.

Steve phoned the Project Office in Trashigang and Rawlinson answered, "Two Roads East." The ensuing conversation between Project Director, Steve, and Project Manager/Chief Engineer, Rawlinson, was one-sided, guarded and brief.

Steve enquired about the project's junior engineer, Martin, and the gruff reply came back, "Out on a field trip, back Sunday. He and Tammy are expecting you Sunday night. You can stay at my place from Monday."

Steve said, "Oh? Okay thanks...by the way, is Narguli out there yet?"

"Yeah…why?"

"Has he mentioned any problems?"

"Huh, Narguli and problems follow each other like day and night, you know that."

"Yes, but anything special?"

"There's some weird stuff happening," Rawlinson said, "but listen, I'm busy, I've just heard the international phone service east of Thimphu will be cut for two weeks from tomorrow. I've gotta get hold of my stockbroker. See you Monday, and hey, I'm out of coffee and sugar and make that two cases of wine will you." He promptly hung up.

Steve looked askance at the dead phone in his hand and gave it back to Namgay. Rawlinson hadn't changed one bit. Steve said, "Rawlinson mentioned a cut to the international telephone service, have you heard anything Namgay?"

Namgay nodded and handed over a printed notice from Bhutan Telecom Limited. Steve read,

Dear Customer, Starting Saturday September 27th, we are upgrading the backbone network between Thimphu and Trashigang to a higher capacity system. During the up-gradation and cut-over, there may be interruptions to the domestic service and the international service will be suspended. Please have our apologies for any inconveniences.

Steve handed the notice back to Namgay and made a sarcastic remark about 'what was new'.

Namgay just smiled and shrugged, "What to do, sir? What to do?"

Out in the car park, Steve said, "Sorry to hurry you Karma, but the Minister's mentioned some problems on the project. What have you heard?" Karma replied abruptly, "Nothing!" and slapped an open hand on the side of the Landcruiser as he

walked to the driver's side. As they drove, Steve tried again, "Anything gone wrong lately?" Karma just shook his head.

Downtown, Steve left Karma sulking in the Landcruiser while he walked into the smaller of the two banks in Thimphu. Inside it was dusty and dark, and busy with the rattle of local commerce. Behind the counters, a row of clerks labored over huge ledgers with ink-pens poised, several others counted, sorted and stacked bundles of ngultrum notes like building blocks, while one attended to the public. After a respectful wait, Steve handed over his passport and three one-hundred-dollar checks. The clerk studied Steve's passport then looked up and said, "Sir's good name is Sydney?" Steve explained that Sydney was where the passport was issued, he leant over the counter and pointed to his name. The clerk remained straight-faced and said, "Wait moment please Mr. Steven. I do the needful." The needful took fifteen minutes, but no one in the line behind Steve was counting.

Outside on the street, Steve and Karma split the money and Rawlinson's shopping list, then went in separate directions with an agreement to meet back at the car in about a half-hour. Steve arrived back at the empty Landcruiser after forty minutes, while Karma staggered back under a pile of shopping nearly twenty minutes later. He was full of apologies and explained how he'd met this one and that one, and that common courtesy demanded he chat with them all. Steve just said, "Of course! No less!" He'd been shopping with Karma before. And mercifully, it seemed to have lifted him out of the doldrums.

After they'd loaded groceries, a few special treats and two dozen bottles of Rawlinson's favorite Californian wine in the back of the Landcruiser, Steve said, "Just one more thing."

"What we forget?" Karma looked puzzled.

Steve said, "A dictionary."

"You wantta buy a dictionary?"

"Not buy one, just look at one."

The glass counters at the front of the bookshop were out of a museum. Down the back was one of the oddest assortments of English language novels ever collected in one place. The bookshop owner looked up; bespectacled, alert and courteous.

"Do you have any English language dictionaries?" Steve said.

"We are having very best dictionary here, sir. I bring." The owner disappeared to the back and sorted through a pile of books on the floor. He chose one, dusted it off on his shirtsleeve and brought forward a dog-eared, Indian edition printed on brown fading paper. The back cover was half missing, and someone had used the front cover as a drink-coaster. He passed the book across the counter with a flourish. Steve took it warily and flicked it open. S… Syb… Sybarite.

"I knew it, it's not a religion." He read aloud, "A person who is excessively fond of comfort and luxury." Steve looked lost for a moment, then laughed. "Huh, that's our dear friend Narguli alright."

Karma and the bookshop man looked at each other and shrugged.

Mystery solved, Steve gave the dictionary back to the shop owner, "Thanks."

"Sir, no like?"

"I like, but I can't carry another thing. Honest!"

Steve moved to leave.

"Sir no take it?" The man's voice was saddened by the prospect of a lost sale.

Steve saw Karma looking at him in a way that said, 'Buy something, anything, *please.*'

A box of music cassettes on the glass topped counter caught Steve's eye. There was a hand drawn sign on the box, 'Two hundred and fifty ngultrums each.' He flicked through the cassette tapes and found one that had a white sandy beach and a brightly colored umbrella on the front. It could have been the

'Beach Boys Greatest Hits on Sitar' for all he knew, it didn't matter. He said, "I'll take the cassette instead."

The bookshop-man smiled and looked at the price on the front of the dictionary. "That one special cassette tape. It'll be four hundred ngultrums, thank you good sir."

9: The God of Difficult Things

The trekking group was on its way from Paro to Thimphu when Farley pointed out the bus window and said, "Sophie, quick, look there. That's blue pine."

It was still early morning, and besides she couldn't have cared what color pine it was, but she knew she had to lighten up a bit, that Nancy was sitting right behind her. She turned and said, "Yeah. Wow. Tall aren't they. Magnificent!"

He picked up on that small token of interest and started a discourse on the two main species, and soon she'd heard all she never wanted to hear about *Pinus wallichiana* and *Pinus bhutanica*. Then, as the bus wound its way around ever tightening corners, Farley ranted about every change in the botanical composition of the forest above them, below them and beside them. Even if she'd wanted to, Sophie couldn't have got a word in edge-wise.

Farley's banter was momentarily put on halt while Anna pointed out a few names and places and then he said in one breathless sentence, "Ohh, I forgot to mention, I met an Australian engineer on the flight into Paro. I sat next to him, he's managing a road project out near Trashigang, it's called Two Roads East and it's funded by the SAIB, that's the South Asia Infrastructure Bank, he's been working on it for a few years now and we're having lunch together today." Farley stopped just long enough to take a breath and added, "I'm sure Steve wouldn't mind if you joined us."

Sophie's blank face slowly framed a faint smile, then she said, "Oh, an Australian! Hmmm, tell me a bit more about him first." Sophie listened hard as Farley dribbled out what he knew of Steve Andrews and his project in the east, and she asked not one question. She didn't need to.

It was mid-morning when the bus slowed above Thimphu and Anna turned in her seat. "We won't get out of the bus here, there will be better places to view the town later." She went on to say how it was now home to about forty thousand people, how most of it had been built in the past thirty years since Thimphu became the capital. Anna pointed out the Trashi Chhoe Dzong sitting riverside at the northern end of town. She explained that it was Bhutan's Capitol Hill, that the king had his offices and throne room there. The dzong had been burnt down and re-built many times over the centuries, and even in the sixties a major extension and refurbishment was completed in the traditional way; with no written plans or nails.

Sophie gazed absently out over the huge white-walled, red-roofed complex of buildings: a central golden tower rose above it and beyond, farmers worked with bent backs in tilled fields. The bus moved off downhill and crossed the Thimphu River while her mind was on meetings and coincidence.

The bus stopped for a goat to move off the road and Farley said, "Well, what about lunch? Will you come along?"

Sophie looked away and shrugged, "I've yet to get a better offer. Why not!"

When they arrived at their hotel, the RiverView, Farley said, "let's explore the shops together," he added, "we've plenty of time before our lunch-date with Steve."

Sophie thanked him but quickly reeled off a list of things she just had to do, unpacking and a phone call amongst them.

Farley nodded his understanding, "Okay, see you for lunch at a half past twelve. Don't be late."

"Sure, I'll be there." Sophie tilted her head, "Hey, where is the Blue Poppy?"

In her room at the RiverView, Sophie had a view over mountains. She stood at the window with her fingers tapping a nervous tune on the glass and butterflies as big as bats flying around in her stomach. Before Farley's offer of lunch, Sophie still hadn't worked out how to stage her coincidental meeting with Steve. Was this offering from the God of Difficult Things, too good to be true? Was she ready?

The *Washington Post* was spread out on the bed, opened at the 'Around Town' column. She'd read it again and her mood was a blend of anger and fright. When she was forced to plan this trip, she knew that it would cause Alex problems he didn't need and possibly end her career in Washington. Worse, Sophie knew who'd leaked that story to the *Post*; it had Stella Borg written all over it. Stella, until very recently Sophie's deputy, had been certain the Coordinator's job would be hers. Now, Stella was running Sophie's office for nine days — nine long days in which to cause her trouble. Sophie had only ever made it to the *Washington Post* once before, and that was when she married Alex eleven years ago. Now she would have been quite happy to leave that as her only appearance in a gossip column. She moved back to the bed and sat on the edge of it. The article was open in front of her and she read again,

'Talk in the corridors of the State Department has it that Sophie Vella, newly appointed Regional Human Rights Coordinator for Latin America and the Caribbean, is already on vacation. She's gone trekking in exotic Bhutan, apparently with the blessing of Under Secretary and former husband, Alex Deloraine. 'I don't know how she does it' said one Washington insider who wonders whether what was once dubbed 'the marriage of convenience' ended with 'the divorce of convenience.' Just a month before their engagement, the Post voted the then forty-year-old rising bureaucrat, Alex Deloraine, 'best dressed and most eligible bachelor in Washington.' In 1986 he made the social pages with his civil ceremony wedding (pictured below) to his twenty-eight-year-old co-worker Sophie Vella. Our insider went on to say, 'since the couple's break-up four years ago, Ms. Vella has made two other career leaps, and lately she and her former husband have been spotted deep in conversation at some of Washington's coziest restaurants; talking work no doubt?"

Sophie left the newspaper open on the bed and moved again to the window and the view over mountains. She watched distant white clouds scud across distant white peaks and slowly her head cleared. On reflection, the way things had fallen into place was better than she could have hoped for. Farley's invitation to lunch was perfect. She had a right to be here and to do what she was going to do, she just needed to keep convincing herself of that; a gnawing emptiness in her stomach told her so.

She checked her watch, subtracted nine and a half hours for Washington time and made up her mind to phone Alex even though it was only two in the morning at home. She needed someone to talk to, he alone would understand.

The telephone was on the desk, and under it was a notice from Bhutan Telecom Limited. Sophie read about the planned up-gradation of the network east of Thimphu and the disruption to international services and thought, 'huh, for once, that won't bother me.'

10: Surprise Surprise

Steve had arrived at the Blue Poppy early and found it empty. He took a table by the window and ordered a fresh lime soda, mixed: sugar and salt, thanks. He'd had an uncertain morning, the minister's note had left him perplexed. Neither Karma nor Rawlinson was aware of anything out of the ordinary, yet everything about his day so far was out of the ordinary. Two Roads East was one of the biggest road projects in Bhutan, usually the minister gave him due priority. And a business meeting at five, in Bhutan, was unheard of.

Sophie had dressed carefully — not so well as to look like she was meeting someone important, but well enough so that it wouldn't matter if she did. She arrived at twelve thirty sharp to see Steve sitting with his back to her and no Farley in sight. She weighed up her options and fought back a desperate, insane urge to leave. She stood by the door and breathed deeply. Her mind went into overdrive and from its deepest hidden recesses, retrieved a school history class that she hadn't thought of for over twenty years. The class was on the element of surprise in battle — how surprise had been used to win many an unwinnable war. Now she faced her own battle, both with herself and the man seated with his back to her.

She took a deep breath and walked straight past Steve to the table beyond his. She sat so as not to face him and didn't move for minutes. Then she casually turned on her chair and spoke as to a stranger, "Hi, you haven't seen a lost trekker with orange hair have you? I'm meant to be meeting him here for lunch?"

Steve looked up and their eyes met for the first time in nineteen years, "No! I'm waiting for someone myself," he began then stopped mid-sentence. He stared as though he'd seen a ghost.

She was straight-faced and outwardly calm, but her heart beat a million times an hour.

He faltered, "Sophie? Sophie Vella?"

Here was her real test. Surprise! She had to be surprised. Her brow furrowed, "Uhh, yeah."

They were only a few feet apart, she couldn't believe how little he'd changed, or how much she wanted to run. He was speechless, staring, starting to stand. She kept a quiet look of complete confusion on her face and remained seated.

"Sophie!" Steve stood and took a tentative step toward her. "What are you doing here?"

"Excuse me, do I...?"

"It's me...Steve."

"Steve? Steve Andrews!" Sophie's eyes were wide open, her face disbelieving. "Farley said he was meeting an engineer called Steve. I can't believe this..." On the outside she was calm and strong, inside though, she was quivering.

Steve took another step, "You're meeting Farley? How? How do you know him?"

"Steve Andrews! It's really you." Sophie smiled, shook her head in an exaggerated state of disbelief and stood at her table, "I'm...I'm going trekking. Farley's part of my trekking group."

Steve took another step. They looked at each other as if neither had the right to be there. He extended a hand, she took it and he put his free hand around her, hugging her tight.

At that exact moment Farley walked into the restaurant and stopped in his tracks, "Hi, umm, Steve...Sophie, umm you two met already I see?"

Steve and Sophie, still in an embrace, turned together. Together their eyes took in an enigma in yellow boots. Sophie hadn't seen anyone dressed like Farley since perhaps, 'The Sound of Music', she laughed, she couldn't help herself, it was part relief, part the way Farley's jaw had dropped and mouth stayed open.

Steve and Farley joined in spontaneously and when the waitress approached with menus in hand, she stopped behind three chilips who seemed to be in stitches over nothing. Or were they laughing at each other?

Once they'd ordered, Farley said, "Hey! Someone owes me an explanation." Steve and Sophie looked at each other uncomfortably, who'd speak first?

After an awkward silence, Steve said, "Yeah, umm, I guess you're wondering how we know each other? I worked for Sophie's parents once. On their vineyard."

First there was disbelief, then discontent in Sophie's eyes and she didn't try to hide it. She glared at Steve and said, "That must have been around...Nineteen seventy eight! My you've got a good memory for faces, Steve. I'm not sure I'd have even recognized you."

Sophie waited for Steve's reply, he looked puzzled, perhaps hurt. Steve said, "Oh, I haven't changed that much. Have I?" Steve shuffled on his chair and bumped the table leg. Nothing spilt.

She said to Steve, teasing him, "And what about me, Steve... Have I changed much?"

Steve hesitated, "Ahh, yeah, you have...You're different... so...so professional looking."

"Well thanks...I think that's a compliment?"

Over lunch, Farley did a masterful job as host and kept polite conversation going against all the odds. Nevertheless, Sophie knew she'd have to be careful. If Steve had just worked for her parents, there was an unnecessary level of tension at the table, it wouldn't be long until Farley said something.

She happily talked about the Napa Valley, her parents vineyard, how her brothers ran the place now and what a good worker Steve had been, but she maneuvered around Steve's questions that might lead to 'where was she living now and with whom?'

Steve was equally guarded, he told her the same story he'd told Farley about his project and his job, but left out everything about his personal life. At the first hint that she might want to know about his family, Steve changed tack in mid-stream; he asked about the trek, had Farley and Sophie met before coming to Bhutan, and what did they think of the place? At regular intervals, Steve shook his head and said he just couldn't believe the coincidence, Sophie and he meeting like this after so many years.

Over coffee and cake, it looked as though the lunch might go on for hours yet, but Steve looked at his watch, frowned and excused himself. He explained that he had to get back to the Zangbo to prepare for a meeting with the Minister for Roads.

Before Farley could respond as host, Sophie blurted, "What! Now!"

Steve replied lightheartedly, "Sorry, business comes first." He stood and shook Farley's hand and joked again about how he'd arranged 'the coincidence of the year'.

Sophie bit her lip, she knew there was an air of desperation about her when she said, "What about after your meeting Steve, we could catch up on old times. Maybe have dinner together?"

Steve's face showed that he hadn't thought that far ahead. He looked momentarily lost, then said, "Yeah, sure, I'd love to, why not?"

"Good, I'll come to your hotel." Sophie added quickly. "What time?"

Steve shook his head ever so slightly, as if to say that this was all moving too quickly. "Umm, say eight."

Sophie's reply was instant, "What about seven? We'll have a drink first."

"Oh! Oh, okay!" Steve shrugged, "Make it seven."

"Where are you staying?"

"The Zangbo, on Jangchhub Lam."

"Looking forward to it," Sophie added, "See you at seven."

11: Old times? How old?
Which times?

Steve didn't hide his inner-most thoughts very well. By the time he'd walked back to the Zangbo, the look of utter disbelief on his face was worn like a mask. Namgay glanced up at him twice and enquired politely, "Everything alright, sir?"

For the second time in two days, Steve opened up to someone he didn't know well enough to confide in. He leant on the reception counter and told Namgay of his strange meeting over lunch.

Namgay took it all in, and as he was wont to do, put a cosmic spin on things, "It's the quarter of the moon, sir. Suspicious!"

Steve wondered if that should have been 'Auspicious', but let it go.

"Meeting an old friend by accident may have a deeper meaning." Namgay paused, then asked casually. "Was she a good friend, sir?"

Namgay's question found Steve without a ready answer. He was the only other person in reception, so he took his time to think about it. Finally he said, "Yeah, more than a good friend...much more. A long time ago."

Namgay's wide smile was almost grandfatherly, he nodded sagely and went back to his work. Steve went up to his room and while he prepared for his meeting with the minister, he replayed every moment over lunch. He examined Sophie's every word and gesture, and tried to put meaning to them. And what about his own reactions, then and now? Why did he feel the way he did? Was it just the surprise of the most amazing coincidence? Or was it more than that? Then his thoughts jumped forward to dinner. Didn't Sophie say she wanted to go over old times? How old? Which old times? What did that mean?

At four he went downstairs to call Karma, his five o'clock meeting was not one to be late for.

Nearly three hours later Steve called the Zangbo from the minister's reception, "Is Sophie there yet?" he asked Namgay.

Namgay replied efficiently, "No, sir, but it's not yet seven."

Steve hesitated, disappointed. "Listen," he sighed. "I still haven't met the minister. He's kept me waiting two hours. I'm going in soon. The minister's PA warned that the meeting could go till late. Please tell Sophie that I can't make dinner, that I'm really sorry. Tell her I'll call her in the morning at the RiverView."

Moments later the minister's door jerked open and the square frame of Lyonpo Rinchen Dorji filled the void. The scowl on the minister's face was worth a thousand words.

The lyonpo was a solid man, he stood no more than five and a half feet, but Steve, at a bit over six feet, felt dwarfed by his presence. The minister's finely woven gho and orange neck-scarf hinted at an imperial presence — on national occasions he wore knee-high woven boots and carried a three-foot long sword, and even though he wasn't wearing it, Steve could almost feel the cold glint of steel hanging at the minister's side. Rinchen Dorji didn't say hello, he gestured with a jab of his thumb that Steve should enter.

The lyonpo closed the door behind them both, then he growled, "Andrews, meet Dasho Tobgay, our Chief of Police."

Steve stood face to face with the largest Bhutanese he'd ever seen. Tobgay was as tall as Steve and stood more like a bear than a man. In contrast to the minister's fine gho, Tobgay's was a dull gray and ill-fitting. His jaw protruded, his forehead sloped back to a stubble of close-cropped gray hair and his smile was crooked — it menaced rather than welcomed.

Tobgay extended a paw like hand and spoke in a surprisingly high pitch for a man his size, "I rather not be here, Andrews, but hello anyway."

The lyonpo gestured towards a small round table with three seats around it. The minister's English was perfect, his tone severe. He said, "Dasho Tobgay's known around here as the happy cop."

Steve shot a disbelieving glance in the direction of the Police Chief: he's happy? What's he look like when he's angry?

Tobgay caught Steve's glance and returned it with a grin, "You know why I usually happy, Andrews?" He waited a moment, "I happy 'cause not much go wrong in Bhutan. I have easy job." Tobgay's grin turned to a snarl, "Now I tell you why I unhappy to be here."

At that moment a cuckoo shot out of the minister's wall clock, Cuckoo! Cuckoo! Cuckoo! Cuckoo! It was seven. Steve knew that bloody bird would remind him of the passing of every fifteen minutes, and on the hour it'd squawk four times.

Tobgay waited for the bird to retreat then leaned forward with hand outstretched, "Please your passport, Mr. Andrews."

Steve recoiled, considered his position for a moment, took a deep breath and exhaled, "What! Why?"

Tobgay didn't flinch, the palm of his huge hand was hovering right in front of Steve, he said, "Police procedures, I must know I talking with right person."

Steve looked from one man to the other, the minister looked distracted but not overly threatening, the Police Chief had a smile of sorts on his face. Steve reached into his inside coat pocket and removed a well-worn, blue covered passport of some sixty pages. He placed it squarely in the middle of Tobgay's outstretched hand.

Tobgay leaned back into his chair, opened the book at the front page and diligently compared Steve's photograph with the person sitting adjacent to him. Satisfied that Steve was indeed Steve, he put the passport on the table in front of him and nodded to the minister, "Let's start."

Sophie started dressing for dinner at six. She'd spent the previous hour deciding what would be appropriate. Finally, a little daring won out over casual conservative and she laid out on the bed a V necked red sweater and a pair of figure-hugging black pants. The boots she chose to go with the outfit were far too good to be part of a trekker's luggage, and the selection of jewelry she'd thrown in at the last minute hinted at anything but the rugged outdoors. Would Steve notice? She wasn't sure, but she was prepared to take the risk anyway.

She started walking toward the Zangbo at six forty-five and she was single-minded; cool, calm and resolute. By the time she reached Steve's guesthouse, she'd decided to get her business out of the way over drinks, it would be a load off her mind. After her success over lunch, she had no doubt she could do it, and do it well. After all, surprise was still a part of her battle-plan, and poor Steve didn't even know what he was walking into.

Sophie strode into the Zangbo and went straight to reception. She checked the four clocks on the wall behind the desk and all of them told her she was on time. She rang the bell and a middle-aged man looked up from his work, he had a name badge, 'Namgay' pinned at an unholy angle across his lapel. She introduced herself and said, "I'm here to see Steve Andrews."

Namgay said, "I know ma'am," and with a pitiful look on his face, shook his head side to side.

He didn't need to say anymore, she leaned across the counter, "What! Where is he?"

Sophie put Namgay's unruffled manner and patience to the test: she paced up and down the reception area, she must have asked ten times was Namgay absolutely sure that Steve wasn't coming back, she asked time and time again had this ever happened before with the minister. She asked lots of other questions too. Questions that judging by the baffled look on Namgay's face didn't make sense. Why, for example, would Steve's old friend want to know was he married, did he have children? How often he made phone calls to, and got faxes from, home?

Namgay's attempt to placate Mr. Steve's old friend was valiant, but by half past seven he'd run out of possible excuses and exhausted his armory of diplomatic small talk.

Sophie slumped down on one of the bench seats in the reception area, jammed her elbows on her knees and her head in her hands and wept, "I should have known. He didn't really want to meet me. He's found an excuse."

Namgay walked around his desk and stood by Sophie's side. He said, "No ma'am. That's not true, ma'am."

She looked up, her face tracked with tears, "How do you know?"

"I know ma'am."

Sophie repeated, "How?"

Namgay said, "Mr. Steve said himself, you were a very dear friend. He was so upset that his meeting is running overtime. There's a big problem on his project. Please ma'am, don't cry."

"I'm not!" Sophie looked up, "He said that? A dear friend."

"Yes, yes!" Namgay nodded earnestly. "Very, very dear."

Sophie's spirits lifted, she almost smiled, "Then I'll wait here, I don't care what time he comes back."

Namgay winced, "No need ma'am. Now I remember, he said he'll call you in the morning at the RiverView."

Sophie eyed him carefully, "You sure he said that?"

Namgay nodded, "Surely sure."

Sophie weighed up her options, spending hours in the Zangbo reception was looking less appealing, she said, "Just to be certain, what time does Steve normally leave?"

Namgay laughed, "Huh...Mr. Steve's driver, Karma, he not good at early start. Mostly they leave after nine. Sometimes ten."

Sophie stood and wiped away tears, "What time is breakfast?"

"From seven thirty ma'am."

"Good! If Steve hasn't called beforehand, I'll be here at seven."

"Yes ma'am."

"Be very sure to tell Steve that...please."

"Yes ma'am. Goodnight. He'll call you ma'am."

12: Dear Sophie, I'm sorry...

The cuckoo bounced in and out of its hole eleven times before the questioning finished. It was nearly ten when Tobgay stood abruptly and snatched Steve's passport up from the table in front of him. His huge hand closed around it and it disappeared from sight.

Nearly three hours of interrogation had left Steve exhausted and fearing the worst. And on seeing his passport disappear into the clutches of the Police Chief, his worst fears just doubled. He'd heard the horror stories, now the nightmare was his. No passport equals no way out.

"You can't take that," Steve said and jumped to his feet. With an outstretched hand he demanded, "Give it to me. Now!"

Tobgay squared his shoulders and growled, "Yeah...You gonna take it? Report me to police, huh?"

Steve was face to face with Tobgay, he felt himself shaking but he was determined not to show it. The Police Chief slid Steve's passport into the inner recesses of his gho, turned to the minister who was still seated and laughed, "Lyonpo, listen to this one...On Steve's project, it's for things gone wrong that we weep. It's Steve's problem, so it's his passport that I keep."

Tobgay laughed heartily while the minister chuckled and tidied his papers. Steve's hands dropped to his sides and his heart thumped. Just as quickly, Tobgay's laughter turned to a snarl. He placed a huge fat finger in the middle of Steve's chest, pushed and then growled, "Now I not happy cop, Andrews. You got till the project wrap-up meeting, Tuesday week, that's just eleven days, to find what happened to our money. If no answer, I get you smallest room at Wangdi Prison. I put Rawlinson and Martin in there too and I lose the key. Got it?"

When Steve finally walked out of the minister's office, Karma was almost asleep. It was the duty of a driver; he'd waited out the entire meeting in the minister's reception room. Steve soon learned that he'd gone without dinner, he'd even gone without company for the last two hours; Dorji Dukpa, the minister's PA, had gone home at eight.

They crossed the car park in silence, drove to the Zangbo in silence and then waited for Steve to collect his thoughts, in silence. Perhaps ten minutes passed with Steve just sitting in the car staring out at the hood, then he turned and said what he knew would be the last thing that a Bhutanese government driver would ever want to hear, "Karma, we're leaving at five in the morning and driving straight through to Trashigang."

At first Karma was too shocked to speak, then he started blubbing, "But, but…that's over twenty hours, I can't…"

Steve cut him off as he opened the door and got out, "See you at five…I'll share the driving."

Namgay was sound asleep when Steve walked through reception and climbed the stairs to his room. He forced himself to concentrate. First he packed his things for an early start, his decision to drive straight through to Trashigang had not been made lightly, it'd be hell, but he had so little time now, he couldn't afford to take the normal two days for the drive east.

While packing, he thought about calling Laudmeir, TRAN-SARCO's corporate lawyer in Sydney. He soon dismissed the idea as too risky, it'd be just like Laudmeir to take control. He'd demand that Steve stayed in Thimphu while he sought a legal remedy. Huh, Laudmeir talked about remedies like they were dispensed by a pharmacy, but he'd never set a legal footprint outside his own cozy justice system. Steve choked again on the impossibility of Tobgay's accusation, 'Narguli's found a problem in TRANSARCO's accounts, over twenty million is missing. Narguli says it's fraud, and I'm thinking to agree with him. You Steve, Rawlinson and Martin are the only suspects.'

As Steve finished packing, he considered his confiscated passport and toyed with the idea of calling the nearest Australian embassy. But that was in New Delhi and what the hell could they do to help him? It'd take them a week just to get someone up to Bhutan. And even then they'd send a fresh-faced second secretary who'd expect Bhutan to operate like India, it'd take another week to explain the differences, it wouldn't be worth the trouble. And he knew whatever decisions he made now would be final. There would be no international phone link outside Thimphu, so if he didn't ask for help tonight, there'd be none.

By the time he sat down to write a letter his hand was shaking and the visceral churning in his guts was impossible to ignore. He took a page of Zangbo Guesthouse letterhead and began, *'Dear Sophie, I'm sorry.'*

When he'd finished it was past midnight and all he'd written was half a page with several words crossed out. Steve put the letter in an envelope and carefully wrote on it, Sophie Vella. He knew his letter would just leave her more confused, but it was the best he could do. He also knew what he'd done to her, and to himself, all those years ago could not be redressed in a letter. Nor could the hurt be sealed in an envelope. Nor, it seemed, could it be forgotten.

13: The essence of the Australian bush

Up in her room at the RiverView, Sophie had paced the floor for hours. Well after midnight she moved to the bed and lay down on her back. She eased off her shoes and let them fall. She let the open newspaper slip from the bed to the floor and an image of Steve from long ago slip into her mind. He was stripped bare to the waist as he worked on her parent's Napa Valley vineyard. The Vella Winery had been home to many a seasonal worker — young and old, male and female, light skinned and dark — she must have watched a hundred young men work with sweat glistening on tanned skin. Why had Steve caught her eye that day?

Steve had a month's casual work on the vineyard. Sophie was home on summer vacation from Stanford. That day she first saw him, she watched him work. He stood and wiped the sweat from his face, their eyes met and for a moment she didn't know what to do. He'd smiled, she'd returned his smile and walked away.

That night she asked about him. She learnt his name and that he was Australian. He was twenty-three and had done vacation work in a vineyard before, at some place called Pokolbin, apparently they grew a reasonable Shiraz there.

She hadn't been able to get the tall Australian out of her mind. Over the next few weeks she found any number of reasons to talk with him. They shared a joke, or talked about the weather to begin. Later on, Sophie sat with him during lunch breaks and he talked about places he'd been. About Australia. About his plans to travel through Central America and maybe further south, depending on how his money lasted.

In those days the vineyard worked six days and rested one; on the third Sunday after Steve's arrival, he mentioned he was going to hire a bicycle and ride around the valley.

"We have some bicycles," she said. "Use ours."

Sophie remembered the way he answered her, "Sure, but only if you'll come along for the ride."

They rode side by side down quiet country roads and talked about everything, and nothing in particular. They shared a picnic under the shade of a huge eucalypt tree, and he told her it was a native of Australia. She hadn't believed him, eucalypts were everywhere in California. He gathered leaves from a few different trees, crushed them between his fingers and held them in his open hands – the fragrance was unforgettable, so were his words, spoken so seriously, 'That's the essence of the Australian bush. It makes me so homesick.' Sophie said in fun, 'Maybe, but don't go home just yet.' He put a strong arm around her waist and kissed her mouth, then he laughed and said, 'I won't, the eucalypts here are just fine.'

Their first formal date was to see a new movie that Sophie's friends had been raving about, 'GREASE'. Was it just a coincidence that the story was about an American and an Australian falling in love? Maybe, but that was the day Sophie first thought that college could wait, that Steve might not travel on alone.

When Steve's month was up, Sophie convinced her father to extend it. Then she talked him into letting Steve move into the old stone cottage that lay vacant fifty yards or so from the main house. It was there that he laid out his travel plans. Together they read the South American Handbook cover to cover. Slowly, his plans became their plans. He offered to help her improve her high school Spanish, she was fluent in Italian so he said it'd be easy. She teased, 'I didn't know Australians spoke Spanish?' He laughed and said, 'They don't, I learned it, but it's a long story and one you probably won't believe...I'll tell you one day.' She made him promise. He kept that promise on the day after her twentieth birthday. It was on a hot, still afternoon. A

Sunday, they had the place to themselves. She'd had one previous lover, another sophomore at Stanford, and compared to his fumbling urgency, Steve had been so slow and gentle that she wondered at first if something was wrong. But later, as they lay in each other's arms and Steve told her about lessons learned from Grace, his Spanish teacher, Sophie sighed, 'That's so beautiful, I love you even more,' and held him closer. The way Steve loved her that day was so different to anything she'd ever experienced, she knew she'd go with him; that what he had to give her, she wanted more of.

14: The chilip's cold hand

Up in the attic room at the Zangbo, Steve threw a final few things into his suitcase and slammed it shut. Then he sat down to reread his letter to Sophie. Yesterday, despite his initial misgivings, he'd been looking forward to their dinner together — it would have been a good chance to catch up on old times, the good and the not so good — and somehow Sophie had kept a place in his heart, he couldn't deny the strength of his feeling for her, even after so many years.

For a moment or two he allowed his mind to drift back to better times, to the first time he saw her and then to the stone cottage at Vella Winery where he'd taught her Spanish and they'd shared a lesson in the language of love for the first time.

A rap…rap…rap on the door brought him quickly back to reality — he heard Karma call out, "Mr. Steve, you awake?"

On answering, "Yeah…coming," Steve knew he'd have to push Sophie to the back of his mind and leave her there. He had just ten days to find his way out of the maze he was caught up in, and no matter how he worked things, only four of those days would be spent with the Project team at Trashigang. What he knew to be certain though was this: he had no passport and no way out of Bhutan, and the Chief of Police had not been joking about finding him a room at Wangdi Prison. And while he loved the easygoing nature of the Bhutanese on the outside, he had no illusions about life on the inside — about how brutal the justice system could be.

Steve jerked his door open. He was packed and ready to move: fast. Karma helped carry Steve's things downstairs. No lights were on. The Zangbo's reception area by day, doubled as the staff sleeping quarters by night. Namgay and his helpers were asleep on bench lounges around the reception area. Namgay alone was under a blanket, and it covered his head but not his feet. The rasping of men snoring was the only sound. Steve refocused his eyes to the gloom, pushed back a pang of guilt at what he was about to do and took three quick strides to shake Namgay awake.

Still half asleep, Namgay fixed Steve's bill and reconfirmed that he had Steve booked in again for the night of October fourth.

Steve said, "Thanks Namgay, see you Sunday week…ahh, do me a favor please, get someone to deliver this letter to Sophie Vella at the RiverView." The words had hardly left the tip of his tongue when he realized that he hadn't called home last night, and that he'd said in his fax he would. He looked at the ceiling, buried his face in his hands and swore under his breath. He thought of making a quick call, then thought again: it was mid-morning Saturday at home and the boys would be at school sport anyway. Sighing, Steve leant across the reception desk, took a sheet of Zangbo letterhead and began a hurried fax home. He apologized profusely for not calling, gave just a hint of a serious problem having arisen from nowhere and finished off with a P.S. *'The international phone service east of Thimphu is down for two weeks, I'll get in touch when I'm back here in around nine days. In an emergency, Namgay can contact me so call him. And don't worry if I'm a few days late, even though the main danger period for landslides is past, you can't be sure.'*

Steve said, "Fax this one to Australia for me please, Namgay. This one is to go to Sophie Vella at the RiverView, and please don't mix them up."

Namgay mumbled, "Yes sir, trust me." He took the letters from Steve and from shoulder height, dropped them on his desk. He asked Leki, his bellboy, to help with the luggage, said goodbye and lay down again with a deep, desperate moan that was meant for Steve's ears alone.

A half-hour from Thimphu the steep mountain road climbed through forests of blue pine and orchards. The Landcruiser slowed in a small village where roadside apple-stalls lined the main street. Karma said, "Even apples better than nothing," and pulled over. Steve had no choice but to follow. Karma chose a makeshift stall staffed by a smudged face girl of fourteen or fifteen. She was barefoot and had a tiny baby tied to her back with a length of colorful cloth. Every time the girl moved, the baby jolted awkwardly, but still it slept. Karma ordered up big. Steve paid with a crisp new note. As the girl knelt to get his change, the baby slid half-out of its sling. Steve instinctively put out a hand to stop the fall. What any amount of jostling on the mother's back couldn't achieve, Steve achieved in an instant. The baby opened its eyes, felt a chilip's cold hand on its head and let out a blood-curdling scream that didn't stop. The young mother was blank-faced, she swung the baby from her back to her full breast — it didn't help. Karma said a thousand 'sorrys' in Dzongkha, the baby cried all the more. People stopped in the street, what had the chilip done? Karma grabbed the bags of apples, Steve said, "Forget the change."

Looking back over his shoulder as they drove away, Karma chuckled and joked, "Maybe your touch with kids is lost just now." It was an innocent enough comment, but to Steve it just reinforced what had haunted him all night: he already knew he'd lost touch with his own kids, and after his meeting with the minister, now he was accused of losing touch with his job as well. And on top of all that, Sophie had walked back into his life and reminded him of his biggest failing, and with it, the unspoken part of his life. He felt the hair on the back of his neck bristle against his shirt collar, and he knew the sick feeling in his stomach was more than just hunger.

15: Namgay offers breakfast
and an apology

When Sophie walked into reception at seven sharp, Namgay appeared to be waiting for her. Ready for anything.

She said, "Good morning, Namgay, I'm here to have breakfast with Steve."

His reply was instant, unapologetic, "Steve's gone ma'am. He left very very early today."

Sophie took some moments to let things register, then she snapped, "What!"

Namgay repeated himself, more slowly this time.

She leant across the reception counter, "Did you tell him I was coming? Remember you promised!"

"Ma'am, the truth is ma'am..."

She didn't let him finish, "You didn't tell him, did you?"

"Sorry ma'am. No." He looked at his hands on the desk in front of him and added as an afterthought, "But don't worry, your breakfast is on the house anyway. Saturday's special."

"I don't want anything," she started. "You told me..." Moments later her voice was terse, and within a minute she was ranting.

"Yes ma'am, I know ma'am," he interrupted firmly but pleasantly, "but it's like this." He explained that Steve had never done this before. He didn't know what had gotten into him. Leki, his assistant sleeping over there (Namgay jabbed a finger in Leki's direction for emphasis), confirmed that Karma, Mr. Steve's driver, was beside himself, that even he had never seen Mr. Steve so contrary. Namgay summoned Sophie closer and whispered, "Some big problem's come up on his project and he's got to get to Trashigang urgently and he's driving straight through to do it…that's over twenty hours ma'am, only the insane…or the desperate, do that ma'am."

Sophie's face showed her utter confusion, her despair. She didn't try to hide it. She was mute, dumbstruck.

Namgay said, "Here let me show you." He laid a map of Bhutan out on the reception counter and pointed to Trashigang. Then he pointed to Jakar and said, "Ma'am, normally they'd stop here for the first night."

Sophie's initial reaction was to scream and hammer her fists on the counter. But she was too angry for that. Instead, reason took over. Cold, hard, unemotional reason. She knew Steve's itinerary off by heart. She knew that he wouldn't be back in town for another eight days, and even then he had a series of meetings — there'd be no free time for her. And she'd always known that her hastily contrived plan didn't have a fallback position. If she waited for Steve to come back to Thimphu, she wouldn't have a job when she returned home. But giving up now, that wasn't something she'd even let enter her thoughts. She slumped against the reception counter like it was a crutch. Her breathing was slow and measured. She could see that Namgay was unnerved, but she just let the prolonged silence sit there.

It took less than a minute for Namgay to break, he pleaded, "Please ma'am, you are having accidental meeting with old friend. Nothing is lost, everything is gained. One cannot expect perchance to repeat itself. Please, try our special breakfast, and then forget about him. Mr. Steve's not himself this trip."

Sophie looked up and blinked away a tear, "I can't."

"You can't?"

"No! I can't!" Sophie choked and swallowed hard. "There's something I have to tell him. Something important."

"Oh is that all," Namgay sounded relieved. "You can try the phone tomorrow. I know where Mr. Steve stays in Trashigang."

"No! No phone calls. This message must be delivered in person."

Namgay stuttered, "But...But ma'am? Nothing makes sense. You met by accident, and you have an important message for him, one that can't be told over the phone?"

Sophie looked directly at him, "That's right. So?"

Namgay pulled his reading glasses down to the end of his nose and rubbed his eyes with his knuckles. He pulled at his earlobes, scratched the back of his neck and said, "Well... If it's that important ma'am, follow him. Find him and tell him."

Sophie hesitated, then repeated under her breath, "Follow him, find him." She lifted her head and said, "Okay, I will. Namgay, where can I hire a car? Right now!"

"Hire a car ma'am? Who would be driving?"

"Me."

"You are having license for driving, ma'am?"

Sophie's response was immediate, "Okay, car and driver... but I need to be quick."

"You are having permit, ma'am?"

"Permit? What permit!"

"Yes ma'am. For traveling east of Thimphu you are having permit."

Sophie's impatience was boiling over, she snapped, "Okay... Damn. I'll get a permit. Anything! Just help me Namgay... please."

"I suppose ma'am...yes, we could try."

"Good...how long does it take?"

"Hmmm...With my help, not long ma'am. Monday we go together. Two, three days maybe. By Thursday you are having."

There was an edge of panic to Sophie's reply, "Thursday! I need to go now. Now! Can't you understand, now."

It took Namgay a half-hour or so to explain the practical realities of foreigners traveling alone across Bhutan. Sophie was most reluctant to listen to reason, but eventually reason prevailed. Namgay finished, "This is why you are coming here with trekking group ma'am. You go with Mountain Adventures, it is quicker."

Sophie sighed and put her head in her hands, "Thanks Namgay. You couldn't know what it will cost me if I do." She turned to go, "And only I know what it'll cost me if I don't."

She was at the door when Namgay called after her, hands waving in the air, "Excuse me ma'am, I forget almost, you are having letter from Mr. Steve. Here...please take."

Back in her room at the RiverView, Sophie sat with Steve's letter in trembling hands. She opened it and scanned the first few lines. His handwriting was shaky, uncertain. She read.

Saturday, early.

Dear Sophie,

I'm so sorry I didn't make it for dinner last night or get a chance to call you before I left this morning. I won't try to explain what's happened other than to say that a serious problem has blown up on the Two Roads East Project and it's my job to fix it. I need to get to Trashigang urgently, so I'm driving straight through. I'll be past Wangdi by the time you read this.

The next line began, 'I would have loved to', but those five words were crossed out. The letter finished, 'Anyway, it was great meeting you again and I hope the trek is fabulous. Maybe you could leave a card with Namgay, maybe we could get together again someplace else. Love, Steve.'

Sophie read the letter several times and didn't know whether to laugh or cry. She said aloud, "Huh, a serious problem on his project. What could that be? Just another excuse!" Her eyes went to the words he'd crossed out, "And what would he have loved to do? Tell me why he left me? Make up for nineteen years of pain?" She was talking to herself and she didn't care, "And why did he cross that line out? He's just the Steve Andrews of old, never able to finish what he started. Oh yes, leave my card. Where's his?" After half an hour or so of staring at the same piece of paper and trying to reason with herself, she felt an overwhelming urge to reconnect with why she'd come to Bhutan — why she was alone so far from home.

Sophie folded Steve's letter and knelt over her softpack. She took out a small photograph album and slipped the letter in the back of it. She'd carefully selected a few photographs to show Steve and as she flicked through them, she knew she had no choice, that her next move was predestined.

Sophie reached for the phone and called the operator. She read out Alex's number and waited. It was late Friday night in Washington, so she began by apologizing then she said, "No word from Marie?"

He replied sleepily, "No, but no news is good news."

"Yeah, I guess...but Australia's so..." Sophie hesitated.

"So what? Foreign?" Alex said and chuckled. "Don't worry, she can look after herself."

"Hmm...yeah, she's yet to prove that. Anyway, I'll call her next."

"Okay, tell her to keep an eye out for sharks, you know how many Australian surfers get eaten every year?"

"Alex! That's not funny. You know I was nervous enough about agreeing to the gap year thing in Bali, and that was organized through the school, now she's in Australia by herself, I'm beside myself."

"Alright, sorry, now, tell me what's happening with you."

Sophie filled in the day's events. When they'd gone around and around every possibility, Alex finally said, "Sophie, you know that I can't guarantee your job if you stay another week? I'm already under pressure. And if it's more than another week, forget it!"

Sophie murmured, "I know."

"It's that important to you is it? To do it your way?"

"Yes," she said and added quickly. "Anyway, I'm trapped. I can't just call Steve and say, oh, guess what I forgot to mention the other day! Now, I've got to meet him by accident...again."

Alex sighed into the phone, "Oh...God, Sophie...you're..."

"I know," she said, "Just do what you can for me, please. And if Stella's name is on my office door when I get back, I'll understand."

Alex said tentatively, "I'm not sure...I just hope you're doing the right thing."

He wished her luck and she said, "Just one more favor please."

Alex said, "Sure, what else?"

"Call MJ at the bank and ask him to find out if something's happened on Two Roads East...something that might explain why Steve left Thimphu in such a hurry." Alex agreed, but reluctantly this time. Then Sophie added, "I'm leaving in the morning, ahh...that's late for you; just fax me the details to the hotel." She stopped for a moment, "Better get that translated to Spanish, I don't want it read at the front desk before I get it."

He said, "That all?"

"Yeah, and guess what? The international phone link beyond Thimphu will be out of service for two weeks. So from tomorrow I can't call you and you can't call me."

"Jesus!" He murmured, "Be careful."

"Sure. Take care."

With the phone still in her hand, Sophie dialed the operator again and gave her the number for Marie.

It was Saturday afternoon on the east coast of Australia, most likely Marie would be working or, Sophie buried the thought, surfing. To her surprise the phone answered almost instantly. It was a young Irishman, who introduced himself as Patrick, on the other end. Sophie explained who she wanted to speak to, to which Patrick replied, "I'm sorry, there's over twenty people in this hostel and I'm hopeless with names, but I'm good with accents. Where's she from? And anyway, who's calling her?"

"She's American, from Washington, and only eighteen, I'm her Mom and I need to speak to her urgently, I'm calling long distance."

Patrick whistled into the phone, "Oh Ho! Now, I know her. Good lord, you got one beautiful daughter there. But, but she's telling everyone her name is Louise."

"Ah! Umm, that's her middle name, she uses it sometimes, please could you get her for me, it's urgent."

At that the phone dropped and Sophie could hear in the background an unmistakably thick Irish accent calling out, "Louise Marie from America…Marie…Louise." Moments later there was laughter and a chorus of different voices calling out "Louise Marie…Marie Louise." A minute or so passed slowly.

Marie answered, "Hey Mom," so sleepily that Sophie wondered if she'd got the time zones wrong.

"Hi darling, umm, it's mid afternoon there isn't it? I hope…"

Marie cut in, "Sorry, I was asleep, I worked until after three this morning then sat around talking until sunrise when a few of us went surfing."

"Oh! Okay! Sounds like you're making a few new friends there," Sophie hesitated, "What about Patrick? Is he…"

"What about him?" Marie said abruptly, "You would get *him* on the phone, he's been hitting on me since the moment I walked in here. Anyway, where are you?"

"Bhutan, in Thimphu, in my hotel room."

"Really, how is it? Have you met Steve yet?"

"It's wonderful, I've fallen in love with the place, everyone is so nice…and yes, I met your Dad yesterday for lunch."

"Great, wow, how is he? I mean, has he changed much?"

"He seems well, hardly changed, he's…"

"Quick," Marie cut in, "did you tell him about me? What'd he say?"

"Marie, umm, look darling, it didn't go quite to plan, I didn't get a chance to tell him."

"What! Why?"

"It's a long story, listen, he's left town to go out to his project in the east, some problem has come up, something urgent. I have no choice now but to stay on with my trekking group and meet him next week sometime, somewhere east of here, in central Bhutan. I haven't really looked at a map, I wasn't planning to go past here. I'll tell him. Promise."

Marie's disappointment was palpable through the phone line. She whimpered, choked back tears and said nothing.

Sophie was closer to tears than she cared to admit, but she put a positive spin on things, "It'll work out, anyway, now I'm here I realized I'd be crazy to miss the chance to see the place. I've told Alex that I'm extending my stay here."

"So, okay, when will I hear from you next?" Marie said. "When can I speak to Steve?"

"Listen darling, there's things I don't know myself. And remember, you set me up for this and I'm doing my best, I'll stay here as long as it takes. All I can promise is that I'll tell him, but you know I can't promise anything on his behalf. Now, I'm going to ask you to promise me a few things."

"Yeah, what?"

"One, I'll be out of contact until I get back here to Thimphu, so I want you to be real careful and to call Alex, night or day, if you need help of any kind. Two, I don't care what it costs, I want you to get that card for your cell phone, I'll pay for it. Three and most important, I want you to promise not to contact Steve's family or to go anywhere near his house or his boys."

"Umm," Marie hesitated, "what about Steve's wife?"

"Yes, of course, her, what the hell, especially her."

"Ahh...I can't...she comes in to the hotel for coffee sometimes. Ahh, I served her the other day...she's quite well known around here, she's a journalist."

"Oh, god. No! You didn't speak to her, did you?" Sophie exhaled in a deep desperate sigh, "Ahh, get someone else to serve her, or, umm, what's she like?"

"Oh Mom, honestly," Marie said in that tone teenagers use when their parents let their guard down, "don't worry, I'm not giving anything away, I said enjoy your coffee, ma'am." Marie hesitated and spoke to someone else, she said, "alright, alright!" then sighed and continued, "Sorry, where was I? Sure I appreciate what you're doing for me, for us, and yeah, she's lovely, slim and blonde and confident and seems half the town knows her. Hold on." Marie spoke to someone else, "Okay, okay, I won't be long."

Sophie was lost for words, she mumbled, "What's happening?"

"I'll have to go now," Marie said. "This is the only phone here and someone else wants to use it. Good luck Mom, love you and don't worry about me, I'll be fine."

"Okay, one more reason to get your cell phone working." Then Sophie rushed through her 'goodbyes' and 'be carefuls' and the phone clicked dead.

Determined, but ill at ease, Sophie reopened the photograph album, took out Steve's letter and started planning again. This time she would not fail, Steve would not escape his destiny so easily this time.

She read again the words he'd crossed out, 'I would have loved to...' She let that thought take her back over nineteen years, back to the stone cottage on Vella winery that she still called her home away from home. Back to the day she'd agreed to travel with him and to see where his need for adventure might take them.

His need to travel; he said he couldn't explain it. It was as though there was some part of him buried somewhere in Latin America, he knew he'd never settle down until he found it. Looking back on it now, it seemed an obscure dream. But then they were young, there were plenty of tomorrows. Their plan was to travel for as long as the adventure, and their money, lasted. Then they'd return to California: she'd get to law school, he'd get a proper job, as an engineer.

For over two months they roughed it on Mexican buses, Guatemalan buses and every other sort of bus between San Diego and San Jose. They'd slept on third class trains, ridden on the back of over-loaded trucks and when things got desperate, hitch-hiked. They'd walked, talked and fought over every difficult mile of the journey. She'd lain her head down in hotels that her parents wouldn't have used as a barn, and learnt the hard way that clean water was a privilege, not a birthright. Finally, when even Steve admitted he was tired of moving every other day, they rented a bungalow by the beach at Cahuita, on Costa Rica's Caribbean coast. It was paradise. They shared a simple village life for the best month she'd ever had, then or now. There were fewer travelers back then, Cahuita was undiscovered, the living was cheap and easy. Time passed in a haze of sun, the beach and each other. It had all been going so well. Then, when Steve finally agreed he'd had enough of traveling, that his curiosity was satisfied, he offered to take the three-hour bus ride into San Jose to pick up Greyhound tickets for them both to Los Angeles. That morning before he left, they walked on the beach before sunrise. As the sun lifted over the horizon, they'd undressed each other, swum naked and made love standing knee deep in water the color of green turquoise.

But when Steve returned to Cahuita late that afternoon, he was a different person: Dr. Jekyll had become Mr. Hyde. He had the bus tickets, but for two different journeys. Sophie's ticket would take her north to Los Angeles, then home. His journey was south to Bolivia. Bolivia! He knew where he was going, but he wouldn't say why. He was so cool, almost cold, about his change of mind. She pleaded with him all night for an answer, but when the sun rose over Cahuita the next morning, neither of them had slept and he was still determined they'd take two different roads for awhile. He said on their final parting at the bus depot in San Jose, that when he'd done what had to be done in Bolivia, he'd see her again. He'd kissed her and held her tight, but more like a brother than a lover. Sophie could not have guessed then, that she wouldn't hear from him again. For nineteen years she'd been haunted by what had changed Steve's mind that day in San Jose. And she was still searching for an answer.

16: Daydreaming of Mexico

As they drove into the morning sun, Steve felt the silence more than heard it. Karma had tried several avenues of conversation, but each time Steve had abruptly brought it to a dead end. He needed thinking time.

In his mind, Steve wrote a postscript to his life-story:

late October, 1997, Bhutan. East of Wangdi, the road skirts round the rim of a dry, windswept valley and clings to the near vertical hillside, it is the only thing that doesn't tumble down into the valley, hundreds of feet below. On the flat valley floor sits an isolated building surrounded by a high wire fence. A passing traveler might stop to ask why anyone would build in such a remote and desolate location? Why the building was so fortified? An honest answer would inform that it's the Wangdi Prison, the only high security lock-up in all of Bhutan. A place affectionately known as Hangrila — the locals joke that while no one has ever been hanged there, the inmates wish there was such an easy way out. The prison population numbers over two hundred, all males. There's one chilip and they say the key to his room has been lost. That he's not coping with prison life.

Steve and Karma had driven by here many times, Steve knew that it was a prison down there, but he'd never wanted to know any more than that. Today though, Hangrila was foremost in his mind. He said, "Karma, ever known anyone that's spent time down there." He gestured to the valley floor with a tilt of his head, hoping his question had sounded casual, remote from his own situation.

"No sir!" Karma looked horrified by the very thought of it, "Hangrila's just for the baddest men."

"Oh!" Steve gagged then joked, "I didn't know Bhutan had any?"

"We do now," Karma said pensively. "Not like in the good old days."

"What do you mean?" Steve said.

"Well, long ago, if the monks had a suspect, they'd tie them up in a jute sack and roll them down the hill there. If they were alive at the bottom, they were innocent. If they were dead, they were guilty. They didn't need prison walls back then."

From the tone in his voice Steve wondered if Karma still hankered for the good old days. He decided to leave it there and glanced down at the prison again. Again his mind twisted and turned; 'when would he wake from this nightmare?' And what scared him most was not the confinement, but the stench of so many wretched souls jammed in together. Earlier in the year he'd read a book by a Nepali woman, a young political activist who'd been locked away for years for expressing her pro-democracy views. What had haunted him about her story was that you could block your ears to the sounds of moaning or torture, or shut your eyes to close out the misery, but that you can't shut out the stench of prison — it invades your senses twenty four hours a day, every day.

Awkwardly, Steve reached for the glove compartment and said overly loud, "Time for some music." Karma immediately started tapping his fingers on the wheel. Steve found his newly acquired 'On the Beach' tape and turned it over several times in his hand. He'd heard of the musician before, but he couldn't remember where. Maybe he should have taken the dictionary instead? He shrugged and pushed the tape into the player, then hit the button. The speakers came to life with the sound of rushing ocean.

"What's that?" Karma said, startled.

"They're waves. Waves washing up on a beach."

Karma pulled over to let a truck pass. He turned, disbelief was on his face. "I've seen photographs of the ocean, but I didn't know it roared and crashed like that."

Steve met Karma's look of surprise with a faint grin. He thought of telling Karma what he'd given up for his view of the ocean. The real cost of his cliff-top house that he didn't feel at home in. But he let it pass and the music played as they climbed up through ever tightening corners. And the music was good. And soon the forest was a splash of color — the first hints of fall were painted in gold, russet and yellow on leaves ready to turn before the winter snows. They drove through the small village of Nobding and the hum of the diesel engine faded off into the forest. As soon as the tape stopped, Karma hit the replay button. 'On the Beach' played all the way to the pass at Pele La and Chris Rea had two new fans.

A giant bull yak jumped from the road cutting, it landed heavily in front of them and stumbled. Karma swerved and braked. The great black beast swung its horns wildly. Steve was brought back rudely from a daydream.

"Shit!" he said, "where'd that come from?" and grabbed for the panic bar. Several more yaks followed. Steve looked up to see a herder taking perhaps fifteen animals down the valley. Soon they were surrounded. "Jeezas! We're over the pass already?" Steve muttered and shook his head to clear it of unwanted thoughts. "Where have I been?" Despite his own question, he knew instantly where his daydreaming had taken him.

Sophie and he were on a back road in southern Mexico. They'd missed the last bus out and faced a two-day wait for the next one. The small town they were in wasn't the sort of place one chose to stay in. He'd joked, 'we could ride on the back of a truck.' Sophie had had no qualms, 'let's do it,' she said and swung her backpack on her shoulder. They went to the market and negotiated a ride on a truck taking bags of corn flour from the Yucatan down to Oaxaca. They climbed onboard and found that part of the load was covered by a tarpaulin, part wasn't. They settled themselves on some flour bags just behind the cabin and got comfortable, then Sophie started looking around. She undid a rope or two holding down the tarpaulin and peeked underneath. She reeled. Amongst an assortment of boxes, there were three wire cages full of jungle parrots; there were probably one hundred and fifty birds in total. They were so tightly packed in they could barely move, and they were strangely silent. She'd drawn Steve's attention to the hidden cargo indignantly, 'I'll bet that's not legal' she'd said with her hands on her hips. Steve remembered laughing at her, 'stay out of it,' he'd warned, 'this is Mexico, remember.'

Before they left, the driver squashed three village women and two young girls in the front seat with him, there was barely room for two of them. When he took off, it was as though he alone was on the road, they'd held on for dear life. Several times the truck veered onto the wrong side of the road, and ran cars, people and an odd assortment of animals off into the ditches on either side. Through the back window of the cabin Sophie could see the driver's left hand holding a cigarette and the wheel, and his right hand exploring the inner-thigh of one of the girls; she was no more than fifteen, and so squashed in, she was finding it hard to push him away. Sophie had taken an instant dislike to the man. Steve had held both her hands and laughed when she'd said, so angrily and seriously, what she'd like to do to men like that.

Later, they slowed to halt in the middle of a dusty little village where a school bus had broken down in the main street. Teachers and kids alike were trying to push the small bus off the road. Their driver's response was to blast his horn and shout abuse out the window. The fracas alerted a young boy selling drinks by the glass, he saw a captive market and approached with his wares on a tray held in one hand. Calling out, 'fresca y fria, fresca y fria,' he pulled himself up onto the running board of the truck, hopeful of a sale or two. The driver leant a great hairy forearm out the window and hit the boy hard across the ear with his open hand. It sent the boy sprawling into the dust, drinks flying. Their driver just laughed. Sophie had had enough; she was ready to intervene. Steve remembered having to hold her back, to restrain her from what inevitably would have led to more trouble for himself than he cared to take on at the time. Sophie had muttered under her breath about injustice and mongrel men all the way to their destination.

When the driver stopped to let them off, she'd said to Steve, 'you fix up the fare, I'll unload our packs.' Steve had climbed off, walked up to the driver's door and wasn't surprised that the price originally agreed had more than doubled. A lengthy negotiation followed, then the driver leant out his window and with a greedy swipe of his hand, finally accepted the wad of notes that Steve was offering. Steve, having so paid up, walked around to the back of the truck to find Sophie standing beside their packs. She had the sort of smile on her face that meant only one thing, trouble. Steve had said, 'what's so funny?' She'd replied, 'wait and see.'

The truck belched a thick black haze of diesel smoke and lurched off down the road, and as it did, one hundred and fifty parrots took flight. Steve would never forget the sight and sound of that moment. The air above them was thick with squawking and the green and red of flapping wings; and Sophie was jumping up and down beside him, waving her arms and yelling, 'go, quick, fly away, far away.'

17: The Takin is a sacred animal

After lunch at the RiverView, when the Philadelphians had gone and Sophie was lingering over her tea, Farley said, "A penny for your thoughts," and laughed.

Sophie was jolted into the moment. She replied distantly, "Oh, sorry. Umm…they're not worth a penny."

Farley joked, "C'mon, let me judge that."

"I was just thinking about our trip. How I've been too busy to really even think about it. I've got a map of Bhutan here, remind me please Farley, where do we go?"

At first, Farley was speechless, then he said, "Umm…Sure."

Sophie folded open the map and spread it in front of them both. Farley used the end of a teaspoon to trace out their journey and point out where they'd be for each night they were out of Thimphu. He said, "And on Thursday morning we start the trek from Jakar. Won't that be just great!"

She didn't reply, a mental picture of Steve's itinerary was in front of her: he was returning from the east Thursday morning for a meeting in the Bumthang Valley early Friday. He'd have to stay over in Jakar Thursday night. Somehow, she'd be there to meet him — but how she would pull out of the trek with a reason that wouldn't just beg more questions, she had no idea. Sophie looked up and saw Farley waiting for her to answer.

She finished her tea in a gulp and said, "I'd forgotten it was a five day trek."

Farley just stared back at her blankly.

"Let's go for a walk," she said. "I guess it's never too late to start getting into shape?"

Sophie and Farley made an odd couple. They walked around Thimphu purposefully but without any obvious plan. They looked in some shops, spent quite a while in the bookshop and then walked around some more. At four they returned to the RiverView and got on the bus with the Philadelphians. Tashi was ready with a grin, he joked, "Who knows what a takin is?" Not even Farley dared a guess. As they drove out of town, Tashi pointed out the Thimphu golf course and said, "It was a gift from the Japanese Government. Now the king's learning to play." About twenty minutes steep climbing later, they stopped high above Thimphu at a small hand painted sign that read 'WILDLIFES PARK'. Apparently they were soon to be introduced to one of nature's strangest looking beasts, the takin. "Takins," Tashi said pointing, "are sacred animals." To Sophie they looked to be half moose and half mountain goat, and while Tashi talked, she thought about taking a journey she'd never planned to take.

Soon her mind flicked back to Alex's closing remark in their phone conversation that morning. He'd sounded uncertain, 'I'm not sure, I hope you're doing the right thing.' Now his doubt was unsettling her. Yesterday when she'd phoned him, he'd been unfazed. He'd referred to the *Post* piece as a 'one day wonder' and finished their conversation laughing. 'Leave Stella and her cheap shots to me, just do what you have to do and get back here quickly.' This morning though, it had been a different matter. Alex had found it hard enough to approve any leave when she'd just started in her new job. But now that she was planning to follow Steve across Bhutan, she knew her job, the job of a lifetime, was at risk. And why had Marie cut their call short? So what if someone was waiting, it had left an empty feeling and now the thought of being without a phone for over a week was threatening rather than liberating.

Laughter brought her back to the takins. She'd missed the start of a joke. Tashi was telling a story about the time the king ordered that all the takins be set free to roam the streets of Thimphu. The Philadelphians and Farley were captivated, she tried to join them but her heart wasn't in it, and her mind wouldn't let go of an image of Stella Borg. The image was of Stella sitting in the Coordinator's office with her feet on the desk and Sophie's telephone in her hand, and she was laughing, laughing out loud.

Alex had mentioned over the phone that in Washington, it was more like winter than fall. She imagined him in his office, reading an appeal against her recent promotion. Ms. Borg was not going to let go easily it seemed. A couple of people on the selection panel for the Regional Coordinators job had asked Alex if there'd be a backlash against her appointment, but he'd insisted, the best person had to get the job and the best person was Sophie. At the time he'd agreed to her special leave, she knew it was against his better judgment, after all, who took 'special leave' to go trekking? But then Alex often joked that everything he'd had to do with her was against his better judgment. She'd swept him off his well-heeled feet. Their marriage had been a roller-coaster of ups and downs. Their separation then divorce had been no different, and even now she couldn't do without him.

Sophie imagined Alex picking up the phone and dialing the South Asia Infrastructure Bank. The woman that would answer would sound Indian, crisply efficient and with perfect English. He'd ask to be put through to Michael James, until a few years ago his boss, and less directly, Sophie's. MJ would answer as though Alex called him every other day. Alex would explain the information that Sophie needed and why, and MJ wouldn't hesitate, he'd say, "Sure, I'll have you an answer tonight." Sophie knew that Michael James wouldn't ask Alex what she was doing in Bhutan and why she needed the information he'd just asked for, after all it was MJ himself that had helped Sophie get hold of Steve's itinerary and quickly plan her trip around it.

18: *Jakar wife is smiling now*

The Landcruiser continued its steady descent, past the village of Tangsibji and into the valley of the Mangde Chhu. Steve noticed a new road being constructed above them, it cut off sharply from the main road and switched back and forth up a forested hillside. Below was a drop-off to nowhere, a thousand feet or more, straight down. Trongsa came into view across the valley. The vast yellow roofs of Bhutan's largest dzong cascaded down the ridge on top of a massive white-walled fortress. A fortress that was once the royal family's ancestral home.

They drove by the Sangyang hotel, normally they stopped there for lunch and just the thought of it made Steve's stomach do somersaults. But he dared not even mention eating lest Karma mutinied. It was at exactly twelve thirty that the Landcruiser entered the switchbacks above Trongsa. The climb up to Yotong La was without incident. The trip east was going according to plan, Steve felt reassured by the familiarity of it, then almost at that instant they were engulfed in a cloud of smoke billowing down the road.

"Road gang," Karma said and stopped.

Steve just sank in his seat and groaned. He knew what sort of delay to expect.

The smoke lifted on a gust to reveal two parallel lines of blackened forty-four gallon drums stretching down the road for thirty feet or more. Between the line of drums a fire was raging. Sitting over the fire and supported by the drums were steaming black trays of asphalt. Both women and men were stirring the black tar with long-handled rakes. As the wind gusted, the workers went into and out of view, the smoke enveloping them, and then lifting to let them breathe again. Soot black from head to toe, they wore makeshift turbans stretched over their faces in faint hope: hope that it might ease the burning in their lungs.

At the end of the first hour they'd waited, Steve was becoming desperate. He'd already walked up and down the road gang trying to find out who was in charge. He'd even asked Karma to find someone who could let them through. Neither of them had got better than a blank look and a shrug of the shoulders. At three thirty, after they'd waited nearly two hours they were waved on. Karma started the motor and said, "I guess it's hopeless now, we'll have to stay over in Jakar after all?" But Steve swore again at the delay and said they'd have to make up the time somehow, that they'd eat dinner quickly in Jakar and then keep moving, even if that meant crossing Thrumsing La at night.

At a crawl, they passed the carriers; men and women taking steaming asphalt in buckets and wheelbarrows to their older children who would spread and compact it on the road surface. The workers, low-caste Nepalis and Indians, lived in makeshift tent villages and led a nomadic life as they followed and fixed the deteriorating road surface across Bhutan. They ate, slept, washed, made babies and delivered them right there by the roadside. The younger children improvised games, or just sat and watched cars go by until they themselves were old enough to pick up a shovel and work. The road gang stretched up to the pass at Yotong La.

The road east dropped from Yotong La through a pristine forest of fir. Grey-green moss hung from the branches like an old man's beard, clouds swirled through the trees and Karma's grip on the wheel hadn't changed. They drove through Gaytsa village and the Chhume valley opened up. Karma pushed in a tape and they listened to music while the miles went by. The mighty Bumthang River came into view as the late afternoon sunlight cut hazy yellow through gaps in the forest canopy. Jakar town was then in sight, and the dash clock showed five p.m. Karma groaned and then stretched in an exaggerated gesture of exhaustion, still Steve was resolute, he just said, "Do you want me to drive now?" Karma didn't answer, his eyes fell again to the dash and at that very moment his expression changed, he said seriously but with an underlying hint of relief, "Diesel we get at Jakar, we won't make Lingmethang." Steve nodded, "Yeah, okay."

They passed the Lhakhang, the six-hundred-year-old village temple, and pulled into the gas station. It was deserted. Karma said nothing as he rested his forehead on the wheel and whistled through clenched teeth. Steve got out and shouted, "Hello, where the hell is everyone?" Karma stayed put. Steve asked who owned the place and where he or she might be. When Karma shrugged and mumbled, "dunno", Steve knew he wasn't getting the truth. He persisted and learnt that the owner was one Nado Yonten, and that Nado was widely known in the town as having a taste for the tipple. On cross-examination Karma speculated that by now he'd be enjoying the first of many arras for the night. Arra, a strong spirit distilled from rice was a favorite in the Bumthang valley. But Steve was not going to give up so easily, he went around to the back of the makeshift office and called out, "Hello, anyone there!" He tried the diesel pump and found it locked, he quizzed Karma again, "You sure you don't know where he lives?" Karma shook his head and the look of feigned disappointment on his face was hard for Steve to miss; or believe. At five thirty Steve kicked at the oil-soaked ground in anger and said, "Shit...we'll ask at the guesthouse. Eric might know." Karma nodded in reluctant agreement and Steve watched as Karma bowed his head to hide the grin on his face.

It was just after six when Karma left Steve at the Eiger Guesthouse with an agreement to be early in the morning. Eric had confirmed that Steve had more chance of finding gold in the valley than finding Nado at that time of day. He'd said, the gas station opened at seven, until then Steve would be his welcome guest. Steve had sworn black and blue but was soon resigned to his fate. He'd made Karma promise not to be late and added that Jakar wife being lonely would not be an excuse.

Karma had offered multiple assurances and wished Steve a good night's sleep. But as he waved goodbye, Steve knew that Karma would be thinking of anything but a good night's sleep for himself — that there was still the risk of a further delay.

19: Only two fingers on the corporate ladder

Outside the RiverView Hotel, Anna Dudinsky had most of her party of trekkers in the bus by nine; the Philadelphians were ready to go but the other two were stalling. Sophie was expecting a fax from Washington, it hadn't come and she was reluctant to leave Thimphu without it; meanwhile Farley had struck up a conversation with the housemaid cleaning his room.

Anna had planned a leisurely drive east with an early lunch at Wangdi. They'd spend the afternoon at a festival, the Wangdi tsechu, and then turn north for the short run upriver to Punakha, where they would stay for the night. It wasn't a long day so Anna agreed with Sophie that they'd wait awhile for her fax to come through. Sophie was in the hotel reception watching the fax machine with a sinking feeling in her stomach — it was nearing midnight in Washington, if Alex was going to get a message to her, it should have been here already.

At nine thirty Nancy tapped Sophie on the shoulder and said, "Come on Sophie, we're all waiting. Leave whatever's bothering you behind, your fax will be here when you get back."

Sophie turned again to the reception clerk and pleaded, "You sure no messages came for me overnight?"

It was the end of a long shift for the night duty clerk and her young shoulders slumped. She so much wanted to help. She said softly, "No ma'am. There's nothing for you ma'am." She stopped for a moment to collect her thoughts, "Only one fax came all night and that was a wrong number, it's in foreign language."

Sophie's heart skipped a beat, why hadn't she been told that before. She leaned over the reception counter and said, "Quick, show me!"

She was aware of Nancy at her right shoulder as the night-clerk rummaged around for a single page written in Spanish. Alex had been so cautious he hadn't put it on departmental letterhead. Sophie took one look at it and said, "That's it, it's mine. It's even got my name on it."

Sophie grabbed the page and quickly folded it in half, "thanks." She was concerned that Nancy had caught a glimpse of the letter and might ask awkward questions. But at that moment Farley raced through reception with a newspaper tucked under his arm and uttering a string of apologies for holding them all up.

They crossed the Thimphu Chhu on the Lungten Zampa bridge and Sophie watched as Farley stuffed a newspaper into his daypack, she thought it looked curiously different to any local papers she'd seen and then thought no more of it. The town was coming to life: buses and Tata trucks were refueling at Thimphu's one gas station, and stall-keepers were scurrying toward the Sunday fruit and vegetable market with heavy loads. As they wound their way uphill on Dechhen Lam, Sophie looked back over the town. Thimphu had a pleasing symmetry about it, it was carefully planned in an unplanned sort of way, and it fitted — Thimphu wasn't yet, too big for its valley. She commented favorably to Farley and while he was distracted by the scenery, Sophie skimmed the one page fax she'd just received. One word leapt off it, *estafar*. Fraud! That one word sent a cold shiver down her spine, and it didn't stop there, soon her legs were shaking. She glanced sideways, Farley was still turned to the window. She looked again at the letter. There was an opening paragraph, then the key lines. She read, *'Steve's passport has been seized by the police. The bank's task manager for Two Roads East, Dr. Narguli, is investigating Steve and two of his staff for fraud. Over twenty million dollars is missing from the project. Steve has less than two weeks to find the money, or he'll wait in gaol until the bank finds it. Michael James says the bank isn't sure what's going on, he says be very careful.'*

Sophie folded the page in one quick movement. Her heart thumped and her mind raced. The police had Steve's passport; they wouldn't take that without a good reason. And she knew enough about the business Steve was in to know what the reason might be. This wasn't just ordinary white-collar crime. She could see the headlines, 'Australian Aid Worker steals Twenty Million from Dollar-a-Day rural poor in Bhutan.'

As she glanced sideways at the sprawling river-valley that Farley was pointing to, the next thought that crossed her mind almost choked her. Had she come all this way to meet a criminal? What would she do if Steve was locked away in a Bhutanese gaol for stealing from an aid project? There had to be a mistake. She knew Steve too well for that. She'd met him just two days ago, he didn't look a common criminal. Or did she know him after all these years?

Farley was talking about how good it was to be on the road again and it was the last thing on Sophie's mind. Within fifteen minutes of Thimphu, bit by bit she brought the conversation around to Steve, to what he'd told Farley during the five-hour flight into Paro. Farley obliged willingly and added a lot more detail than Steve had been prepared to impart over their lunch on Friday. By the time they stopped to buy apples, Farley's memory for detail was a godsend. Sophie heard about Steve's designer house on a headland overlooking the Pacific Ocean. And his two boys and how he doted on them. And how hard he was working to keep it all going.

As their bus wound its way around ever tightening corners, Sophie probed deeper and Farley was a willing talker. He kept talking until they reached the top of the mountain pass at Dochu La, "Though he'd stumbled into it, Steve loved his job to begin. He told a wonderful story about his first project abroad, in Vietnam, how he'd helped design and build a road into some remote mountain villages, how he felt that his work made a difference to the lives of hundreds of people. How the smiles on the kid's faces made up for the tough conditions. His best days at work were like that and he had the freedom to balance it with family-life. But then TRANSARCO merged and Steve got a new boss. Some guy called Bradshaw who regarded anyone doing less than nine months of the year away from home a life-styler. The one most likely to be hurled off the middle rung of the corporate ladder was the way Steve put it. Sophie, I got the feeling that Steve's grip on that ladder is just a couple of fingernails at the moment."

The bus stopped and Anna said, "Bring a coat, it'll be cold outside." They all got out and followed her to a line of white prayer flags on the edge of a clearing in the forest. The flags, tall and narrow and attached to freshly cut wooden poles, were printed with ancient Buddhist prayers. The wind, they were told by Tashi, carried the prayers far and wide and spread them for all to hear. Behind the row of flags was their first view of the main Himalayan Range. While cameras whirred and clicked, Anna pointed out Gangkhar Puensum at twenty-five thousand feet. She said that it was now the highest unclimbed mountain peak in the world. Farley asked Anna to take his photo by the chorten and Sophie took that as her cue to go. Within moments she was back in the bus reading Spanish — one crumpled page that she folded and put away as soon as Farley sat next to her again.

The road dropped through forests of spruce and hemlock; rhododendron, daphne and magnolia scattered the understorey and Sophie said, "We were talking about Steve, where were we?" Only here and there did dappled sunlight touch the forest floor. Where it did, it spotlighted ferns, mosses and creepers hanging like garlands from low hanging branches. Flame-colored minivets and rosefinches darted about while Farley filled in the last few details he'd heard from Steve, he said, "Steve's married to a

Miranda," as if the name denoted a species. "She's a journalist and does her own thing. And Steve's not a happy man."

Sophie said, "He told you that?"

"What?"

"That he's not happy?"

Farley grinned, "Well, not exactly. But I'm an intuitive person, I know these things."

20: Taken in by 'The Land of the Thunder Dragon'

One hundred and seventy miles to the east of Thimphu, the Eiger Guesthouse had long been Steve's chosen accommodation in Jakar. And despite his thwarted attempt to bypass it last night, he'd once again been grateful for its comforts. A Swiss carpenter named Eric had built the guesthouse by hand, he'd visited Jakar over twenty years earlier and never quite left.

It was just on six thirty a.m. and Steve was making his reservation for the return journey, on the Thursday and Friday nights of that same week.

Eric ran his finger across the page. The guesthouse was booked out by Mountain Adventures for Tuesday through Wednesday, but the group was leaving on a five-day trek on the Thursday morning. Eric said, "You're lucky, they'll be gone."

Steve's reaction was immediate, he blurted, "Mountain Adventures! They're staying here?"

Eric looked up, "You know them?"

"Ah, sort of, yeah. One of them is an old friend, but looks like I'll miss her again."

Eric just smiled and nodded.

A minute or so later Karma arrived, and to Steve's chagrin he was both immodestly cheerful, and early. With Karma whistling a tune, Steve sat in a stony silence as they drove out of the guesthouse, refueled in town and turned east. From the Bumthang Valley to the Ura Valley they listened to music and hardly spoke.

Steve continued the line of thought that had been right there at the front of his mind from before first light: he'd been thinking about Sophie Vella and coincidence. Now that he knew she'd be staying at the Eiger the night before he returned. That she'd be going trekking for five days and their paths wouldn't cross again, it just reconfirmed what he'd already convinced himself of. Their chance meeting in Thimphu had been just that, anything further was not meant to be.

It did cross his mind as curious that Sophie had come on the trip alone, but then it didn't surprise him that much. Sophie had always been a free spirit. He shook his head and scoffed. A team of takins couldn't drag Miranda to Bhutan, trekking was not her style. Sleeping in tents! No hot showers! No thanks!

Just outside Ura they crossed the Liri Zam Bridge and began the climb to Thrumsing La, the highest pass on their journey. Tight corners followed each other so closely that Karma's hands were a blur on the wheel. Steve held onto the panic bar and forced his mind into neutral: soon, as clear as if it were yesterday, an image formed itself in his head and wouldn't leave.

He was sitting in his office at home, at his desk but with his back to it. Facing him was a wall of framed photographs. There were many, but only one had been taken nearly twenty years ago in Guatemala. In the foreground were two young children in traditional dress. With their jet-black hair and eyes, and colorful costume, they made for an interesting talking point. A casual observer would assume that he'd taken the photograph of the children, but a closer look revealed a young woman in the background. She carried a backpack and had her dark brown hair tied in a red bandana. Her face was in profile, it was a face that demanded a second look. It was possible that he'd taken the photograph without knowing the woman; she wasn't looking at him. But it was just as possible that he knew her. Miranda took very little interest in his photography, and even less in his travels of bygone days — the budget that Steve had traveled on was not to her liking. Years ago though, when he'd first put that photograph up on the wall, Miranda had pointed to Sophie and said, "Who's that?" Steve, caught by surprise, answered, "Oh, just another traveler." Even back then, he wasn't about to start the one story that he knew he couldn't finish. Miranda had shrugged and walked away. She'd never asked again. The photograph was still there. It was a reminder of the only time in his life that he'd been truly free. That freedom had come on leaving Australia and the confines of a loveless family that lived as though every new day was a task to be endured. The contrast when he'd been taken in by Sophie's family, was stark. His own father was a small wiry man, an elder in the Methodist church for whom the color gray did not exist; Sophie's father was larger than life, he could find something good from any adversity, he'd turn up a joke from anywhere, anytime. Steve's mother never set foot in the local church, by choice the family home and the business attached to it was her prison. Glossy magazines, alcohol and cigarettes were her only escape. Sophie's mother, Maria, was one of those warm, caring women for whom the heart of the family home was her kitchen. His older brother Bill was his only sibling. But from as early as Steve could remember, Bill had chosen to fight him rather than befriend him. Sophie's brothers, Tony and Louis, were men that could laugh out loud, hug each other and even cry together. Emotional expression that Steve secretly envied. Just months after that photograph was taken, Steve's newfound idea of freedom had been stolen from him and never returned. That day in San Jose when he'd had to turn his back on Sophie and walk away, he'd lost a lot more than the best friend he had ever had.

After an hour and a half of steady climbing, Karma rounded the chorten on Thrumsing La at twelve thousand three hundred feet and bowed to it respectfully. Then began the plunge to the Kuri River. The road here could not be said to descend, for that was far too mild a verb to describe the feeling of dropping from over twelve thousand feet to six hundred feet in less than sixteen miles as the eagle flies. They crept downhill at a little over ten miles per hour. At the village of Sengor, Karma pulled over for a tea break and that image of Sophie and freedom was still foremost in Steve's mind.

Soon after Sengor, the road is etched into the side of an overhanging cliff a thousand feet above the valley floor. At an altitude of five thousand feet, they stopped in a grove of oaks and ate a picnic lunch that Eric had prepared.

While Karma was busy with his third helping, Steve picked at his food and bit by bit, forced Sophie out of his mind and work into it. He cursed himself; Two Roads East had been going so well. His trips to Bhutan had been easy, and he'd been captivated by the country, the people and the mystery of the place. Most places he worked he knew that he had to watch every project dollar, corruption and greed were everywhere, but he'd never felt that in Bhutan. Now he wondered if he'd been taken in by the 'Land of the Thunder Dragon'. He knew he hadn't had his mind fully on the job this last twelve months. That he'd been preoccupied with problems at home. His own innocence, he was certain of. But the possibility that one of his own team might have siphoned off project money was so foreign to him that he hardly knew where to start thinking it through.

The bank and TRANSARCO kept separate accounts for the project. The bank's accounts showed draw-downs on the loan. TRANSARCO's, recorded project expenditure. When reconciled, the two sets of books were meant to match. Recently however, Narguli had found that the bank's accounts showed just over ninety five million had been spent while TRANSARCO's own accounts rounded up to seventy five million. And neither of the 'Two Roads' was finished, it would take at least another ten million to finish the job.

Steve's immediate suspicion jumped to kickbacks. The project buys say one million dollars worth of pipes. The project and the supplier agree to an invoice being issued and paid for one and a half million. The staff of the project and the supplier share the half million — it's simple but it works. Steve had seen it before, but the beneficiaries always left the project before the problem was discovered. If Rawlinson or Martin had tried that one, they wouldn't still be in Bhutan. It had to be something more sophisticated.

First, John Rawlinson came to mind. Steve had found Rawlinson in TRANSARCO's Seattle office. His CV looked perfect for the project manager's job, Steve remembered it well: 35 years experience in 45 countries, he'd worked for every development bank, bi-lateral and multi-lateral known to man, he'd managed mega-projects and his civil status was proudly spelt out in capitals - DIVORCED. As Steve later discovered, to Rawlinson this was a badge of honor in the industry; proof that he'd put his career ahead of his family, a sign that he was free to travel and work unencumbered.

But Rawlinson had several other offers on the table at the time. Changing his mind had come down to one thing: money. At that thought, Steve winced again at how much he was paying Rawlinson, it was one of the reasons he'd cut a few corners in other areas of the project — like cutting out a fulltime project accountant.

From Rawlinson, Steve had learnt a hard lesson: CVs don't always tell the full story. There was no question that Rawlinson was a great engineer, but what his CV hadn't mentioned was that his best work had been done with a support team bigger than many medium-size engineering companies. In Bhutan, with Martin, a junior engineer from TRANSARCO's Sydney office as the only other team member, Rawlinson had struggled with the administrative side of things. But Martin had been helping with the project accounts. How, between them, could they lose track of so much money?

The stench of Hangrila was in Steve's nostrils when his thoughts turned to Martin Pickel. A twenty-nine-year-old Tasmanian, Martin had been with TRANSARCO since graduation. This was his first posting abroad. Both Steve and Rawlinson had found him to be a pleasant and capable engineer. He willingly took on the arduous duty of camping out with the field crews, sometimes for a week at a time, and he had great rapport with his Bhutanese colleagues. What most impressed

Steve though, was the way Martin had offered to help with the project accounts when it became obvious that Rawlinson couldn't (or, more likely, wouldn't) keep the books. Martin had said, "I'll do it, I'll learn how." Martin hadn't made too much of it, but Steve knew that he did most of this extra work at home, after hours.

According to the women in TRANSARCO's Sydney Office, Martin was 'one hell of a good-looking guy.' A real catch. Those that had mothered Martin, and that was the majority, had differing opinions on Tammy, his wife. When they'd married, the less generous said that at four years Martin's senior, Tammy was just looking for another man to help her achieve her dreams. And her dreams were not modest. Her first husband, Tammy openly joked, 'was going nowhere fast.' The minority said that Tammy was just what Martin needed, 'she was a woman with ambition and big ideas, things Martin lacked.'

In their first year in Bhutan, Tammy had been a model of support and enthusiasm. She was helping with English teaching at the local primary school, and she even tried to pick up some Sharchop, the language of the East. But the gloss was starting to wear off by the second year. It was mid-way through year two that Rawlinson reported his concern about how much they were drinking. Steve had hinted at it in a roundabout way, but Martin and Tammy had laughed it off, 'what else was there to do?' By the third year, Tammy was into complaining. The money TRANSARCO was paying Martin wasn't enough. Steve hadn't explained how difficult the living conditions were, how remote it was. Martin left her alone while on field trips. There was no social life, the food was limited and if she wanted to work, the pay was at volunteer rates. She complained more when she'd been drinking, and lately she'd been drinking most times Steve spoke to her.

On his last visit, Rawlinson and Steve had been invited to have a drink with them. There was no doubt that Tammy had had several gin and tonics too many. They'd been there less than half an hour when the conversation drifted to Bhutanese names, and how a monk or lama gave them, how there was no such thing as a family name. Tammy was laughing about how one of the local engineers had just had a son, and how confusing it was that Sangay Yonten and Mindup Kesang have a boy named Dawa Dorji. Then (still laughing) she'd said that Martin would have been better off as a Bhutanese. No child of hers would ever be a Pickel. Her surname, Davis, was her first husband's name, and she and any children would be keeping it, thanks.

"After all," she'd said, "who'd take on a name like Pickel? As if life isn't hard enough!"

Martin had tried to laugh it off, explaining that Pickel was the name of a proud Tasmanian farming dynasty that'd worked the same fertile acreage for five generations.

"Oh yeah, a farming dynasty," she'd chided, "my horse-shit covered boot. Your family grows a paddock or two of opium poppies. Big-time farmers indeed."

"At least we grow them legally," Martin defended. "And they're big paddocks."

"Christ Martin! You're such a lightweight," Tammy had scolded and then offered Steve and Rawlinson another drink. Both had declined, and on that note the party ended.

After thinking it through, Steve decided that he was as convinced of Martin's innocence as he was of his own. That Martin hadn't found a twenty million dollar shortfall before Narguli did, worried him. But incompetence was easier to believe than criminal intent. There was a slight gnawing doubt about Rawlinson, why for example had he been so adamant that he wouldn't take on the responsibility for the project budget? And money was such a big thing to Rawlinson? But to end a thirty-five-year career with TRANSARCO by dipping sticky fingers into the project till, it just didn't stack up.

That left Tammy, but she couldn't do anything unless Martin was complicit, and he knew in his heart that Martin wouldn't steal from the Bhutanese, or TRANSARCO, even if Tammy would.

Steve sat up with a jolt, a churn in his guts. He'd be staying with Martin and Tammy tonight, then with Rawlinson, Monday through Wednesday nights. He was their houseguest and he'd be looking at them as possible suspects.

21: The Dance of the Twenty One Black Hats

Over lunch at Wangdi, Sophie had had too much time to think through what Alex's fax from Washington had told her. Farley's story on Steve just added to the muddle. Knowing what she knew now, how would she approach Steve when they met again in Jakar? Could he really be a criminal? Or was there some huge mix-up? Or was Steve being framed for a crime he didn't commit?

Around her were eleven people having fun, she knew it would be just a matter of time until one of them, probably Nancy, said, 'Why so glum, Sophie? What's on your mind?' She also knew she'd have to wait until Thursday to answer any of these questions. She decided to push all her doubts to the back of her mind and leave them there. Looking for a distraction, she sipped her coffee and opened Bhutan's national weekly newspaper, the *Kuensel*. There were stories on blessings given by His Holiness the Je Khenpo; an accident where a bus had plunged off the road killing 40 people; the difficulty of keeping Dzongkha alive as the national language; and a captioned photograph of the king and youngest queen's recent visit to the east. The one page of international news was dominated by an account of the life and times of Mother Teresa of Calcutta. Sophie tried to read the article through, it was well written, but all she could think of was Steve with the bank's Audit Department hot on his tail. Michael James was a good friend to have, but she could hardly think of a worse person as a foe. Since MJ had taken over as head of audit, he'd been relentless in the pursuit of thousands, let alone millions. MJ was building a reputation; in search of twenty million, Sophie knew he'd stop at nothing.

She needed another distraction, quickly. She scanned the back page of the *Kuensel* again and that got her thinking about the *Washington Post* — had she brought it with her? Where had she put it? Moments later, to Sophie's relief, Anna called them together.

Tashi started telling them about the tsechu — the main festival of the year being held in the courtyard of the Wangdi dzong. How important it was to Bhutanese culture.

"What's the festival for?" Farley asked, amongst many other questions.

"It's to honor Guru Rinpoche, the founder of Buddhism in Bhutan." Tashi continued, "The monks dress up as deities, heroes or demons and perform dances to bring blessings to all the onlookers. It's a religious festival, you're blessed by attending."

When they arrived at the tsechu there was a group of barefoot dancers (probably deities) being pursued and harassed by another group (clearly demons). The costumes were wildly colored and flowing, and the music of drums and horns echoed through the ancient courtyard like a cymbal clash up-close. Tashi leaned over to Sophie, "It's the Dance of the Twenty-One Black Hats." She thanked god; she was being drawn in, distracted.

When the first dance finished, the air was electrified by the sound of children yelling and laughing. Clowns had appeared from nowhere — clowns with long red noses that poked and prodded, and brought screams of delight.

After the tsechu they'd looked around Wangdi and then driven north. Sophie found it easier to get involved in the tour than to think about where she was headed and why. About thirteen miles out of Wangdi the Mountain Adventures' bus rounded another sharp corner and the Punakha Dzong came into view. It sat on the opposite bank of the Mo Chhu, with a cantilever footbridge joining the dzong to the town. The dzong's central *utse* glinted golden in the late afternoon sun and its fortress-like walls were high and impenetrable. Anna began their tour of the dzong by saying, "They started building this dzong in 1637..." Sophie moved closer, she didn't miss a word after that. "The original name meant Place of Great Happiness." Anna kept them spell bound for over an hour. It was almost dark when they arrived at the Punakha Inn. For a couple of hours at least, Sophie had hardly thought about Steve's problems and what they meant for her.

She went to her room and unpacked. Strangely, she couldn't put her hand on the Washington Post she was hoping was in her suitcase so she began reading a novel she'd picked up at the airport in Bangkok. But no matter how hard she tried to follow the story, she soon found herself drifting: to a bicycle ride in the Napa Valley, a beach in Costa Rica, a bus station in San Jose.

22: The loneliness of the unwanted guest

From five thousand feet, the Landcruiser dropped straight down to six hundred feet. It was hot and sultry at the Kuri Chhu — the river gave the impression it was perpetually in flood. Rice paddies were terraced into the hillside and mangoes and bananas were growing an inch a day. Temperate Bhutan was suddenly tropical, and fraud was back on Steve's mind.

"How are things going with Martin and Tammy?" Steve said as casually as he could.

The faintest of smiles crossed Karma's lips, "To tell you the truthfully, Mrs. Tammy is not happy just now."

"Yeah! What's up with her this time?"

"Mr. Martin has been spending too much time away."

"More than usual?"

"Yes sir, much more. He's hurrying to complete Section 101. Lately his crew work from sun up, to sun down."

"Hmmm," Steve found a note of sympathy, "they should have got a house in Trashigang town. At least then she'd have some company."

Karma nodded. "They have a beautiful house down by the river, but how much time can you spend looking at the water rushing by?"

They passed a lemongrass distillery on the banks of the Kuri River. The sweet aroma of distilled oil hung in the air.

"Ahh good," Karma said in exaggerated delight, "Lemongrass has the best smell."

"Yeah," Steve said. "Hey, is your brother still in the business?"

"Yes sir. Still Dechen travels all over the east buying oil. He's in Thimphu now arranging a shipment."

Steve nodded and thought 'good', that meant he probably wouldn't meet Dechen this trip. They left the river behind them. An hour-long climb to Mongar lay ahead. With the town in sight, Steve said, "How's Rawlinson at the moment?"

"Good, he's always good." Karma's response was automatic. "Everyone enjoys working with him, even Mr. Nigel Smyth-Jones."

Steve frowned. "Smyth, who?"

"Jones." Karma turned to Steve, "He's the expert that the minister sent out with Dr. Narguli."

"Expert! Expert what?"

"Not sure, sir. But Mr. Rawlinson says he's not an engineer."

Steve bit back, "Why didn't you tell me about him?"

Karma considered the question a moment too long.

Steve butted in, "Well?"

"You didn't ask Mr. Steve."

"I did," Steve said angrily. "I asked if there were any problems you'd heard of."

Karma slowly shook his head side to side, "Mr. Nigel's not a problem, he's a funny old chap."

"Chap!" Steve echoed. "Where'd you get that from?"

Karma smiled. "That's what he calls everyone. Old chap."

Karma pulled up beside the hand-pump at the Mongar gas station and they both got out. Karma pumped while Steve held the diesel hose in the tank. The slow process of re-fueling began.

"Tell me more about Mr. Nigel," Steve said so pleasantly it was an apology and question in one.

"Well, he doesn't seem that happy with Trashigang. He's been complaining about the accommodation, and the meals, and umm, just about everything else in town."

"Hmm, is he staying at the PORC Hilton with the others?"

Karma shook his head in the affirmative. "He looked at the hotel also, but he soon realized that PORC's is the best place in town."

While Karma paid for the diesel, Steve reflected on how lucky he'd been that Rawlinson had taken a three-bedroom house and invited him to stay when he was visiting Trashigang. He dreaded the thought of staying at PORC's. In the early nineties when the Pan Orient Resources Company had started prospecting for gold in the Radi Valley east of Trashigang, they'd taken over an unused army barracks as their staff guesthouse. They'd spent a little money renovating it, but the emphasis was on 'little', not money.

The road tilted up toward Kori La, the final pass for the day. Thereafter, it would be downhill to the Dangme Chhu. And soon after, Martin and Tammy's house which overlooked the river and the Chazam Bridge.

"And what about our friend Dr. Narguli," Steve said. "Did he bring his assistant as usual?"

Karma balked at Steve's use of the word friend, sarcasm wasn't much used in Bhutan. "Yes sir, Miss Ollie is here as usual."

As the bank's task manager for Two Roads East, Narguli had checked off every invoice, every major purchase and every subcontract. Narguli also had Olivera Ramos, a project economist to help him. But now it appeared that Steve would shoulder the blame for every unaccounted dollar. And why had Narguli only now raised the alarm?

They passed over Kori La where clouds swirled cool and moist through the towering oaks. Steve was tight-lipped and distracted.

Just on nightfall they drove north along the west bank of the Dangme Chhu, a huge brown river draining most of eastern Bhutan. Looking up and across the river, Steve could just make out the Trashigang Dzong silhouetted against the fading evening sky. Finally the Chazam Bridge came into view. "Not far now," Karma said. They'd been traveling for over ten hours, and that was a quick trip from Jakar. They rattled across the old bailey suspension bridge and Steve glanced up to see Martin and Tammy's house with no lights on. What would they be talking about right now? What they'd need to hide from him?

Steve sensed trouble. Danger was in his nostrils as soon as they pulled up in front of the two-level home. He'd noticed that Martin's HiLux was not there: he feared the worst if Martin was late home today.

They alighted and looked up. Tammy was leaning over the balcony-rail, drink in hand. "Hi boys," she called too pleasantly. "Come on up, Steve. Martin's not home yet."

They unloaded the luggage that Steve would need for the night, Karma wished Steve well and then drove off in a hurry. Steve knew that Tammy had always unsettled him, but even so Karma's haste to get going seemed extreme — perhaps it was more to do with the welcome that Trashigang wife would have waiting. Steve looked and felt like hell, but his senses were on full alert. He walked into the house and glanced across at the stairs to the top floor. He hesitated, knowing that the balcony Tammy was on was only accessed through the main bedroom. Looking at himself in a mirror on the wall, he saw a man that had just traveled for ten hours straight: unwashed, uncomfortable and under-dressed for the occasion.

"Can I come through, Tammy?" Steve called out as he peered around the bedroom door.

"I'm on the balcony, Steve. Come on out."

He had not detected anything in her voice that was cause for concern, but something wasn't right. On the balcony, Tammy was reclined in a deck chair. She eased herself to her feet. In very high heels she stood five feet six with more curves and sharp features than a geometry lesson. And she was dressed all in black.

She shook Steve's hand once then let it drop. "It's a long drive for one day, isn't it?" Before Steve could answer, she said, "I'm having gin and tonic. Want one?"

"Uh, yes thanks."

Tammy skirted round him and out through the bedroom. Steve watched her go, her movements feline and confident. He sank into a deck chair and looked over the river. The evening cloud was tinted pink and orange. Tammy came back with his drink. She took the chair opposite Steve's and rested her head back with a long deep sigh.

"How was your trip?"

"Fine thanks, one of the quickest ever."

"How's the drink?"

"Ahh, it's very strong." He added quickly, "just what I needed."

Tammy smiled, "More gin than tonic, huh?"

He nodded. "What time are you expecting Martin?"

Across the rim of her glass, Tammy's green eyes caught Steve's. She almost spelt the words she spoke so slowly. "When he gets here."

He cast around for a change of subject. Lights in the villages along the opposite bank of the Dangme Chhu were sparkling across black water. The rush of the river was the only sound.

"The river's beautiful, isn't it?"

"Is it?" Tammy replied bittersweet and finished her drink in one long mouthful.

He had no answer. He sipped his drink and even the ice-cubes were warm in comparison to present company. Without a word, Tammy stood and walked out. Her short auburn hair bounced around her neck and she accentuated the swagger that annoyed the hell out of him.

She came back with two more drinks. "Martin tells me you've been away a lot this year."

"Yeah, too often."

"It must be tough on your family?"

"It is. Since I was here in April, I've hardly been home."

"You must miss the boys terribly."

"Yes, I do."

"And poor Miranda! That's a lonely bed you're leaving there, Steve."

He stared into his drink. When he looked up, her eyes were right on him. She expected an answer.

"It goes with the job."

Tammy cut in coldly. "So I'm learning."

He wanted to crush his glass with his bare hand. He could match Tammy if he had to, but to do so now was to win the battle at the risk of losing the war. He said nothing and tried to smile as if he hadn't heard her.

Tammy sipped her drink and let the silence just sit there. She tapped long, claret-painted fingernails on the side of her glass. In the still night air the sound was chilling. She waited for the right moment, then demanded, "Steve, I want Martin sent back to the Sydney office."

"What! What do you mean?"

"I mean I'm sick of this place and your project, I want to go home."

"But...but, Martin's career...he's loving it here."

"Yeah...and I'm not. I want my own life again. I want my job back."

Steve hesitated, this was totally without warning. He knew Tammy called the shots, if she wanted out, Martin would probably follow her. He said tentatively, "When? The project finishes next..."

Before Steve could finish his sentence, Tammy was out of her seat and leaning over him, she was so close he could smell her gin-breath. She snarled, "I don't care, I want out now."

She straightened and walked out through the bedroom. He heard angry footsteps clatter on the stairs. He couldn't move. Was there any lonelier feeling than being an unwanted guest? And he was trapped in the house until the following day. The blackness of nightfall enveloped him and the only sound was of Tammy in the kitchen downstairs. He was still sitting in the same chair when he heard Martin pull up outside and walk into the house below. He could hear Tammy and Martin talking. He couldn't follow the conversation fully, but Tammy sounded fine, she was playing up to Martin and laughing about something he'd said. Ten minutes later Martin came out onto the balcony with a drink in each hand. He took the chair Tammy had been in and said, "Hi Steve." He handed across a drink without asking if Steve wanted it. There was nothing in his manner to suggest a problem, he was the usual happy-go-lucky Martin. It appeared that leaving Bhutan was Tammy's idea alone.

The conversation began normally enough. They talked about the weather and how the road-work was going. Steve asked a few questions about some of the Bhutanese engineers they were working with then he said, "How's Narguli been this last week?"

Martin tossed his drink back and grinned, "Just the usual asshole."

Steve tried to smile, it didn't work. He had no idea how much, or how little, Narguli would have told Martin and Rawlinson. It seemed from the flow of Martin's casual banter that it was very little, that it would be up to him to break the news.

Steve began by leaning forward and lowering his tone. In ten minutes he summarized what the minister and the police chief had taken three hours to tell him. Martin's jaw dropped and his strong hands gripped his knees so hard that the muscles on the back of his hands stood out like ropes. Martin said nothing to begin, nor did he move. Finally he looked up at Steve with eyes that didn't blink, that had nothing to hide and said, "Twenty fucking million! Twenty fucking percent of the project budget! So, Nigel Smyth-Jones is here to do a check-up on a fuck-up?"

Steve didn't flinch. He held Martin's gaze and said, "It's you, me and Rawlinson they suspect. They've taken my passport, but there's no way out for any of us. We'll all be guests at Hangrila unless we find out what's happened by Tuesday of next week. That's just nine days away." He stopped and watched for

Martin's reaction. There wasn't one. Then the opportunity was lost as Tammy suddenly appeared. Her long fingers slid over Martin's shoulders and she whispered in his ear, "dinner's ready, darling."

23: Old friends - New friends

Over dinner at the Punakha Inn, Sophie helped Farley make some new friends. He'd been invaluable as far as she was concerned, but in just two days she'd be out of the picture anyway — it was time for the Philadelphians to adopt him into their group. Earlier, he'd mentioned that he'd spent every Sunday since May in the Brooklyn Public Library studying the flora of the Eastern Himalaya. What Farley didn't know, but Sophie did, was that among the Philadelphians at the table were the president (Nancy, Jim's wife); secretary (Jim) and treasurer (Tom) of the Linnaeus Garden Club, and that the one passion that bound the eight of them was botany. Sophie had also been told, somewhat indiscreetly by Tashi, that on a number of recent trips the one negative that Mountain Adventures had picked up on was that neither Anna nor Tashi knew much about the flora of Bhutan. Apparently, Mountain Adventures had been bringing tour groups to Bhutan since the early nineties, but only recently had client surveys started to show that visitors to Bhutan in particular were interested in the mountain flora. That they wanted guides who could identify at least the major families and genera.

All Sophie had to do was make the connection, she knew Farley would be too modest to announce his own botanical credentials so she waited for the right moment and did it for him. Sophie sat back and smiled, she was all but ignored for the rest of the evening as the discussion ranged across botanical themes well beyond her interest and understanding. She didn't mind though, she had bigger things on her mind.

Later, as they went to their rooms, Farley apologized for ignoring her. Sophie assured him it wasn't a problem, but Farley wouldn't accept that. "No, I was selfish," he insisted. Then as she tried to close her door, he said, "I've got an idea for the morning. Just you and me."

24: The Bookkeeper

Tammy had created a masterpiece, but Steve hardly ate. Tammy poured wine, Steve barely touched it. Martin was contemplative, but not as distracted as Steve might have expected; he ate with good appetite, but refused a second glass of wine. Tammy tried her hardest to get some conversation flowing, but her best efforts met with little success. She gave up after a while and turned her attention to the wine bottle. It was empty when the dinner was over and Martin had had only one glass, and Steve a half a glass. By the time Tammy served cake and coffee she was spilling as much as she was serving and her speech was slurred. When coffee was over she offered port. Martin and Steve refused politely, Tammy poured herself a large glass and it was gone before a dozen words were spoken. They said goodnight with Tammy slumped against Martin's shoulder and his hand under her bottom, holding her up.

Steve showed himself to the spare bedroom on the ground floor. As he readied himself for bed, he heard them talking above him. The wooden floor boards in their bedroom, were the wooden ceiling boards in his. He checked his travel clock, it was after eleven. He set the alarm for half past six and lay down. He realized how tired he was as soon as his head hit the pillow.

Steve lay still and tried to put his mind to rest. He could hear Martin talking in hushed tones, but he couldn't hear enough to get the gist of the conversation. He heard Tammy more clearly, she was interjecting at regular intervals, her speech was loud with a terse drunken edge to it. The first word that Steve heard unmistakably was '*fraud*', then '*twenty million*'. Tammy shouted it again, 'Who's fucken frauded who?' Then he heard Martin say, 'Quiet, keep it down.' Tammy responded angrily, 'Don't fucken shush me. Who's Steve think he is…To come here and accuse us of stealin' twenty fucken million? How do we know he's not the fucken guilty one?' Martin spoke firmly, 'Tammy… Shut the hell up!' She shrieked, 'No…fuck Steve…I should know…I done those fucken books for nearly three years now and I done them fucken right. There's no mistakes. No fraud.' Tammy's cursing was suddenly muffled, it was as though Martin had his hand over her mouth. There were heavy footsteps and Tammy was either pushed, or fell heavily onto the bed: it creaked, she groaned. She sobbed briefly then all was deathly quiet.

Steve lay frozen in a cold sweat. His senses were on full alert. He listened hard, but heard nothing. The room above him was as quiet as a graveyard at midnight. His mind went into overdrive, what was Tammy talking about, 'doing the books for three years?' Slowly, inexorably, the rushing of the river outside was the only sound and Steve finally slept, but his dreaming was of questions. Questions he'd ask Martin in the morning.

Down by the river, the morning after the night before was anything but normal. Steve overheard Tammy refuse to get out of bed while he was in the house. Martin got ready for work as usual, Steve though, was finding it hard to get going. He couldn't find the clean socks he knew he had. Nothing was where it should be. He'd hardly slept. His head felt too heavy for his neck, his whole body ached. But in the sleepless predawn he had at least resolved one thing for himself: he wouldn't confront Martin just now, he'd wait a few days and see what was offered by way of explanation. If Martin said nothing about Tammy having done the books, or wanting to leave in a hurry, Steve's presumption of Martin's innocence would need to be reviewed, and quickly.

Martin was in the kitchen making tea when Steve stumbled in, desperate for coffee, strong coffee. Their greeting of each other was far from warm. Martin served them both with tepid, sweet tea and toast and they ate without a word exchanged. It was soon a competition to see who could withstand the stony silence longest.

Steve broke first, he said, "How's Tammy today?"

Martin looked up, "Okay! Why?"

Steve balked, then decided he should at least give Martin an opening. He said, "Oh...she seemed a bit upset last night...that's all."

Martin pushed his chair back and moved to the kitchen sink, he turned on the tap and replied with his back to Steve, "We'd better get moving."

Outside, Steve lifted his suitcase into the back of the HiLux and then turned his attention to a gray sheet of cloud scudding in from the east. He could smell far-off rain and a restless breeze was swirling leaves and dust. He turned back to the house to see Martin kissing Tammy goodbye at the doorway. She, deliberately, did not look in Steve's direction.

Martin and Steve drove down the driveway and turned uphill. Almost immediately Martin started talking roads and weather. Steve didn't want to hear about either, the only thing he wanted Martin to talk about was Tammy doing the project accounts? He'd thought it through, under normal circumstances it wouldn't have been such a big thing if she had helped him with the accounts, it would be more that Martin hadn't mentioned it. That he'd let everyone believe it was his work. But circumstances were now anything but normal.

Martin wheeled the car round one corner and into the next, he was intent on driving, not talking. Unlike in western Bhutan where the towns and villages are built in the valleys, in the east they're built high on the hills. After about twenty minutes of steady climbing they arrived in Trashigang, a pleasant, white-washed village set around a brick-paved plaza. Steve glanced up and the first thing that he noticed was that the 'w' had fallen off the sign above their office door.

25: The born leader

As they climbed the hill behind their hotel, which to Sophie looked more like a mountain, Farley led the way by flashlight. His idea had been to catch the sun rising over the valley, the highlight he'd assured Sophie would be the first rays of golden sunlight hitting the golden central utse of the dzong.

That he lost the trail and they missed the sunrise in a maze of thick forest, was a mere detail, a mistake anyone could have made. But he took it hard. He apologized time and time again as they searched for a way out.

When it was obvious that they were going round and around in circles, Sophie suggested they sit for awhile; catch their breath and get their bearings. Farley agreed and they sat side by side on a fallen log. As soon as they sat down he began apologizing again, his shoulders were slumped and he looked a defeated man, "I'll never change. I thought coming here might change me."

Sophie, at his side, said, "Farley, you mentioned the other day that you'd come here to face a challenge, to prove yourself?"

Farley nodded, "Yeah."

She followed quickly, "Who to?"

"Georgie, my partner back home."

"Oh! Oh I see," Sophie said. She leant forward on the log and matched Farley's lowered tone. "And what are you going to prove, to Georgie?"

Farley bent his head. "That I can change."

The sun was fully up now, and as they talked the shadows retreated from the clearing in front of them. He said, "It all started to go wrong back in May. I get one day a week off work: Sunday. Georgie and I go walking in the Brooklyn Botanical Gardens on Sundays. After spending six days with cut flowers,

I need some balance. I find that in the gardens, in trees rooted in Mother Earth, the same one week as the next. We both love the Cherry Esplanade. In early May the blossom is still out, but it's starting to fade, it's past its best. Every year I find the impermanence of it harder to take. It's beautiful. Then gone!"

Farley glanced up, birds were chirruping in the forest around them; welcoming in the new day.

"That day in May I said to Georgie that I was tired of things changing all around me all the time; that I wanted the cherry blossom, that feeling of spring to stay all year. I didn't want anything to change."

Sophie nodded and Farley cleared his throat.

"A north wind was blowing and it was starting to rain. The petals were blowing all around us. I held Georgie closer. I didn't want wind and rain. Not on my one day off. I said, 'The cherry blossom isn't going to last, but we'll never change, will we?'"

Farley peered through blurred eyes. "You won't believe what she said, Sophie."

"She! I might. Try me."

"Georgie pushed me away. She turned on me. Her eyes were as cold as ice. She said, 'F you, Farley. The world's changing, I'm changing and I can't stand this any longer.' She walked away. I just stood there in the wind and rain and the cherry blossom kept falling. Now Georgie's in Boston for six months. She said if I'd changed when she got back, she might stay with me. Otherwise it's all off." Farley slumped until his head was almost on his knees.

Sophie rested her hand on his shoulder, "Change just for yourself…you'll have a better chance of pleasing someone."

26: *Just another day at the office*

The Two Roads East project office sat above the plaza, next to the telephone exchange. Steve knew that once he got into the office the opportunity to talk to Martin in private would be lost. As Martin reached out to open the door, Steve said, "Martin, anything you want to talk through before we get in there with Rawlinson and the others?"

Martin let his fingers rest on the door handle, he turned and looked directly at Steve. He took a long moment to answer, "Why would you ask that?"

Steve wanted an answer, not another question, he said brusquely, "Just answer me will you."

Martin rubbed the half-shaven stubble on his chin. His intense blue eyes met Steve's determined gaze without blinking. He said, "There's no secrets in this place, Steve." He swung the door open, then closed it deliberately softly and took the stairs up to the office two at a time.

Steve didn't move until Martin was inside. He had his answer, but what would he do with the information? He'd always managed by the golden rule: keep project families and project work separate, now it looked as though he had little choice in the matter, he'd have to break his own rule. He got out and slowly walked up the two flights of steps to the office door. On the top step he found himself face to face with a complete stranger. They sized each other up as men do in an awkward spot. The man spoke, "Well, well, you must be Andrews, I'm Nigel Smyth-Jones."

Before Steve could reply, Smyth-Jones said, "You're looking a little disheveled this morning, old chap. Everything all right I hope?"

"Hi...yeah, I'm Steve Andrews. Ahh...it's been a long trip."

They shook hands. Steve felt a gentlemanly rather than a firm handshake, and he looked into a kindly round face with pale blue eyes, eyes that had seen a lot of the world but were not yet weary of it. Smyth-Jones was immaculately groomed. He wore a tie and tweed jacket, and though probably twenty years Steve's senior, he looked the better man on the day.

"I was just coming out to enjoy a pipe." Smyth-Jones looked Steve up and down. He put his unlit pipe in his mouth and reached over to Steve's crumpled shirt collar. "Here, let me fix that collar for you."

Steve recoiled but Smyth-Jones didn't notice. The older man leant forward and Steve felt velvet smooth fingers brush his neck. Nigel said, "There...that's better. Now let me introduce myself properly."

Steve mumbled, "Thanks. Yeah."

"The bank and the Minister have asked me to come out here and help Dr. Narguli with the little...ahh, kerfuffle we all now find ourselves embroiled in."

Steve was dumbstruck, his passport had been confiscated for a little kerfuffle? His expression must have given away his inner thoughts because Smyth Jones patted his shoulder and said reassuringly, "Never mind old chap...we'll find it...every last penny of it." With that Smyth Jones pulled a tobacco pouch from his pocket and began filling his pipe.

Steve took the final step into the office still pulling at his shirt collar. He already felt sticky and uncomfortable, now he was confused as well. Martin's summation seemed spot-on: the weirdest auditor he'd ever met! A single light globe hung from the center of the room, it was the only source of illumination save for the one small window. The floor was made of pine boards, some nearly a foot wide. The walls and ceiling were no different to the floor, except they'd been stained and polished. On one wall was a large paper map, Two Roads East was printed across the top. The map showed Trashigang town in the center, a road south to Wamrong and a road north to Trashi Yangtse.

Rawlinson rose from his desk. He stood and stretched himself to full height, then shook Steve's hand very firmly. He was a little man with big features and a big voice. Balding and gray, and with thick black-rimmed bifocals balanced on a long nose, Rawlinson had long given up on looks to impress. He said, "Hi Steve, how was the trip?" and before Steve could answer, "Did you get my shopping?"

Steve just nodded.

"Good," Rawlinson croaked and sat heavily.

Martin was half hidden behind the screen of his laptop in the far corner of the office. He sat at a small wooden desk, one leg of which was propped with a wad of cardboard. Rawlinson said, "You're unusually quiet today, Martin? What'd Steve do, throw the damn TRANSARCO rule book at you?"

Steve scowled and Martin didn't even lift his head.

"Just joking," Rawlinson said and pushed a pile of monthly reports across his desk, "There Steve, you'd better get reading."

Steve, glad to have somewhere to start, sat opposite Rawlinson's desk and opened the August report first.

Minutes later, Smyth-Jones said from the doorway, "Horrid weather coming, hey chaps?" Three pairs of eyes were instantly on him. He pointed at Steve with the stem of his pipe. "I should have mentioned, Andrews, Dr. Narguli and Miss Ramos will be along later." He walked to his desk and added for good measure, "They worked late again last night. Heavens knows what a mood our good doctor will be in today."

Steve's head dropped and his neck ached all the more. They settled to work. Smyth-Jones bent over a stack of accounts, Martin tapped at his computer keyboard, Rawlinson drew lines on a map while Steve's eyes chased blurry words across a page.

Not five minutes had passed when Smyth-Jones said, "Careful, Andrews. I really don't know how you can read in here. The light's so poor."

Steve looked up and nodded, "Yeah."

Smyth-Jones laid out a handful of spreadsheets across his desk and spoke to no one in particular, "Oh, dear me. Back to the wretched numbers." He muttered to himself, "this is such a puzzle. Really..."

Steve looked up and caught Rawlinson raising his eyebrows. No one spoke.

Minutes passed. Steve worked his way through Rawlinson's August report, all the usual detail was in it, plus an annex on safety management.

Smyth-Jones stood abruptly and put his hands to his lower back. "Curses, Rawlinson old chap. Isn't there a better chair than this? My back will never be the same."

Rawlinson looked up and scowled, he said nothing. Steve shook his head, he thought, the minister and the bank have sent this guy out here to audit us? He'll be lucky to find his way home.

Fifteen minutes later Steve had read the briefing notes for the September reports. There was nothing on the shortfall in the project accounts. He said, "John, let's go and have a coffee. You can fill me in on the rest of it."

Steve stood to go and said, "Nigel, I notice you're adding those columns with a calculator. I'm sure that would be easier using spreadsheets." Smyth-Jones peered up and raised his eyebrows. Steve saw misunderstanding and added, "Is your computer broken? You can borrow my laptop if you need it."

"Awfully kind of you, Andrews old chap," Smyth-Jones replied and smiled half-heartedly. "But good heavens no thanks, I don't trust computers."

27: The mandala

Anna had her group in the bus and on their way mid-morning. Sophie felt distracted and distant. Beside her, Farley was unusually melancholy and that didn't help things. Behind her, the Philadelphians were in high spirits and that didn't help things either. The morning's program included a stop at the Wangdi Dzong again, but instead of watching a festival, this time they were to witness a rare event. A sand mandala had been started a week ago and today it was to be finished. They'd be amongst the first to see it.

A young monk was waiting to greet them, his head was freshly shaven and his smile was wide and welcoming. They left their bus and shoes a respectful distance from the huge main gate to the Dzong and followed the monk across an ancient stone forecourt. Way below them the Punak Chhu carved its way through the fertile valley and the only sound was of bare feet on warm stone, the wind and a distant chanting...Om Mani Padme Hung...Om Mani... As they crossed the vast expanse of the court and approached the intricately decorated main gates, the chanting grew louder. They followed single file up a set of stone steps that led into an alcove over painted wooden double doors three times the height of the monk. He pushed the left-hand door and they were bid to enter behind him. Soon they were in a small passage, it made two sharp right angle turns before it led them into a main courtyard. Tashi spoke first, "this is called the dochey." He pointed up at a tower like structure off to one side, "that's the utse, in it is the lhakhang, the main chapel." All around the courtyard were balconies and rooms overlooking it, but their attention was immediately drawn to the source of the chanting. At the far end of the main-court a group of kneeling monks came into view. There were six in a circle, their maroon robes hung to their knees. They were crouched over something in the middle of the group and they stopped chanting as soon as Tashi spoke behind them. Five of the six stood and greeted him, one remained kneeling, he was pouring colored sand from his hand onto the outer rim of what at first glance appeared to be a brightly colored circular painting on a large flat stone. It was about four feet in diameter. A closer look revealed that the geometric pattern was made entirely of colored sand: there was white, black, blue, green, yellow and red. "The mandala," Tashi said. "It's taken six days to create." On one side of the mandala stood a semicircle of robed monks, quietly chanting a blessing; on the other side a semicircle of American tourists, too stunned to speak. They just stood there, mouths agape.

It took a long moment for the first of them to say something, it was Farley, he said, "Oh that's so beautiful, so perfect."

Nancy added, "But...but, how can they move it? It could be ruined out here...there's the wind, and the rain?"

Tashi shifted from one foot to the other and rocked his head side to side. He looked to Anna and she nodded toward Sophie, then Farley. Tashi said, "The wind and rain can't ruin it because it's finished, it's served its purpose."

The look of confusion on their faces said no one had understood.

Tashi moved toward Sophie and without saying a word took her hand and led her into the center of the circle. He gestured for her to kneel beside him, then he pointed to the mandala and said, "Using your open hand, I want you to sweep this into a pile in the middle."

Sophie uttered a long drawn out, "No..." She looked up at the others. They were as stunned as she was, but Anna and the monks were smiling, urging her on. She glanced around, the monks that had taken six days to make the mandala were now beckoning her to sweep it up. She looked back to Tashi, her face said I can't do this.

Gently, he leant forward and whispered in her ear. The creation was in the teamwork that built it. The message in this form of Bhutanese art was in its destruction. Nothing is permanent. We live with impermanence. Learn to let go, move on. The sweeping of the sand is symbolic of the letting go.

Sophie's heart was thumping in her chest. The work of art she was about to destroy was speaking to her. Deep down, she knew she had to do it and why. She looked up at Farley again, he was shaking his head, he didn't understand. She put her open hand at the outer rim of the circle and started sweeping slowly towards the middle, just as slowly the colors melded, bright blues and yellows mixed with black and white and turned to gray. More quickly now she swept her hand again, and then again. What had taken six men, six days to build, she'd undone in less than a minute. All that remained was a pile of colored sand. But none of the colors stood bright. Mixed like they were now, they were lifeless. Still kneeling, Sophie bowed her head onto her chest and her eyes filled with tears. All around her was the silence of nothing.

Sophie was still kneeling, her head bent, when she heard Tashi say, "Farley, I want you to put the sands in this jar. Now the sands must be spread on the water so that the message is taken far away."

The next thing that Sophie was aware of was Farley crouched down beside her. He was scooping up the sand and pouring it into an earthen jar.

The road east from Wangdi clings to the hillside as it climbs and descends a series of small valleys. Sophie had her eyes on the road ahead. Farley was beside her with an earthen jar firmly held between his knees. To begin the landscape is dry and windswept, but further up-valley it is fertile country and the farmhouses show it; built in traditional style they stand on small hills overlooking the terraced fields of green and gold. Most of the houses are of two stories. The ground floor is built of stone and white washed. The top floor is of hand-hewn timber, with huge intricately decorated windows on all sides. Above the top floor and beneath the roof is a loft, a place for drying and storing hay for the long winter months. The roof is made of hand-cut wooden shingles. Large stones are laid over the top to keep it all in place. Red chilies dry on the roof and on mats around the roughly fenced yards.

As they left the valley floor and began the ascent into the forest just beyond Tikke Zampa, Tashi talked more about the sand mandala, about the spreading of the sands on moving water. Soon they passed through the village of Nobding and saw six grey langurs playing aerial acrobatics in a birch tree. Higher up Farley identified spruces, yew and cypresses and just under the pass at Pele La, they stopped to get photographs of yaks grazing in an almost pure forest of rhododendron.

Over Pele La and over lunch by a clear mountain stream, Farley asked Tashi where they would spread the sands in the jar that he still had clutched in front of him. Tashi laughed, "There's a river, Farley. It flows deep and wide. It drains to the Bay of Bengal. From there, who knows where our blessing will go."

28: The wisdom of beggars

The two engineers walked from the office and crossed the plaza. It was starting to drizzle. As soon as they were out of earshot, Steve turned to Rawlinson. "The minister called me in on Friday night for a three hour meeting. He'd kept me waiting all day. Narguli's told him that the loan is almost fully drawn, and that that could only mean one thing: TRANSARCO's lost twenty million dollars somewhere. Narguli's talking fraud. He's pointing the finger at the three of us. The police have my passport."

"Yeah," Rawlinson responded casually, his hands deep in his pockets. "That explains a few things."

"Shit, thanks for your concern," Steve said and huffed loudly, "did you know the money was missing?" His tone threatened, "Well, did you?"

"I knew nothing." Rawlinson stopped. Steve had to turn to catch his reply. "And listen buddy, Martin's your man and it's your problem. I told you at the start I'm an engineer, not a bloody accountant. Ask Martin!"

"I will, and I'll do my own audit, starting this afternoon."

They climbed the stairs to the Yanchen teashop with the police chief's stupid rhyme ringing in Steve's ears. 'On Steve's project, it's for things gone wrong we weep. It's Steve's problem, so it's his passport I keep.' While the coffee was coming, Rawlinson talked about engineering things — how the road as far as Shali was on schedule and how well the new section south of Khaling was holding up. How the training was producing good results. How Martin had the 'touch' for development work. It went over Steve's head, there were bigger things on his mind: a police chief who doubled as a childish poet, an auditor who didn't use computers and a trusted employee who

125

he no longer trusted. The waiter boy placed two small glasses of creamy milk coffee on the table.

"What do you make of Smyth-Jones?" Steve said, "They wouldn't be paying him, would they?"

"Try, nine hundred a day."

"Shit, and he's never used a computer?"

Rawlinson sipped his coffee and nodded, "Yep. And that's just the start of it."

"What's Narguli saying?"

"He hasn't said anything so far. He didn't even tell us what Smyth-Jones is doing here."

Steve said, "How's Ollie this trip?"

"Miss Olivera Ramos is still the loyal lieutenant to the big general. She doesn't say a thing unless Narguli asks her to." Rawlinson smirked, "And, they keep the oddest of hours."

Steve raised his eyebrows but let Rawlinson's comment pass. He said, "Seriously, you've been in this business a long time, John. What do you reckon has happened?"

Rawlinson let his bifocals slip and stared at Steve over the top of thick black rims. He said, "I'll tell you what's happened. Money's gone missing because you're too soft-headed for this business, Steve."

Already Steve was regretting that he'd asked, he said, "You think so?"

"I know so. You're not filling potholes for some two-bit NGO, change your thinking and you might see what's happening."

Steve sat in a brooding silence. He needed help, not another bloody Rawlinson lecture. He got one anyway.

"Let me tell you about business in this part of the world. About being hard-headed. On my last trip over here I had to overnight in Calcutta. I was sitting in the back of a taxi on the way from the airport to a half-decent hotel I've stayed in a few times. We were caught in a traffic jam, three lanes across; everything gridlocked. Every second driver had his hand on the horn. It was as hot as hell. A beggar-woman was making her way down the line of cars, she was working the middle lane. It was hard to tell her age, her head was draped in a tattered gray shawl and she carried a baby over her shoulder. The baby was wrapped in rags and asleep, only god knows how in that heat and noise. When the beggar-woman saw me she made a bee-line straight to my window; a white face, money for jam. She tapped on the glass. Her face was dark as chocolate, her eyes sunken and piercing. She kept pointing to her sleeping baby and putting pinched fingers to her mouth in a gesture that said, 'feed it'. I turned off as I always do. She kept tapping on the window. I stared straight ahead — to make eye contact with a beggar is to lose the game. She kept tapping, her bony hand doing the food for the baby routine. Finally she was getting on my nerves. I turned and shooed her away with the back of my hand, her eyes bore right through me — but she was no closer to even one rupee. I turned away again and moments later I heard a thump on the window rather than a tap...tap. Her baby howled. She'd hit the back of its head on the window. I put two hands up: stop! She held the baby under the arms, like a rag-doll. She hit its head again. Thump. The baby screamed and even above the din of the traffic it cut cold fear into me. She hit the baby's head again, harder this time. She had my full atten-tion. She hit it again, she had twenty rupees."

Steve's jaw dropped, Rawlinson was straight-faced. This was no tale, this had happened.

"She had one hundred rupees and a smile on her face before she moved on."

Steve felt a shiver down his spine. He'd never waited that long to hand a few rupees out of the window.

Rawlinson leant forward and banged two fists on the table, "When I got to my hotel I mentioned it to the concierge, he just smiled and said, 'she's one of Calcutta's richest beggars sir, she hires those babies by the day.'"

Steve just stared at the expressionless, pale face opposite him. Where was this leading?

"See what I'm getting at. Her business was begging, her attitude to it smart, and uncompromising. You're the wrong man in the wrong place, Steve. Start thinking like that beggar before it's too late."

Steve sat motionless and speechless. A minute may have passed before he shook his head and sneered, "You're a hard bastard, Rawlinson."

"Am I? You still don't get it, do you?" Rawlinson said. "Two Roads East's got the biggest bank account in Bhutan at the moment, there are people here that want their share, just like that beggar wanted her share of my money. We're being framed, Steve."

Steve stood abruptly and glared back at Rawlinson, "No! You're wrong. Bhutan is different."

Rawlinson looked up. "I'll give you that," he said. "But people aren't, they're the same everywhere."

"We'll see," Steve said and shook his head, ready now for a jab at Rawlinson's soft spot, "Bradshaw said the bank has sent the auditors into the Sydney office, they're talking about a black-listing."

Rawlinson's eyes bulged, "Shit Steve, that happens and my stock holding is worthless. Fuck, remember Kinimonth Partners, they were bigger than TRANSARCO before they got listed by the bank for their fuckup in Bangladesh. They're half our size now. Fuck." Rawlinson shoved his chair back, stood and left his coffee unfinished.

Steve settled the bill then climbed down the ladder-like stairs. He walked out onto the street. The misty rain had withdrawn, but black clouds were building to a storm. Rawlinson had his back to the teashop and his arms folded, watching a boy and girl aged about six playing catch with a green orange.

Rawlinson spun around, "You still missed my point."

"Did I?" Steve snapped, "When I need that sort of fucking help I'll ask for it."

"It's up to you, buddy" Rawlinson shrugged and added, "just keep reacting…and never acting…and you'll never see your passport again." He started walking towards the office.

Steve stayed a few yards behind. They crossed the plaza without another word spoken. Thunder rolled over distant mountains. A rustle of leaves floated down from a grove of eucalyptus and the air was static with the expectation of a storm. 'Reacting…and never acting', Rawlinson's words were stabbing at Steve's subconscious, was this the story of his life?

At the steps to the office, Rawlinson turned and said, "Anyway, I don't know what you expect to do in three days. You just get here, then you leave."

Steve looked up at the amassing thunderstorm, pretending not to hear. He'd tried to get here earlier, and he hadn't set Friday as the date for the bridge inspection back in Jakar; Bradshaw and the World Bank had, and they hadn't consulted him when they agreed it. He couldn't miss it. Steve started up the stairs, knowing full well that the treadmill he'd been on for years was set on fast forward: impossible itineraries had been his life for too long now. Reacting, but never acting.

Rawlinson followed at his heels, "What happens if you don't find anything?"

"Huh, you'll find me at Hangrila!" Steve stopped and turned, "And hey, the police might have *my* passport, but it's the three of us they've got tagged. Just remember will you, we're supposed to be on the same team."

Rawlinson feigned a punch at Steve's shoulder and pretended an Australian accent, "Sure thing, mate."

Steve and Rawlinson entered the office to find Narguli standing over, and Smyth-Jones sitting at, a desk covered in spreadsheets. The pages contained columns of numbers, dollar signs sat importantly at the head of each column. They also had the two sets of project books open. The bank's accounts, showing the loan draw-downs, were spiral-bound; TRANSARCO's, recording all project expenditure, were loose-leaf and held by a bulldog clip. Narguli and Smyth-Jones were trying to match the entries one by one, nearly one thousand of them. They'd been at it for a few days now and they were still less than a quarter of the way through. They'd come to realize that TRANSARCO and the bank had often recorded the same item by different names. So what was a pipe on SAIB's accounts, might be a culvert, tube or drainage channel on TRANSARCO's. In some entries asphalt was called bitumen, occasionally both were called black tar. Crushed stone was variously recorded as gravel, rock, aggregate, crushed stone or just stones. Narguli's patience was being sorely tested, and Smyth-Jones was learning a whole new vocabulary; to begin he'd thought 'Plant Hire' had something to do with office decoration.

Steve shivered, a chill followed Narguli like a shadow. Narguli, on noticing Steve and Rawlinson enter, glanced up from the desk, scowled and screwed his face up as if someone had farted. He said, "So, you're finally here, Andrews," and turned back to his work.

Steve, having received the welcome he expected, crossed the office to where Martin sat talking with Ollie.

Ollie said, "Hello Steven," then with a smile so false it was counterfeit, walked away to stand beside Narguli. Soon she was entered into the discussion that was taking place over the meaning of this number and that.

Martin and Steve talked about the accounts. Martin put a copy of the thirty-two TRANSARCO spreadsheets on two disks. He put the bank's accounts on another two disks and labeled them. He handed them all to Steve and wished him good luck.

Narguli raised his head, he was a viper ready to strike. He cut in over Steve and Martin, saliva oozing like venom at the corners of his mouth, "Good luck!" Narguli's beady black eyes scanned the room. He brushed a lock of immaculate gray hair from his forehead and strode to the center of the room. The single light-globe was a halo just above him. He called a project meeting by clearing his throat loudly. Steve, Martin, Rawlinson and Smyth-Jones looked up like school children from where they sat. Ollie sensed the importance of what was to come, she crossed an imaginary line and stood at ease behind her boss.

"You'll need more than good luck, Andrews." Narguli ran the tip of a sticky tongue around his lips, then his voice rasped, "I've waited until you were all here. Consider my words an official statement of the South Asia Infrastructure Bank. I'm investigating fraud. Mr. Smyth-Jones has been retained by the bank to assist me. We believe that there is a criminal in this room. And let me tell you, I find it distasteful to have to work with such people as yourselves, but that's my instruction from the SAIB, the work must continue, at least for the time being." Narguli berated them in this vein for another ten minutes, and they were left in no doubt about their future if the missing money was not found.

Narguli had worked himself into a lather. He adjusted the tidy paunch that was bulging over his belt, dismissed the meeting with an imperial flick of his fingers and took three quick steps back to his spreadsheets. Every head bent to work. An hour or so passed before Dr. Narguli summoned Ollie to return to the PORC Guesthouse where they would lunch and continue their work. Narguli suggested (somewhat impolitely for the comfort of an English gentleman) that Smyth-Jones might start 'getting to the bottom of things'. Ollie collected up their papers and (like a lieutenant) obediently followed the big general.

Narguli stopped at the doorway. He turned to Steve and sneered. "I want to work out how much money is needed to finish this damn project." Narguli had a bad taste in his mouth, it looked like he was ready to spit it on the floor of the office. "We'll take the south road tomorrow, make a field visit to Wamrong. Wednesday we'll go north and visit Trashi Yangtse early. We'll return here for our meeting with the dzongda at three. This afternoon, I suggest you three get busy. Real busy!"

29: *Whatchadoin Mista?*

The bus wound its way downhill through the Longte Valley. They stopped in the village of Sephu and bought finely woven bamboo baskets, and this time Sophie joined in the fun. The bus crossed the Nikka Chhu and tracked alongside the river, and just past the village of Tangsibi, where the mighty Mangde Chhu winds deep and rushing though a narrow gorge, the bus stopped. They parked at a small trailhead leading down into deep forest. Tashi turned and said, "Farley, don't forget the jar."

The trail led steeply downhill. Sophie commented that it looked well used for a trail that seemed to come from nowhere, and lead nowhere. They walked in single file. Sophie was near the end, but she knew they'd stumbled upon something when the Philadelphians, led by Tom, stopped abruptly and gasped, "Oh, my God."

The trail had come from dense forest to the edge of a river gorge hundreds of feet deep. They stood at one end of a narrow wire rope bridge dangling over the gorge. Way below, the thundering rush of the Mangde Chhu made it hard to hear. They gathered close in to Anna and heard that the trail led over the bridge to a village from which the kids walked three hours each way to go to Tangsibi, their nearest school. The bridge, which the king himself had ordained, was suspended between four thin wire ropes. The ropes were tied into obscure footings in the hillside, the top ropes were just far enough apart to provide the handrail and the bottom ropes held the decking of narrow wooden planks: planks tied in place with vines and frayed rope; planks just wide enough for one foot in front of the other; gaps in the planks wider than a foot in places.

"Okay," Anna said, "who wants to spread the sand on the water?"

"What?" Jim said on behalf of all of them. "From that bridge?"

"Yep, right in the middle. Otherwise it'll just land on the rocks."

Everyone was looking at everyone else. Jim teased Tom, "Come on," he laughed, "you were a Boy Scout." Nancy was voicing the obvious for all of them, "you'd be mad to even try it..."

Sophie shook her head and smiled, she didn't need to say no.

A hushed silence came down over the group. Anna and Tashi pretended dismay — no one was going to take up their offer? Would they have to do it themselves?

Then a man's voice was just audible over the rushing and crashing of the river far below. "Sophie, can I have a word, in private."

Of the eleven faces that turned toward Farley, Sophie's showed the most surprise. She mumbled, "Of course," and walked away from the group a few paces.

"I thought about what you said this morning," Farley began. "Here's my chance to prove myself...just for myself. What do you think?"

"No! Umm...ahhh, maybe, I guess so, yeah," Sophie tried to sound reassuring, "But, umm...you sure you can do it?"

Farley looked at his feet and said, "Heck no...I've never been good with heights. But if I don't, well, I guess that proves something anyway?"

Sophie couldn't draw on experience because she'd never been placed in a position like this before. If she erred on the side of caution, Farley would too. But if she said 'do it', was there any guarantee he could? She looked back at the group and could tell they knew exactly what was on Farley's mind. Nancy was shaking her head and talking in Jim's ear, and it wasn't hard to read her lips, "He wouldn't dare. Not Farley. He wouldn't even think it, surely?"

Sophie turned the other way and saw a structure that in the wildest stretch of her imagination could hardly be called a bridge. She saw gaps in the planking that Farley's foot would surely fall through. She glanced down and the void under it seemed to go on forever. Way below, the rushing and crashing of whitewater over rocks was thundering and ominous. And she was aware of Farley beside her, waiting for her to answer. She turned slowly and said, "The school kids do it twice a day, everyday. So can you, just don't look down, okay?"

But in the moments she had had her back to him, Farley's initial enthusiasm for the challenge appeared to have waned a little. He mumbled, "Oh, okay, sure. Thanks." He hesitated, cleared his throat, straightened himself and adjusted his hat, then with the earthen jar firmly held under his right armpit and not as much as a glance at the uncertain faces of the Philadelphians, he took a first tentative step onto the bridge. His free hand held the guide wire like a vice. He forced one foot past the other, feeling for the gaps rather than looking down at them. He'd taken ten or so steps and still the bridge was holding, although disconcertingly, it was starting to sway under his weight.

Not a word was said between the eleven people on the edge of the gorge. Their feet were on solid ground, Farley's were in mid-air. He was almost to the middle. A few more steps and he could tip the sand from the jar over the side of the bridge.

Farley had the jar in two hands and one hundred and twenty degrees of the turn behind him when Sophie saw it happen; four bare-foot, gho and kira clad school kids appeared from the forest at the other end of the bridge. The three boys and a girl, all aged under ten, stood and surveyed the scene. They saw a man in suspended motion in the middle of their bridge. He was holding a jar and turning so slowly that he might have been a ghost spreading his own ashes. Sophie saw the children look at each other and shake their heads. She guessed they'd seen chilips before, but never one dressed like Farley, never one as ghostly white as he was now.

There was a confused moment of silence at each end. Then Anna yelled, "Stay where you are. Let him get off first."

The three boys looked at each other and shrugged; while they did so, the girl ran onto the bridge. She crossed quickly towards Farley.

Farley sensed instantly that something had changed. Sophie saw him tense up and close his eyes. His hands were shaking so hard the sand was spilling of its own accord.

The girl yelled from just behind him. *"Whatchadoin Mista?"* Farley froze. His boots shook violently, Sophie could picture his feet and even his toes shaking within them. The decking boards clattered. His hands were blue on the jar he was holding it so tight.

The girl must have decided that since he hadn't answered her, she'd squeeze past him and ask him face to face. The boys, seeing what fun their younger sister was having, decided they'd join her. By the time she was in front of Farley, the three boys were behind him. The girl asked again, "Whatchadoin Mista?"

Sophie could see Farley trying to speak, but strange gasping movements of his mouth uttered nothing. Then the boys started to swing the bridge. To and fro. To and fro they rocked and the bridge went with them.

Farley's trembling knees finally gave way. He knelt first on one knee, then the other. He tried to cry out, but he was mute.

The boys clambered past him, over him, they all asked together, *"Youalright Mista?"* Sophie could almost hear Farley's teeth chattering, his heart pounding. The boys looked at each other and three heads shook. Then the girl shrieked. "He no talk chilip demon, *RUN.*" The four of them turned and raced across the bridge, each yelling louder than the other. They didn't even stop to acknowledge the horrified faces of eleven chilips watching from the side of the steep gorge. The kid's voices faded off into the deep forest above.

Gradually, the bridge stopped swinging. Gradually, Farley's heart started beating again. Sophie saw him start breathing, saw life flow back into him. She was saying under her breath, "You can do it, you can do it." First he straightened one knee, then the other. He was standing again. He hadn't looked down through that ordeal, and Sophie knew he wouldn't now. He put one hand on the guide wire and with the other held the jar at arm's length. Slowly, the sands tipped and floated down and down and down until they were swallowed and swept into the rushing torrent way below. When the last grain of sand had fallen, Farley turned and began walking toward the group. After a few steps he managed to smile, and he straightened his shoulders.

Sophie clapped her hands above her head, and with that the Philadelphians, all of them, joined in.

30: Spreadsheets and other puzzles

Steve spent a long afternoon behind Martin's desk. He opened spreadsheet after spreadsheet and the numbers all started to meld and look the same. A couple of times he glanced up at Smyth-Jones working on his set of the same numbers, once their eyes met, neither knew which way to look. When he'd had enough of formulae and linked sheets that didn't seem to link properly, Karma delivered Steve and his luggage to Rawlinson's house just on dusk. Rawlinson opted to walk the quarter mile from the office, it was his daily exercise he boasted. Martin was allowed to go home, relieved that he'd got through the afternoon without too many questions from Steve.

Rawlinson's two-level house was on the road to the hospital, it was set back in a small garden where his housekeeper grew some vegetables and flowers. Behind the house were several rows of eucalyptus trees. Steve sat on the upstairs balcony and looked out at nothing in particular. The sky was heavy and gray. Clouds rested halfway down the mountains, a lid over the valley. Rawlinson brought two mugs of coffee out to the balcony, he set them on a small table. Neither man dared talk about work. They each asked about the other's family and neither told the full story in reply. Steve asked about the only non-pelf passion in Rawlinson's life, classical music, but that fell flat. So while Steve mulled over his twenty million reasons to worry, Rawlinson put on some music and ranted about his stock investments, how he'd be doomed if TRANSARCO crashed.

"Who are we listening to?" Steve asked just to change the subject.

"Debussy." Rawlinson said to keep the conversation going.

They listened to the music and ate as outside the heavens opened. Lightning flashed across the sky and it rained like it would never stop. At eight fifteen Steve excused himself and went to his room. He opened up the project accounts on his laptop and stared at the screen. There had to be a smarter way of comparing the two sets of accounts. He tried grouping the items by supplier. Starting with the largest first he wrote; Veejay Industries; Calcutta Pipe Works; and Hindustan Corporation; each one at the top of a new page. He started listing the invoices one by one. But some were in dollars, some in Bhutanese Ngultrums and some in Indian rupees. Then he discovered that the ngultrums and rupees had been converted to dollars using different exchange rates. The deeper he went into it the more he began to drown in the detail, detail he was supposed to know. At nine his head was spinning, then the power failed, or was simply turned off at the sub-station. At ten, Steve's battery went dead and the screen of his laptop died. At ten thirty he lay awake and listened to rain beating on a shingled roof. Thunder rolled across the valley and echoed back from the mountains beyond. The single window in Steve's room lit up as lightning flashed behind it. Spreadsheets and Tammy Davis were on his mind and sleep was a long time coming.

At the Norbut Hotel in Trongsa, a party was in full swing. Farley, being the cause for celebration, was the center of attention. As soon as he'd finished one Red Panda beer, Jim, Tom or Anna was buying him another. Farley was asked time and again how it felt when the boys started to swing the bridge, and each time he answered his story grew upon itself.

But while there were twelve at the party, two weren't drinking, or laughing. Tashi and Sophie sat off to one side and their conversation was intense.

Sophie, though pleased for Farley to be celebrating his metamorphosis, had been unsettled all day. Now she was pumping

Tashi for everything he knew about sand mandalas, Buddhism and its concepts on detachment. She wanted to know why he'd chosen her to destroy the mandala. He was trying again to explain she hadn't destroyed it. The monks that made it can always make another one. They live with impermanence, not fight against it. He said she was chosen because he sensed there was something in her life that she hadn't let go of. He didn't know what it was, but he hoped her time in Bhutan would help.

She was left speechless, shaking. She so much wanted to share her burden, but she knew she couldn't. She excused herself and went back to her room. There, she read Steve's letter again and then tore it into pieces. She'd detached. Impermanence! It didn't help; she still felt permanently torn between the job she'd come so far to do, and the confused feelings she had for a man she once loved.

31: Mozart or Haydn?

Steve knew the story off by heart, it came from the bidding documents prepared by Narguli at the start of the tender process.

'The Two Roads East Project will rebuild two arterial roads running north and south of Trashigang...It is thirteen miles from Trashigang to Wamrong as measured off the map. By road, the distance is some fifty miles. The drive takes over three hours and there are frequent delays due to landslides. The road was built with Indian Government assistance as a single lane suitable for light transport only. The section from the Indian (Assam State) border to Wamrong is just over sixty-two miles. It traverses easier terrain with more stable geology, its condition is considered reasonable. But north of Wamrong, the road is inadequate. The Royal Government of Bhutan has agreed to borrow from the South Asia Infrastructure Bank (SAIB) to finance the rebuilding of the Wamrong-Trashigang section. The feasibility study noted that the project would assist the development generally of the most populous and remote part of the Kingdom, and particularly Bhutan's ambitious plans to export hydroelectric power.

A number of consultant reports have identified prospects for the development of hydro-power to supply the Indian market. A site has been identified on the Kuri Chhu, near Lingmethang; the problem was, how to build a power station when heavy transport is impossible beyond Wamrong, and all the heavy equipment will need to be brought in from India by road? Several independent studies have shown that the hydro factor alone justifies the eighty million earmarked for the Wamrong-Trashigang section of the Two Roads East project.'

When Steve wrote the winning tender for the project he had high hopes, he'd spoken to Narguli by phone and he'd seemed reasonable – pedantic, but human enough to work with. Now, three years into the project and dreading yet another road inspection with Narguli at the helm, Steve was wondering what he'd done in a past life to deserve his current lot.

Karma waited in the Landcruiser. Rawlinson and Steve walked up the office steps and found the door open. Martin was already at work. In the ensuing discussion of the day's plans, Martin agreed to stay back and complete his training report. Steve and Rawlinson would go to Wamrong with the bank team. They waited for Narguli and they waited some more. Twenty minutes after the agreed time, Jochu, one of three per-manent drivers for the bank in Bhutan, bounded up the stairs to the office. Breathless, he bowed slightly from the waist and said to Steve, "Dr. Narguli and Miss Ramos are working on things, they go separately. We meet at Deshi restaurant in Wamrong for lunch. We look at roadwork on our return."

Steve turned to Rawlinson, they both shrugged, "Okay."

Nigel came up the stairs laden with accounts in one hand and a briefcase in the other, he muttered something about Tues-day already and wretchedly impossible deadlines and stress, and went straight to his desk. While cleaning his pipe, he con-firmed that neither Narguli nor Ollie had made it to breakfast.

Rawlinson suggested Steve and he leave anyway, there was something he wanted to show him on the way to Wamrong.

National Highway No. 3 ascends about three thousand six hundred feet from Trashigang to a first pass at Yangphu La. First it climbs through fields of corn and potatoes. Higher up, it passes small farming villages. Along the way, Rawlinson told Steve they were heading for a little-known airfield built by the Indian Army during the Sino–Indian war. The Indians wanted an airfield close to the Chinese border, but of course couldn't find any flat land to build it on. The solution was to create some. They bulldozed an airfield out of the side of a mountain.

"It's kept pretty hush-hush," Rawlinson said. "We discovered it on aerial photos we're using for the road alignment."

"I'll believe it when I see it," Steve said. He'd been on the brunt end of Rawlinson's humor before.

They were almost up to the pass at Yangphu, in deep forest, when Karma swung hard left. They climbed on a side road for perhaps twenty minutes, the road leveled off and they came out of the forest at a huge cutting through the side of the mountain.

"Jeezas!" Steve said. "You weren't kidding." They were at the end of a runway that stopped at a sheer cliff, a man-made cliff where blasting and bulldozers had eaten into solid rock for a hundred feet or more. Steve's eyes wandered down the length of the blacktop. At the other end of the runway, in the hazy distance, there was nothing but thin air. Cloud swirled and eddied across the side of the mountain and the end of the runway went in and out of view.

Rawlinson said from the back seat. "Karma, I want to show Steve what's down the other end. I'll drive, you wait here."

The exchange of drivers happened so quickly that Steve hardly had time to contemplate Rawlinson's strange request. Rawlinson wheeled the Landcruiser out onto the deserted runway and accelerated. The left side of the runway was cut into the cliff-face. The other side dropped off into a void. One moment they were in the clouds, the next clear of it. "Hey," Steve said, "this is the best bit of road in Bhutan."

Rawlinson kept his foot flat to the floor and said nothing.

The speedometer wound round, fifty, sixty, seventy miles per hour. After traveling at average speeds of less than twenty, this felt like flying. The distant end of the runway was suddenly less distant. Steve could see that a jet aircraft would be at one thousand feet right on take-off; the runway just stopped at the edge of nowhere, it was coming up quickly now. "Okay," Steve said. "Time to slow down."

Rawlinson was blank-faced. Hadn't he heard? The runway was now disappearing at an alarming rate.

"I see what you mean. Let's stop." Nothing happened. Steve gripped the panic bar with sweaty hands. He turned, Rawlinson's face in profile had an almost maniacal edge to it. "Stop now!"

The end was just up ahead, it was right there, then nothing but blue sky.

"*Bloody well stop*!"

Rawlinson looked around as if that was the first he'd heard. He said, "Do you want me to stop?"

"Shit! Yes! Now!"

Nothing happened.

"Brakes!" Steve roared. "Now!"

Slowly, the speedometer responded, fifty-five, forty, thirty, twenty.

The end was just ahead. Steve was certain they'd go over it, "Shit! Rawlinson! *Stop*."

"We are, Steve."

Agonizingly long moments passed until they came to a dead stop. Rawlinson sat there as though he was waiting for a red light to turn green.

Steve was shaking. He got out without saying a word. He looked around, orientated himself and took two steps forward. He walked further, not bothering to turn back. His heart caught up with his brain and he started to breathe normally. He walked maybe fifteen yards. He got to the end of the runway and got down on his hands and knees, he peered over the sharp drop-off. He turned and looked at the Landcruiser, momentarily it was lost in a swirl of cloud.

Rawlinson hadn't moved. The expression on his face hadn't changed.

Steve knew he'd been tricked by a magnificent optical illusion. The end of the runway was a convex curve and the scale of the airfield and its surroundings was beyond comprehension: fifteen yards had appeared as one or two. Steve froze in anger, he strode up to the driver's side door, jerked it open and shouted, "What the fuck did you do that for?"

Rawlinson turned slowly. Just as slowly he took off his thick bifocals and his eyes, puffy and bloodshot, met Steve's steel-eyed stare with almost complete detachment. He said in a voice that didn't quiver, didn't change tone, "Just wanted to wake you up...like I said...time to stop dreaming." With that Rawlinson started the motor and gestured for Steve to get in.

Steve closed the driver's door with a thud and walked around to the passenger side, he climbed in and said angrily, "Thanks for nothing. As I said yesterday, when I need that sort of help I'll fucking well ask for it."

Rawlinson just shrugged and drove slowly back down the runway.

Steve looked over his shoulder, he knew they'd already driven a hundred yards, it looked like ten.

Neither man spoke again until they pulled up beside Karma who was sitting on a rock at the edge of the runway. He could have been waiting for a bus. Rawlinson got out and Karma got back in behind the wheel without speaking, it was as though it had been rehearsed.

Rawlinson climbed into the rear behind Steve and looked at his watch, he said, "We'd better move it."

Karma put his foot to the floor as they drove out through the cutting and out onto National Highway Number 3, where he turned hard left and uphill. He said, "Mr. Steve, blame me, sir. I told everyone about this place. How two drivers were sharing one wife. That the wife said she only wanted children to one of them, the bravest. How she decided that they'd race to the end of the runway and it would be the last to stop that would put the children in her belly. It's become a local legend."

Steve sighed. He wouldn't have believed it anywhere else. He said, "Yeah. So what happened?"

Rawlinson butted in from the back seat, "She's still childless, Steve. They both went over the end."

Karma drove over Yangphu La at just above seven thousand feet. Cloud swirled across the top of the pass and down to the south. The road circled around on a ridge top and skirted forested gullies on either side. They passed through Khaling to a background of serious road talk between engineers, there were only three things you had to get right — the drainage, more drainage and then even more drainage — it was Rawlinson's by-line. Steve was talking about Section 309, and how well it had held up after the storm. Not one landslip had come onto the road, the batters were well stabilized.

Rawlinson said, "We'll soon be onto section 308. We had some major blasting to manage, and some difficult drainage issues."

Steve nodded his acknowledgement. They drove on slowly, discussing the features of the new roadwork as they went.

"Mind if I play some music?" Karma said.

"Only if it's classical," Rawlinson shot back.

Karma pouted.

Rawlinson searched through some tapes and said, "What would you prefer Steve, Mozart or Haydn?"

Steve, not in the mood for small talk, answered abruptly, "Is there any difference?"

Rawlinson leaned forward and spoke just behind Steve's ear, "I hope you're joking?"

"Let's see," Steve said. He kept his eyes straight ahead. "Haydn is more considerate of the listener. He's calmer in his approach, more traditional. There's time to breathe between the notes. Mozart is demanding. He hardly gives you time to think before one note finishes and the next starts. In his day he was criticized for having too many notes."

"That's better," Rawlinson said. "I have taught you something useful."

"So!" Steve said and hesitated. "Considering the state of my nerves, Haydn!"

Rawlinson handed over a tape, Haydn's Surprise Symphony. Steve pushed it in and turned the volume down. As they drove the two engineers talked roads and yet more roads.

Rawlinson pointed ahead a quarter mile or so. "We've got some widening going on past that cutting. I wonder if we'll meet..."

The blood drained from Steve's face then he ducked his head. He saw it before he heard it. Dust. Rocks. Tree branches. Fragments spraying into the air from behind the road cutting. "SHIT!" was all Steve could utter.

The *boom* of the blast blocked any other sound. The shock waves bit hard, mercilessly hard. Karma hit the brakes. They skidded on the loose surface. Rawlinson knew immediately what had gone wrong, he didn't open his mouth to speak, instinct drove him to the floor. The shattering of the windscreen sprayed broken glass like shotgun fire. Steve groaned. No one moved. Haydn's Surprise was the only sound.

Karma spoke first, voice quivering, "Mr. Steve. You okay?"

Steve was slumped across the front seat. Ahead of him was a shattered front windscreen. Around him he could hear leaves and branches falling, and smell dust and dynamite settling. "Not sure, Karma," Steve moaned. "I'm bleeding...bad."

Karma hit the tape player button. Haydn's Surprise died. Steve's head and face were streaked with blood. His shirt collar was red. Blood oozed between his fingers where he held his hand to the wound. His breathing was erratic, shocked.

Rawlinson leant over the front seat. "Stay still! Let me see." He moved Steve's bloodied hand from above his left ear. It covered a flap of mangled flesh peeled back to the skull. Calmly, Rawlinson laid the torn flap of skin back over the wound, replaced Steve's hand and said, "A piece of rock must have come through the windscreen. You're lucky to be alive."

Steve just groaned.

Rawlinson said, "Karma, where's the first aid kit?"

The question met with an uncomfortable silence. Karma mumbled, "The what? Mr. John."

"First aid, the bandages, cotton wool..."

"Ahh...no got, sir." Karma hesitated, "I lend to cousin in Thimphu."

A murderous silence spanned a second or ten. "Dammit," was all that Rawlinson said as he opened the rear door and leapt out. As he did so, he found himself face to face with a road worker holding a red flag on a stick. "Where the fuck were you and your flag?" he snarled and grabbed at the front door handle.

The small man reeled back in surprise. He rambled incoherently in a local dialect, the look of desperation on his face said that he knew what he'd done.

Karma cradled Steve's head in his hands.

Rawlinson leant into the front of the Landcruiser and said, "Steve, look up at me. Can you see okay?"

Steve opened his eyes, "Yeah, you're blurry, just stop the bleeding, will you."

The flagman at the open door was gibbering madly.

"We need something clean to put on this, Karma." Rawlinson said and looked around for bandages that he knew weren't there. Blood was running down Steve's fingers, dripping onto the seat.

Steve groaned and said as he lifted himself off the seat, "Ohh...for Christ's sake." With bloodied fingers fumbling he took off his long-sleeved shirt. He tore the right sleeve off at the shoulder. He folded the cleanest part of it into a bandage and jabbed it at Rawlinson, "Use this!"

Rawlinson said nothing as he took the wad of shirt cotton and held it to Steve's head, too gently.

Steve cursed then shoved Rawlinson's hand away and held the bandage himself, he applied more pressure and a shot of pain found every raw nerve he had. As he sat there, Steve slowly became aware that the flagman was still at the door, pleading. The man was almost sobbing. "What the hell's he saying, Karma? Tell him to piss off."

Karma spoke firmly. The man bowed slightly from the waist, then with his flag over his shoulder, ran off downhill.

"What happened, Karma," Steve demanded. "Where was he?"

Karma sighed. "He was standing back there for over an hour, the blast must have been delayed. He ate something bad last night, he had to go quick. He was crouched down in the bushes under the road cutting when he heard us drive by. By the time he had his pants up, the blast hit him as well. He's so sorry."

Steve's mind raced, it turned over all sorts of things he might do with a flag on a stick.

Jigme Pemjo, the Bhutanese engineer-in-charge, arrived out of breath and close to tears. He surveyed the damage. "Sorry so much, the flagman was here, but he…"

Steve cut him off. "Jigme, we know. You did all you could. It was an accident…"

"Steve'll be okay, Jigme." Rawlinson added casually, "How'd the blast go?"

Jigme turned and his face lit up. "The granite boulder, the huge one. We moved it, moved it big."

Rawlinson looked delighted as he said, "Good work. Well done."

Steve took the wad of cotton from his head and saw that it was blood-soaked, the bleeding wasn't going to stop easily. He closed his eyes and grit his teeth. He said, "John, I'll have to get back to Trashigang. I need stitches."

Rawlinson nodded, "Yeah, I guess you do."

As Karma knocked the shattered glass out of the windscreen, Steve struggled to put his one-sleeved shirt back on. The movement caused a sharp stab of pain.

Karma and Jigme said together. "Mr. Steve, better for other sleeve to go too."

Steve shrugged and tore the other sleeve off his work shirt. He stuffed the spare sleeve in the pocket of his jeans, at the rate he was bleeding, he'd need it before they got back to Trashigang.

The blue project Landcruiser crept up the slight hill towards Khaling. They'd traveled about a mile when SAIB's white Landcruiser rounded a corner ahead. Karma and Jochu stopped opposite each other. Both drivers nodded, but neither spoke.

Narguli, seeing the shattered windscreen, asked what had happened. Steve leaned across toward the driver's window and explained in as few words as possible.

"Where are you going now?" Narguli asked curtly.

"Taking myself to hospital. I'll need stitches."

Narguli leaned out the passenger window and surveyed Steve's injuries, he said, "Do you *all* need to go? What about the road inspection?"

Rawlinson cut-in keenly, "Steve, I'll go with them. Karma can take you back."

Steve glared at Narguli who was looking straight ahead with arms folded. Ollie, in the back seat, at least looked a little concerned. Steve turned and said, "Thanks, John."

Rawlinson got out of the blue Landcruiser and replied, "No problem, hospitals aren't my scene." He crossed the road and climbed into the back seat next to Ollie.

Jochu took off downhill, south, and Steve just caught the beginnings of another Narguli lecture on how many more things can go wrong.

Karma drove uphill, north, with a passenger that groaned at every bump in the road.

32: A California Girl

They were entering the Chhume valley. A valley of meadows and wildflowers, a small farm here and there, a place where monasteries sit high on rocky hilltops and mountain streams splash over boulders, and Farley said, "So you grew up in the Napa Valley, Sophie?"

She turned and smiled, this was a bolt out of the blue, "Yeah...I'm a California girl."

"Oh! I've heard it's beautiful there. Sunny and warm."

"Yes. It is."

The bus was meandering along quietly with the sleepy afternoon sun tilting into the treetops and Sophie would have been quite content to daydream, but it was not to be, Farley it seemed, wanted to chat and nothing would put him off.

He said, "You mentioned at our lunch with Steve that your brothers still run a winery there..."

Sophie shrugged, what was the point in resisting, "Both my parents have passed away, my two older brothers, much older, have run the Vella Winery for years now. It's become a local success story. But it wasn't always like that."

Farley said, "I love hard-luck stories turned good, tell me."

"My father was a risk-taker, a true believer. He staked the family's life savings on a piece of dirt he thought could grow grapes. That was just after the Second World War when the Californian wine industry was in its infancy. He planted the vines and built the winery from the ground up. But even at his death, way too young, the vineyard was still very hard work for little return."

"Oh, what a pity your father didn't get to see..."

"Yeah...but it was much later that Napa Valley wines really found their place in the world market. Along with Napa's international recognition, Vella wines made their name and my brothers are right up there with the best of them."

Farley said, "How do you feel about that? Your brothers get a thriving family business, and you have to work, in Washington?"

Perhaps it was the way he said, 'In Washington' that sparked her reaction, or perhaps it was the suggestion that her family was like so many others she'd heard about. Sophie replied with just a hint of 'mind your own business', "No, no it's not that way. My brothers and I get on just fine. If I'd wanted to stay I could have, but it's changed. I've changed too."

Before Farley could open his mouth to apologize, she added quickly. "Anyway, I still own a third of the land and a cottage. I go there every year, sometimes twice a year."

Sophie was amazed at how deftly Farley changed the subject. Before she knew it she was telling him about studying law at Stanford and her long-held interest in human rights. "I was appointed to a junior position in the State Department and I've worked there now for fifteen years," she said and added a bit about the sort of things she worked on and the countries she traveled to.

When they crossed the Bumthang River and Anna said not long to go now, Jakar's just up ahead, Farley said "Umm, Sophie, something's been on my mind. I've been waiting for the right moment, there's something I have to confess."

"Oh! What?"

"On Sunday when we were leaving Thimphu, I picked up a newspaper that had been thrown out...it was on the maid's trolley, it was a Washington..."

"Post!" Sophie butted in, "You took it? That's where it went!"

"I...I wasn't sure it was yours. And I didn't take it, the housemaid had found it under a bed and assumed it was trash. She gave it to me."

Sophie whispered, almost fearing the answer, "Did you look at it?"

Farley nodded, "Yeah…sort of."

"The 'Around Town' column. You read it, didn't you?"

"Ahh…Yes."

Sophie turned away from him and stared out the window, her hands gripping the sides of her face. She let him wait like a criminal anticipating his sentence. A minute or more passed by and she could feel Farley beside her, squirming on his seat.

He said, "I was just wondering, the photograph under the article, the one taken on your wedding day?"

Sophie just gazed out the bus window and let him simmer.

He stumbled and stuttered. She turned as the color rose in his neck and face. "The caption said that the flower-girl was your daughter from a previous relationship?"

Still Sophie said nothing. She turned away again. He placed three fingers ever so gently on her shoulder. Gradually she turned, "I want that paper back, and I want you to promise me you won't mention it again."

"Sure. Of course." Farley leant closer and whispered, "She's Steve's daughter, isn't she?"

33: Singh the Sikh

The Project Landcruiser crept uphill. Steve held his head in his hands. Every movement, every bump in the road, sent a bolt of pain jarring through his head. Without a windscreen and without sleeves on his shirt, he soon started shivering. Karma was full of apologies, but there was little he could do to make Steve's trip more comfortable. For a few miles, Steve tried lying on the backseat. But he soon found that jarred more than when he was sitting up. By the time they arrived at Trashigang hospital, Steve looked every inch the urgent casualty that Karma booked him in as.

They sat together in a cramped, dark waiting room for fifteen minutes or so. The hospital only had one doctor, an Indian veteran of the business. Dr. Singh, a Sikh, was a huge man with poor eyesight, nimble fingers and a wicked sense of humor. The turban he wore accentuated the latter — when asked by the local kids what he kept under his strange hat, he'd often scare them with stories of spiders, scorpions or even snakes. He'd attended to the medical needs of the local community for so long that there was hardly a person in town that he hadn't delivered, stitched, de-itched or cured of a lingering malady. His rooms were spartan, but clean. His equipment was limited, but he knew how to use it. His manner, reassuring and caring. His fee, whatever Steve cared to offer. For those with nothing, Dr. Singh worked for the love of it. For those more fortunate, a generous donation to the Trashigang Hospital Fund was eagerly encouraged. The whole procedure only took a half-hour, but after it, Steve felt so much better than when he'd come in, he handed over enough ngultrums to keep the place running for a month. Dr. Singh, on seeing such generosity, joked that Steve should use half the money to buy himself a shirt with sleeves.

Steve laughed, then stopped, it hurt too much. Dr. Singh apologized and immediately lifted the level of service to match the payment. He was already done with the stitching and bandaging, so he moved onto the diagnosing and prescribing. He talked about mild concussion, possible temporary amnesia and dizzy spells. He handed over two small bottles of pills, he'd typed the labels himself. One bottle, the brown one, contained about thirty off-white colored pills, the label read, 'SINGH'S HEADACHE SPECIAL - FOR MILD PAIN – TAKE NO MORE THAN SIX PER DAY. LOTSA WATER.' The other bottle, of clear glass, contained just two huge pills, they were a pinkish-gray in color and oddly shaped, they had a homemade look about them. The label read, 'SINGH'S SLAMMERS — FOR ACUTE PAIN ONLY – TAKE ONE TABLET AND LIE DOWN IMMEDIATELY. ABSOLUTELY NO ALCOHOL.' The good doctor administered two of the HEADACHE SPECIALS, which Steve washed down with milky sweet tea.

When Rawlinson arrived home, Steve was stretched out on the lounge with a crepe bandage wrapped around his head. Martin was in the kitchen making tea. Karma was sitting by Steve's side, in a worse state of shock than the patient.

"All okay?" Rawlinson said as he walked into the room.

Steve didn't look up. He groaned, "Yeah, I think so."

"You want tea?" Martin said from the kitchen.

"Nah...whisky," Rawlinson replied. "I see you met Dr. Singh?"

Steve raised his eyebrows, they disappeared under his bandage. "Yeah, him and fifteen of his yak-hair stitches."

Rawlinson took a glass full of whiskey from Martin and said, "Thanks, hey, how lucky was I that Steve was sitting in the front seat."

Martin shook his head, "I hope you choke on that you old bastard."

Rawlinson just chuckled and lifted his glass.

Steve asked about the road inspection and Rawlinson opened fire, "Narguli started as soon as I got in the car. 'Rawlinson,' he barked, 'it looks as though your team has been totally incompetent in managing health and safety.' I shot back, roadwork's dangerous business. Anyway, our August monthly report says health and safety management is still unacceptable. Narguli turned on me. You know those black agate eyes of his. He said, 'don't just write about it, Rawlinson. *Manage* it man!' For the next four or so hours, Narguli criticized, sneered at, argued over and derided just about everything he saw while Ollie, with a face as blank as a passport photo sat silently in the back seat and took notes on everything that I said."

Rawlinson cooked dinner for them both. Steve hardly spoke, he ate even less and retired early. Back in his room, he desperately wanted to just lie down and sleep it off, but he knew he couldn't do that. He opened up the TRANSARCO accounts on his laptop and took another two of Dr. Singh's HEADACHE SPECIALS, this time with water.

He started with the page headed, 'Veejay Industries'. He searched every entry. They hired heavy plant and equipment. He listed out their invoices one by one, it was slow and tedious work. By the time he'd totaled up nearly thirty six million dollars he was cross-eyed and had a headache that defied gravity. He closed the laptop and rested his forehead on the lid. While he didn't like what the spreadsheets were reaffirming, there was one thing he had to admit to himself, they were beautifully set up and presented. And the more that Steve thought about it, the less likely it was that they were Martin's own work. Martin was much stronger in the field than in the office, his reports were poorly presented, his attention to detail woeful. They had Tammy written all over them.

At the Eiger guesthouse in Jakar, Sophie and Farley sat side by side on the verandah overlooking the town and the Bumthang Valley, the rim of which was a silhouette under starlight. Anna and Tashi were downstairs checking and re-checking their equipment and supplies. The Philadelphians had gone to their rooms to read with Nancy saying for all of them, "we'll leave you young ones alone now".

Farley poured tea from a thermos, produced a chocolate bar from the pocket of his jacket, broke it and handed half to Sophie. He said, "Thanks for trusting me."

"You didn't give me much choice, did you?" She added, "Is the likeness really that strong?"

"I knew she was Steve's daughter instantly, it's unmistakable. What's her name?"

"Maybe I never wanted to see it," she said to herself, then to Farley, "Marie. Anyway, it really is the coincidence of a lifetime, isn't it?"

"You and Steve meeting here like that...it's just so uncanny. I love it...I just love it so much I wish I could tell someone."

Sophie's reaction was immediate, "No, you don't. You promised remember!" The flow of conversation had Sophie unsettled. Losing the newspaper and having to confide in Farley was already a chink in her plan, to take it any further was out of the question. She needed an excuse to pull out of this exchange, pull out of the trek and get on with her business. That excuse she needed right now. She feared that Farley's next question would be along the lines, 'Hey, I've been thinking, Steve didn't ask you about Marie at our lunch, how much does he know about her?' To make matters worse, Farley was talking about a walk for the following day. Some plan he'd hatched with the Philadelphians, he'd give the details over breakfast. But a walk with Farley would surely lead to more questioning. There'd be questions she didn't want to answer.

She sipped her tea and nibbled at the chocolate bar Farley had given her, and her mind was a blank until Anna said from below, "Sophie, Farley, could one of you give me a hand with this tent, please?"

Farley stood to move, his mouth was ready to form the words, "Sure, coming," but Sophie beat him to it. She almost pushed Farley back onto his seat and called out, "On my way!" She ran across the verandah, took the steep stairs two at a time and on the bottom stair, tripped. She cried, "Help!" as she sprawled across the stone pavement, breaking her fall with outstretched hands. All was quiet, then she let out a yelp, "Oww, my ankle. Oww!" She rolled around on the ground in agony and let everyone know it. "Owww, Owww!" She lay on her back and held onto her ankle with both hands, "Aghh, Aghh!" Anna, Tashi and Farley all leant over her and said simultaneously, "Sophie, what's happened?"

"Agh...My ankle." Sophie grimaced and writhed a little more, "I think I've sprained my ankle. Oww it hurts!"

By now the commotion had alerted Eric and the Philadelphians as well, in total twelve people were now standing around her and wringing their hands until Anna took command, "Quick, someone get ice. Tashi, the bandages, hurry! Sophie, don't move."

34: An unexpected lesson
in good manners

Though Narguli's tender documents for Two Roads East didn't say as much, it was clear to Steve on the first reading that the northern road was something of an add-on, a second thought. Trashi Yangtse Province, or Dzongkhag as the political sub-division was called in Bhutan, was relatively undeveloped. So it was with development in mind that the Royal Government allocated twenty five million dollars from the Two Roads East project to upgrade the road between the Chazam bridge and Trashi Yangtse town. Steve knew that this was the reason that Rawlinson had all but handed over this part of the project to Martin. From Day One it had been Martin's baby and he'd cared for it accordingly. Now though, with the project budget in question, it was clear that upgrading the twenty-five miles of winding single lane blacktop would be delayed at best. At worst, it might never get finished.

No project supervision mission was complete without meetings to appease the local politicians, and as Two Roads East was working in two Dzongkhags, duty required that Steve meet the Dzongdas, the political leaders, of both of them. It was the aspect of his job that Steve enjoyed least, and today he couldn't have felt less like the two meetings that were ahead of him. He had a throbbing headache and he was only managing to stay on his feet courtesy of Dr. Singh's painkillers.

At a quarter to nine outside the project office, Dr. Narguli ordered that he, Ollie, Steve and Martin would travel to Trashi

Yangtse in the bank's Landcruiser. Their meeting with the Dzongda was scheduled for eleven and he wanted the roadworks discussed as they drove, there being no plan to stop along the way. Smyth-Jones and Rawlinson, Narguli demanded, would prepare themselves for the afternoon meeting with the Trashigang Dzongda, while Karma could start the search for a new windscreen.

At ten fifty, just three miles from Trashi Yangtse town, they swept round a corner and stopped abruptly. An orange Tata truck was parked across the road, blocking it from both directions. Jochu turned off the engine.

"What did you do that for?" Narguli said. "We're not stopping here."

"I can't get past, sir."

"Then get out and tell them to move," Narguli ordered.

Jochu approached the four burly Bhutanese men who were lifting bags of potatoes off the truck, two were on the ground and two were on the tray-back. There was a brief conversation, then he slunk back to the Landcruiser.

Narguli asked sharply, "So?"

"The men said that the truck driver is having a meal, somewhere."

"Are the keys in the truck?" Narguli snorted, "Tell them to move it."

Moments later Jochu was back again, "The keys are in there, sir. But they said if we want it moved, we can move it ourselves. None of them drive." Jochu's eyes sank to the road.

"*Then move it*," Narguli demanded.

"But, but sir! I don't know how...I don't drive trucks."

"Then learn. *Now!*"

Jochu climbed onto the running-board, opened the door and sat in the driver's seat. He reached for the ignition and without warning the truck's starter motor kicked over, rarr...

rarr. The truck lurched forward, frog-like and stopped dead. The workmen on the back were thrown off balance and fell heavily. The largest of the men jumped to his feet, furious, he thumped closed fists on the roof of the truck and roared obscenities. Jochu threw open the door and tumbled over four feet to the ground. He scampered back to the Landcruiser, jumped in and locked it. His eyes were closed tight and he was shaking so hard his teeth rattled.

Narguli leapt out. He ran to the side of the truck and screamed abuse. He stomped in the dust. He kicked the tires and banged the side of the truck with open hands.

Ollie, who was sitting in the middle of the back seat, reached over and put an understanding hand on Jochu's shaking shoulder. "Don't worry," she said, "Dr. Narguli is a bit anxious today."

It wasn't much, but Steve didn't miss it. Ollie had expressed an independent opinion, almost a dissenting one. Steve turned to Martin whose raised eyebrows said he'd seen it too. Finally Steve said to Martin. "Help the poor bugger will you, before he has a heart attack."

Ollie glared at Steve, it was almost as though Narguli's heart attack was exactly what she was waiting for. But then, Steve could have misread her, perhaps she was angry that it had taken him so long to offer help?

It took Martin all of two minutes to move the truck so there was just room to pass at the front.

Narguli quickly composed himself and strolled back to the Landcruiser with his head held high and hands in his pockets, and said loudly enough for Martin to hear it, "So, the boy's useful for something after all."

The Trashi Yangtse District Administrator, Dasho Leki Deki, was expecting to greet the bank supervision mission at eleven. They arrived at the dzong nearly fifteen minutes late.

The dzongda's staff was pacing the car park. Chief Engineer Pema greeted the delegation, and on noticing Steve's bandaged head, wanted a run-down on what had happened. Steve filled in the details in as few words as possible while Pema led the way across a newly paved forecourt to a steep set of wooden steps. Although the dzong had not long been inaugurated, it was built in the traditional style and already had a touch of the ancient about it. In single file they followed Pema along narrow corridors, through curtained doorways and into the dzongda's ante-room. They had hardly taken their seats when Dasho Leki Deki greeted them formally, but warmly. He opened the door into his large office overlooking the town. They took seats on cloth covered benches that paralleled a row of low tables. Dasho Leki was immaculate in a midnight-blue tartan gho and knee-high woven boots. Even his staff looked scrubbed up for the occasion. There was a huge photograph of the king hanging behind the dzongda's desk. Colorful drawings of Buddhist gurus and a large map of the dzongkhag decorated the other walls. The first sign of trouble came when the dzongda offered tea to everyone, and Narguli refused it for all.

"Oh! Alright," the dzongda said still smiling but clearly taken aback by Narguli's rudeness. "On to business then, as you wish."

Steve gave a brief run-down on progress but stopped short of mentioning delays, or even worse, a full shutdown of the project.

There was a moment of confusion. Who would speak next? The dzongda sensed it was up to him, he said, "There's a rumor going around...The project's run out of money?"

Steve was unsure of himself, it wasn't his job to answer. Narguli's closely shaven face was impassive, he didn't move until he yawned with mouth wide-open and hands at his side.

Dasho Leki waited for a response, when it was clear he wouldn't get one, he stood and adjusted his gho. He sat again, all eyes were on him. "So, the project's not going to get finished?"

Narguli sighed out loud. "Ohh…look Dasho…we have an inquiry under way. There will be a delay, yes. But it's only the last few miles into town that aren't finished. Surely you can live with that for a while?"

Dasho Leki almost choked on Narguli's cool rebuttal. He said, "It depends on how long we have to wait. We can't bring large trucks into town. We have to load and unload at the three mile post. There's a lot of double-handling."

Narguli cut in. "We've seen that for ourselves. But such a minor inconvenience, really!" He signaled to Ollie for her agreement. She glared back at him. No one in the room missed it.

Dasho Leki snapped back, "Minor for you maybe, but major for us. You mentioned an inquiry, who's conducting it?"

"Mr. Nigel Smyth-Jones, he's been jointly appointed by the minister and the bank."

The dzongda said, "Where is he?"

Narguli didn't hide his irritation, this was sounding like a challenge. "I asked him to stay back, he's preparing for our meeting this afternoon at Trashigang."

"Oh, he's too busy to come all the way to Trashi Yangtse, is he?"

Narguli's reply was immediate and hostile. "We appreciate your concern, Dasho. But this part of Two Roads East is rather minor."

"As I said before, minor for you maybe, major for us. When will the inquiry finish?"

The tension was measurable. Narguli scanned the room. It was as if Ollie was waiting for him to choke on his answer. Even Narguli had noticed the change in her. "My dear Dasho," Narguli began, he was obviously buying thinking time. "The bank has its procedures, and of course due process must be followed. The inquiry will finish when we find what we are looking for."

The air was suddenly heavy, laden with looming confrontation.

"Please excuse me if I am out of order, Dr. Narguli." Dasho Leki stood and paced the floor, his hands were clasped behind him, his head bent forward. "We signed up to your loan in good faith. The loan included a generous contingency. Now the contingency is spent, the road's not finished and you're asking me to tell my people to wait while you work through bank procedures and processes that we're not even part of?"

Steve shuffled uncomfortably on his seat, hoping he wouldn't be drawn in, his head was throbbing already.

Narguli's jaw firmed. He shook his head and blinked several times in rapid succession, "Are you suggesting, Dasho," Narguli waited and bared his yellow teeth, "that an official bank inquiry alter its course because the occasional truck can't come right into Trashi Yangtse? Because one or two trucks have to be unloaded three miles from town for a while?"

The dzongda, still standing, faced Narguli from across the room. "I'm saying that, as partners in this project, we have a right to know what's happening and when we can expect results."

Narguli cleared his throat, went to speak, then stopped. He thought some more. Hesitated even, before getting to his feet. It was as if there were only two people in the room. "Dasho, I will remind you we are talking about the South Asia Infrastructure Bank, one of the largest financial institutions in the region."

The Dasho took three steps towards Narguli and facing him said, "Dr. Narguli, *sir*, your bank and my people are equal around here. I am working for my people. My dzongkhag."

"And what do you think I'm doing here, Dasho?" Narguli sneered. "Let me remind you that I turned down Bangladesh and Sri Lanka to work with you people."

"You're a banker, sir…you're here selling money…and debt."

Narguli barked in reply, "And development, and opportunity!"

"Yes sir, but the debt always follows you sir, the development and opportunity sometimes do…they're optional extras."

Narguli stepped backwards and fell into his seat, his voice raised a notch or two in pitch, "Dasho, I'm not sure what Russian textbook you've learned your high-school economics from, but let me warn you, a little knowledge is a dangerous thing."

The Dasho smiled and leant towards Narguli, he spoke softly, in control, "Yes sir, but not nearly so dangerous as a whole lot of arrogance."

Never had a project meeting at the Trashi Yangtse Dzong finished so quickly, so unexpectedly. Narguli would have walked through the door had it not been opened for him. The only words that were spoken on the return journey were Narguli's order, which he barked at Jochu. "Get us out of this moronic place. Quickly!"

It was just on two when Jochu pulled up at the office in Trashigang. Narguli turned to face Steve, Martin and Ollie in the back seat. He said, "Miss Ramos and I have some things to discuss. We'll meet you at the Trashigang dzong at three sharp."

Ollie sat between Steve and Martin in the back seat. She hadn't moved an inch, or said a word since they'd left Trashi Yangtse, so it was with surprise that Steve heard her say, "Steve, Martin, I'll join you both for lunch."

"NO!" Narguli shouted, his face purple with rage. He pointed at Ollie, his shaking finger was only inches from her face, "You'll come with me."

35: *Alone with thoughts*

Breakfast at the Eiger was served buffet style on the open verandah overlooking the valley. Sophie opened her door and looked out, a soft morning light was hovering above a valley mist and birdcalls were welcoming in the new day. Despite the early hour, Farley and the Philadelphians were already engaged in conversation that sounded as though it had been going for some time. As soon as they heard her door open, all nine of them turned and said, "How's the ankle?" Sophie grimaced and, balanced on the walking stick that Eric had given her, said, "I guess I'm lucky it's not broken."

She hobbled across the verandah and squeezed in next to Jim on a bench seat already holding four others. All conversation stopped while Sophie was served with tea, toast, butter and honey. Was there anything else she wanted? Was she comfortable?

Concerned faces were all around her, but most concerned of all was Farley. He was even blaming himself for Sophie's accident; it was he that should have moved more quickly, Sophie shouldn't have had to help with the tents. Sophie told them all not to worry, to go hunting rare orchids without her, that she'd rest for the day and would be okay, it was only a sprain.

Farley and the Philadelphians had been gone for mere minutes. Sophie sat on the verandah at the Eiger and she was in pain, but it wasn't her ankle that was troubling her. The pain she felt was of her own making. Now that she was alone, especially that she was alone in the very place she'd meet Steve in a little over twenty four hours, her mind was playing games.

Dangerous games. She'd tried to meditate, to follow Tashi's advice and 'let go.' She'd tried reading. She'd even tried just sitting on the verandah and staring out over the valley at the river and the dzong and the fields of pink and green. But nothing was working. She just couldn't let go of the fact that all she'd come for was to deliver a message for their daughter, and now, like it or not, she was involved in Steve's life again.

Her mind cast back again to that last day at Cahuita. To a beach at sunrise, to Steve undressing her, to swimming naked and then standing knee deep in turquoise green water, to feeling the urgency and strength of Steve's desire for her. To wondering if it was possible to be any more in love with someone. Then his return from San Jose entered her mind, then a sleepless night of pleading with him to tell her what had changed, then a bus station and a farewell. Then the last time that he kissed her. A kiss on the cheek, not the mouth, and more tears. For nineteen years she'd been haunted by what changed Steve's mind that day in San Jose. And she was still no closer to an answer.

Their need for each other that last morning was unstoppable, and unprepared for. And whatever regrets she'd had in her life, having Marie wasn't one of them. They'd shared so much. Marie had been her inspiration for so long now it was impossible to imagine life any other way. Though lately it seemed, change had entered her otherwise ordered life without even knocking on the door, and once inside, like a cyclone, it wasn't going to leave until it had lifted her roof.

It was pride that had stopped her contacting Steve during her pregnancy. She'd told Steve when he left her that she would never be the first to make contact. He'd agreed and she'd stayed true to that vow for over three years, until Marie's first questions about her daddy got in the way. But after she'd phoned Steve's home and spoken to his brother Bill, only to be told that no one knew where Steve was, but that he was with another woman, Sophie had put off the inevitable to another day. And while Sophie had never denied her daughter the right to know her father, she'd never wanted to face that inevitable day either.

But year by year Marie's insistence to exercise her right had been growing. In July they'd had an argument that scared both of them. Sophie had suggested a party for Marie's eighteenth birthday and offered to invite a whole bunch of Marie's friends along. Marie had replied, 'No, I don't want a party. You know what I want and you won't let me have it! And if you can't give me that, then give me a ticket to Australia and I'll go meet him myself.' They'd ended up in tears with Sophie promising that she'd do something, but that she had to wait until the time was right. She'd reminded Marie that she was applying for a new job, a promotion, and that she needed some understanding. But understanding is a hard word for an eighteen year old obsessed with meeting her father, Marie had shouted, 'I've been understanding now for fifteen years, how long do I have to wait, another fifteen?'

Then followed a standoff of sorts. Marie started spending hours on the internet, researching anything she could find on her father, the company he worked for, where he lived and the projects he was working on in places as far flung as Cambodia, Indonesia, Bhutan and China. The pressure she applied to Sophie was gentle, but relentless. Then in early August, Sophie opened her front door and Cyclone Change came in at force five; she got the job she'd wanted so much for so long, and that same day Marie came home with the news that Josie, one of her school friends had been accepted into a gap-year Indonesian language course in Bali and that Marie wanted to join her for three months or so — that Josie was more an acquaintance than a friend, that Marie's Indonesian was several levels below Josie's and that the course started in less than three weeks didn't even enter Marie's head as a problem. Sophie had discussed it with Alex at the time, he was much more upbeat than she was about the value of Marie improving her Indonesian and the arrangements were made in such a rush that Sophie's second-sense reservations about the whole thing never got a proper airing. Sophie wondered now, after the event, how much that second-sense was to do with Bali being too close for comfort, to Australia.

Marie's determination in the matter reminded Sophie of her own when she'd first told her parents that she was joining Steve on his trip through Central America. She knew there was no point in arguing, Marie was her baby; Sophie had brought her up to be determined and it seemed that a somewhat useful trip to Bali was the price she'd have to pay for a few months of peace and a chance to settle into her new job.

Sophie had farewelled Marie and Josie on their flight to Indonesia and left the next day for a three country visit to South America. She was in Venezuela when she heard via Alex that Marie had left Indonesia bound for Australia. The flight from Caracas home had never seemed so long and the phone message that greeted her had confirmed her worst fears, but it couldn't have forewarned of what was to come. Here she was, just weeks later, alone in central Bhutan on mission impossible, and she had no one to blame but herself; she was doing it, her way.

Her way had involved some high level help at work. Convincing Alex that she had to leave so soon after starting her new job had been the hardest part. Through Marie's research on the internet she knew where Steve worked and generally what he was doing. Then Alex, through Michael James, discovered that Steve was scheduled to visit Bhutan from September 25th for two weeks. He got hold of the full itinerary for the bank supervision mission to Two Roads East, and with that, Steve's itinerary. From that point on her plan to meet him in Bhutan 'by accident' seemed almost sensible. She'd suffered a slight setback when she was told that tourists could only visit Bhutan in organized groups, but then she realized that booking herself with a trekking company was the perfect alibi at work. She'd stay with the group just long enough to do what she had to do, then pullout on the pretext of a problem back home. Luck had it that Mountain Adventures had one place vacant on a Bhutan trip that overlapped with Steve's. Overlapped too well, she'd have preferred not to be on the same flight as him, but with Steve in Economy and her in Business, it had worked out okay.

Not only did she know what flight he was on and where he was staying in Thimphu, but when he was to meet the minister and when he should have some free time. That free time was to be hers. That was, until an unexpected hitch in Steve's plans became an even more unexpected hitch in her own.

Whether or not Steve was guilty of fraud, whether or not he'd been set up, now mattered to her, and it would also matter to Marie. In her work in Latin America she'd had to help a number of US citizens who'd been framed for crimes they didn't commit. Sophie knew the story well — in a place like Bhutan, when they had your passport, they had your freedom.

That someone could change over nearly twenty years she didn't doubt. But she did doubt that someone like Steve could go from being the most authentic man she'd ever known, and that was notwithstanding the way he'd let her down in San Jose, to a criminal trying to defraud a country like Bhutan of loan funds on an aid project.

36: An unexpected lesson in road safety

It was a warm, sticky afternoon in Trashigang. Rawlinson and Smyth-Jones sat in the shade of a tree in the forecourt of the Dzong. Martin and Steve walked down from the office to join them. Steve had finished his lunch with another two of Dr. Singh's HEADACHE SPECIALS. They were helping, but he was far from well. He was dreading what the afternoon might bring. At three precisely, Narguli came in with Ollie following a few feet behind. Even from a distance it was clear that she'd been crying. The dzongda's staff asked them all to follow. As they walked across the open forecourt a young monk stood on the white-washed stone wall surrounding it, he was using his robes as a kite to catch the wind blowing up from the valley. He turned to watch the procession of chilips, then his face was lost in a wave and flap of maroon cloth. They entered the vast passageway in the outer wall and walked in half darkness past the huge frescoes of the Kings of the Four Directions. At the end of the passageway there was sunlight again. They followed solemnly across the paved court of the inner sanctum.

The Trashigang Dzongda, Dasho Ugyen Penjo, appeared. With a bow he invited everyone into his office. Dasho Ugyen was an elder statesman, what he shared though with his younger counterpart at Trashi Yangtse, apart from their 'Ivy League education', was a wish to serve his people and his king in a traditional Bhutanese way. The Bhutanese way with foreign advisers and their aid programs was to be very selective. Development would come to Bhutan on its own terms, and in its own time.

Dasho Ugyen chaired the meeting. He began by welcoming everyone, expressing his sincere regrets for Steve's accident and then offering tea. This time Narguli did not refuse. Some of the dzongkhag engineering staff were also in attendance. In all, twelve people were seated on benches that formed a rough square around the room. Ollie was the only woman. The streaks of recent tears still marked her face.

Dasho Ugyen took the meeting through the agenda efficiently and courteously. Martin spoke on the training program and presented a draft report to the dzongda for his review. Steve stood to speak, his head began swimming, and for a moment he thought he'd faint. He covered progress with the road south to Wamrong, but deliberately didn't discuss what might happen on the last four or five miles that would hardly be started: that was Narguli's job. His account was met with serious nods of Bhutanese heads and a whispering of concerned voices.

After an observed silence, the dzongda said, "There's a rumor going around…Something about a twenty million dollar shortfall?"

Narguli butted in, "Dasho! We have launched an inquiry. Mr. Smyth-Jones is running it."

Dasho Ugyen turned to Nigel and said, "And how long might your inquiry last, Mr. Smyth?"

Nigel stood to speak. He straightened his tie. "Sir, the task is considerable and our resources are limited, but we will do our best." He remained on his feet for the dzongda's response.

Dasho Ugyen bowed his head to consider Nigel's reply. When his head lifted, his smile was gone. "We're widening the Trashigang to Wamrong road so that we can build a hydroelectric plant at Lingmethang. It is to be Bhutan's largest ever investment, an investment underwritten by the Indian Government and with a guaranteed market for all the power we can produce. Now we're told it all has to wait for an under-resourced inquiry."

The color drained from Nigel's face. He mumbled, "Yes sir," and almost fell backwards he sat so heavily. Five of the six chilips shot uncomfortable glances at Narguli. It was his job to respond, surely? He just wrote importantly in his notebook, he refused to look up. Ollie grinned sarcastically and shook her head. No one else spoke or moved.

A lengthy silence brought the first agenda item to a close. Dasho Ugyen said, "Oh, okay then, let's keep things moving." The penultimate agenda item was the itinerary for the supervision mission members, the Dasho always liked to know what the chilips in his part of the world were doing. "Dr. Narguli," the dzongda said, "what are your travel plans, please?"

Narguli answered without making eye contact. "I've agreed that Miss Ramos can return to Thimphu tomorrow. She wishes to prepare for Tuesday's project wrap-up meeting. I'll travel back with Mr. Smyth-Jones on Sunday as planned."

"Thank you, Dr. Narguli." The dzongda turned to Steve. "Mr. Andrews, your travel plans, please?"

"I'd planned to leave tomorrow for Jakar and stop over there Friday for a meeting, then drive to Thimphu on Saturday. But our Landcruiser won't be ready, I need to..."

Steve was interrupted in mid-sentence. "Excuse me, Dasho," Ollie said. All eyes were instantly on her.

"Yes, Miss Ramos?"

"Mr. Andrews can travel to Jakar with me in the morning."

Narguli glared at Ollie, then at Steve. He started to speak then checked himself. Steve turned to Ollie and nodded a thank you. Ollie looked up, anywhere but at Narguli. Her legs were stretched out in front of her and her hands were on her knees, it was as though she was inspecting the ceiling for flaking paint.

The dzongda wrapped up the first part of the meeting. While a second round of tea was being served, informal discussions broke out around the room. Steve and Dasho Ugyen talked about Steve's meeting on Friday with the Chief Engineer for Bumthang Dzongkhag; how he was collecting the bidding documents and doing a site inspection for the Upper Bumthang Bridge project north of Jakar town.

The dzongda brought the meeting to order again. The final agenda item was safety management. Dasho Ugyen referred to yesterday's accident and expressed his concern again over Steve's bandaged head.

Steve thanked the dzongda and assured him that he would be okay, although the dull thudding ache behind his eyes told him differently. He remained seated and referred to an annex in their August monthly report. He read the title. "Ten simple steps to safer roadwork in Bhutan." He drew specific attention to Recommendation Number Two, 'There shall always be a flagman on duty at both ends of a blasting site'. Jigme Pemjo, the dzongkhag's Chief Engineer almost slid off his seat in an attempt to disappear. The dzongda, noticing this, intervened. He said, "What was our flagman to do? He was suffering loose bowels. These things happen." Dasho Ugyen looked to Steve. Steve had no answer, he turned to Martin and then Rawlinson, both were blank-faced. He bit his bottom lip then thanked the dzongda for his question, he agreed they hadn't thought that one through, they'd look at it again.

The meeting finished with a thank you speech from the dzongda and then he played his trump card. He did it so well it had to be deliberate. He said casually, "I believe a SAIB Director is to attend the project wrap-up meeting next Tuesday. That's just six days away, I hope your inquiry has an answer by then."

It was hard to say who was most surprised. Narguli's jaw dropped open and he blabbered, "What? A Director? Why?" Ollie was no more composed, her eyes opened almost as wide as her mouth. Rawlinson and Martin shot furtive glances to Steve who just shrugged and raised his palms. Only Nigel Smyth-Jones took the news with equanimity, he muttered, "Well, well, we *are* under a little pressure, hey chaps?"

Steve and Martin walked silently back to the office. Steve's day had begun badly, and trouble had stayed with him all day. His headache was slowly working its way down his neck and spine, and the further south it went, the worse it got. He'd thought several times of mentioning Tammy's drunken outburst to Martin, but what he really wanted was for Martin to say something first.

Steve switched on the light at the office door. Martin sat behind his desk as though it drew a defensive line between them. Steve moved a chair to sit opposite him and said, "Well, where do we start?"

"How would I know," Martin said. "I'm not the project director or the project manager. I just offered to keep the books, and shit, don't I regret it now."

This opening set the mood for the meeting and it went downhill from there. An hour later, with Martin's defensiveness still leading them round and around in circles, Steve exploded. He said, "Shit, Martin, is this even your work?"

Martin shoved his chair back, slammed his tightly clenched fist on the desk and shouted. "Don't fucking blame me. The accounts are right. Shove it, Steve!" Without looking back he walked out the door and slammed it so hard the office walls shook.

Steve sat in the loneliness and chill of the empty office and rethought his position on Martin and Tammy. Now he was certain that what he'd overheard on Sunday night at their house was the truth. And under the circumstances, that truth placed Tammy as his chief suspect. Whether or not Martin was involved in the scam was irrelevant at this point, he was guilty by association anyhow. Steve slowly closed his laptop and felt sickened by the thought of going to the wrap-up meeting on Tuesday and having to admit to Narguli, and now also a bank director, that one of his own staff was most probably guilty. It just reconfirmed how badly he'd let the project slip, and how much his own problems had been on his mind over the past year. Bradshaw was right, he'd been asleep at the wheel.

As he walked from the office to Rawlinson's house, Steve decided that he wouldn't even mention his suspicions to him. Rawlinson had never been a friend, or even someone that Steve had looked up to, but on this visit Rawlinson had been even more self-interested than usual: if it didn't affect Rawlinson's pocket directly, it wasn't his business. That neither Martin nor Rawlinson appeared the least bit concerned that they might end up in gaol with him was perplexing, the worst part of it though, was that they might be right. If there was no resolution at the wrap-up meeting on the seventh, Steve was starting to convince himself that it would be he alone on the hot-seat, and he wasn't about to let that happen without a fight.

By the time Steve walked through the front gate, the next part of his strategy was set. He needed more evidence than words he'd overheard through cracks in the floorboards; he'd go over and over the spreadsheets and invoices until he'd worked out how Tammy had siphoned off the money. Hopefully, this might give some clue also as to what she'd done with it. Then, when he got back to Thimphu, he'd call Laudmeir, TRANSARCO's corporate lawyer and ask his advice. Tuesday was less than a week away and bearing down on him fast; he had a lot to do before then.

While Rawlinson cooked rice and a yak meat stew for dinner, they talked about the World Bank Bridge project near Jakar. Steve and Rawlinson had their differences on many things, but they agreed that on the Upper Bumthang project, TRANSARCO should be very competitive, in fact, hard to beat. But, Steve lamented, if we don't sort out the problems with Two Roads East, the minister will strike TRANSARCO off the shortlist for bidding.

Rawlinson turned a paler shade of gray. He sneered, "Fuck, dammit. We've got work worth hundreds of millions a year at risk with SAIB, and if that ends in a blacklisting it'll flow on to the World Bank, and they're a much bigger client. TRANSARCO will be fucked, and I'll be fucking ruined."

Steve put his hands to his head to hold in the pain. He said, "It had crossed my mind," then he shrugged, just a little too casually for Rawlinson's liking.

"Shit, Steve," Rawlinson snapped. "It's easy to see you haven't taken up your stock options!"

"My options! Fuck! It's staying out of bloody gaol that I'm worried about."

Rawlinson fidgeted all through dinner. He made Steve promise to get a message to him straight after the wrap-up meeting on Tuesday. He said. "If I have to sell TRANSARCO at a loss, I'll hold you personally accountable. Thanks for nothing, buddy." He excused himself abruptly and went to his room. The door closed with a dull thud behind him.

Steve sat still for minutes, the pain in his head was hammering closer and closer to a raw nerve. He fixed up in the kitchen, and as he did so the house felt as un-welcoming as his own. He went to his room and picked up the bottle labeled SINGH'S SLAMMERS, he read the label and decided he wasn't that desperate yet. He took two more HEADACHE SPECIALS and opened his laptop again. By the time he'd added all the payments to Veejay Industries on the TRANSARCO books, he had a grand total of nearly thirty six million dollars on one hundred and eleven separate invoices. He started the same exercise on the SAIB accounts. It was just past midnight when he'd recorded one hundred and sixteen separate payments totaling just on forty six million. He compared the two sets of results and thought, that's strange? How'd I get that so wrong? Or is it wrong? He weighed up the option of checking his work or sleeping. Dr. Singh's pills were wearing off and he'd already taken the daily dose: sleeping won. I'll go over it again in Jakar he promised himself as he packed away his laptop.

At two thirty in the morning a cold shiver ran through him. He thought of home, four and a half hours ahead. The boys would be waking; they'd be counting the days until he was home. If anything, he dreaded letting them down more than he dreaded the thought of Wangdi prison and how long it might take TRANSARCO to get him out of there. That thought led him again to Tammy. He was convinced that the answer lay in the accounts that he had with him. Somehow she'd doctored them to hide discrepancies that now totaled ten million just on one supplier, and she'd even managed to hide that from her husband. He had just five days now to find out how she'd done it, then he'd gladly pass the whole thing over to Laudmeir and his legal team, they could sort it out from there.

37: Too many fishermen, too few fish

At six a.m., some one hundred and seventy-five miles to the west of Trashigang, Sophie was already at breakfast, her bandaged foot prominently propped up on a chair in front of her. She turned as Farley opened the door of Room 2. She looked him up and down several times then blinked hard, she opened her eyes again but he was the same. He had his full trekking outfit on, the one he'd bought out of a catalog. He dipped his feathered hat in traditional style then sat down to a huge breakfast. The Philadelphians were checking everything off, lists were read and re-read. When seven-thirty approached, nine people expressed their disappointment that Sophie wouldn't be coming, and one looked as if he might shed a tear. Eleven hugs later (Anna and Tashi joined in) Sophie was downstairs and waving them good-bye. Suddenly she was the only guest at the Eiger. She hobbled back up to the verandah and gazed absently out over the valley. She felt both ready for, and frightened by, what lay ahead.

Despite a thudding dull ache in his head, Steve reapplied his bandage and tightened it. At six a.m. he opened the bedroom door. Rawlinson was already up and the aroma of freshly brewed coffee filled the house. They hardly spoke over breakfast. It appeared to Steve that all that was on Rawlinson's mind was the possible impact of 'the problem' on TRANSARCO's bottom line, and hence his stock value. If there was to be any negative reporting on TRANSARCO's prospects, Rawlinson wanted to beat the market to it. It was now obvious that Steve's chief value to Rawlinson was as a harbinger of bad news, as if that was inevitable. Steve washed down two HEADACHE SPECIALS with strong coffee and Rawlinson scoffed, "You'd be brave, or stupid, or both, to take anything that crazy Indian gave you."

Ollie arrived at ten past seven. She was sitting in the back seat of a four-wheel drive HiLux TwinCab, the driver was a lanky dark-skinned man with a red-and-white checked cotton scarf around his neck. He wasn't Bhutanese, Steve wasn't sure where he was from but introduced himself anyway in English. The man shook his head, he hadn't understood. The driver pointed a finger at himself and said, "Jalal". Steve shook his hand and repeated, "Jalal" to make sure he'd got it right. Ollie stayed in the car. Steve loaded his luggage in the rear and then realized he had a decision to make. Should he sit in the front seat with Ollie behind him, and travel for ten hours in what would be surely stony silence, or should he ignore convention and sit in the back with Ollie, where there might be at least a chance of conversation.

Steve shook hands with Rawlinson and again promised to phone him with a report on Tuesday's wrap-up meeting. He turned, and without hesitating opened the back door and climbed in next to Ollie. Her look of utter surprise confirmed that she'd expected him to take the front seat. She turned away.

They drove by the turn-off to the dzong. Steve said, "Well Ollie, we've one hundred and seventy-five miles, or ten hours driving ahead of us. Which do you prefer?" Without turning she gave the barest hint of a smile.

As they dropped toward the river, Steve made a bet with himself; he'd get Ollie talking, or go hoarse trying. They crossed the Chazam Bridge and tracked down along the river. Ollie gazed out the window, distracted and distant. Steve eased into the silence. He started to think about his day in Jakar. About bridges and World Bank tenders, about TRANSARCO and what would happen if the minister dropped them from the shortlist for the Upper Bumthang Bridge project.

They drove through the road camp at Rolong. Ollie had her back to Steve. To get any further away from him, she'd have had to get out of the car. Without warning, Jalal wrenched the vehicle off to the left. He stopped with a screech of tires and clouds of dust. A speeding Tata truck passed by within inches.

After a moment of silence, Steve leaned over and said, "Use the horn on the corners. It's safer."

Jalal grinned and bared a mouthful of crooked yellowed teeth framed by dry, cracked lips. He shook his head, he hadn't understood a word.

Steve leaned over further and pointed to the horn, he gestured. "You know, *Toot*! *Toot*!" He immediately felt a fool and out of the corner of an eye, he saw Ollie giggle.

"Even after all these trips," he said. "I'm still nervous about hitting a truck on one of these blind corners, especially with a driver I don't know."

Ollie said, "Me too," and smiled faintly. "I cross myself and pray to the Blessed Mother Mary before every trip."

Steve didn't know much about Catholicism, but he felt comforted anyway by the thought that Mother Mary was looking out for them. And he'd managed to get Ollie to say something. There had to be more, but he had all day, he wouldn't rush it.

They crossed the Sheri Chhu and started the climb uphill toward Yadi. Jalal pulled half off of the road and stopped. He turned around to face Steve. "Pee, sir. Please I pee?" He threw the door open and scrambled off into the bushes. Ollie blushed and stared out the front windscreen, she hadn't said a word for over fifteen minutes. Jalal pulled at the fly of his ill-fitting pants as he crossed the road and got in behind the wheel.

Steve leaned over the back of the front seat and pointed to the tape player. "We have music, okay?"

Jalal shrugged. Steve turned to Ollie. "Okay if I play some music?"

Her face lit up, she smiled and nodded, "Please, go ahead." The tape player clicked on and music played as the HiLux labored up through the switchbacks. Jalal had hardly finished turning out of one corner before he was into the next. He heeded Steve's warning and sounded the horn on every bend which, on this stretch of road, meant every ten seconds or so.

Steve was wondering if Eva Cassidy accompanied by a car horn was worse than silence, when Ollie said, "She's a favorite of yours, Steve?"

"Oh...sort of. Do you like her singing?"

"It's very beautiful. Her version of 'Over the Rainbow' almost made me cry." Ollie stopped, but it was clear she hadn't finished. Almost to herself she said, "It always does that to me, it's a song of unfulfilled dreams."

Alone, Sophie sat on the verandah at the Eiger, reading. She was more than halfway through her book about horses and accidents, but the dilemma in her own life seemed much more immediate. She wondered what her own story would reveal this time tomorrow and wished she could skip a few pages to see what happened. She caught herself drifting and sat up straight. She shook her head to clear it and repeated Tashi's mantra over and over, 'let go...detach...let go.'

The HiLux climbed up out of the switchbacks. Pine forest gave way to small farms. Ollie hummed along with the music as they drove through the village of Yadi. The views stretched back over the deep river valley and Trashigang was almost in sight. After two hours driving, they were less than ten miles from where they'd started. The road passed through cornfields and into the forests of oak, chestnut and maple on the way to Kori La. The music stopped.

"Do you have any other tapes?" Ollie asked with a warm smile.

Steve glanced over at the serious young woman he was sharing the back seat with, "Yeah sure," he said. "Classical, okay?"

"Yes anything, I love music."

Steve leaned over and pushed in another tape. They talked about how it made the miles go by. How Dr. Narguli refused to allow music in the car. She even asked Steve how his head was feeling, and almost expressed sympathy for his accident.

He kept it going, "Have you studied music, Ollie?"

She looked away, he thought she wouldn't answer. Moments later she said, "No, where I grew up there was no opportunity. I would have loved to learn singing."

"Oh, where'd you grow up?"

"In the Philippines, on Cebu Island. I lived in a fishing village."

Steve willed her to say more. Looking straight ahead, she told him there'd been no time for music when she was young. Every waking minute was spent just trying to survive. Much later, her father moved from fish catching to fish marketing and had made a fortune. He'd spent most of it supporting poor fishing families in the area. "There are too many fishermen and too few fish now," she said, turning her head away.

Steve wasn't going to let it stop at that. "Cebu! What a beautiful place to grow up."

She looked out at the road. "Yes, the tourists love it." She turned toward him. "They pay good money to walk along our beaches. To watch fishermen like my father in his early days, trying to eke a living out of paradise." Her words were overtaken by the hum of the motor.

Steve's mind jumped back to his work on the Visayas Rural Roads project. He'd taken a few days off at the end of a mission to do some diving. He'd stayed on the beach on Mactan Island, just off Cebu City and watched the 'bancas', outrigger canoes, bringing in the catch. The fisherman were small and muscular, their brown skin shining under sweat and dried seawater. He'd been enchanted by it, but he'd never stopped to think of bringing up a family on the catch of the day.

He said, "What was the name of your village? I might know it."

She hesitated. "You've been to Cebu?"

"A few times. I worked on the Visayas Rural Roads project in the early nineties."

"I don't want to talk about it." She looked away. "Too many memories."

A Cebuan fishing village was about as far from this high forest pass as you could get. Steve wondered how Ollie got from such a humble beginning into one of the biggest development banks in Asia. Lulled maybe by the music and the dull hum of off-road tires, on-road; he got her talking again. She told him about the catholic school she'd gone to in Cebu City. She'd loved the music there, but had always been too busy to study it. She talked about college, how a Sister Carla had said to a young and impressionable Miss Olivera Ramos, 'You've got to follow in your father's footsteps young lady. The arts won't put food on the table of the poor. Study economics.'

She turned to Steve. "That's what I did. My father agreed I could study in America if I would use my education in development work. I had an auntie in Las Vegas, I went to live with her. I topped my year in Economics at the University of Nevada. I'm an American citizen now, but my heart is still in a fishing village in the Visayas."

Jalal muttered, "Mongar. Stop we?"

The HiLux pulled into the dusty main street of Mongar. Jalal scurried across to the Samling Hotel, Steve hoped it was only to use their facilities. They bought some bottled water and food for the trip. Soon they were winding steeply downhill from Mongar to the Kuri Chhu, at Lingmethang. The fields of corn and potatoes around the town yielded to the broadleaf forest then to the pine. Music played. Jalal drove. The back seat passengers looked at the road ahead.

The Kuri Chhu came into sight. The huge brown river crashed over boulders and turned to white foam as it plunged south. They rumbled across the rusted and patched bailey bridge and turned left toward Lingmethang. Down along the river, Steve and Ollie talked about the possibility that hydropower could bring sustainable development to Bhutan. He noted her grasp of the financials attached to the project and winced when she added, 'if the road is ever finished, that is!' The HiLux veered away from the river, the road tilted sharply upward. Jalal notched down a gear and the climb began. A troop of rhesus monkeys crossed the road.

"Crazy monkeys," Ollie said, "Hey Steve, now you've heard all about me, tell me about yourself."

He hadn't expected this. Where to start? He said, "You know I'm Australian. I was brought up in a country town in a place called the Hunter Valley. It's a few hours north of Sydney by car." He turned to her. "Have you been to Australia, Ollie?"

She shook her head and a gold-chained cross danced above the perfect small swell of her breast. She was less scared, more open.

"Well, you wouldn't have heard of it anyway. Maitland was where we lived. My family was in business, in hardware. We lived above our store."

Pretty asian eyes said, yes, go on.

"My brother still lives there, he took over the business while I went to Sydney to study engineering."

"I've heard Sydney is beautiful."

"Yeah. I guess it is…around the harbor at least."

"So. Did you work there?"

"No. Two weeks after my final examination, my then girlfriend left Australia for home. I left home too. I packed my bags and flew to California. I missed my own graduation and traveled for over a year in the United States and Latin America."

"Traveling is so expensive, you must have worked there?"

"Yeah, a bit, on a vineyard in California. I had a small inheritance, and I traveled on a budget."

Sophie snapped her book shut and dropped it down on the table. She gazed absently out across the Bumthang valley and sighed, neither the outlook nor the book was helping the mood she was in. By midday she had little appetite for lunch and felt guilty at the effort that the Eiger's kitchen had gone to just for her. The tranquility of the morning had been fine, but now it was too quiet, it gave her too much time to think. Sophie put her left foot up on a chair and undid the bandage that Anna had put on so carefully. She moved her foot back and forwards, round and round and decided to leave the bandage off for awhile. And she started planning again. In a few hours she had to stage her second accidental meeting with Steve. How would she do it? Would she just be sitting right where she was when he arrived? Let him get the surprise and explain himself. After all, she'd already justified her being there, her bandaged foot would be testament to that.

The HiLux was revving hard, mostly in second gear. The first colors of fall were a random pattern on the wall of green above and below the road. Ollie hummed to the music, prayed all along the dangerous bits of road and talked on the easy bits. They were delayed for over an hour by a truck broken down in the middle of a narrow stretch of road, otherwise it was an uneventful trip into the clouds.

"Stop we?" Jalal asked in Sengor. Steve turned to Ollie, she nodded. Jalal had half a yak and rice. Steve and Ollie declined eating, but they all took tea. Steve washed down two more HEADACHE SPECIALS and hoped that would see him through to Jakar. All the jolting and turning was playing havoc with the delicate state of his headache. From Sengor to Thrumsing La, Jalal's stomach gurgled and he belched almost non-stop. The downhill run from Thrumsing La to Jakar is just over fifty miles. Jalal seemed to be on automatic pilot. They listened to more music (some of it for the third time), drove through villages where children waved, drove through forests where branches waved in the wind and forded mountain streams where the water was up to the doors. And even when there were long periods of silence, it was now a comfortable silence between them.

Sophie closed her book just before five. She showered and ate early, then re-bandaged her left ankle. Just on dark, car headlights beamed over the bridge on the Bumthang Chhu. She froze, then relaxed as she realized he wouldn't be coming from that direction. She double-checked with Eric that Steven Andrews was still booked in for the night, and that he'd be in Room 2, directly across the upstairs verandah from her room. She said thanks and reminded him not to say a word about her being there. Eric didn't even think to ask why, or how she knew Steve.

Safely before seven Sophie closed the door to Room 4, lay on the single bed and picked up her novel again, determined to finish it this time. But after little more than a chapter, she gave up and replaced her bookmark less than thirty pages from the end. She crossed the room, parted the curtains and knelt in front of the window overlooking the car park. She'd watch Steve arrive then decide her next move from there.

38: Visitors, one expected, one not

The HiLux came in through the apple orchard at seven twenty. A shaft of dull yellow light shone through one of the upstairs windows of the guesthouse, otherwise all signs of life were downstairs. The diesel motor died. Steve put on a cap to cover the bandage sitting just over his ears, he wasn't in any mood to explain his accident to Eric. He opened the door, bent his legs out and stretched. Every muscle was knotted and tight and he knew the dull ache behind his eyes was just the calm before the storm. Ollie mechanically opened her door, pulled her legs around and tipped herself out onto solid ground. She groaned, "What a trip, I'm so tired." Jalal sat and waited further orders, which were simply to fill the HiLux with diesel and get back there by seven thirty in the morning. The yak he'd eaten at Sengor was still troubling him, he seemed anxious to get going.

The parking area was unsealed and under spreading oak trees. Steve undid the tarpaulin over the back of the HiLux and started unloading their luggage. He looked around the car park, there appeared to be no other guests. He gazed up at the first floor verandah and thought of a hot shower, a meal and sleep. He knew that spreadsheets would figure somewhere in his evening too.

Ollie was now by his side. She said, "Thanks Steve, I enjoyed today...getting to know you better." She stood on her toes, put her hands on his shoulders and kissed him. He didn't pull back, her smooth skin brushing his was electrifying, her lips were moist and warm. The sensation lingered.

Eric's eldest son, Eric Junior, came out to help with the luggage. One of their several Tibetan mastiffs followed close behind at a low growl. The lower half of the Eiger was of heavy stone in traditional Swiss fashion. The first level was built of local pine, with intricate woodwork and attention to detail in every feature. The window frames were the work of artisans. The doors solid and unpainted, and the smell and feel of pinewood permeated all. The stairs were more like a ladder than stairs, but young Eric insisted on carrying their suitcases, despite Steve's offer to help. The ladder delivered them onto a large open verandah.

Room 2 was at the front of the building and off to one side of the verandah. Room 4 was opposite. The common verandah served as the outdoor eating area, it afforded spectacular views across the valley.

Eric Junior's sister joined him on the balcony. She was a plump, sweet and smiling cherub-faced girl of about fourteen. She said, "Dinner you want now, please?"

"We need a hot shower first," Steve said and looked to Ollie. She grinned. "Do *we?*"

"Oh, sorry."

"Just joking," Ollie said. "Make that dinner in half an hour, okay?" She went out through the dining room to Room 3.

Steve crossed the verandah to Room 2.

In her room, Sophie was kneeling in front of the window. She held the curtains almost closed, there was just enough of a gap to peer out without being seen. And what she'd just witnessed left her shaking. It was bad enough that Steve had arrived with someone else, but when Sophie had seen him and whoever it was that he was with, kiss; her heart started thumping and her blood ran cold as ice-water.

It was half past eight. Steve was in the dining room a minute or two before Ollie came in wearing leather sandals, a mid-length skirt and a snug-fitting, low-cut casual lemon colored top. Her hair was still wet and simply combed back from her face, and on second glance, Steve noticed she wasn't wearing a bra. She smiled when she saw Steve and glided over to take a seat opposite him. "That feels better," she said. He didn't reply, it seemed there was nothing he could do to make himself feel better. The cherub-faced girl asked if they wanted a drink. Ollie ordered a coke. Steve, desperate for something to ease the dull ache that was creeping down his neck again, ordered a beer. He'd have been happy with a small bottle, but got a large one and managed to finish it anyway. The meal was a buffet of yak meat cut into strips, red rice and local vegetables. Ollie ate with good appetite and talked freely. She even laughed once or twice, but as soon as the meal was over she put up a barrier. They ordered tea and sat looking at each other like strangers.

Ollie played nervously with the chain around her neck. She said, "Ohh! The thought of driving all the way to Thimphu tomorrow."

It was more a passing remark than a seriously thought out alternative when Steve said, "Why don't you wait over here tomorrow, and come with us on Saturday."

Ollie looked startled, she said immediately, "I've too much work to do. Thanks anyway."

"You could just as easily work here tomorrow. You could send Jalal back to Trashigang."

Ollie squirmed on her seat. "No. I can't. Dr. Narguli might think...things." She looked away. "It's difficult Steve. Let's leave it, please."

"Sure."

Just the mention of Narguli's name changed her mood. She said, "Anyway, sore head or not you'd better get on with it Steve, Tuesday will come around very quickly." With that Ollie stood up and made ready to go. Dinner was finished. They agreed on breakfast at six thirty and wished each other good night.

Steve pushed open the pine-paneled door to Room 2 and switched on the light. He closed the door and rested his back against it, the pain in his head was now so acute it was making him feel sick. He now wished he'd had water rather than beer with dinner and swallowed two more HEADACHE SPECIALS. He sat at the desk for minutes before opening his laptop. He clicked on Excel. His screen was soon full of spreadsheets, but his mind was filled with images of Ollie — first as a brown skinned child on the white sand beaches of the Visayas Islands, then in the uniform of a strict convent school in Cebu City. Her motivation for studying economics crossed his mind, he'd really misjudged her.

Then he thought about meeting Ollie and Narguli at the wrap-up meeting in just five days time. This thought brought him sharply back to reality. Soon he had spreadsheets on his mind and all over the desk. Last night he'd left off with a difference of ten million between the two sets of books for just one supplier, Veejay Industries. Even the number of invoices from Veejay didn't tally. The bank's accounts had registered five more invoices than TRANSARCO's — he needed to find those five invoices, or had he made a simple error in his arithmetic, or got a function wrong, or applied a formula in the wrong cell? He closed his eyes, put his hands over his ears and listened to the sounds of the night. His head swirled. A dog barked a long way off, wind blew in the trees and he could almost hear leaves falling when his mind went swimming, then blank. He slumped slowly forward. His forehead came to an abrupt stop on the keyboard of his laptop, but he wasn't aware of that.

While Steve was at dinner, Sophie had time to think things through. It was time to get rid of every issue she'd ever had with Steve, except one. So what if he was here with someone else, that wasn't her problem. Her job was to deliver a message on behalf of their daughter, no one, nothing would stop her doing that now — now that she'd come this far.

Marie would have to accept that her father might not fit the image that she'd developed of him. There was nothing that Sophie could do about that. She sat at the desk and pulled out a sheet of thick, handmade paper she'd bought in Thimphu. She wrote,

Today

Dear Steve,

Coincidence plays some mighty tricks on us at times. This morning I should have left here with my trekking group, instead I stayed back alone to nurse a sprained ankle (be careful on those steps, I found out by accident how steep they are).

Anyhow, I got talking to Eric today, I couldn't believe my ears when he said I'd have some company here, that an Australian roads engineer named Steven Andrews was booked in for tonight and tomorrow night.

It seems fate has determined that we should meet again.

If you're not too tired to say hi, I'm in Room 4.

Yours,

Sophie Vella

Sophie sealed her letter in a plain envelope and wrote 'Steve' in an elaborate cursive in the middle. She waited until she heard Steve's door open then close. She counted to sixty slowly, then she walked ever so softly across the wooden verandah. The dining room had been cleared and Eric's family was downstairs. Her footsteps approached Room 2, they were very light, very cautious. Sophie knelt and slid the envelope underneath Steve's door. Her heart raced and her footsteps retreated. Back in her room, she picked up her novel again and forced herself to read. How long would she have to wait? Ten, twenty minutes? Surely no more!

After ten minutes she was pacing the floor. She'd dressed carefully for the occasion: black pants and a (tight) white V-neck sweater. On her feet, the sandals she'd chosen didn't hide the bandage that she wanted Steve to see. She checked the mirror, not a wisp of hair was out of place. After another ten minutes Sophie decided that Steve must have missed seeing the envelope. She couldn't wait any longer, she'd just knock on his door and get it over with. Purposefully this time, she crossed the verandah and made ready to knock.

In Room 2, Steve regained consciousness with a jolt. First his eyes opened. Then he lifted his head and groaned low and long, almost primally. He tried to move and moaned in agony. It was the blurred thinking of a desperate man that led his hand toward the only thing that might save him. And just that movement, the reaching of an unsteady hand, caused him to groan again. He picked up the bottle of SINGH'S SLAMMERS and dropped one into the palm of his hand. He didn't look at it, nor consider the pros and cons of taking it. He tilted his head back and the movement sent a bolt of blue lightning down his spine. He moaned again as the pill slipped down his throat. He washed it down with a mouthful of water and sighed in relief. He staggered to his bed. He sat on the edge of it and it creaked, he groaned and lay down. He tossed side to side, trying to make himself comfortable. Each time he moved the bed creaked and squeaked. It creaked again as it swallowed him up soft and warm and held him in a suspended state of delirium. He sighed again, a deep and contented sigh of relief: something was taking him away, and within minutes he'd slipped back into unconsciousness.

Outside Room 2, Sophie had her fist clenched, ready to knock. First she heard Steve moaning and groaning; moaning low and long. Then she heard sighing. Then moaning again. Then she heard a bed creaking. Sophie froze and let her hand drop to her side. She listened again. More moaning, then a bed squeaking and creaking and then more sighing. She shook her head and let her chin drop to her chest. Her shoulders slumped. Sophie shuffled back to Room 4 in a state of suspended disbelief.

Back in her room, Sophie went to the window and rested her forehead on the glass. There were no lights outside, but the gibbous moon cast an eerie shadow over the valley below. Was she really here? Was this really happening? Her mind snapped; yes, this was happening, to her. She turned on her heel, opened her door and crept silently across the verandah again. She passed the door to Steve's room and descended the stairs. She tried the door to Eric's office and it pushed open. The light was on, she was hoping Eric would be there at his desk. She had a question for him. But the room was empty. Sophie swallowed hard and pulled her shoulders back, then she entered the room. On Eric's desk she found what she was looking for. The Guest Register was open, there were two new entries. Sophie read,

NAME: Olivera (Ollie) Ramos
Age: 28
CITIZENSHIP: USA
PLACE of Birth: CEBU City, Visayas, Philippines.
REASON FOR TRAVEL: SAIB Project Accountant/Two Roads East/Returning from bank supervision mission, Trashigang.
GOING: Thimphu

Three things rankled. She's Filipina. She's twenty eight. Steve's wife is at home alone, a single mom.

39: The young professional

It was the hour where light and night intersect. That time of day when yesterday is not quite gone, and the new day is yet to take shape. Steve and Ollie had been on Sophie's mind when, through sheer exhaustion, she had drifted off to sleep, and they were there again as soon as her eyes opened. She still couldn't believe what she'd heard to be true. Just how much Steve had changed? And if he was capable of cheating on his wife and kids, what else was he capable of? Defrauding the aid project he's managing?

The merest hint of sunlight crept under the ill-fitting curtains. The only sound was of breakfast being prepared in the kitchen below. Sophie edged out of her single bed, showered and washed her hair then dressed for a purpose. She pushed open her door and stepped out onto the verandah. She wanted to be out there first. She wasn't.

Ollie was alone at the main table on the verandah, idly gazing out across the valley, one foot on the seat, her chin resting on her knee. The day was heavy in morning mist, and quiet. Dew lay on the grass and hung from spider's webs, so still. The massive oaks in the car park spread boughs, not shade. Everything was normal for a new Jakar day until the door to Room 4 opened. Ollie swung her head and stared as though Sophie had no right to be there.

Sophie, balanced on one foot and still holding her door open, said uncertainly, "Good morning, umm, I'm Sophie."

Ollie said nothing at first, then tentatively, "Oh...hi... I'm Ollie."

Sophie looked around for a spare table and quickly realized that the only table set for breakfast was the one that Ollie was at. They both paused too long for it to be comfortable, eventually Ollie said, "Please, won't you join me?"

"Thanks." Sophie pulled her door shut and without thinking added, "Oh! You're alone here?"

"No, I'm with a colleague," Ollie smiled, pouted and then tilted her head. "I guess he's sleeping off a late night."

It was an innocent enough gesture, but to Sophie the sexual overtones were too close to the surface to ignore. Sophie thought 'brazen, aren't we,' as she slid along the bench seat opposite Ollie.

They smiled at each other across the table and tried to ignore the awkward silence separating them. Sophie, having made the effort to be up and out the door at six thirty, had been expecting at least a few minutes alone — a chance to survey the scene and set things up for breakfast with Steve. She'd thought it through. When his door opened she'd be sitting there just as natural as could be, she'd say 'Hi Steve, did you get my note? I slipped it under your door last night.' But now, unexpectedly, she was sitting opposite Steve's young lover and a new opportunity had presented itself — she just had to use it, and use it well. Here was a once-in-a-lifetime chance to really understand what made Steve tick now, the new Steve. But how to start? One of them had to speak first, Ollie obliged, "Your foot," she said, "what happened?"

Sophie grimaced, "Tripped, on the stairs a few days ago. My ankle's sprained."

"You've been here a few days," Ollie said with eyes wide open. "You were here last night?"

"Yes, my trekking group left yesterday morning."

The cherub-faced girl climbed the stairs while balancing a fully laden tray, she said, "Breakfast you take?" They both nodded and turned to each other again.

"Oh?" Ollie said. "What bad luck."

"Maybe," Sophie said, "but better to hurt my leg before the trek, than on it."

The breakfast things were being laid out in front of them, the table was set for three, the cherub-faced girl said, "Mr. Steven take breakfast too? He late? Sleeping maybe?"

It was sign of her unease, a fault-line in her preparation, Sophie blurted, "Steve! Late! Never!" She knew straightaway that she'd laid her soul bare.

Ollie jumped on it. "Do you know him?"

Sophie, pinned by the weight of her own transparency, gagged, "Steve Andrews? Sure! Yeah!"

Ollie recoiled, obviously catching her breath, then she covered with a grin, "I didn't know he was that famous." She faced Sophie square-on, clearly waiting for an explanation.

Sophie put her elbows on the table, she needed thinking time. She hadn't planned to be on the defensive. She joined her fingers, rested her chin on her hands, and said blithely, "It seems strange doesn't it. I'd heard that in Bhutan everyone knows everything about everybody. Maybe it's true?" Sophie let the moment linger then smiled and added, "Well actually, Steve sat next to a mutual friend on the airplane coming in here. We didn't see each other, even though we were on the same flight. Farley, that's our mutual friend, invited us both to lunch in Thimphu last week. You can imagine Farley's surprise, and mine, when Steve recognized me, remembered we'd met years ago." Sophie saw that Ollie was still unconvinced, so added quickly. "I knew that Steve was in Bhutan, working somewhere in the East. But it was Eric who mentioned that an Australian engineer named Steve Andrews was booked in here last night."

Ollie leant forward, there was a hint of a challenge in the way that she held her mouth, "You knew Steve years ago?"

Sophie armed herself, her reply had to finish this, "Yes, casually, he worked for my parents, on their vineyard in California."

Ollie processed that information and it seemed to fit, she relaxed and said, "Does he know you're here?"

Sophie highlighted her unease by the time she took to answer, she said, "I'm not sure, maybe?" It was the truth, she had no way of knowing if Steve had picked up her note. Then it hit her, Ollie had been in the room with him, had she seen the envelope slip under Steve's door first?

Ollie answered Sophie's question without words, she gestured to the toast, butter and cheese and said, "Sophie, tea or coffee?"

Sophie said, "tea thanks," with a sigh of relief and hoped she was over the worst of it, she wasn't here to defend herself.

Ollie began pouring and said, "If you were here alone, why didn't you join us last night?"

Sophie jerked backwards; she was immediately annoyed with herself, why was she so on edge? She gulped and replied, "Umm, I was too tired. I was in bed reading." She needed to change direction, but subtly. She said, "What about you, Ollie? Are you on a project here too?"

The younger woman sipped her tea thoughtfully, "Yes, I'm working on Two Roads East. The same as Steve."

Sophie nodded and said too quickly, "Oh, and what is it you do at the bank?" Her *faux pas* stuck in her throat like a chicken bone.

Ollie hesitated and quizzed Sophie with wide eyes, "Umm… I'm on the Young Professionals Program. I'm an economist."

Sophie bounced back, "Fabulous, I've heard that it's very competitive though. I know a lot of good people miss out."

"They do," Ollie agreed readily. "Fifty jobs amongst fifteen thousand. You need something a bit special to get in these days."

Sophie's false smile said, 'How modest of you, Ollie'.

Ollie added quickly. "It was my background that got me in. They give preference to people from developing countries. And what about you, Sophie, where do you work?"

"In Washington D.C., in the State Department. I'm a lawyer working on human rights issues." Ollie's raised eyebrows demanded to know more. Sophie added the minimum, "I'm in the Latin America section, working on women's and children's issues…You'd know the things that come up?"

Ollie nodded. "Hmm. Yes, I sure do."

Sophie poured more tea for herself and without asking, another for Ollie. She busied herself cutting a square of cheese into rectangles. The cherub-faced girl climbed the stairs to see that everything was okay, she sensed the moment wasn't right for questions and disappeared as quickly as she'd appeared.

"I'd better eat some more," Ollie said. "I've got a long trip ahead of me today."

"Oh, you're going, where?" Sophie asked, hardly hiding her relief.

Ollie talked freely about driving to Thimphu with Jalal while she spread more toast and sipped her tea. From the flow of conversation it was clear to Sophie that Ollie would be traveling alone, and given her relationship with Steve, Sophie was intrigued at how casually Ollie had accepted that Steve might not join them for breakfast.

Ollie even joked about it as she ate toast spread with butter and jam, "Boy, Steve can sleep, I didn't think I'd been that hard on him last night."

Sophie felt a pit in her stomach, but giggled in complicity and then asked as though it was the most obvious follow-on, "How long have you two known each other?"

"Hmm," Ollie pondered, "I guess we've been working on Two Roads East for three years now, but it was only yesterday that I really got to know Steve. There's more to him than first meets the eye."

Sophie swallowed her immediate disapproval and mumbled, "Oh, oh, yes there is…Umm, did he talk about his family?"

Ollie's face lit up, she said with almost childlike innocence, "No…no he didn't. Does he have a wife, and kids?"

Sophie kept a straight face but felt her fingernails digging into the skin above her knees. She thought, how could you? But before she could answer, the clack of a diesel-motor turned both their heads. Ollie looked down over the car park and said with more than a hint of annoyance, "It's Jalal. Heck, he's hurrying me." She checked her watch for reassurance, "It's only seven fifteen." Ollie took a last mouthful of toast, gulped it down with coffee and wiped her mouth with a napkin. She stood and excused herself, "Been nice meeting you Sophie. Take care of that foot."

Sophie went to stand, but Ollie said, "Hey, don't bother. Say bye to Steve for me please, tell him I'll see him in Thimphu on Tuesday, and that I hope he found what he was looking for last night."

Sophie choked and said to herself, 'Dear God, do I need to hear that, on top of everything else?' Ollie turned and made her way to her room at the back of the guesthouse.

Within minutes Ollie was back again, this time wheeling a suitcase behind her. She smiled again at Sophie and handed her luggage to Eric Junior who'd climbed the stairs to meet her. Ollie said cheekily over her shoulder, "You two have fun…If Steve ever wakes that is."

Sophie had no reply but a forced smile, she watched from the verandah as they walked into the car park. She saw young Eric load Ollie's luggage in the back seat of a twin-cab HiLux, Ollie got in next to it. Then she saw a tall, coarse-looking man get in behind the wheel and they were gone.

Sophie watched the HiLux move through the apple orchard and out into open fields, then her gaze turned to the door of Room 2, behind which Steve supposedly slept without a care in the world. Ollie had been remarkably unconcerned that Steve hadn't made it to breakfast; she'd exhausted him in bed last night, now she'd left him without as much as a goodbye. Sophie shivered, Steve's new lover may be young and beautiful, but she had a heart of stone.

Sophie poured herself more tea and thought through her next step. While Ollie had been a surprise, an unplanned intrusion on her plan, there'd been little real damage. She still felt sorry for Marie, her father was not going to fit the image Marie had of him, but at least she had the day ahead of her in which to carry through with her promise. By nightfall, Steve would know about his daughter.

It was almost eight a.m. when Sophie heard a vehicle approaching. She watched another HiLux pull into the car park, this one a well-used, single-cab utility. A gray-haired Bhutanese got out and looked around, he looked lost, as though he was expecting someone to be waiting for him. He scratched his close-cropped head and leant against the side of his truck and waited. He'd noticed Sophie looking down from the first floor verandah but taken no notice of her, so she watched to see what would happen. Maybe five minutes passed before Eric walked out to greet his visitor. The two men embraced, Sophie figured they were old friends. Very soon thereafter, they were climbing the stairs.

"Morning, Sophie," Eric said. "You haven't seen Steve have you."

Sophie shook her head, "I think he's still asleep."

The two men exchanged disbelieving glances, Eric said, "I hope not, Dorji and Steve are meant to be inspecting a bridge site this morning." In the ensuing introductions, Sophie learnt that Dorji was the District Engineer, that he was to show Steve the site and plans for a new bridge. Steve's company was to tender for its construction.

Eric quickly summed up the situation and decided he'd have to wake Steve, if indeed he was asleep, which would have been most unusual. According to Eric, Steve was an early riser. Dorji reclined on the bench seat next to Sophie while Eric crossed to Room 2 and knocked. He waited and knocked again. He put his ear to the door, nothing. Eric waited some more and knocked again, louder this time. He turned to Dorji and Sophie and shrugged, "I didn't fit locks here for a good reason." He opened the door and peered inside. Eric was rigidly still for perhaps twenty seconds, then he shook his head side to side and withdrew, leaving the door ajar. He turned with confusion on his face, "He's in there, sound asleep on his bed, fully dressed." Eric shrugged and walked over to sit opposite Dorji. They looked at each other with blank faces, what to do next?

Sophie's imagination went into wild overdrive. Steve was with Ollie last night? She's left, mysteriously without wanting to see him. Now he's fully dressed on his bed. Was he asleep? She jumped to her feet, her bandaged ankle taking its full share of weight without a whimper. "I'll wake him." Eric and Dorji nodded okay in unison.

She was trembling as she pushed Steve's door open. She stopped at the threshold and called out, "Steve. Steve wake up." He was motionless, his left leg was hanging off the side of the bed, his shoes were still on his feet. His head was bandaged, blood had oozed through in a clot twice the size of a quarter. She took a tentative step inside, knelt and picked up her envelope which lay unopened just inches inside his door. She pushed it into the pocket of her jeans and moved quickly across the room to stand beside him.

Steve was a lifeless gray in color and Sophie couldn't even make out the rise and fall of his breathing.

Steve felt his shoulder being shaken and heard, "Steve, wake up. Please, wake up." In that lapse between the unconscious and the conscious, Steve was certain he'd died and been reborn in times past. It was Sophie's voice by his side, she was shaking his shoulder to wake him, just like she'd done so many times before. He let the moment linger, let the lovely soft tones of her voice soothe him. Soon though, he realized there were no soft tones, if anything there was an edge of panic to Sophie's calling of his name. One eye dropped open, red and blurred of vision. It was Sophie all right. Angel Sophie. His other eye opened, she was leaning across him, her breasts heavy against his chest, her face close enough to kiss. He shook his head and blinked, dying wasn't so bad after all. He felt the cool of her open hand on his forehead. She was near tears, saying over and over, "Steve, are you okay? Steve, speak to me!"

Slowly, surely Steve's blurred vision cleared and the reality of his day came into sharp focus when Sophie said, "Steve, there's a Mr. Dorji here to see you, he said you were expecting him?"

40: *Bridge Design 101*

It was nearly nine thirty when Steve opened his door and crossed the verandah toward Sophie. His mind was a jumble, Dorji was not a person to be late for, but then Sophie had reappeared in his life like a miracle. The morning light was softly outlining her face in profile and, despite the immediacy of his work, nineteen years seemed to disappear before his eyes. She was on the beach at Cahuita. Were they in Costa Rica, or Bhutan?

She smiled as he slid along the bench seat opposite her and said, "Thanks nurse."

"I'll bet that feels better."

Steve laughed, "I'll tell you what, I'm buying a truck load of Dr. Singh's SLAMMERS. They saved my life, I've never slept so well."

Sophie shook her head and scolded, "It said 'NO ALCOHOL' on the label."

Steve said, "You know me, I was never a great reader." He could hardly believe how much better he felt, he'd even dispensed with his bandage. He said, more seriously this time, "What are you going to do this morning while I'm at work?"

"Oh, I'll be your assistant of course."

He wasn't ready for her quick answer, "Sorry?"

"I'll join you. It'll be fun…Watching you and Dorji work."

He saw Sophie looking back at him defiantly and stumbled for words. "Ah! Okay, but…"

"But what?" Sophie echoed.

"Your ankle…We'll be walking?"

"It's feeling much better now, a day's rest was all it needed. I'll go and put on some walking shoes." She slid off the seat and stood with two hands on the table. "See you downstairs in five."

Steve watched her walk comfortably to Room 4 and close the door behind herself. Then he covered his face with his hands and shook his head to try and clear the thoughts that were coming at him from all directions. Had he taken the better of two roads nineteen years ago?

Apparently, Steve had only met the Chief Engineer for Bumthang Dzongkhag a few times, but his welcome and handshake were as warm as yesterday. Especially, Sophie thought, when they were running nearly two hours late. Dorji climbed in behind the wheel of his HiLux utility. Sophie took the middle position and Steve squeezed in beside her. She felt their legs press together.

Steve and Dorji quickly engaged in engineering talk as they drove northwards up the west-bank of the Bumthang Chhu. It was as though Sophie wasn't there. She gleaned that Steve was the last of six company representatives to inspect the site and collect the World Bank bid documents for the Upper Bumthang Bridge project. From the flow of conversation, Sophie picked up that both TRANSARCO and Steve were well known and highly regarded in Bhutan. But when Dorji asked how Two Roads East was going, she felt Steve tense up immediately. He said, "Okay I guess," and added unconvincingly, "There are a few problems, you'd know how it goes with a major project coming to a close?" Dorji said, "Yes, so I heard. A few problems." His expression didn't change, his eyes were on the road. "Maybe twenty million problems?" He shoved the gear lever into third and revved the diesel motor into the steep left-hand corner they were entering. Sophie saw Steve's jaw clench and the color drain from his face. She knew exactly what Dorji meant and what Steve was thinking; why was it that only bad news traveled fast?

They stopped on a grassy flat beside the Bumthang River. Dorji stood with his back to the water. With rolled-up-plans in hand, he spoke to the assembled audience of two (if it had of been two hundred, Sophie was certain that his delivery wouldn't have changed). Steve took notes. Sophie watched as he scribbled and wondered how he would ever read what he'd just written. Dorji described how the new bridge would join the roads up the east and west sides of the river, how the bridge design was fixed, and that the tender would be decided on price and technical considerations in the usual way. Dorji stressed that Bhutan was borrowing all of the money for the bridge from the World Bank. He added, poignantly Sophie thought, that they'd be paying it off long after he was gone. Sophie followed as Steve and the old engineer walked up and down the riverbank. Steve asked questions about geo-technical surveys, abutments, spans and flood levels. He scribbled notes and took a roll of film. After an hour or so, Dorji announced that they would now look at the other side.

They all got back into the car and drove south, crossed the river and drove north again on the east-bank, an hour later they were opposite where they'd been before, and perhaps two hundred yards away. Sophie watched as Steve and Dorji went through the same procedures again. She overheard Dorji saying that the bids were due on December sixth, a decision would be made early in the New Year. Work was expected to start by February, with completion expected by mid 2001. Steve nodded and the two men shook hands again. She couldn't tell whether or not Steve felt confident, his demeanor hadn't changed.

They had a late lunch on the verandah at the Eiger. Sophie was trying to bring the conversation around to the 'twenty million problems' that Dorji had referred to, but Steve wasn't cooperating, his answers were monosyllables or deliberately off-putting. She'd made up her mind that before she'd tell Steve about Marie, she'd clear her mind on a few things. Things like whether or not he'd explain his sudden departure from Thimphu and the cryptic note he'd left her. She said, "It was a pity we missed each other for dinner in Thimphu last week."

The delay in his response showed her that he'd either forgotten it entirely, or wanted to. He bit his lower lip and put his fingers to his head to remind her of the accident he'd yet to recover from. He said, "Oh, sorry, yeah, umm…How about dinner tonight instead, here?"

She had to smile, "How generous of you."

"That's okay," he said, "hey, did you finish law school?"

She nodded in reluctant reply and he led the conversation onto where she was working now and what she was doing there. She didn't want to go down this track, and told him as little as she could of her work and regular visits to Latin America.

He said, "How's your Spanish now?"

She felt like kicking him under the table, but answered, "Okay, gracias."

Steve tried to avoid her steady gaze, and said, "So you're in Washington now?"

She had time on her side, he could play games for awhile. She said in a purposefully pleasant voice. "Yes, have been for fifteen years now."

"Hmm, you must have moved there shortly after graduating?"

"Yes, graduating amongst other things," Sophie said and saw immediately that she was unsettling him.

"Ahhh…I've been to Washington at least once a year for the last six or seven years."

"Oh!" Sophie feigned surprise even though Alex had already helped her to discover this for herself. "And what do you do there?"

"Visit the World Bank, they're one of our major clients."

"Well done, Steve. It seems that you've turned a lifestyle into a career."

"Huh? What do you mean?"

"Traveling of course, your first love. Now you get paid to do it."

Steve laughed. "Oh come on! There's more to it than…"

"I'm sure there is," Sophie said. "I'd love to hear about it, later."

She had plans for the afternoon. She'd reasoned that it would be easier to get him to open up if they were walking side by side, she wasn't going to just sit there and let him lead her around in circles. "Hey, we're wasting a perfect afternoon here," she said. "Can we walk somewhere?"

"Uhh, I'd love to, but I've got so much to do."

It took Sophie fifteen minutes to turn him around, "You owe me," she said. "Standing me up in Thimphu the way you did."

Finally he relented and agreed on a gentle walk up past the dzong to Lamey Goemba, then over into the Chhume Valley.

41: The making of choices

They walked out through the orchard and down along the narrow winding road. Steve carried a small daypack, he had a thermos and some apple cakes onboard. They were in fields one moment and in forest the next. A boy and girl came up the road toward them. The girl, who looked no more than eight, led a milk cow by a ring through its nose. She was in a bright blue kira. The boy, perhaps her older brother, wore a reddish-orange gho over long socks and polished shoes.

Sophie looked ahead and saw a road winding its way to the river. Beyond, a soft fall sun lit the valley and the whitewashed dzong stood out on a knoll forested in pines. In the mid-ground, fields of pink flowering buckwheat were cut geometrically by green hedgerows. Further on, the Bumthang Chhu sparkled as it crashed over boulders and eddied into cool deep pools. They walked downstream along the east-bank of the river and crossed the single-lane bridge. Prayer flags were hanging, but not fluttering, from the handrails and Sophie recognized an Ibis balanced on long legs in shallows by the riverside. Upstream a lone woman washed clothes and lay them on boulders to dry.

Steve pointed to a hill in the far distance, "That's where you're taking me...You know I really should be working."

Sophie seized on the opportunity he'd opened, "What, on the bridge project we just looked at?"

"No...On Two Roads East."

"Oh, hey, did you ever sort out the problem that you mentioned in your note...The one you left Thimphu so urgently for?"

She slowed to catch his reply, "Ah, yeah...I'm on the right track, but I've got more spreadsheet work to do...Umm...I...."

"What happened?" Sophie said.

"Ahh, there's a problem with the accounts, some money has gone missing."

"Much?"

"Yeah," Steve sighed, "twenty million, someone's been fiddling the books. And I won't stop till I find out who."

"Twenty million! Steve! Any suspects?"

"Ah, one of my own staff…Anyway, let's not spoil a good afternoon talking work, we've got a lot to catch up on."

There was no point in going further, anyway, she'd heard about as much as she needed to, she said, "Sure, where do we start."

"Well," Steve said. "Tell me about yourself, what…"

Sophie ignored him and even though she knew the answer, said, "Steve, are you married?"

He answered, "Yeah" and followed with, "how about you?"

"Not now," Sophie said, "so what's your wife's name?"

He turned to her, but her eyes were hidden behind sunglasses. He said, "Miranda. Why?"

She responded by asking how long they'd been married.

"Just on fourteen years."

"And children?"

Steve talked about Ric and Tim and mentioned Ric's thirteenth birthday, on Saturday week. She asked lots more questions and even heard about the famously mischievous Clancy, the boy's black and white border collie.

As they entered Jakar town, she asked if Miranda worked, "as well as looking after the boys," she added quickly. He told her about Miranda's lifestyle column in a national weekend newspaper, "she shares a page with a self-help guru, Tristan Troy. He's well known on the corporate speaking circuit, you know the type, one of those motivational crusaders. Between them, their three thousand words and their faces in photos fill a page. And for that she earns more than I do," Steve said. Sophie picked up on hurt rather than pride. She made a mental note to explore this further, later. She continued the questions. "Where do you live?"

He turned the question back on her, "Did you ever get to Australia?"

"No," she said. "But I learned a lot about it from an Australian I once knew."

He grinned, then told her about Byron Bay and long stretches of white sand beaches, their home overlooking the Pacific Ocean and his favorite fishing spots.

They walked by the Jakar Lhakhang, the small temple at the fork of the roads and turned right. A group of children ran after them. "Hello mistas. What your name?" They were walking fast. Steve commented that she was in good shape, especially for someone who'd recently sprained an ankle. She said, "Thanks...How did you and Miranda meet?"

He said it was a long story.

"Good, we've plenty of time."

She saw him shrug and he began, "I got back to Australia from Rio De Janeiro, flat broke of course. I needed a job. I answered an advertisement for a junior civil engineer to supervise a road-widening project in northern New South Wales. I got the job which was based at Byron Bay." He told how Miranda had met him, rather than the other way around.

"What do you mean?" she asked.

"Miranda moved to Byron Bay from Sydney at the same time I did. She had a job as a cadet reporter on the local newspaper. We met at the Byron Realty. We both wanted the same house, and rental properties were in short supply at the time. She was too quick for me," Steve said and without taking a breath added, "The guy running the real estate office suggested we sort it out between us. He had one property and two people interested, he didn't care which of us took it. Before I could say a thing Miranda had grabbed the keys. She said to the real estate guy, 'I'll take the place but he can come to dinner anytime. That's fair isn't it?' The real estate guy said that he reckoned I was onto a good deal and that was it. She got the house, I lived in a caravan for several months. We had dinner together, and it all went from there."

"Come on, tell me more," Sophie said.

"Well, we dated. Miranda had big plans. I hadn't quite found myself. I went to dinner one night and she had an ocean-front property advertisement cut out of the local paper. It was a rugged block, covered in scrub. Miranda had it all worked out, she reckoned together we could clear it and build later. By morning we'd agreed to buy the land and move in together. Suddenly I had plans too. Her plans."

"Hmm," Sophie mused. "Miranda gets her way, huh?"

"Always has, always will!"

The road had dwindled to a trail winding through a forest of blue pine. They were climbing steeply. The trail followed the sharp edge of a ridge high above the valley floor. The shadows of the pines were long as the sun edged westwards. It was too narrow to walk side by side, Steve led the way. They glimpsed an ancient building through a break in the tree canopy. "The goemba is just up ahead there," Steve said.

Sophie was behind him, a little out of breath. "Thank god... What's a goemba?"

"It's a Buddhist monastery," he said. "I'm not sure if it's still in use."

Sophie came up and stood right next to him. She looked up through the trees at the goemba, then looked at her watch. "Let's have our picnic up there."

"Sure. Need a rest?"

She shot back. "No more than you do. It just looks a good place for a picnic."

"Actually I'm quite impressed. You're doing well...For a city girl that is."

"*Steve!*"

"Hey, only joking."

They reached Lamey Goemba in a clearing in the forest. The old monastery was traditionally built with a row of prayer wheels along one wall. There was a small brook and a grassy flat in the shade of some trees. They stretched back on the grass. A light breeze was fluttering the prayer flags that flew from the buttress above them. Steve took the thermos and some apple cakes from his pack. Sophie's legs were tucked up beside her on the grass. She was a little flushed. She took off her hat and ran her fingers through her hair, then unbuttoned the blue denim jacket she was wearing over a white tee shirt. The generous curve of her breast pushed against the thin cotton fabric. Steve tried not to notice, but his mind jumped back to Costa Rica, to day hikes in the thick tropical jungle around Cahuita, to picnics just like this, to Sophie stripped down to bikini pants in the searing tropical heat.

They ate simply, but well. Side by side they lay back on the grass. Steve put his hands behind his head and looked up into the vast blue above him. Clouds skipped by on a higher breeze. They talked about Bhutan and Mahayana Buddhism. Sophie said that this was the first truly Buddhist country she'd visited. He assured her there was nowhere else the same.

She led the conversation from Buddhism back to his home life and he talked easily enough about the lifestyle trap Miranda and he had fallen into; how just as they'd finished building their dream home, his big highway widening project came to an end. TRANSARCO offered him two options. He could move to the Sydney or Brisbane offices and work on domestic engineering projects with better prospects for a promotion. Or, he could stay at Byron Bay, join the International Development Group and commute to Asia. He grinned as he recounted how Miranda had made the decision for them. There was really no choice, Miranda wasn't leaving Byron, and that was that. "So now I spend up to nine months of the year away from home. The boys have grown up without a father and Miranda's career has blossomed. She has one hell of a lifestyle to write about and lots of friends to fill the house."

Sophie smiled, she knew Steve too well to let that pass without comment, "If we're talking about the Steve I knew, I can't imagine him choosing to give up the traveling life for a steady day job…you sure it was just Miranda's choice?"

Steve choked, "We'd better get moving." He jumped to his feet and spluttered, "All those spreadsheets waiting and Tuesday's meeting just four days away."

Sophie stood and brushed off her jeans. She stuffed her denim jacket in the daypack and said, "you haven't changed one bit." He laughed as she followed him onto the trail that soon started to switchback up the steep hillside. The forest floor was cool underneath an almost pure canopy of blue pine. They were walking on a bed of pine needles, it was soft underfoot. Steve said hello to a short, stooped woman carrying firewood on her back. She was dressed in a tattered brown Kira and was barefoot. Her graying black hair was hacked rather than cut, and her face wore the miles of a thousand such journeys. The woman's load was heavy and awkwardly strapped around her back and shoulders. As she trod the steep downhill path, the load was swaying from side to side, trying its hardest to pull her off balance. Sophie turned to watch and by the time she turned back to the trail Steve was twenty or thirty yards ahead. She pushed on up the steep hillside. By the time she caught up with Steve, he was sitting at trailside at the top of the hill. The trail went over the tight pass and steeply down into the forest below. Through the treetops they could just make out the roof of the Tharpaling Goemba, it looked similar in design, but smaller than Lamey Goemba that they had already passed.

"There it is," Steve said. "Not long to go now." He stood and readied himself. The trail beyond led steeply downhill.

"There's what?"

"Tharpaling Goemba."

"If we go down we'll have to climb back up again." Sophie turned to Steve and said, "We can see it from here. Let's turn back, remember, just this morning you were almost dying."

Steve was caught off-guard. The walking was actually helping to clear his head, but he wasn't about to argue the point.

He knew he still had hours of work ahead of him, so said, "Sure, okay. City Girl."

Sophie scowled. He laughed.

They were back down to the Lamey Goemba before they spoke again. The sun dipped quickly, the trail was behind them. Their shadows stretched out on the road as they walked side by side.

"Now tell me about yourself," Steve said. "What happened after you got home?"

Sophie walked on without saying a thing, it sounded so simple put that way. How could Steve know what it was like for her to get home, by bus from Central America, alone?

"Okay. I guess it's my turn to fill in the years," Sophie began. "It was difficult, we'd explored a world that none of my family or friends understood. My family knew only one thing, hard work. Finding oneself through months of travel was a foreign idea. My parents and even my brothers tried to share it with me, but really I felt more alone than I ever had."

Sophie took a sip from her water bottle, she hoped Steve was not looking at her and kept her sunglasses on even though the afternoon light was pale and soft. She talked firstly about how she continued the Spanish lessons they'd begun together. "And in nineteen seventy nine, friends convinced me to go back to law school. I just buried myself in it." Mom and dad gave me all the support they could, but in my third year, dad died in an accident.

"Oh, no!" Steve turned to her, "what in a car?"

She fought back tears and sketched out the accident on the vineyard. The tractor had rolled over in a place her dad had driven it a thousand times or more.

Steve said he remembered the spot, one sharp steep incline on an otherwise gently undulating property.

Her brothers, she said, had taken over the vineyard okay, but her mom never really got over it. She died a year later. "That was just a few months before I graduated."

They stopped, Steve took both her hands in his. "I can't believe that, your mum was so good to me."

"There was little for me to stay around for," Sophie said. "I wanted to go someplace else and get my career moving quickly. I applied for a position with the State Department and within a month, I moved to Washington."

They walked through the main street of Jakar as the town was closing down for the day. Steve said, "I've often wondered what happened to you, Sophie."

She surprised him by asking, "How often?"

He looked at her to make sure he'd understood.

She repeated, "How often have you thought about me?"

Steve mumbled, "Oh, you know, every now and then."

She bit her lip and said nothing.

They walked over the bridge and the Bumthang Chhu was steely gray in the fading light. The Eiger guesthouse was in sight high above them. Sophie was tired, her gentle walk had turned into a trek and she longed for a hot shower. Steve asked what part of Washington she lived in. When she replied Georgetown, he said he'd walked around there a bit.

"You've probably walked past my townhouse," she said, "it's in the West Village, just up from Wisconsin Avenue. It's three stories high with red brick at the front. You couldn't miss it," she joked, knowing that every third house was the same.

The sound of a diesel motor came up behind them, Sophie was too tired to look around. A familiar voice called from an open window, "I'm going up to the guesthouse. Hop in if you want a ride." It was Eric. Sophie was saying to herself, 'Thank you God for small mercies', she was moving toward the car.

Steve answered back, "Thanks Eric, but we'd rather finish the walk." Sophie swung around, her eyes were wild. Before she could hit him, Steve had her by the arm, "Come on, climb in there."

Sophie took a hot shower and took time to think. Was Steve guilty of fraud? She thought not, more than likely he'd been set-up. Anyway, she agreed with herself, it wasn't necessary to know any more right now. Just as Steve would soon have to accept Marie for who she was, Marie would have to accept her father for whatever he was. As she dried herself, she reflected on the day. The ruse with her sprained ankle rankled a bit with her conscience, but she reassured herself, 'Under the circumstances, a girl's gotta do what a girl's gotta do.'

As to Steve and Ollie's naked night of intimacy, of moaning and sighing and squeaking beds, Sophie felt almost laughably guilty. Her imagination had got the better of her. But, had she also imagined her relief at learning the truth? Was it relief for Marie, or for herself?

She dressed for dinner in a black polo-necked top and a pair of gray tweed trousers, then she talked to herself in the mirror. She'd enjoy the meal and Steve's company, get to know him a bit better, then over coffee when it'd be too late for lots of questions, she'd have to tell Steve what she'd come here to tell him.

42: Ema Datse

Steve was sitting at the table on the verandah, gazing out over the valley and the lights of Jakar below. He was thinking how he could finish dinner quickly and get back to his work. He knew he was on the trail of something with Veejay Industries, he wanted to finish what he'd started. When Sophie joined him, he suggested they have a drink before dinner, "just one" he said, and offered Red Panda beer or local whiskey. Sophie said she had a better idea, she went back to her room and returned with a bottle of Cabernet Sauvignon. Steve checked the label, Vella Reserve Collection was printed in off-white on an almost black background. He opened the bottle and poured two glasses. Sophie said, "Let it sit awhile." They talked about the day and Bhutanese cuisine. When she said that she was hungry enough to eat a yak. He assured her that's exactly what they'd be getting. There'll be red rice as well, and *daal*. A thick lentil soup they serve like a sauce. If we're lucky there'll be some fresh vegetables and of course *ema datse*. Bhutan's national dish made from chilies and cheese. Steve added, "Watch the *ema datse* if you haven't had it before. It's so hot it cooks itself."

They moved into the dining room and sat opposite each other. The cherub-faced girl had placed a large bowl of red chilies in the center of the table. Sophie said, "I hope the chilies are a decoration, and not our dinner." Steve grinned and suggested a toast, they touched glasses and he said, "To celestial coincidence in the Land of the Thunder Dragon." Sophie laughed, openly. This could be a long night Steve thought, cautiously aware of the work he should be doing.

Hot and sour soup was served first, it was spicy and hot and good. They finished the soup and Sophie sipped her wine, she said, "I should have decanted this. It takes a while for the full aroma to open up."

"If it was any better," Steve said. "It'd be too good to drink."

"Tony sent me a dozen bottles just before I left. This is the first I've tried. He said it'll be a classic."

Sophie swirled the deep red liquid in her glass, but he could tell she hadn't come here to talk about classic vintages. Steve said, "I hope you don't mind me asking?"

"Depends what it is you're asking," Sophie said over the rim of the wineglass lifted to her lips.

"Well, when I asked if you were married, you said not now."

"That's right."

"Oh, I'm sorry to hear that...I hate to think you're living alone?"

"Well...Work keeps me so busy." Sophie straightened up and put her glass down slowly. "And I don't have time for a new relationship just now, if that's what you're asking."

"Ahh...What happened?"

"With what?"

"Your husband, your marriage." He hesitated at his own lack of subtlety, "I'm only asking because I care."

"Do you?"

"Of course."

Sophie held her glass in front of her face, she twirled the contents hypnotically. Without looking at him, she said it was a common enough tale in Washington. "Alex is a senior bureaucrat. He's always busy. I'm always busy. Alex wanted me to give up my career for his. When he was away, I'd manage the house and my job. But when I was away, his life would fall to pieces. I'd be blamed for everything from the cat dying of starvation to the cupboards being empty." Steve nodded. Sophie added, "After being separated for six months, I guess you could say we split amicably."

"And kids?"

It was as though she hadn't heard. She seemed momentarily lost for words then looked away quickly, "We didn't have children," then Sophie added, "Alex is nearly twelve years older than me, there was no place for kids in his life."

Steve sipped his wine and wondered at the color rising in her neck and face.

"When I'd finally accepted that he didn't want to be a father, ever," Sophie said, "he was even too busy to look after things in that department. So I had to. Alex took it all for granted, and with that I moved out."

Steve shuffled on his seat uncomfortably. He thought of Miranda's and his own (never to be concluded) discussions in that area of their own lives. He hoped that Sophie wouldn't pursue the subject.

She raised her glass. "So there you are, Steve. Not quite what I had in mind when we were backpacking through Central America, but my career has had its rewards."

He returned her gaze uneasily, it was his turn to say something. "I hope you're not lonely," came to mind first.

She hesitated and joined her fingers in a knot, "No...I'm too busy to even think about that." She looked past Steve to the wall beyond.

Suddenly the room was too big for just two people. Sophie sipped her wine, deliberately avoiding eye contact. Steve looked around the room and willed the cherub-faced girl, dinner would be a welcome distraction.

"You said in Thimphu that your brothers are managing the business, do you see them much now?"

Sophie smiled faintly. "Yes, we're still close, I go out there often. They've expanded the vineyard and built a new winery. Tourism is a big part of the business now, Louis's wife runs a restaurant there. You'd hardly recognize the place, it's grown so much."

"What's Tony do? He had a great sense of humor."

"Tony's in charge of the vineyard operations. Louis looks after the wine making and marketing."

"That's great. Say 'Hi' to them for me. They were good to me, your whole family was good to me."

"They were, weren't they?" Sophie said in a voice that seemed to ask whether Steve had been good to the Vella family. Steve squirmed on his seat, he was saved by the sound of footsteps.

The main course was delivered buffet style, there was enough food for four. It followed Steve's prediction closely enough, the only change to the menu was the addition of a thin pizza topped with local cheese. They served themselves and ate and drank heartily. Sophie tried the *ema datse,* quite bravely Steve thought. She needed a jug of yogurt and a few large spoonfuls of red rice to quench the fire. They shared more wine and the banter of polite conversation, but Steve knew something was wrong.

He sought neutral territory by asking, "Sophie, what encouraged you to come to Bhutan of all places?"

She hesitated, and said, "I've always wanted to see the Himalayas."

"You could have gone to Nepal?"

Sophie lowered her eyes, "Everyone goes there, I wanted something different."

To Steve's relief, desert was served with tea and coffee. He poured coffee for them both and they ate apple pie without so much as a word. Steve could feel a storm brewing and felt powerless to stop it, but he tried anyway. "This is good, but nothing compared to the pies your mother made." If he'd looked up at Sophie's face he would not have continued. "If there's one thing I'll always remember about the Napa Valley and the Vella vineyard, it's your mother's cooking."

Sophie fixed him with a withering look and rolled her eyes, "Is that your main memory, Steve?"

He stopped. He sensed the danger and carefully tried to untangle himself. "No, of course not, there's you. But that's difficult to talk about now, you and me. You must see that, Sophie."

"I know, I just wanted to hear you say it." Sophie put her elbows on the table. "That I wasn't just another interesting, but forgettable part of your travel experience."

Steve squared his shoulders. His hands tensed under the table, his senses were on full alert. He looked at Sophie, there were no tears, but there was no denying it either, the hurt was still there after all these years. "Sophie, we had some good times. Really good times. It was just the wrong time in my life."

"We could have worked it out."

"We tried! Remember, you made the ultimatum, 'Come back to California with me now. Or go south and walk out of my life forever'. They were your words."

"You were the one that changed all our plans in one day, not me." Sophie added, "I hope you haven't rearranged that truth in your mind?"

"No! I can't rearrange the truth of that day," Steve reached over and put both hands on hers. "You could never know why I had to go, why I changed my mind."

"Of course I couldn't!" She pulled her hands away. "You wouldn't tell me why!"

Sophie was looking right into his soul. His life's greatest failure was before him.

It was minutes later when Sophie spoke. "Steve, look at me, please. Was there anyone else?"

"No! No, it wasn't that," Steve stopped and held her gaze. "There was no one between you and Miranda."

"I'm glad to hear that," her face lightened a little, she almost smiled. "So, can you tell me now why the sudden change of plans?"

Steve balked, "No! Please Sophie, not now, let's not spoil tonight."

"Oh! So nothing's changed hey?" Sophie sat rigidly still, her eyes bore through him. "Then why didn't you contact me? You could have written."

Steve hesitated. "I did, I started so many letters. I never knew what to say, I wrote but I just never sent them. I don't know." He could almost taste the bitterness in the air. "You could have written to me, Sophie." He said without looking up, "I gave you forwarding addresses that last day."

"I had a shoebox full of letters I'd written." Sophie ran her fingers through her hair, she held her hands over her head. "There was just too much happening in my life, you wouldn't..."

He stared at his empty glass, there was no answer there either.

"What about when you got home, Steve. Why didn't you write then?"

"I thought about you a lot at the start. I was really flat. I had no money, the few friends I had left were married or in steady relationships. I don't know really. I guess you just seemed so far away, and I thought you probably meant what you said. That I had my choice in Costa Rica. That I'd walked out of your life."

Sophie picked a long red chili out of the bowl in front of them. She held the chili in her fingers and stared at it as though it was the cause of her anger.

"For God's sake, Sophie. I didn't know myself then."

"What about when you called once and didn't call back. Did you know yourself by then?" She ran her fingers angrily along the length of the chili.

"What do you mean?" Steve said defensively.

"I mean when you phoned home to check that I'd arrived safely?"

"Yeah, and?"

"*And*," Sophie snapped the chili in half. "*And* you got my mother. *And* she told you I was away for a couple of days. And you never called back?"

"Well I..."

"You called to satisfy your conscience. To make sure I'd arrived. You probably felt a sense of relief to think you didn't have to talk to me then. How lucky for you that I was away at the time." She glared across the table and dropped the broken chili in front of herself.

"Be fair, Sophie. I couldn't have known you weren't there, I..."

"Be fair! Mom said you didn't even say 'Give Sophie my love', or anything that showed you cared. I waited by the phone for weeks after your call. I was sure you'd call back. You never did." Sophie grabbed another chili from the bowl, she held it in two shaking hands. Her eyes were on fire.

"I know. I should have. But it wouldn't have changed anything."

"How could you know? If I'd been able to speak to you. To hear your voice, to know you cared."

"Look, I should have called back, yeah. I'm sorry, but I wasn't going to turn around. I was going to Bolivia and that was that."

"Well I made the right decision then. *Didn't I, Steve?*"

"I dunno! What decision?"

"To get on with my life…To be self-reliant."

Steve shrugged, "Maybe," and then watched helpless as nineteen years of unresolved anger ignited in a flash.

"Maybe!' Sophie squeezed the chili then bit the end off it. It burned. She spat an inch of red chili into her hand then threw it on the table. "Ugh." She shoved her chair back and it fell heavily behind her. She stood and glared at him. "*Maybe! Maybe* I've had enough of you and your sulking selfish secrets. *Maybe* I'd rather go for a walk…*alone!*"

Before he had a chance to reply, to try to calm her, she grabbed the bowl of chilies from the table and upended it in his lap.

She said, "I hate you," and slammed the bowl on the table. She took a gulp of her wine and emptied the rest of the bottle into Steve's glass. "You decide if it's got a long lingering finish. I'm going."

He was still trying to work out what had happened.

She turned on her heel and walked heavily to the door leading onto the verandah.

He stood and red chilies spilt everywhere. He said after her, "*Go on then, walk out.*"

She stopped and faced him, her black eyes volcanic with anger.

Steve yelled across the room. "You've been angry with me for nineteen years now. Stay angry for the next nineteen. We'll both be too old to worry then."

Sophie looked back at him defiantly. "Eat the chilies Steve — the whole bowl — they might thaw you out, you cold-hearted ass." She stormed out across the verandah and took the steep stairs two at a time.

Steve waited for twenty-five minutes for her to return. He looked out over the balcony for any sight of her. He thought of going to find her, then thought the better of it. He went to his room, sat at his computer but didn't turn it on, and listened. He waited another fifteen minutes before he heard her footsteps, then the door to Room 4 open and shut. Then he thought about how he might explain things in the morning.

In a way he was glad that he was leaving tomorrow. He had enough problems of his own just now. But then he didn't want to leave her this way. Sophie had reawakened that 'sulking selfish secret' that troubled him from time to time. But it was impossible to tell her the full story now. He should have done that nineteen years ago.

43: Over the edge

Sophie had been sitting alone at the table on the verandah for fifteen minutes. She had a cup of sugary tea in her hand and cool morning air gently ruffling her hair. She turned at hearing the door to Room 2 open and said just pleasantly enough, "Morning, Steve, late again?"

Steve stood at his open doorway and checked his watch, "Hey, it's not even seven thirty." He said, "Anyway, are we at peace?" as he slid along the bench seat opposite her.

Sophie said without a hint of regret. "Yes, as much as we can be under the circumstances. Perhaps I wanted to know too much too quickly."

"Yeah. But that's not why you walked out."

"I know. I shouldn't have done that." She smiled, it was an apology and truce in one. "So what's happening today? What are your plans?"

The valley was already awash with the full light of day. There was an out-of-season warmth, despite the early hour. Steve replied, "With luck, Karma will be here around nine, then I'm leaving for Thimphu. I've got an important meeting on Tuesday and a lot to do before then."

"Karma?"

"Yeah…my driver."

"Oh, and after?"

"Depends, I guess. I hope to go to Paro Tuesday afternoon and stay there overnight." Steve added, "I'm flying out to Bangkok on Wednesday morning."

"Hmm. My trekking group doesn't get back here until Monday afternoon," Sophie counted the days on her fingers. "We'll be back in Thimphu Wednesday midday, but you'll be gone by then?"

"Yeah, I guess," Steve said and added quickly, "so we've only got a couple of hours left together. Let's part friends."

Sophie weighed a 'couple of hours' in her mind and said, "You mentioned, with luck, Karma will come at nine? Where's luck come into it?"

Steve saw his chance to relax things a little, he laughed and reeled off his story about Karma's three wives, how Jakar wife saw the least of Karma and was therefore the hardest for him to leave…how timeliness was not Karma's strong point anyway.

Sophie laughed along for awhile, but uncertainly — even if Jakar wife was successful in delaying Steve's departure, it would only be for an hour or so, and under the circumstances that was nothing. Her moment was near — she had to tell him soon. But first, deliberately and subtly, she started talking about her work, about regular trips to Latin America, in particular to Venezuela and Colombia. She went on to say she liked Ecuador and found Peru daunting and then she mentioned Costa Rica. She'd been there recently for a conference on Central American women's health. She wanted to gauge Steve's reaction and was pleased when he asked a few general questions about the place and how it had changed over the past nineteen years. He was looking out at the valley, so didn't see how carefully she watched him as she casually said, "I had a free weekend on my last trip to Costa Rica. I hired a car and went to Cahuita. I booked into a small hotel and spent the weekend there."

She led him to talking about that time in their lives, when they could have taken the one road together. They talked about the beaches they'd walked on, the crystal waters they swam in and the bungalow they'd rented for a month.

"Is it still there?" Steve said. It was an innocent enough question.

"Yes." Sophie moved her distant focus down to the shimmering light reflected off the river, "I found our place. It's much the same. No one was there so I went and sat on the porch. I looked out through the coconut trees and over the beach to the water."

"And?" was all that he asked.

"And then I cried."

Steve reached over and put his hand on hers. They just sat there. Neither looking at the other. Neither ready to move. Minutes later Steve stood and walked aimlessly around the verandah. Sophie remained seated, the beach at Cahuita was right there in her mind. She could see the bungalow, feel the tropical heat and the salt water dried on her skin. Their last day at Cahuita was vivid in her memory, a walk on the beach before sunrise — Steve undressing her and a swim in a turquoise sea — then their desire for each other. But she wasn't here to reminisce. Her moment had come. She had to tell him soon. Now! His back was to her, she started, "Steve…there's something…"

Steve turned and footsteps clattered on the steep wooden steps. The cherub-faced girl appeared balancing a breakfast tray. "You take breakfast now, out here?" They both nodded. She set the tray down and stood by at attention.

Steve served tea for Sophie, he made a strong coffee for himself and said, "Yeah?"

Sophie leant forward, "The girl, does she need to stay?"

Steve turned and nodded, "Kadinchhey." The cherub-faced girl smiled, bowed and left. He turned back to Sophie, "What have you got planned for today?"

Sophie said, "I haven't really thought about it."

"There's lots of other walks to do. You could take a trail to the east, to Tamshing Goemba."

He drank his coffee eagerly. She hardly touched her tea, her stomach churned. This was the part of her plan that she hadn't quite worked through. She should have told him last night. Now she'd have to just come out with it, Steve guess what, we've got a daughter? Instead she heard herself ask, "What about when you come to Washington next? Could we have dinner or meet somewhere?"

His face showed that he hadn't even thought of this possibility, he mumbled, "Yeah, I'd like to, but…"

She noted his unease. "Surely Miranda wouldn't mind. We're just old friends."

Sophie watched him think through his response, he didn't even try to hide his confusion. "It's not, ahh, Miranda. I've never even told her about you."

Sophie reeled. "*What?*"

Steve caught his breath and held it. She could read his mind, he didn't want to go where he knew this could lead.

"Are you joking? Have you told Miranda about your time in the Napa Valley? Your job on the vineyard?"

"Yeah, but..."

"What about our travels in Central America?"

"My travels, yeah. Listen..."

"Oh! So Miranda heard a version of your life-story, without me in it?"

"Uhh, ahh, yeah, I guess she did."

"I should have known."

"Sophie, it's not that simple..."

Sophie fought back a desperate urge to scream, this was leading her off-track. She hadn't come all this way to talk about what Steve did or didn't tell his wife. And she couldn't leave it until he came to Washington either, if nothing else, she'd promised Marie. She had to tell him now. She closed her eyes and willed away her anger. She opened her eyes again and faced him but without eye contact. She started, "Steve, there's something you..." She choked and her voice was so soft she couldn't hear her own words. She put her hand to her mouth and tried to clear the logjam in her throat. She started again, "Steve, I..."

The sound of a vehicle caught Steve's attention and he turned. Sophie stopped mid-sentence.

With his back to her he said, "That's Karma!"

Sophie said, "Then he's early?"

"Yeah...and I've never seen him in such a hurry." They both watched as the Landcruiser pulled into the car park in a cloud of dust. The driver's door flung open. Karma jumped out and looked up to the verandah. He signaled alarm without even noticing that Steve had company. He ran across the courtyard and clattered up the stairs. Karma was halfway to the table before he even noticed Sophie. He stopped and gathered in his surprise, he gasped, "Mr. Steve...Mr. Steve."

"What is it, Karma?"

Karma's face was white. He was shaking, almost incoherent. "It's Ollie. She's gone. Gone over the edge."

"Karma, calm down. What's happened?"

Karma slumped himself onto the bench seat. He looked up. "Bad things, Mr. Steve."

"Slowly Karma," Steve said. "Tell us what happened."

"Ollie's driver, Jalal, has reported in to the Trongsa police. My brother got the message to me. Jalal told the police that on Friday when he was driving Ollie to Thimphu, he stopped on the road to meet a call of nature. Because he didn't want to pee in front of the woman, and there was a steep cliff beside them, he walked up a side road. As he was emptying himself he heard a huge explosion above him. He ran back to the HiLux, there was nothing, a landslide had taken it over the edge and down into the forest way below."

"Over the edge?" Steve's jaw dropped open. "With Ollie inside?"

Karma just nodded. His head stayed bowed. Sophie's face was buried in her hands.

"Karma, maybe your brother got it wrong?"

"No sir! On this sir, brother Dechen is good."

"What about Ollie, did they find her?"

Karma looked up at Steve. "Dechen says that where the accident happened the cliff is maybe one thousand feet. It will take days just to get someone down there."

Steve sighed. "She wouldn't have a hope."

Karma repeated. "Not a hope."

A gust of wind came from nowhere. Sophie shivered, Steve didn't even notice it.

"Where'd this happen?" Steve demanded.

"This side of Pele La, sir. People are saying it was set off by blasting on that new road near Tangsibji."

"Jeezas! We've got to get there, Karma," Steve said. "We've got to do something!"

"What can we do, Mr. Steve?" Karma looked up, his face drained of emotion. "The road is blocked, we can't get through. Trongsa Police are asking people to stay away, to wait till the road is cleared."

"I don't care," Steve said. Anger was taking over from reason. "There must be something."

Karma just bowed his head, under his breath he began his puja. His slow chanting in Dzongkha had a lilting tone.

Steve glanced over at Sophie, her face was still hidden in her hands. He looked again at Karma, head bent in prayer. Steve waited, then said, "We'll leave tomorrow morning, Karma. We'll stay in Trongsa if the road is still closed. I'll talk to the police myself."

Karma lifted his head and rose slowly. He looked restored, somehow suddenly above it all. He said, "Yes, Mr. Steve. I'll come early." He bowed to Sophie and said, "Sorry, ma'am, I'm Karma."

Sophie introduced herself and watched as he crossed to the stairs, and without looking back, climbed down and walked to the Landcruiser. They both watched him go and Sophie felt a silent space that Karma still occupied, as though his prayers had a presence all of their own.

"I'm going for a walk," Steve said. "I need to think things through."

"Can I come...please...I don't want to be alone here."

44: A quick change of plans

"I'd only met her for such a short time," Sophie said as they walked out through the car park. "But I could tell Ollie was different."

Steve walked slightly ahead, it took him some moments to stop and say, "You met her?"

"Yeah, at breakfast yesterday morning, while you were sleeping."

He paled, then said, "Other than Jalal, you were the last person to see her alive."

"Yes, and her last words haven't left me. Ollie said, 'Tell Steve I'll see him in Thimphu on Tuesday, and I hope he found what he was looking for last night.'"

Steve's jaw dropped, "Oh!"

"She meant the money did she?"

"Yeah! She meant, if I don't find how it went missing by Tuesday, that's three days away now, I go to gaol."

"Gaol?"

"That's right! The whole lot's been blamed on me. The police have taken my passport."

"No! Steve, have you ever been inside a gaol in this part of the world?"

"No, but I've heard..." He shook his head, "I can imagine..."

Sophie cut in, "Believe me...You can't imagine." She turned and met him face to face, "Listen...I've had to visit gaols in South America, I'm sure they wouldn't be much different here. You're not taking this seriously enough."

"Don't worry, I am. But I think I'll be okay. Like I said, I'm onto a lead and I'll call our corporate lawyer as soon as I get back to Thimphu."

"Your corporate lawyer should already be onto this. Surely you've heard of the 'Black' case. Ian Black, the engineer from Florida who's still doing time in Bombay. We're sure he's innocent, that he was set up. State Department's been working on that one for three years now and we're no closer to getting him home."

Steve's look of utter desperation, the way he shook his head, said what she already knew. That he hadn't heard of Black and it wouldn't help to tell him anyway.

In a way Sophie was relieved that he was confirming what she already knew, but now it was all too real. And Ollie's supposedly accidental death didn't help things. Was this part of a set-up? Should she get involved? Did she even have a choice now?

They crossed through the orchard. The sun was fully up now and their shadows stretched out behind them on the narrow road.

"Steve, wouldn't they put up warning signs for an explosion as big as that?"

Steve kicked angrily at a rock on the road. He said, "Sometimes they don't, look at me!" He pointed to the still obvious wound on the side of his head. "Anyway, if I'm correct the accident happened where they are putting in the new road near Tangsibji. The new road's above the existing road."

"You'd think they would stop the traffic at least."

"Yeah, the blasting wouldn't have been on the main road, but they should take precautions. It's just the way it is here."

"What will happen?"

"Probably nothing. They'll get Ollie out somehow. They'll do puja and nothing will change."

They walked on in silence.

"Something doesn't sound right," Sophie said. "The driver's need to relieve himself was too well timed."

"No, Jalal has a bladder problem. He stopped four or five times on the way across."

"I'm still not sure it was an accident."

"Sophie! You're thinking like a lawyer."

"That's the way I think."

"Yeah! But don't forget that this is Bhutan, crazy things happen here."

They walked further down the road. They were just above the river. Sophie couldn't get Ollie out of her mind. She kept coming back to a picture of Ollie sitting patiently in the HiLux, when out of nowhere thousands of tons of rock and dirt crashed down from above. Would that have killed her before it swept the vehicle over the edge? She hoped so. It would be kinder that way: Ollie was too young to die slowly. Sophie said, "Would anyone want Ollie out of the way?"

He snapped back, "What do you mean?"

"Could Ollie know something that she shouldn't? Something about the twenty million? Be serious here Steve, it just doesn't add up."

"Jeezas! *No*! To murder her!" He turned to face her and said gruffly, "That stuff doesn't happen in Bhutan."

At the Bumthang Chhu, Steve pointed to a grassy flat. They sat near the water's edge and let the rushing of the river block out any sound. Some wading birds were foraging in the shallows on the opposite bank, were they herons Steve wondered? Sophie's question would not leave him. Now he started asking questions himself. Narguli agreed to Ollie traveling back alone, that was unusual. Where did Jalal come from? He wasn't a project driver, nor was he with the bank. Ollie and Narguli had argued the day before they left Trashigang, what was that about?

Steve idly threw stones into the water and watched them splash. Whatever the answer to his questions, tomorrow he'd be on his way, and, as good as it had been to spend this time with Sophie, they'd be taking two different roads again. He hadn't even mentioned his planned trip to Washington in December.

She seemed to have forgotten her own question, and there was just too much going on in his own life at present, too many problems. Anyway, problems were a personal thing. He was better off alone. Wasn't he?

When they returned to the Eiger, Eric had lunch ready for them. Neither felt like eating but they made an attempt anyway. Over coffee, Sophie listened while Steve explained to Eric what had happened. Steve said, "Later on I'll need to use the phone to call Trashigang, I'll have to tell Rawlinson about Ollie's accident, and ask him to tell Narguli." Eric agreed and said all the kind words that fitted the occasion, then cleared their table and left them alone again.

Almost immediately, Steve went to his room on the pretext of having to work on his spreadsheets. He told Sophie just enough of what he was doing to be convincing and then left her with an agreement to knock on her door when he was done.

She agreed, somewhat reluctantly, and went to her room determined this time to finish the last thirty pages or so of the novel she still hadn't finished.

Less than two hours later, Steve knocked on her door. He called out, "It's hopeless, I can't concentrate. I'm going to walk downtown. There's an archery match on. It's Bhutan's national sport, you shouldn't miss it. Umm…what did Ian Black do wrong, the guy from Florida?"

Sophie agreed readily and said she'd tell him about Black while they walked. But now she knew she'd have to wait to tell Steve about Marie — clearly he had enough on his mind already. But then how long could she wait? And while the archery match was fun, and the underdog had won the un-win-nable contest, and it had distracted them both somewhat; she still hadn't answered her own question. How long could she wait to tell him?

On the way back up the hill they agreed to meet for dinner at seven, and Sophie wondered if there'd be an opening for the two things now on her mind: Firstly Marie, and secondly her growing conviction that Steve was being framed for a crime she was sure he hadn't committed.

Steve sat deep in thought — a glass of water in his hand, a lot on his mind.

"How was the news of Ollie's death received?" Sophie asked as soon as she reached the table.

"I couldn't get anyone," he said. "I tried Rawlinson several times, and Martin and Tammy. No one's home. I even tried the office, but that's shut Saturday afternoon. And I can't call Narguli because the PORC guesthouse doesn't have a phone."

They ate in silence, both locked away with private thoughts. After dinner their conversation hedged around what each of them knew hadn't been talked about yet. When it couldn't be avoided any longer, Steve said, "What are you going to do for the next few days?"

Sophie was ready for him, "I've decided to go to Thimphu with you." She waited for that to sink in and added quickly, "You mightn't know it yet, but you need help. I believe that, that landslide was no accident."

"Oh," Steve said. It was as if he hadn't heard correctly. Slowly it sank in. "You're...you're coming with me? I need your help?"

"Yes, yes to both...if that's okay?"

"But...but..."

"Please Steve, I've got no reason to stay here alone," Sophie said.

Steve started to speak, then stopped and just stared at her. He noted her determination, he'd seen it before.

"And I can help you stay out of gaol."

"I'm not planning on going there."

She didn't respond. The look on her face was resolute, he knew it well.

"But what about your tour group?"

"I'll meet up with them in Thimphu," Sophie's eyes held his without blinking. "I mean it. This time I'm coming with you. You need help, even if you don't know it yourself."

He knew he should say *No*! But something deeper inside took control. Was it the look on Sophie's face? Her determination? Or did he really want her help, and a friend? Could Sophie be right? Did Ollie know too much? He murmured, "Okay. Sure."

In Room 4, Sophie packed for the morning. As she put away her things, she thought about how she would lead Steve through the events leading up to Ollie's supposedly accidental death. She needed to find out a lot more about his project and the people involved, but now she had several days to do that. The thought was comforting, and Sophie didn't dare admit to thinking it, even to herself, that this turn of events fitted into her plan better than she could have ever hoped. She'd help Steve solve his problem first, then she'd deal with her own. "Marie would approve", she said to herself.

In Room 2, Steve tried to distract himself with spreadsheets and the re-counting of Veejay Industries' invoices, but his mind kept coming back to Ollie sitting in the backseat of the HiLux, then being buried alive by a landslide. The image wouldn't leave him.

After a wasted half-hour he closed his computer and lay on his back on the bed. First he thought about Sophie, then about Ollie, then Miranda. He was sure he was doing the right thing in the wake of Ollie's accident, Sophie could help him. He didn't have the mind for questioning things the way she did. And while he wasn't convinced that the missing project money and Ollie's death were linked, he had to admit that if they were, Sophie was right, he needed all the help he could get.

He stared at the ceiling and thought of home, of Miranda in bed asleep at two in the morning. That thought led to the last time they'd slept together, over fifteen months ago. From there his mind went to the way that she had broken her news on his arrival home from three months in Cambodia. It still hurt that she'd wanted him to drive home from the airport so she didn't have to face him, and that was knowing that he hadn't slept for thirty hours. It still surprised him how calm she'd been as she told him that he was still a good man and a good father, but that it was now 'Trist', Tristan Troy, who would share her bed.

He remembered gripping the wheel so hard it hurt. Trist rolled around in his brain and it rhymed with Trust. Trist and Trust, Trist and Trust were going over and over in his head and it was all melding and clanging with the frantic rush of the traffic and his own sleeplessness. When he finally found his voice, he said angrily (with eyes fixed on the road ahead and knuckles white on the wheel), "So, the great self-help guru has been helping himself to my wife, hey?"

Miranda told him not to be childish. She said that these things happen.

These things happen. Things happen. He drove for five or maybe ten minutes before he spoke again. Then, with bitter tears burning his cheeks, he said, "And when are the self-help adulterer and the lifestyle adulterer starting their new life together?"

Miranda had shouted in reply. "You're absolutely wrong, Steve. It's not adultery because I'm never going to sleep with you again. Trist and I talked about it. If I don't sleep with you again, then it's not adultery."

With his brain rattled and the flow of the highway traffic humming a dull monotonous tune, it had all seemed so unreal, but so believable, even convenient. Miranda wasn't going to sleep with him again: how proper of her.

He'd been overseas most of the past year. When he was home, he slept in a single bed in the office off their bedroom. The boys were not to be told yet. Miranda had promised that she and Trist would play lovers during the day, while the boys were at school, they'd know nothing until the time was right. Miranda had it all planned, as she always did. Ric and Tim would go to boarding school in Sydney next February. She hadn't planned what Steve would do, but she had suggested he keep working: she'd chosen one of the best private schools in Sydney for the boys, it would not come cheap.

Trist's wife Heidi had already left town. Trist had plenty of money to pay Steve for his half of the house, and Mr. Tristan Troy would move in as Miranda's new husband the day Steve moved out.

45: The grandmaster policeman

Seven on a Sunday morning, Steve knew would not be a good time to call Rawlinson at home but he did it anyway. The phone rang out again, just like it had done last night. He tried Martin's house just after seven and both of them again at eight. There was no answer at either place. Just to be sure he called the project office, nothing. There was no other way to get a message through, but at least he'd tried. Narguli would learn of Ollie's fate soon enough anyhow.

Karma pulled into the Eiger's car park at eight fifteen. As they loaded their luggage, Steve glanced twice at Sophie's Vuitton softpack and thought it was an odd choice for someone coming to Bhutan on a trekking expedition. Sophie stood at the front of the Landcruiser, she was out of hearing range. Steve whispered to Karma, "Sophie's coming with us to Thimphu."

"Truly, sir?" Karma said and put his hand on Sophie's already loaded luggage.

"She's a lawyer." Steve said. Then noticing that Karma was still unconvinced, added, "She can help me investigate Ollie's accident."

"Yes, of course Mr. Steve," Karma's white teeth and dark brown eyes sparkled; he winked.

Steve met Karma's gesture with a stone-faced glare and turned quickly.

They thanked Eric for his hospitality and Steve paid his account. Sophie double-checked that Mountain Adventures covered hers and reminded Eric to pass on the letter she'd written to Anna. Steve offered Sophie the front seat, she accepted and the three-hour journey began.

As they crossed the Bumthang Chhu, Steve said, "Damn! I haven't made forward reservations in Trongsa."

Karma shrugged, but said nothing.

Steve said from the back seat, "The Norbut Hotel might have spare rooms. What do you think, Karma?"

"Don't know, sir. I never stay in Trongsa." Karma spoke to the rear vision mirror where he had Steve in his sight. "No wife. No stay." He laughed happily at his own joke.

They drove slowly through Jakar town and turned left to track alongside the river. The fields lay golden in the morning sunlight, the slightest breeze pushed waves across them. Sophie, looking out over the valley, said, "What's the crop, Karma?"

He replied, "Barley, Miss."

"Why don't you just call me, Sophie?"

Karma glanced sideways and nodded deferentially, "Okay, Miss Sophie, I try."

Steve, in the backseat just shook his head. Some things would never change.

On the climb up through the pine forests towards Kiki La, the tape of Rawlinson's Classics played, the sun shone and the diesel motor hummed a comfortable, powerful tune. They crested the pass and began the descent into the Chhume Valley. Steve listened to Karma and Sophie talking occasionally about something they passed by, or the name of a village. Otherwise, he watched Sophie from the back seat — the shine of her hair as it caught the morning sun, the profile of her face, the sound of her voice and the proud way that she held her head, it was all coming back to him.

The tape of classics stopped. Steve passed 'On the Beach' to Sophie and the music started again with the sound of waves crashing on the shore.

Karma said after a moment, "This is 'On the Ocean'!"

"You're close," Steve said.

"Yes sir, one day I take my wife to see the ocean."

"Which one?" Sophie said.

"Jakar wife."

She laughed, "Not which wife. Which ocean?"

Karma hesitated, he turned to Sophie with confusion written all over his face and said, "The blue one."

They passed by the village at Gaytsa and started the climb to Yotong La. The oaks and chestnuts, walnuts and maples were starting to turn yellow, red and russet. They climbed up through the fir forests and came upon the road gang that had been on Yotong La a week or so back. Steve considered commenting, but he could see that Sophie was somewhere else, that she was lost in deep thought. The Landcruiser circled the chorten at the pass, then began the steep descent into Trongsa. Sophie played the whole Chris Rea tape again as they wound downhill through the fir forest. The Trongsa Dzong came into sight, and soon after, the watchtowers above it.

Karma stayed in the vehicle while Sophie and Steve went into the Norbut Hotel to register for the three of them. There was no one in the reception area, so Steve walked into the kitchen and found a boy of perhaps ten who spoke reasonable English. The boy said that he could check to see if any rooms were available. He mentioned on the way to the desk that they were particularly busy, a number of travelers were waiting over until the road reopened. Sophie leaned over the desk as the boy ran his finger up and down the guest register for three vacant rooms.

He looked up. "Two rooms only, two beds in each. Okay?"

Sophie was ready to say fine, that'll do, but Steve frowned and said, "There's another hotel just down the road, maybe they'd have three rooms?"

Sophie turned to him, "Is it as good as this one?"

"Ah, no."

"Oh! You mean it's like those half star rooms you took for us in Mexico and Guatemala?"

"Sort of, yeah, but the rats are bigger in Bhutan."

"Forget it. Let's stay here, you share with Karma."

Steve nodded. "Yes Ma'am."

She laughed. "That's better."

They checked in and took lunch in the restaurant.

Steve led the way to the Police Station which was next to the checkpoint on the road into town. There was no sign, everyone knew it. A junior police officer was outside watering geraniums that grew behind a waist-high stone wall running the length of the station. Karma spoke in Dzongkha and the police-boy signaled to the door with a pronounced shift of his head. Steve knocked and waited. Nothing happened. He knocked again. There was no response. Finally, Steve pushed the door slowly ajar and stuck his head into the gloom to see two uniformed officers playing chess by candlelight.

The most senior of the men looked up, his teeth and mouth were stained with betel nut. "Wait moment. Check-mate almost."

Steve withdrew, "They're in there. Playing chess."

"Who's winning?" Karma said.

Steve held his palms aloft. The three of them waited in the warm afternoon sun with the unmistakable scent of geraniums behind them. After perhaps five minutes there was a muffled shout of 'check mate' from inside. Moments later the Police Chief poked his head out of the doorway, and said, "You are wanting some helping?"

Karma introduced Steve and Sophie in English, then broke into Dzongkha to detail their relationship to each other and to Ollie. They were there to find out about the accident.

The chief smiled broadly, his teeth were either crooked and betel-stained, or missing. He shook hands firmly with Steve.

As he held onto Sophie's hand, he mumbled something about sincere regrets on the tragic accident. Steve thought they'd be invited into the office and formally briefed, but instead the chief beckoned them to sit on the stone wall of the flower garden. He hoisted his short, slightly rotund frame onto the wall. Steve and Sophie sat either side of him, the sun warm on their backs. The chief explained in slow but reasonable English that he had inspected the accident site and taken a statement from the driver, Jalal, who had now returned to Trashigang. The road works supervisor had also been questioned. The chief's eyes narrowed to slits as he explained they were making arrangements for a specialist team to recover the HiLux, "It might take us a week," he said. It would be difficult enough just to get to the vehicle, and given that it fell over a thousand feet, there was no possibility of Ollie being alive. The chief concluded by saying that his statement would report a most unfortunate accident, and the road will be re-opened tomorrow.

After wishing them well on their forward journey, the chief stumbled rather than jumped off the wall. More surprised than injured, he collected himself, straightened his gho, bowed slightly then disappeared back into the office. As the door shut they overheard, "My move. You're black this time."

On the way back to the hotel, Sophie said to Steve, "You'd think the police would at least keep an open mind and consider murder as a possibility, that they'd investigate whether the landslide was planned."

Steve shook his head and said, "Tell me how you *plan* a landslide and I'll take you seriously."

Landslides were still on Sophie's mind when they arrived back at the Norbut less than half an hour after leaving it. At the entrance, Karma said he wanted to go to his cousin's place, as much to get an update on local gossip about the accident as to see his brother Dechen. He asked Steve and Sophie to go along with him. Steve, Sophie noticed, was reluctant. She, on the other hand, would have gladly taken up the invitation.

After a moment of indecision, Steve said that Sophie and he had a number of important things to talk about. He quickly added, "About the accident, of course."

Karma added another "of course", then Sophie settled the matter by suggesting that Karma go alone, but that he bring Dechen along to dinner that evening.

When Karma had gone, Sophie said, "What's wrong with Dechen, don't you two get on?"

"Ahh…It's not that. I need to talk things over. I thought we could go for a walk and talk some more, that's all."

Sophie shrugged, she had an inkling that Steve wasn't telling her the full truth about Karma's brother.

It was after three when they started walking slowly down through the town. It was a sleepy, warm afternoon. Sophie saw clouds building to a storm on the mountains across the valley and heard the sounds of a village at work lift and fall on the ruffling of a breeze: Trongsa was going about its business without hurry. People peered at them out of dark windowed shops and homes, dogs opened their eyes, then went back to scratching or sleeping, kids laughed and called out, "Hello Mistas," and the occasional car or bus went by. A hundred yards down the road, the houses and shops thinned out to one every now and then. On the fringes of town, red chilies dried on big woven mats laid out on the roadside while old men sat idly chatting to neighbors with toothless grins. Further on, huge eucalyptus trees cast a foreign shade down the road and the distant rumble of thunder warned of change.

As soon as they'd left the town behind them, Sophie said, "What was it you wanted to talk about?"

"Ollie, and your ideas from yesterday."

A gap in the trees opened up views over the valley. Sophie was drawn to the side of the road and stood looking out over the forest and the farms and the winding river way below. Steve stood at her side and she said, "Good, I want you to tell me everything you know about her."

"I misjudged her to begin," he started. As they stood there looking out over the valley, he pieced together the fragments of Ollie's life that he knew about. Sophie's questions took him as far as he could go, then she turned the conversation toward Ollie's boss, Dr. Narguli. They walked on again, and Steve told her all he knew about Narguli. One thing that Steve said stuck in her mind.

"This is the sixth supervision mission for Two Roads East, each time we have a wrap-up meeting in Thimphu at the end, but never before has Ollie gone back early to prepare for it."

Sophie said, "Other than the obvious, anything different about this meeting?"

"Yeah, a director of the bank is coming."

"Oh!" Sophie said with deliberate surprise, "Do you know any of them?"

"Are you kidding?" Steve said. "I see their photos in the annual report. That's as close as I'd ever get."

As they walked, Sophie heard about the one hundred plus some million dollar loan the SAIB had made to the Bhutan Government to upgrade two roads in the east. Steve told her how the bank monitored the loan through regular supervision missions by Narguli and Ollie, and that he'd prepared the bid for the project nearly four years ago. She also learnt that the bank was one of TRANSARCO's biggest clients. That they did work worth hundreds of millions a year for SAIB all over south Asia, and that the development banks talk to each other. Steve said, "A problem with the South Asia Bank soon becomes a problem with the World Bank, the Asian Development Bank, the InterAmerican Bank and others, and that these clients provided over a billion dollars of TRANSARCO's annual revenue." A few well placed questions revealed that the working relationship between Steve and Narguli was terrible, and that Narguli had made open accusations of fraud. She made a mental note of everything Steve said. Parts of the puzzle were starting to fit together.

They came to a narrow bridge over a rushing stream. Sophie suggested they should walk back. "The sky's very dark, it might rain."

He assured her it wouldn't, but agreed to turn around anyhow.

They hadn't gone fifty yards uphill when Sophie said, "Yesterday, you mentioned you were onto something...You had a lead?"

He told her about Rawlinson, then Martin and Tammy, what Steve had overheard in the spare bedroom when he'd stayed over with them. He laid out his evidence piece by piece and when he'd finished, she said, "That's hardly convincing, there are lots of good reasons...And I guess not so good reasons, that people keep things to themselves. Tammy kept the accounts and Martin didn't tell you, so?"

His shoulders slumped, "So why? If they were honest they wouldn't do that."

"Maybe! What's the payment approval system?" Sophie said like a prosecutor.

"The government covers the cost of all labor and their own engineering staff. The loan pays for the TRANSARCO fees and expenses plus major procurement, which includes the hire of heavy plant and equipment and materials. The major suppliers are all Indian firms, mostly from Calcutta. Rawlinson and Martin check-off the invoices and then send them to Narguli and Ollie for final approval. Once approved, the invoices go to the bank's treasury for payment direct to the suppliers."

"And the two sets of accounts?" Sophie said.

"Well," he began, "TRANSARCO enters up every invoice that we pass on to the bank for approval. Our records show that we've spent around seventy five million. We were okay with that, we reckon there's about twenty five million needed to complete the job. We were hoping to come in under budget. The bank keeps its own account of the draw-downs on the loan.

After they'd processed all the recent invoices, they advised the minister that the loan of one hundred and five million was almost fully drawn. That there was less than ten million left."

She stopped in the middle of the road and turned to him. "Have the accounts been reconciled? Don't you compare them regularly?"

"I did to begin with, but then everything seemed to be okay." He looked blankly at his feet, "The last reconciliation was, ahh, over a year ago."

"Hmm. When's the inquiry going to finish?" Sophie said.

"The minister's lost faith in us, he's brought in an outside expert."

Sophie pumped him for everything he knew about Nigel Smyth-Jones and suggested caution when Steve concluded that he was the least likely person to find anything. "Eccentrics sometimes see things we don't, believe me," she said.

Steve shrugged, "Okay, but he's more than eccentric. He's nuts."

Sophie looked sideways and frowned, "Narguli's an unusual name, where's he come from?"

"I dunno, hell or thereabouts."

Sophie stopped and said, "I meant nationality."

Steve kept walking, he turned, "Sorry, it's just that..."

She caught up to him and said, "I need to know."

"Honestly, I'm not sure where he's from. In all these years he's never said a thing about himself."

Sophie made a mental note to follow this up.

As they reached the outskirts of town a light rain was starting to fall. Soon they were jogging and the rain came down more heavily. They were getting drenched. Without thinking about it, she took Steve's hand and they ran the last hundred yards or so up through the main street of Trongsa. They jumped the half-full gutter and stood under cover at the doorway of the Norbut Hotel. Sophie's face and hair were dripping, they were both panting. He gave her hand a gentle squeeze as he let go of her. She lingered as his fingers slipped from hers. Their eyes met and held each other's briefly.

"Thanks Steve," she joked, "For the walk, the talk and the cold shower."

"Sorry."

"It's okay!" Sophie laughed as she ran up the wooden stairs to her room, "You can order a hot chocolate for me while I change."

46: Dinner with an Oil Baron

Sophie and Steve were alone in the ground floor restaurant, the boy manager served them hot drinks. There was a row of windows in front of them, they sat side by side, their backs to the table and their feet on the windowsill. The view stretched out to the rain soaked roof of the dzong, and into the cloud-filled valley below.

After talking about the weather and how good the hot chocolate was, Sophie said as though it was a natural extension of the conversation, "I don't know what your exact role as project director is, but I can't believe that you wouldn't have picked up on something earlier."

Steve looked straight ahead. Sophie waited then repeated the question.

Their eyes met, he said, "You haven't changed, have you?"

"As I said, I'm just trying to help," Sophie's determination in the matter was obvious, "you know, sometimes an outside opinion..."

Steve interrupted. "Yeah, I know."

She touched his hand and said, "Excuse me Steve if I've got this wrong, but as project director isn't it really your job to know where the money's going, to track the project finances?"

It was not a cross-examination, she'd asked more as a friend, but it cut to a raw nerve anyway. She saw Steve grit his teeth. He said nothing.

She wasn't going to let this go, "How did you let it get so out of hand? Didn't you notice anything on previous trips?"

Her question remained unanswered for an uncomfortably long time. She was just about to say forget it when he looked back to her and barely whispered, "Yeah, it's my fault alright.

It'll be my fault when TRANSARCO's black-listed by the Bank. You know what that means in this industry?"

"Yes, I do, but it's you I'm thinking about, they'll survive, you may not."

"All my stupid bloody fault, but..."

"But what?"

He sighed long and deep. "If only you knew what's been on my mind the last few trips here, you'd understand why things are falling apart. Why I've lost track of the accounts...and just about everything else as well."

This time she reached out and took his hand. She said nothing for awhile, then bit by bit started him talking. It was dark when he finished telling her about the news Miranda had delivered him just over twelve months ago. How he'd been playing her game to keep it from the boys. That the day he returned from this trip, on Friday the tenth, Tristan Troy, the great self-help guru would be taking Miranda away for ten days to a 'Wholeness' retreat.

"What!" Sophie said. "You return and she retreats on the same day?"

"That's her plan."

"And your sons aren't to notice anything?"

Steve just nodded. Sophie tangled her fingers in his.

They were sitting there still hand in hand when Karma and Dechen came in. Karma spoke from the doorway behind them. Their hands parted and she heard Steve say, "Well, well, if it isn't Bhutan's very own oil baron."

Karma's brother roared laughing and clapped his hands. Karma joined in. Sophie waited to be introduced.

The conversation over dinner had Sophie enthralled. The two men opposite her looked and acted so differently, it was hard to believe they were brothers. Karma, she'd already gleaned, was the family comedian. Dechen was gregarious and funny, but he had a serious side as well.

When she'd asked Dechen, early in the night, if he was really in the oil business, he looked seriously back at her and nodded. "Yeah. I bet you didn't know Bhutan was a big oil exporter did you?"

Sophie played along, she said, "Next you'll be telling me you're Bhutan's representative to OPEC?"

Dechen laughed and said he hadn't a clue what OPEC was, but that he'd gladly join if there was an easy ngultrum in it.

Sophie and Karma laughed out loud. Steve chuckled along with them, but it was obvious to all that his heart wasn't in it.

Sophie asked lots more questions. Finally, Dechen agreed to tell her about his business buying and selling lemongrass oil. She heard that Karma and Dechen's family lived in Tangalang, in far-eastern Bhutan. They'd been collecting and distilling lemongrass since the early eighties. Dechen had gotten into the trading side of the business by selling the family's oil, and then realizing it was a far easier way to make money than by collecting and distilling the oil itself. Now he traveled all over eastern Bhutan buying oil for the export markets in Europe and India.

By the time desert was served, the dinner was a three-way affair. Karma and Dechen asked as many questions of Sophie as she did of them. Steve tried unsuccessfully to look interested. When Sophie enticed Karma and Dechen into talking about their family, Steve stood and excused himself. He said he needed some fresh air.

So while Steve walked alone along the main street of Trongsa, Sophie heard that Dechen only had one wife (Tenzin) and two children who lived with the family. The family also comprised Dechen's and Karma's mother (Kunzang), the two men they called father (Tshering and Dawa), and of course Karma, who rarely visited now. Perhaps he was too busy with his three wives, Dechen joked and ruffled his brother's hair.

Sophie hid her surprise well.

Karma chipped in, Tshering and Dawa were brothers and they were both married to Kunzang. She sat speechless as Karma and Dechen joked about which one might be their father. Karma she learned looked more like Tshering, and Dechen like Dawa, but one could never be sure Karma joked, it made life more interesting that way.

By the time that coffee and tea were served, there wasn't much about the family history of Dechen Phuntsho and Karma that Sophie didn't know. She asked Karma if he was jealous that his brother had been given two names and he only one. The brothers looked at each other as though they'd never considered the question before. Then Karma said with a grin that it was a question of balance. He'd been given the good looks so he only needed one name. The monks that had named Dechen had obviously taken pity on him, he needed his two names. Dechen punched Karma's shoulder and they seemed to compete for the loudest laugh.

Steve came back to the table and shortly afterwards Dechen said he'd better be going. He had an early start in the morning; he was traveling right through to Tangalang and it might take fourteen hours he said without a hint of concern.

Karma said he'd take Dechen back to their cousin's place, and that Steve shouldn't wait up, they might talk a bit or play a hand of cards. Then, with a flourish of gallantry, Dechen handed Sophie a small gift wrapped in hand-made paper and shook hands firmly with Steve. The brothers left arm in arm, they were still laughing and joking as they walked onto the street and the heavy front door closed behind them.

"Why'd you leave, Steve?" Sophie said as soon as they were alone. "Karma and his brother are the most fascinating men. Did you know that their mother is married to two brothers. That they don't know which is their..."

"Yeah, I know," Steve interrupted coolly.

"Don't you find that interesting? That's fraternal polyandry. I've read about it, but I never thought I'd meet..."

"Sophie! I don't really care what it's called."

"But, I thought..."

"Look, it works here, but so do lots of things that wouldn't work anywhere else."

Sophie considered a worthwhile reply, but then thought the better of it as she recalled the mood of their conversation just before Karma and Dechen arrived. She reached out and put her hand on his arm. "It's been a long day. Let's get some sleep."

They said goodnight at about ten, just as the lights downstairs began flickering. Shortly thereafter the power failed and they went to their separate rooms by candlelight.

Back in his room, Steve snuffed out the candle with bare fingers and walked to the window overlooking the main street of Trongsa: it was as dark outside as his thoughts were inside. Meeting Dechen did that to him every time — or was it more, that when Dechen and Karma were together it brought back memories that he preferred stayed buried — that unspoken part of his life.

In the gloom of those thoughts, his mind wandered to Sophie and to the warmth of her hand in his when Karma and Dechen had walked in on them. He tried to recapture that moment, but all that would come to him was the reason he'd had to leave her nineteen years ago and how different his life might have been if they'd been able to stay together.

47: Looking over the edge

Steve woke and was surprised to see Karma in the bed just a few feet away. It took some seconds for yesterday's arrangement to re-register. He lay still and wondered what time Karma had come in, he certainly hadn't heard him.

Karma peeped sheepishly from under the blankets, his eyes blood-shot, "Morn'n Mr. Steve." He moaned, "Shhh, I so stupid. We play cards till one." Karma closed his eyes and screwed-up his face in anger at himself, "never again, I lose bad." With that he disappeared under the blankets and began reprimanding himself in Dzongkha.

Steve said, "See you at breakfast."

Karma groaned in response.

Sophie was already in the restaurant, she asked, "Where's Karma?"

"He had a late night. Got himself cleaned up by the Trongsa card sharks. Best not to mention it."

Sophie winked. "Okay."

Toast and an omelet was served with tea and coffee. Karma joined them on cue, and shortly thereafter the conversation turned to the trip ahead. Karma confirmed with nods and grunts that yes, they had about seven hours driving ahead of them, provided of course, that the road was open when they got to the site of the landslide. The shared thought of passing by Ollie's body, alone in the wrecked HiLux a thousand feet below the road, pulled down a pall of gloom. They finished breakfast on that low note and agreed to meet downstairs at leisure. The road was not going to be re-opened until mid-morning, there was no point in leaving too early.

Downstairs, Sophie found Steve paying the hotel bill, she said, "What's my share?"

"Don't worry about it, it's not much."

"Thanks Steve, but I'll pay for myself."

Karma thanked Steve for taking care of his room and food bill (again) and they packed their luggage into the Landcruiser (again). The heavy rain of the previous day had cleared the air, it was a fresh sunny morning. Steve offered Sophie the front seat, she said, "Let's share it, you first."

As they passed by, the vegetable market was alive with the sounds of commerce and chatter; latecomers were still arriving, their vegetables tied to their backs in bundles bigger than themselves. The road from Trongsa down to the Mangde Chhu clings to an unstable hillside for four miles. They crossed the river and after another four miles climbing up the opposite bank, looked across the valley at Trongsa. It seemed to be only a stone's throw away. The road climbed through a series of switchbacks until several miles later, they approached the landslide.

Steve looked up at the mountainside above them, it was heavily forested, but with large outcrops of rock jutting prominently from the otherwise unbroken tree canopy. "This side is all metamorphics," he said, speaking almost to himself, "it's all stable geology."

Sophie quizzed him, "How big an explosion would it take to set off a landslide here?"

"Bigger than what was needed, that's for bloody sure."

Ahead of them was a sharp scar through the forest, the exposed sub-soil of the landslide hung precariously above the road. A road gang of four women bent double as they swept off small rocks and dirt with besoms fashioned from the branches of nearby bushes. A huge rubber-tired Caterpillar tractor was jammed up against the rock-face on the topside of the road.

Steve asked Karma to stop. They got out just below the point at which the HiLux and Ollie would have been swept over the edge. Karma and Sophie stayed beside the Landcruiser. Steve walked up and down the road then got down on hands and knees to look over the cliff. The landslide had ripped out a section of forest about twenty yards wide, below that, the cliff was overhanging. Steve could just make out a white speck of tangled metal amidst a sea of green — the wreckage of what was once a vehicle on the forest floor. More clearly, circling above it, were Himalayan griffon, the scavengers of death in these parts. He dwelt a moment on the thought of Ollie's body down there, alone, then on the job of retrieving it. If the vultures got to Ollie first he knew there'd be nothing but bones to carry out. He shuddered at that thought then eased back from the cliff edge. He stood and turned. The source of the landslide was just under the new road being constructed above.

Steve walked back to the vehicle, his face drawn and angry. He got in without saying a word. They moved off uphill. Karma bowed his head as they drove over the remains of the landslide still on the road. Several minutes went by, no one spoke. The steady hum of the powerful diesel motor was a welcome distraction.

"I just can't believe Ollie's bad luck," Steve said finally. "That landslide was only twenty yards wide. Jalal could have stopped anywhere else on the road, and Ollie would still be alive."

"Steve," Sophie asked from the back seat, "Would they really use explosives on that new road above there, without stopping the traffic down below?"

"Yeah, it could happen."

"So, you could plan a landslide that way?"

"Hmm," Steve shrugged and said, "give me a day to think on that one."

He reached over and tuned in to All India Radio; they listened for a minute or so to a heated discussion about Indian involvement in the war against the Tamil Tigers in northern Sri Lanka. He flicked it off, pushed in a cassette tape then turned up the volume. They drove for nearly an hour with hardly a word exchanged. Near the top of the mountain pass at Pele La, Steve turned to Sophie. "Want to take a short-cut?"

"Depends," Sophie replied tentatively, "after what we've just seen, I'm not interested in taking a back road."

"No, this is by foot."

Karma circled the chorten and stopped the car. "You walk to Nobding, Mr. Steve?"

"If Sophie wants to," Steve said. "It's a beautiful day, why not?"

Steve explained. "There's a trail from here down to Nobding village. Because the road is so winding we can walk it as fast as Karma can drive. It's steep, but downhill all the way."

"Have you done it before, Steve?"

"Almost every time I come through here. Unless it's raining I'd rather walk, it's less than an hour."

They got out at the roadside and Karma drove off downhill. The blue-black smoke of diesel exhaust followed him until he changed into second gear.

Sophie and Steve began down the steep winding trail, she went first. They followed a pebbled streambed through high fir forest, the trail was stony and narrow. Sophie slipped a few times but caught her balance before she fell. Almost as soon as they left the road the silence of the mountain forest descended, it was eerie but at the same time welcoming. Small birds darted here and there, otherwise the only sound was of their careful footsteps. They passed by a far clearing where yaks were grazing on alpine pasture. Closer in, the gnarled branches of rhododendron and daphne stood ready for the harsh winter to come.

Further down, the trail leveled out to run around the side of a small glade. The tree trunks and fallen logs were covered in moss, creepers hung from the branches above, only here and there did a shaft of sunlight cut through the dense canopy to the forest floor.

"Did you bring a camera?" Sophie said.

"Sure, it's in the daypack."

"You're still a keen photographer then?"

"Yeah, when time permits."

"Where are all the photos from your trip through Latin America?"

"In a box at home," Steve replied without thinking.

"What about the photos you took of me?"

Steve stopped. "Why?"

"Well, haven't you shown the photos of your trip to Miranda and your boys?" Sophie asked with her hands on her hips.

"Yeah, of course."

"And the photos of me? What did you do with them?"

"Don't start it again, Sophie. Please."

"I'm not starting anything." Her voice raised a pitch. "Did you throw them away?"

"No, I've still got them. I was just careful not to show those ones."

"Do you ever look at them yourself?"

They faced each other in the middle of the gently sloping trail. He could see that she wanted an answer. If he said 'No' he was trapped. But what if he said 'Yes'? Or should he just tell the truth; I've got a photograph of you on the wall of my office.

Instead of answering, Steve put a finger to his lips to signal quiet. He pointed. There was a deer no more than thirty yards away from them, its head was lifted, antlers high; it sensed danger.

Steve whispered in Sophie's ear. "It's a sambar." She sensed his presence beside her and felt the warmth of his breath. She moved closer to say something but her new running shoes slid on the mossy trail. She slipped, lost her footing altogether and grabbed at a tree branch, it broke off in her hand. Steve caught her by the waist and held her firmly. She regained her footing and the strength of Steve's hands around her waist caught her by surprise. The deer bolted.

They had come down through fir and spruce, and were now entering the upper limits of the broadleafs. Ancient oaks towered above them as they walked. Too soon for Sophie, the steep winding trail finished abruptly and they stood in filtered sunshine on a narrow dirt road.

"Nobding is just a mile down there," Steve gestured to his right.

Sophie turned and walked with the warmth of the sun on her back and glimpses of the valley opening through breaks in the forest, she said, "Pity we didn't get a photograph, I loved that."

Steve laughed and quickly changed the subject. The rest of the way into Nobding they talked about how the trekking group might be going. Sophie smiled as she thought of Farley, how he'd be keeping the Philadelphians entertained with his botanical this and that on everything green they saw.

Then Steve turned the conversation closer to her home, and her heart. He asked if she'd gotten out of Washington much on weekends. Had she been to Shenandoah National Park, the Blue Ridge Parkway?

"Huh! No way!" Sophie laughed. "Being married to Alex put an end to that. His idea of adventure is having coffee at an outdoor café on Pennsylvania Avenue."

Steve didn't react and her mind raced ahead, "Perhaps when you come to Washington, we could go for a drive?"

Steve put his hand gently on her lower back. "There's Nobding, we're almost there."

48: Boys fight, real men duel

The Landcruiser glided into one corner, then the next. They hardly needed the motor. Steve was in the back seat. No one spoke, music played.

On their approach into Wangdi, where the road skirts round the side of a forlorn hillside dropping into an even more forlorn valley, Steve glanced down at the prison and decided not to comment. If Sophie asked 'what's that horrible place down there?' he'd tell her the joke about Hangrila, but otherwise he'd keep his thoughts to himself. When he'd left Trashigang, he'd more or less convinced himself that if anyone from TRANSARCO would end up behind bars, it'd be Martin and Tammy. But Sophie had heard his evidence and dismissed it, now he wasn't so sure anymore. And he had to agree with her, Ollie's death just raised the stakes in the dangerous game he was in. And now on his mind were landslides of the manmade kind.

Lunch took a little longer than usual, so by the time they were on the road out of Wangdi town, it was a quarter of three. Despite a clear run into Thimphu, they pulled into the car park of the Zangbo Guesthouse at five to six. Steve was only half out of his seat when Namgay rushed out the door. His small round face was twitching, his arms were flapping wildly, "Mr. Steve sir, please hurry. Mr. John need speak with you very urgent."

"Oh," Steve sighed, "what now? Is he on the phone?"

"No, you call him," Namgay blustered. "He say strange things are happening."

It was then that Namgay saw Sophie. He seemed to forget the urgency of the moment as he bowed deep and low and said, "Welcome ma'am, as my guest this time."

Namgay bustled around to the back of the reception desk, he picked up the phone and dialed the home of John Rawlinson in Trashigang. The phone rang and rang, it dropped out unanswered after a minute or two.

"Try the office," Steve said. "But first, Namgay, a room for Sophie, please."

Namgay fumbled the telephone and dropped the guest register. "Oh, umm, so much to be done," he mumbled. "We are having two twin rooms on the second floor."

"Good. Give Sophie one, I'll take the other."

Steve suggested Sophie go up to her room while he called Rawlinson. He turned to Karma, "The wrap-up meeting is at half past nine, see you tomorrow at say nine?" Karma nodded and backed his way out. One of Namgay's boys helped Sophie with her luggage, while Steve dialed the Two Roads East project office.

The phone answered. "Rawlinson here."

"Steve here, John."

There was a moment of hesitation, then they both spoke at the same time. "Have you heard about Ollie?"

"Yes," Steve said. "Who told you?"

Rawlinson's voice was so loud Steve hardly needed the receiver, "It's all over Bhutan, where have you been?"

Namgay sat behind his desk and timed the call.

During the whole of twenty two minutes, Steve offered just three utterances. Near the beginning, he said, "Was Martin drunk?" At about the twelve minute mark. "I can't believe that!" And just before he hung up. "Shit No! Not Wednesday."

When Steve finished, he handed the phone back and said, "Not a word of that to anyone, promise me, Namgay."

Namgay nodded as if his neck was a tightly coiled spring, he said, "Yes, sir, I only hear one side anyhow sir."

Steve glanced up at the row of clocks behind reception: Rome, New York and Thimphu all told him it was six forty-five, London had stopped at ten to two. Though there was no clock for Sydney, his mind flicked to home. He did a quick calculation, it was after eleven on the east coast of Australia. "Too late to call now," he cursed. Suddenly, urgently, he wanted to talk to the boys, to hear Ric's voice, to share a joke with Tim.

Namgay stared at him. "Everything okay, sir?"

"Yeah, I'll fax home later."

Namgay blinked and said, "Surely, but not too late, please sir."

The cool emptiness of the reception area was like a wet net over him. He was hungry and needed a shower, but first he had to talk with someone. Thank God Sophie's here he said to himself as he hurried up the stairs.

He knocked on Sophie's door, there was no immediate answer. He knocked again, harder this time.

"Who is it?"

"It's Steve. I've got to talk."

"Right now?"

"Yes. Please."

Sophie inched the door open. "I'm just out of the shower."

"Doesn't matter," Steve said, "this is urgent."

He walked in to the room and sat on one of the single beds. Sophie closed the door behind her with a thud. She was dressed in black jeans and a red t-shirt, but barefoot and her hair was wet. She walked across the room, sat on the other single bed and faced Steve. He was immediately aware that he'd invaded her personal space. The clothes she'd worn that day were strewn on the chair, her bra was on top of the pile.

"Sorry," Steve said, "I didn't mean to barge in, I have to talk."

"What is it? Is something wrong at home?"

"No, I was too late to call home, I'll send a fax later. It's the project, you won't believe it."

Sophie toweled her hair dry while he talked.

"It started Saturday night at the PORC Guesthouse in Trashigang. Nigel held a farewell party for himself and Narguli. He invited Martin and Tammy, and Rawlinson. He spared no expense on food and drink, there was too much of every-thing."

"Ah ha." She leant forward, "So?" Her wet hair fell over her face.

"So that's why I couldn't get anyone by phone from the Eiger, everyone was there." He talked, she listened and brushed her hair.

Rawlinson said the party got underway before seven. At least that's when Narguli knocked the top off his first bottle of Mountain Cloud, a potent local whiskey brewed from God knows what. Narguli was meant to be in charge of the decora-tions, but drinking got in the way and he soon figured that nothing would lift the drab surrounds of the PORC guesthouse, so why try? Nigel took charge of the catering — he ordered in momos of every variety and arranged them on fancy plates.

As Rawlinson tells it, he was the first of the guests to arrive and the first to leave. His gout started playing up after the first drink and he was gone by nine thirty. Tammy was in a 'mood' from the moment she arrived. She refused all strong drink, found the momos too spicy to eat and the music too 'last cen-tury'. Undaunted, Nigel made busy playing host while Martin and Narguli drank enough to make up for the five of them.

Apparently it was just after ten when Tammy said to Mar-tin, 'come on Marty, time to go.' Narguli raised his half-empty bottle and sneered, 'Yeeah, com'on Smarty, Mummy says it's bedtime.' Martin flew into a rage. He swore black and blue, strode across the room and grabbed Narguli by the scruff of the neck. He said, 'What's up with you old man, your pretty little girl's left you has she. Couldn't keep it up to her, hey?'

Martin wanted Narguli to fight him, but Narguli's too clever for that. He said, 'boys fight, real men duel.' He chal-lenged Martin to a duel and Martin accepted without even knowing what he was getting himself into. Tammy and Nigel tried to stop them, but Martin's pride was at stake.

The duel turned out to be a race down the Yonphula airfield, with the first to touch the brakes the loser. Yonphula airfield, the local proving ground, has already claimed two drivers this year and it was ready for a third.

Narguli, suddenly sober, announced the duel this way. 'Pickel, you and I and our HiLuxes will line up at the southern end of the runway. When I blast the horn we'll begin the race towards the sheer cliff at the northern end. Once we've begun, the first to touch the brakes is the loser.' Narguli and Martin sealed the duel with a stiff whiskey each and no amount of abuse from Tammy would stop them. It was ten thirty when they tore off uphill with Narguli in the lead.

Neither of them returned on the Saturday night. Tammy was beside herself. Smyth-Jones had to sit up with her all night. He didn't have a vehicle or a phone. At first light Sunday morning, Smyth-Jones and Tammy walked to Rawlinson's home and organized a search party. They found Martin's HiLux at the end of the runway, the front wheels were hanging over the edge of the cliff. It was only just balanced there and Martin was still behind the wheel, he'd been there all night, too afraid to move in case the HiLux toppled over the edge.

According to Rawlinson, as soon as Martin heard Tammy's voice, he broke down. He started babbling about how hard it had been on her, how he loved her and how if he lived, could she ever forgive him. Tammy was in tears too, she was at the edge of the runway, talking to him through the open window. It was as though Nigel and Rawlinson weren't even there.

Rawlinson and Nigel tied a rope onto Martin's HiLux and pulled it back onto the runway. Tammy wrenched the door open and almost had to lift Martin out, he was so stiff from sitting there all night that he could hardly move. They stood there just hugging and crying.

Then as soon as he could talk, Martin turned to Rawlinson and said, 'I quit right now. We're outta here!' Tammy's smile was a mile wide.

Sophie began to say something, but stopped. She walked slowly to the window and parted the curtains. Behind her she heard Steve say, "To make matters worse, Rawlinson said the minister's postponed the wrap-up meeting until Wednesday morning."

Sophie turned to him, her hands deep in the pockets of her jeans, her shoulders pulled back, "What about Dr. Narguli?" she said.

"Oh, him!" said Steve. "Narguli didn't show his face until Sunday night, then he just strolled into the PORC guesthouse as though nothing had happened. He's denying he was even involved and said if Martin hadn't quit already, he would have had him fired anyway. Smyth-Jones and he left Trashigang this morning. Narguli will get here tomorrow, for the wrap-up meeting on Wednesday."

49: Project Management 101

Sophie was already seated when Steve walked in. As soon as he sat down she said, "The restaurant's called the Royalty Room? What's that all about?"

"It's about the proudest day of Namgay's life."

The tilt of Sophie's head said, come on, tell me.

"The Prince of Wales visited Bhutan recently. He chose the Zangbo for a banquet he hosted for about fifty people. Don't ask Namgay about it unless you've got a spare hour to hear the full story."

Sophie grinned as Bijaya came out from behind the bar and Steve ordered for them both, then she brought things straight back to business, "Smyth-Jones, the British expert? I want to hear more about him?"

"I already told you he's an eccentric."

"Tell me why you think that."

"Well," Steve said. "He's a hell of a nice guy really, but the last person you'd send out to eastern Bhutan to go through three years of project accounts." He told her all he knew and finished, "I can't see how he got the job."

"Who selected him, and how?"

"The minister, I guess," Steve said. "I don't know how he found him. I suppose the bank would have approved him, after all they'd pay his costs."

"Okay, so if the minister wanted to bring someone here who would be guaranteed not to find anything, Nigel Smyth-Jones might be a good choice, huh?"

"Forget it!" he said without hesitation.

"Why?"

"Because the minister is above suspicion, that's why." She noticed Steve's voice raise a level or two, "He's the best client I've ever had, that's why!"

"Okay, okay, just raising possibilities," Sophie said.

Soup was brought to the table, it was milder than Sophie expected and tasted good. Almost before they were finished, Bijaya took the plates away and returned with the main meal. They hardly spoke, Sophie was trying to impose some sense on the news that Steve had delivered less than an hour ago. Had Narguli planned the fight at the party? Was Martin meant to go right over the edge? If Narguli could organize that, could he also organize a landslide to get rid of Ollie?

Bijaya came to the table again and Steve ordered coffee for them both.

Sophie adopted her classic pose, her elbows on the table and fingers clasped with her chin resting on her hands. She closed her eyes, but she could feel Steve watching her. A minute or so passed then Sophie opened her eyes again, "Tell me if I've got this right.

Twenty million dollars goes missing, but you aren't even sure it's missing, maybe there's a simple accounting error in the bank's records for the loan. You have a project manager who has managed his own money brilliantly, but with project money, he doesn't want to know about it. Narguli and Ollie audit the project every six months, and they have to sign off on all major expenditure and contracts. She obeys him as though her life depends on it, he orders her to return to Thimphu early and then she dies in a mysterious accident on the way. We have two mature professional men, one works for the bank, the other with you. They agree on a death-defying car race down an airfield that ends at a sheer cliff. Martin, or more correctly his wife, has been keeping the books for the project, at home. After nearly three years here, they've quit with no notice, now they can't get out of Bhutan quick enough. The minister responsible for organizing a complex audit of the project chooses an international expert on nine hundred a day who is a lovely 'old chap' who doesn't 'trust computers', who, in your words, 'hardly knows what day of the week it is?' And to top it all off, the Police Chief who took your passport talks in riddles and his investigating officer for Ollie's accident, would rather play chess than do his job." Sophie raised her eyebrows, as if to say, is that all?

Steve listened hard. "Right," he said, "and unless there's a miracle, the whole mess will be blamed on me. I'll rot in gaol while TRANSARCO's lawyer, a soft little guy called Laudmeir who's never been out of his legal comfort zone, untangles it all at snail's pace."

Sophie wanted to hug him. She reached across the table and put her hand on his, she felt him trembling. "I'm going to make a call to Washington. I have a contact at work, I think he could help us."

"Us?" Steve said. "But…"

Sophie beat him to it, "I don't want to answer questions, just let me help you."

Steve withdrew his hand and folded his arms. He looked down and spoke as if to himself, "Okay. But I don't know how anyone in Washington could help."

"Well then, call Laudmeir and explain your problem to him." Sophie smiled, "Ask him to hop on the first flight over here."

Steve bit his lip and the faintest of smiles followed, "Ah, why don't you call Washington first."

In his room, Steve kicked off his shoes, lay on his bed and thought about the spreadsheets he hadn't touched since Thursday night. Did he have the energy to start on them again? He was sitting at his laptop when, twenty minutes later, there was a knock at the door. He walked across the room and opened the door. Sophie was there.

She said, "Steve, don't forget to fax home."

"Oh God, I'm so distracted." His hands shot up to cover his face, "Thanks."

Sophie said, "Goodnight again," and turned toward her door just a few feet away.

"Hang on...did you get through to Washington?"

"Yes." She smiled and took two steps to her door. "Steve, your fax."

"Well...can whoever you called help me?"

"Not sure yet, I've set a few things in motion, I'll have to call back tomorrow...I should have an answer then."

Steve sighed. His shoulders slumped and he went back into his room. He sat at the desk and wrote,

Monday night, late.

Dear Miranda, Ric and Tim.

I wanted to call today but got back here too late.

I'm fine, but there are a few problems with the project. It's too complicated to explain by fax, also I don't know the full story yet.

I promise I'll call tomorrow. I'm really missing you all. It's been a long eight weeks.

Love

Steve/Dad.

PS. The minister has postponed the wrap-up meeting till Wednesday. I'll have to change my flights. I'll go to Druk Air in the morning before I call so that I can tell you what's happening.

Steve smiled (a little evilly he would admit) at the thought of Miranda reading the bit about the delayed flight. Miranda did not welcome changes, especially if they were not of her making; she had no time in her life for things going wrong. Steve padded downstairs in bare feet, the lights were out. Namgay was lying on a bench seat in the reception area, he was readjusting his blanket after having attended to Sophie's overseas call.

"Sorry Namgay," Steve said into the darkened room. "Urgent fax to go to Australia."

Namgay sighed desperately from under his blanket and murmured, "Mr. Steve, you send please."

Steve thanked him and crossed to the fax, he dialed in the country code and his home number and put the handwritten fax on the machine. He pressed send and stood there in the dark thinking of home, thinking that he should tell Ric and Tim just what was happening.

Then as he stood listening to the fax go through, he felt a shiver run the length of him — he wasn't sure himself, what was happening.

50: *In quest of a scholar*

Steve and Sophie hadn't finished breakfast when a summons came via Bijaya. A boy downstairs wanted to see Steve, 'right now please, Mister.' He had a message that he would not give to anyone else.

Steve drained his coffee and said, "Be back soon." He walked heavily across the wooden floor.

The messenger-boy was standing off to one side of the reception area. He was immaculately dressed in a dark formal gho, his shoes were polished leather and his hair was carefully combed and parted. Steve guessed his age as early teens and soon discovered that the boy was very well spoken and confident about his errand.

"Are you Mr. Steven Andrews, the Australian engineer?"

"Yes, why?"

"I have a message for you."

"Who is it from?"

"I can't say."

"Oh," Steve said. He was taken aback by the boy's self-assuredness. "Well, what it is?"

"I can't tell you here."

"Then how do I get it?"

The boy lunged his hand into the deep recesses of his gho, searched around for a moment, then brought out a single sheet of unbleached hand-made paper. It was folded in the middle and stuck together with beeswax.

The boy handed the note to Steve. "If you wish to follow me after you've read this, I'll be at the clock tower on Wogzin Lam at nine sharp. I'll leave there at five past nine exactly, whether you are with me or not."

With a polite bow the boy was gone. He ran down through the car park and turned right at Jangchhub Lam.

Steve turned to Namgay at the reception counter. "Who was the boy, Namgay. Do you know him?"

Namgay looked up with a wad of bills in both hands, he replied, "What boy, sir?"

"The boy that gave me the message."

Namgay looked blankly across his desk, "What message?"

It was too early for jokes; Steve held the notepaper up in his hand, "This one."

Namgay looked vacantly at the piece of faded paper in Steve's hand. "Ah! A letter paper, where did you get it?"

"The boy gave it to me."

Namgay said, "What boy, Mr. Steve?" and went back to counting his money.

Steve looked over the reception counter at Namgay's head, it was bobbing to and fro over a stack of ngultrum notes. He decided it wasn't worth the effort and climbed the stairs with the feel of the paper rough in his fingers. He walked over and sat opposite Sophie.

"What's the message say?"

"I haven't opened it."

"Who gave it to you?"

"A boy of perhaps twelve, although he spoke like someone much older."

"Open it, Steve."

Steve took a clean knife from the unoccupied table next to them, he slit the beeswax seal and unfolded the notepaper. He stared at the five-line message, there was one word on each line.

"What's it say?"

He looked up blankly and passed the letter across. Sophie stared at the ancient handwritten script. "What's this? Dzong-kha?"

"I don't know," Steve raised his hands, palms up. "I guess so."

"What did the boy say?"

"He said when I'd read this, if I wanted to follow him he would be at the clock tower at nine. He would wait for five minutes then leave."

Sophie looked at her watch, it was almost eight thirty. "Are you going to meet him?"

"Are you joking? It's Tuesday already, the wrap-up meeting is tomorrow, just one day away. I've got too much to do."

"I know that, but this could be important." Sophie added urgently, "Let's try and get this deciphered. I wonder if Namgay reads Dzongkha?"

Steve rolled his eyes and shrugged, "No harm in asking I guess."

Downstairs, Steve leaned over the front desk and beckoned Namgay. "Do you recognize Dzongkha when it's written?"

Namgay nodded keenly and his glasses slipped down his nose. He prodded them back into place with a jab from his index finger and held out an open hand.

"Can you read this for me please?"

Namgay took the page, readjusted his glasses and squinted. He turned the page upside down and on its side, he took off his glasses, it made no difference. "This is not Dzongkha. It's an ancient Tibetan script. Only a scholar will be able to read this."

"Where will we find such a scholar?" they asked together.

Namgay considered the question carefully. He looked at Steve differently now, he was no longer just an ordinary chilip guest. "Where did you get this, Mr. Steve?"

"The boy?"

"What boy?"

Steve was ready to shout. "Just tell me Namgay, and quick, where will I find a scholar who can read this?"

Namgay's eyes rolled. His head nodded side to side. He turned and pointed obscurely behind him. "Up there, at Tangsangkha Lhakhang."

"Write it down please, Namgay," Sophie said.

Namgay scribbled, Tangsangkha Lhakhang, near Motithang.

"What is it?" Sophie asked.

"It's the ancient monastic school. It's high on the south hill."

"Have you been there yourself?"

"Oh, no Ma'am," Namgay said, his dark eyes wide with the fear of the unknown.

Steve looked at Sophie and shrugged. "I haven't got time to run around getting strange messages deciphered. I've got to get to Druk Air to re-book my flights, then tell Karma the meeting's delayed, and I've got to phone home around midday. I'll have to ignore it."

Sophie said, "No Steve, you can't."

He looked over at her, read the determination on her face, then sighed. "What can we do? I can't pronounce Tangsangkha, let alone find it."

"The messenger-boy! We'll meet him at nine."

Steve carefully folded the note and stuffed it in his shirt pocket. There was no point in arguing.

They sat on the steps at the base of the clock tower at eight fifty-five. An old man lay on the lone park bench, he looked as though he was sleeping off a hangover. A couple strolled by. The woman had a woven basket on her elbow, the man held a live chicken by bound, still-kicking legs. A mangy dog loitered up, scratched, peed then walked on. Steve sat there not daring to think how foolish he would feel if this was a joke. He wondered if Karma could be behind it, then he remembered he'd asked Karma to meet him at the guesthouse at nine. Hell, he thought, this is crazy, but his eyes were scanning every movement for a sign of the boy. "Your good name please, Miss?" a voice asked behind them. Steve and Sophie swung around together. There crouched behind Sophie, almost whispering in her ear was the boy. How did he get there?

"Sophie Vella, and your name?"

The boy didn't answer, "Mr. Steven. You follow me. Alone!"

Steve read Sophie's face and said, "No! Not alone."

The boy hesitated, clearly Sophie had not been expected. He bit his lip and spoke to Steve as an equal. "We are having Miss Sophie with you?"

Steve balked, "Yes."

The boy looked around, he looked back to Steve. "We three go. Quickly."

Sophie looked to Steve, she mouthed the word, "Where?"

Steve said, "First tell us where you are taking us."

"Tangsangkha Lhakhang."

"What?" Steve said. "Spell it."

Sophie reached into Steve's shirt pocket, she unfolded the piece of paper that Namgay had written on and showed it to the boy. "Is it this place?"

"Yes," the boy said uneasily. "Who wrote this?"

"I'll tell you that," Sophie said, "if you tell us who sent you."

"It will all be known." The boy smiled confidently, he was way beyond his years. "You will meet the all knowing."

Steve and Sophie didn't have time to talk, or consider their next move. The boy led them down an alley beside the book-shop.

On Chang Lam the boy doubled back and hurried along a narrow winding alleyway. He led, they followed, down Nor-zin Lam and through the southern traffic circle. They darted through narrow streets hardly stopping to talk. Their direction was westward and uphill, the boy was wasting no time.

Steve glanced over at Sophie a couple of times. She seemed relaxed, it was as though she was exhilarated by the fast walk, the mysterious boy they were following and the unknown of it all. As the town of Thimphu lay beneath them and the open fields started to give way to a forest of pines, the boy slowed his pace a little. He asked if they were okay, was he walking too fast? Steve took the opportunity to ask his name.

"Dendup."

"Dendup," Steve said. "This place we are going, is it far now?"

"Not far now, sir."

"Can you tell us now, who we are going to see?"

"The Compassionate One, sir."

"Umm, why does the Compassionate One want to see me?"

"All will be known soon, sir."

"What should we call 'The Compassionate One' when we meet him, or her?" Sophie asked breathlessly, as she strode to keep up.

"He is the great lama, Desi Gampo. But you should call him 'lopon', revered teacher."

The road passed through pine forest, then open fields. As the temple came into view, Dendup pointed. "There it is, Tangsangkha Lhakhang. It was built over seven hundred years ago." They looked up at the white-washed temple, huge and stark against the blue sky behind.

"I will leave you here," the boy said. "A senior monk will guide you from the top of the steps. Please remember a few rules; remove your shoes when the monk removes his, always move in a clockwise direction and do not speak loudly."

The temple rose fortress-like among a forest of pines. The inward-sloping stone walls housed intricately carved and painted doors and windows. The roofs rose in a series of steps to a central spire rising heavenward, and on the corners were dragon heads to scare away evil spirits. A set of steep stone steps led from the road up to the courtyard wall that surrounded the temple.

Steve and Sophie looked up at the steps and looked back at each other. They turned to thank Dendup, but he was gone. They looked again at the steps, they couldn't see the top or what they might walk into should they climb them.

Steve motioned his head and asked with his eyes. 'Are we going up?' Sophie nodded, her jaw was firmly set and her hair tied back. Turning around was not an option.

They climbed one step at a time, Sophie was right behind him, but Steve checked every few steps to make sure she too hadn't disappeared into thin air. Sophie counted every large step, there were ninety-nine exactly. Near the top they approached a high stone wall around the outer courtyard. A middle-aged monk leant his shaven head over the wall, he was taken by surprise and said, "I see two, not one?" They entered through a narrow gap in the wall onto a large flat courtyard, it encircled the temple — a dry moat, cut stone laid out in an ancient pattern.

The monk welcomed them. *"Kuzo zangpo la."* He looked Sophie up and down several times and scratched his shaven head. He shrugged and with a ceremonial flourish of his maroon robes, led the way across the courtyard. The monastery towered above them as they walked beside a stone wall with no doorways. Prayer wheels were set into the wall, the monk sent each of them spinning as he walked by. They followed to the southwest corner of the building, then walked along the south-facing wall. Ahead an ornamental stairway led towards a huge, richly decorated set of double doors. The monk took them to the top step, turned with a great swish of robes and led the way through the door. The doorframe and the walls either side of the entrance were intricately painted with the *Tashi Tagye*, the eight signs of Himalayan Buddhism: the Golden Wheel and the Lotus Flower were either side of the door. Through it they entered the inner sanctum. Inside was another courtyard, a group of perhaps forty red-robed monks was sitting on the steps along one side. They appeared to be taking a lesson from a senior monk who was striding up and down in front of them.

Their guide pointed to a towering, eleven-headed, many armed statue in the center of the courtyard, *"Chenresig,"* he whispered. Steve and Sophie bent their heads way back to take in the statue towering above them. The monk said, "Chenresig, the Buddha of limitless love and compassion." He began a slow chant. "Om Mani Padme Hung...Om..."

When they'd crossed the courtyard and climbed more steps leading to another pair of doors, the monk stopped his chanting and bowed. He said warmly in perfect English. "The principal deity here is the God of Compassion, you will be very welcome. I will leave you now, please remove your shoes before you enter the doors up ahead." With that he turned and left them dwarfed by the ornate wooden doors ahead.

The scale of the building and the quiet reverence were unnerving. They placed their shoes next to three other pairs that were on the right of the door. Steve pulled the huge brass handle on one of the doors but nothing happened. He pushed and it gave. He pushed a little further and peered around the door, he was beckoned to enter by the smiling face of another monk. Steve reached for Sophie's hand and together they entered a vast altar room. The room was darkened and at one end sat a statue of the sitting Buddha, it was over eight feet tall and gilded in gold. Richly woven tapestries hung on either side. As their eyes adjusted to the light, the intricate paintings and decorations all around them came to life. The smiling monk looked at them as if he was seeing double, he tilted his head to the left, then to the right, he stopped smiling. Something was wrong. Sophie moved closer to Steve, her hand stayed clenched in his.

The monk blinked several times, shook his head and smiled again. "One is now two," he said and beckoned them to sit opposite him in a yoga pose. The monk lifted a brass cup and handed it to Steve, he took it straight to his lips, ready to take a sip. The monk signaled, no! Steve looked in the cup, it contained three dice. He looked back to the monk who gestured that Steve should throw them, not drink them. Steve obliged and the monk studied the result. He nodded and smiled, but there was an aura about him that said the result was not particularly auspicious.

Scooping up the dice in one hand, the monk put them in the cup and passed it to Sophie. He said, "Your good name,

Miss?" She said, "Sophie." He repeated her name a few times, she nodded when his pronunciation was close enough. He gestured, throw the dice. She shook the cup and the dice scattered. The monk followed their progress, he bent way over to see the fall of the final dice. He considered the result, then his face broke into a wide grin, his eyes sparkled and his hands came together at his chest, he bowed.

The smiling monk all but ignored Steve, he said to Sophie. "You are the strength for Kaka Dawa."

Steve and Sophie looked at each other, Kaka Dawa? The monk stood and asked them to follow. The sound of their footsteps in bare feet was barely audible, but it was the only sound. The monk passed through a curtained door on the side of the altar, Steve brushed the curtain aside, Sophie was behind him.

From the darkness he heard, "Steve, thanks for coming."

He swung around. There in the gloom of the poorly lit, smallish room, was a short, round, bald-headed, bespectacled monk dressed in plain red robes. Next to him was a younger, orange-and-yellow robed monk; trim of figure with head freshly shaven.

The young monk extended a hand and said, "Hello Steve." It was unmistakably Ollie's voice, and the facial features were Filipina, not Bhutanese.

51: *The snake charmer and the snake*

Steve took the outstretched, slender hand in his. Everything he knew about reincarnation whizzed and whirred around in his head: it didn't happen so quickly, surely to God? Or Buddha?

Sophie passed through the curtains and stood at Steve's side. There was a moment of silent confusion. The young monk, Ollie, looked at Sophie as though she'd just seen a ghost. Sophie looked back at Ollie the same way.

"Sophie!" Ollie blurted, "What are you doing here?"

Sophie was too stunned to speak. The old monk just swayed on his feet and chanted under his breath.

Seconds ticked by until Steve and Sophie said together, "Ollie! You're alive!"

"It's Kaka Dawa," Ollie said with a manufactured smile. "And yes, I'm very much alive."

Sophie moved to touch Ollie's arm, she said, "Thank God, Ollie, ahh Kaka Dawa. We thought you died in the landslide."

Ollie's face glowed, she took on the mantle of an angel. "Mother Mary, Santo Nino and a few special saints were looking after me." She waited for the impossibility of it to convince. "Let me introduce you to Lama Desi Gampo. Then I'll explain what happened."

Both Steve and Sophie remembered what the boy had told them. They bowed low and said, "Lopon." With the introductions complete, they moved through yet another curtained doorway to a small sitting room.

There were cloth-covered benches around the walls, knee-high tables were pushed up in front of them. Almost as soon as they were seated, tea was served. It was hot, black and salty with a large blob of yak butter floating on the surface. The smiling monk, the one that had guided them to the room, rose and shuffled over to the lopon. He whispered in his ear, it was something about Sophie and her roll of the dice. The lopon adjusted his spectacles lower on his nose and fixed his gaze on Sophie. He grinned and nodded his approval. Sophie, not knowing what else to do under the circumstances, did likewise. The gesture was well met. The smiling monk then whispered something to Kaka Dawa, bowed deeply to the lopon, bowed to Steve and Sophie and took his leave.

The lopon gestured toward the tea and picked up his cup, he slurped at it eagerly. Steve and Sophie followed suit, but sipped, less eagerly. Kaka Dawa left her cup where it was. When they'd finished their tea and the sour taste of yak butter was biting at their throats, the lopon stood. Ollie, then Sophie and Steve did likewise. "I'll leave you now," he grinned, "Kaka Dawa will explain why she asked me to send such a cryptic note to the Zangbo. You showed good spirit to come here."

"Excuse me, lopon," Steve said. "What language was it?"

"Choekey, an ancient Tibetan language. The only place in Thimphu you would get it translated is here."

Steve pondered a moment on the lopon's unusual method of summonsing them, he said, "What did the message say, lopon?"

The lopon laughed as he walked out through the curtained door. "It was a shopping list...just the usual, rice, tea, sugar."

The room took on a different feel after the lopon left, it became just a room: the one small window needed cleaning and there was dust on the floor.

"Have you both recovered?" Ollie said. "Can I start?"

Steve and Sophie nodded, both were to stunned to speak.

Ollie spoke matter-of-factly, almost as though she was reading the evening news on TV. "Last Friday the trip with Jalal was going according to plan. As he had done the previous day he needed to relieve himself every few hours, even so we were making good time. We took tea in Trongsa and he used the facilities. We traveled on, and about an hour later he pulled up on the side of the road and indicated that he needed to relieve himself again. I felt annoyed but nodded my consent, what else could I do? He got out and walked quickly up the new road being built there. I was sitting in the rear left hand seat, I looked out and almost fainted, he had pulled up within inches of the side of a sheer cliff. The vehicle was so close to the edge that when I looked out the window, there was nothing between me and the valley floor way below. I'm not good with heights, so I took my shoulder-bag, gently slid across the seat and got out on the right hand side of the vehicle. There were no other cars in sight. Jalal was nowhere to be seen, so I thought I would walk up the main road a little. I hadn't gone ten yards when I heard an explosion above me.

Steve felt fear rising in his throat, he had no voice to express his thoughts. Sophie put her hands to her face, she said, "Oh my God."

Ollie's bald head nodded several times in rapid succession. "My instincts took over, I ran uphill as fast as I could go. I heard, and felt, the landslide coming down behind me. The sound was terrifying. I screamed and ran. I didn't look back. I ran maybe one hundred yards and saw a dark green Landcruiser coming slowly down the road toward me."

Ollie stood and adjusted her robes, she ran her hand over her shaven head and sat again. "The driver stopped and asked what was wrong. I explained as best I could, I was sobbing and shaking. The car belonged to an Indian businessman, he invited me to get in. The driver then edged down the road until we could see the landslide, the road was clearly impassable, and the HiLux was nowhere to be seen, it had gone over the edge. I was in panic, my luggage was gone, but my life was spared. Loose rock and dirt fell from the landslide above the road, it was impossible to cross safely, even by foot. We knew it would take days to clear. The businessman had no choice but to return to Thimphu, he offered me a ride back here. I accepted and must admit to not even thinking about Jalal, whether he had lived through it or not."

Steve and Sophie sat on the edge of their bench seats, words seemed trivial under the circumstances. Steve eventually voiced the obvious. "Ollie, someone up above is looking out for you." Ollie smiled and nodded tacit agreement, she bent her shaved head solemnly.

Almost simultaneously, Steve and Sophie said, "Ollie, your hair, the robes, the new name, what's happening?"

"All will be known," Kaka Dawa said. "But first let's eat. We start the day here before five. I'm so hungry."

They walked out the way they had come, put on their shoes and followed Ollie across the courtyard. She climbed up a set of stairs and the sounds of conversation filled the air. They entered the student monks' dining room. There were perhaps fifty monks taking their meals at long tables. The chatter and laughter was not unlike a college canteen, except that everyone was dressed in a robe and had a shaven head. No one turned to look at them. They took their meal from a buffet laid out on the head table and blended into the crowd. The food was hot and spicy, and there was plenty of it. Large thermoses of hot sweet tea were on each table, Steve served Sophie and Ollie, then himself. With no audible signal that Steve noticed, the laughter and spirited conversation turned to silence. It was as though a switch had been turned off. The young monks stood and filed out. Within a matter of minutes, the three of them were alone in the room. Instinctively, Steve looked at his watch and it seemed to say, what place does time have here? But if you must know, it's eleven fifty eight. After the monks left, Ollie wasn't in a hurry to move, it was as though she was buying thinking time. They sat for another hour drinking tea and talking, and in all that time Ollie only asked Sophie one direct question. In reply Sophie only offered half the story, she said, "Oh, I thought it would get a bit quiet at the Eiger all by myself. Steve and

Karma had a spare seat so I accepted their offer and here I am in Thimphu."

Sophie noticed Ollie's demeanor change before they had even taken off their shoes and re-entered the room they were in before. Once inside, Ollie asked them to come closer, Sophie sat at Ollie's side, Steve took a seat adjacent to them.

Ollie hugged her elbows, she fought back tears. "Sophie, I'm so pleased that you came also."

Sophie glanced at Steve, she couldn't read the look on his face.

Ollie sobbed. "I've got no one else I can trust."

Sophie put her right hand on Ollie's left arm, she didn't need to speak.

"I don't know where to start," tears rolled down Ollie's cheeks. "You'll think I'm so bad." She reached into the deep recesses of her robe and took out a handkerchief, she wiped her eyes. With no hair, her head was strangely round and small, almost childlike.

"I don't expect your sympathy," she began, "but I do need your help. Dr. Narguli is my supervisor for the Young Professionals Program. Each year the supervisor writes a report. Every YP knows that one bad report is enough to end a career at the bank, it's so competitive." Ollie hesitated, she collected her thoughts. "At the end of my first year, Dr. Narguli said he wanted to discuss my progress over dinner. I agreed of course, then he said, 'tonight, at seven at my apartment'. At first I said no, but then he said all his YPs had their end of year interviews over dinner at his place. He can be very charming, very reassuring, I soon found myself accepting."

Ollie's face was streaked with tears. "Over dinner it soon became obvious what I had to do to get a good report."

Sophie's hands gripped each other as if it was Narguli's neck she was holding.

Ollie bent her head, she stared down at her bare feet, which were just visible under her robes. "You couldn't know what my job means to me. So I went to his bed that night. When he had finished with me, he said he wanted to look at me, he asked me to stand naked at the end of his bed, and..." Ollie buried her face in her hands and sobbed. "And he asked me do things in front of him as he lay against the bed-head, watching me."

Ollie lifted her head on trembling shoulders. Her face was frightened, but her voice was stronger now. "Two days later he invited me to his home again, but I refused. Then he said he had something to show me that might change my mind. He had photographs of me, naked at the end of his bed. He has a hidden camera in his room. He said, 'from now on, I'll have you whenever I want you, or these photographs ruin you. They'll go to your family first'."

Sophie felt a familiar sickening wrench in her stomach — this was too much like work, how many such stories had she heard before?

Steve rose and walked nervously around the small dark room.

Ollie sighed and took a deep breath. "In the first year of Two Roads East, Dr. Narguli asked me to turn a blind eye to an invalid foreign exchange transaction, it added twenty eight thousand dollars on expenditure of a half-million. It was a test he assured me, he wanted to see if you were on top of things, Steve."

Steve and Sophie exchanged quick glances, her heart sank.

Ollie paused then spoke with rising anger. When TRANSARCO didn't pick it up, Dr. Narguli said it proved his point. He said there'd be no money lost. He just wanted to break you, Steve.

"Why?" Sophie and Steve said simultaneously.

"I don't know, but I do know that TRANSARCO was never his first choice for Two Roads East. He has many contacts in the business." Ollie collected her thoughts. "When I said that was wrong, he said 'do you want to see the photos again?' He taunted me about what I'd done." Ollie's shoulders shook, she fell forward and sobbed over her knees. "Only God knows how much I hate that man."

Sophie's mind was spinning. How did Narguli do it? And why? Her heart thudded in her chest, but she noted Ollie's every word, her every gesture. She had to stay removed from any emotional attachment, bitter experience had taught her that much.

Ollie slouched over her knees and held her bare head in her hands, her fingers seemed to be searching for hair that she couldn't believe had gone. "That was the small start and it just went from there. The second time was the same as the first, but much larger." Ollie shuddered, "Dr. Narguli said I didn't need to see the paperwork, he said he'd send the photographs if I asked too many questions. In some ways it was easier for me not to be involved in the detail, I felt removed from it, as though by just signing papers, I couldn't be doing anything too wrong. Once that started, then it became regular. Dr. Narguli would ask me to sign, he wouldn't tell me how much money was involved. He said minor amounts. He said he'd stop the game when TRANSARCO started doing the job properly, that others were in on it too, there were some senior people that wanted TRANSARCO out of Bhutan. If I challenged him, he became angry, then he'd threaten me; he reminded me that he had the evidence to destroy my career, my life."

Without looking up Ollie said, "So you see, there's not really any money missing." The reason the two sets of books won't reconcile is that the dollar amounts that have gone through the bank's payment system are different to the one's TRANSARCO's recorded. That difference is sitting in the bank's Foreign Exchange Hedge Fund."

Steve held his head in his hands. "I just don't understand."

Ollie glanced up at him, then lowered her head again. "It's so simple really. Take that first example I gave you. TRANSARCO recorded it as a five hundred thousand dollar transaction and passed it to Narguli for approval. He waits a little while to enter it, and then alters the exchange rate for the transaction so that it records as five hundred and twenty eight thousand dollars against the loan, the twenty eight thousand automatically goes to the bank's Hedge Fund. You would have never picked it up, and as for Nigel Smyth-Jones, he's still trying to work out how the foreign exchange system works, he hardly knows the difference between Pounds Sterling and Indian Rupees.

Ollie lifted her head. Sophie looked at Steve with raised eyebrows. He shook his head, closed his eyes and turned away from her.

On hearing her own words, at knowing now that others knew, Ollie wept openly and her shoulders shook. She spoke between sobs. "I've been a slave to Dr. Narguli for the last three years. He's taken advantage of me in ways you could hardly imagine." She looked over at Steve. "I don't know why he wants TRANSARCO out of here, or what's in it for him. How can I trust him? How can anyone trust him?" She didn't wait for an answer.

Ollie brushed tears from her eyes with an angry sweep of her fingers, she took a deep breath and took control. "Until that meeting in Trashi Yangtse, where Dr. Narguli was challenged by Dasho Leki, I thought Narguli had power over everyone. The Dasho showed me I was wrong. That was the day I changed. I felt so angry at that meeting, then in the Landcruiser on our return, I decided to take my life back into my own hands."

Steve said, "I remember that..." But his voice was barely audible, Ollie's sobbing cut him short.

"When we got back to Trashigang that day, Dr. Narguli and I had a terrible argument. We were in his room at the PORC Guesthouse. I said to him, the Dasho showed you up for who you really are, what you stand for. Dr. Narguli sneered at me. 'That fool, I'll have him removed. He'll be crushing stones by the roadside next time I come here'. Then I lost my temper, I was so angry I slapped his face."

Ollie glanced up at Steve, her cheeks streamed with tears, her whole body was shaking. Sophie put her arm around Ollie's shoulders. Ollie chewed her fingernails. "It just gets worse." Sophie pulled her closer and held her like a sister. "After I hit him," Ollie said. "He stormed out. I locked myself in his room. Later, as I looked around, I decided how I'd get my own life back. I searched through his things and I found a concealed compartment in the lid of his suitcase. It took a nail file to open it, there was a black plastic file inside. The photos I wanted were in there, but so were other things, things I never thought I'd see. I emptied the file and put it back where I found it. As I was screwing the false lid back in its place, I heard him coming down the hallway. I hid the contents of the file under my shirt. He tried the door and called out for me to open it. I closed his suitcase and turned to face the door — he barged into the room, the chain-lock gave way. Strangely, he wasn't all that angry. He said he was sending me back to Thimphu early, that he'd arranged with a driver to take me. I broke down and ran to my room, I hid his things — then we went to the meeting at the Trashigang Dzong, you know what happened from there." Ollie looked straight at Steve, it was a look that demanded a response.

"I wondered about that," Steve said.

"That's why I asked you to travel with me, Steve. I was scared, really scared."

Ollie stopped, straightened her back and looked right past Steve. "That landslide was no accident. Dr. Narguli paid Jalal to kill me."

At the saying of it, Ollie slumped over her knees and covered her head with her robes. Her sobbing was the only sound in the room. Steve was on his feet in an instant, he pushed clenched fists into his pockets and walked in tight circles. Sophie stayed seated, sharing her strength and comforting someone she hardly knew. The sound of tears died away slowly. Ollie lifted her head and said with rising spirit. "I've long known it. Dr. Narguli is both the snake charmer, and the snake." She sat upright, her face was stronger, her voice firm. "Until the snake is captured, I'm Kaka Dawa. The shaved head, the robes, my refuge here, it's my only hope."

52: The dice were right

There was so much to absorb. Sophie had a thousand questions on her mind and her bare feet on a cold stone floor. She held Ollie's shaking shoulders and felt the ancient silence of the monastery swallow her. The only sound was of Steve speaking softly to himself. A butter lamp in the corner of the room burned out, it flickered as it died, and the darkness that followed enclosed them.

Steve went to the one window in the room and pulled back the dusty yellowed curtains. Sophie wanted sunshine, but there was a bare stone wall just outside — the little natural light that found its way into the room was scarcely enough. Steve said with his back to them. "We've got to get help. I'll talk to the minister. He'll get the police involved."

"*No!*" Ollie said. Her face was resolute, she pushed Sophie away and walked to the center of the room. "*No.* No minister. No police."

Steve backed away from the window. "Why?"

Ollie's voice was strong now. "Steve, I can't believe that you haven't seen it. Do you think Dr. Narguli could do all this alone?" Ollie let her question sit unanswered.

The stunned look on Steve's face said that Ollie was right, he hadn't suspected a thing.

Sophie stood and took a few paces backwards, she watched both of them, every movement and every gesture. Steve slumped onto the nearest bench seat, put his elbows on his knees and held his head in his hands. He said, "I can't believe this."

Ollie was by his side, her hand on his shoulder. "You're just too honest, Steve. Too honest to see the obvious. Bhutan has taken you in with its Buddhism and its beauty. It's easy to think otherwise, but corruption is here, the same as every-where."

Ollie kept her hand on his shoulder and moved around to sit next to him. Ever so slowly she brought her hand down to his knee.

Sophie stood to one side, almost hidden in the gloom. Steve didn't move for minutes, finally he looked up and without turning, said, "Why did you ask me to come here?"

Ollie's reply was immediate. "I told you. I need your help. I need you to take something to the project wrap-up meeting tomorrow." Ollie took her right hand off Steve's knee and thrust it deep inside her robes. She brought out a sealed, manila envelope about eight inches by six: SOUTH ASIA INFRA-STRUCTURE BANK was printed in the top right hand corner. She held it in two hands in front of her. Sophie watched them both closely from across the room.

Ollie said, "In here are the photographs Dr. Narguli took of me." She turned her face to Steve, there was pleading in her eyes. "I want you to promise me that you won't look at them."

He said, "Of course not."

Ollie almost smiled, "I know you wouldn't." She sat so still it was hard to pick up her breathing. "I haven't told you what else I found in Narguli's suitcase, what's made me more determined than ever to get even with him."

Steve pulled away, clearly not ready for anything more.

Ollie lowered her voice, she held the envelope in two hands. "There are other photos in here also. When I saw them I wanted to kill him, but that would be too kind. Anika is Narguli's new secretary, she's just twenty, with five months in the job. Devi is personal assistant to one of the directors, she's been with the bank for years. He's photographed both of them the same way."

Steve grimaced. He glanced up at Sophie who was almost lost in the murk of the room. Her face gave nothing away.

Ollie said, "Sophie. Steve. It's a cultural thing. I know nudity is not a big deal in America, nor I guess in Australia. But for me, for Anika and especially for Devi, we'd rather die than know that our families had seen photographs like these. Believe me, what Narguli has done to all of us, has robbed our souls."

Steve said, almost inaudibly, "The snake and the snake charmer".

Ollie held the envelope at arm's length, "That's why you must take it. Please Steve. Take it to the meeting."

Steve groaned from way down deep. He shook his head and looked at the brown paper envelope that Ollie held in front of him. "Does Narguli know you've got this?"

"I don't know. I don't know if he planned to kill me anyhow, or if he found that I'd taken the photos, then decided I had to die."

Steve stared back at her, his eyes pierced the small distance between them. Sophie was stunned by how calm Ollie was. She watched as Steve put an unsteady hand on the envelope and said so quietly she could hardly hear him. "Who do you want me to give this to?"

The determination on Ollie's face was beyond challenge, even beyond questioning, "I'm not sure which director will come to the meeting tomorrow. It could be James, he's head of Audit. But it could just as easily be Schmidt or Lee. It's unlikely to be Fujiieda, she's just returned from a stint in hospital. Whoever it is, I want you to give them this and I want it opened in the meeting. You can tell me later about the look on Narguli's face."

She pushed the envelope into Steve's hands and said, "Dr. Narguli has to pay for what he's done. He'll be back in Thimphu by now, that's why I'm staying here until I hear that the snake is behind bars."

Steve took a deep breath then exhaled in a long sigh. His eyes met Sophie's across the room and she signaled that it was time to go.

Ollie added urgently, "I hope it is James that comes tomorrow. Devi is his PA. He might strangle Narguli on the spot. He's strong enough to do it."

Sophie knew that Ollie's wish would be granted, last night Alex had said on the phone that M.J. was already on his way to the meeting. The barest smile crossed her face at the thought of it; the fabled Dr. Narguli was to meet his match.

Steve and Ollie both stood. She turned and hugged him, her head resting on his chest. She looked into his eyes. "Tomorrow, deliver the envelope and we'll both be free of Narguli. Don't let me down. Please." Steve said nothing, but Ollie seemed to sense victory. She let go of him and smiled.

Ollie hugged Sophie warmly and said through tears, "The dice were right."

They counted ninety-nine steps down and turned right towards Thimphu. Dominant in the valley below them, the dzong shimmered in the late afternoon light.

There was a minute or so of stunned silence, then Steve said, "I can hardly believe it." He looked at the envelope in his hand, it was the only proof he had that he hadn't been dreaming.

Sophie didn't respond.

Steve spoke his thoughts aloud. "I knew Narguli was a bad ass, but I didn't think he was a killer. And the minister's in with him? What could be in it for them both — to get rid of TRANSARCO and me that way?"

"It may not be all that it seems, Steve. Remember what you told me about Bhutan."

He glanced sideways at her. A part of him felt relief; he'd found the answer that would return his passport, that would keep him out of Hangrila. Another part of him still had some niggling questions unresolved. Ollie's explanation accounted for the differing amounts of money that went through the two sets of books, but it didn't account for the different number of invoices that had gone through?

On the way downhill, Steve quizzed Sophie about the possible legal avenues open for Ollie. Should he, or shouldn't he, look in the envelope?

Sophie answered some of his questions but said a lot of things didn't add up, that what she needed first was a chance to call Washington again.

53: Work, life and no balance

They were almost back into Thimphu, Sophie said, "When are you going to phone home? It's already a quarter of four."

Steve added four and a half hours. "*Damn*! There's no point in calling until I know about my return flight, that's all that Miranda will ask about. But if I don't call soon, I'll miss the boys." Steve frowned. "I'll have to go straight to Druk Air."

A low sinking, sick feeling told him how much he needed to call home — to touch base with reality, to ask Ric about the surf and the fishing and to see how Tim was going.

Just on three fifty p.m. they stood awkwardly at the intersection of Doendrup Lam and Jangchhub Lam. Steve looked at the envelope in his hand and thought of what was in it, and what he'd promised to do with it. Sophie said, "Do you want me to take that back to the Zangbo for you? It's not something that you would want to carry around, especially if Dr. Narguli is back in town now."

He tried to see the lighter side of things and grinned half-heartedly as he handed the envelope to Sophie. She put it in her shoulder bag, turned and said, "See you back at the Zangbo." She smiled and walked off toward the main town. He watched her go and wished he'd kissed her, then he turned and strode purposefully down Doendrup Lam.

At the Druk Air office, the big glass doors banged shut. Steve looked mournfully at the smartly uniformed woman on the other side of the glass.

"Please let me in," his mouth was almost on the glass.

"We're closed sir, come back tomorrow. Wednesday we open at eight." She pointed to the sign which said, HOURS of OFFICE 8 a.m. UNTIL 4 p.m.

Steve clung to the door, his fingers gripped the glass. "Please. You wouldn't believe the day I've had."

The Druk Air woman was unmoved, she'd seen this sort of funny behavior from chilips before. The office supervisor walked over and joined her. Together they gazed through the glass at Steve.

He spelt out the words. "It is urgent."

The supervisor opened the sliding doors a little. "It's okay, sir. We can help you in the morning."

Steve pleaded with the middle-aged woman as if his life depended on her. "PLEEEZ."

"Why didn't you come earlier if it's so urgent?"

He ignored her. "It's a matter of life and death."

The two women went into a huddle. The supervisor checked her watch, she looked back to Steve and sighed. "Come in and sit down." She turned and said, "Kesang you go home, I'll do the needful."

Over ninety minutes later she let Steve out the door with new tickets in hand. He bowed, he said "Kadinchhey" three times and turned on his heel toward the Zangbo.

Back at the Zangbo, Sophie gave the operator Alex's phone number. The operator, who hadn't made so many international connections in a year as she'd made in the last few weeks, said, "same number again, Ma'am? I am now remembering code for Washington, DC. Ma'am, what's DC mean?"

Sophie explained about District Columbia then as she waited for the connection, her mind replayed her call to Alex yesterday. He was in the regular Monday morning meeting of the Latin America and Caribbean branch, the meeting was being run by Stella Borg filling in for Sophie. And there was a hot issue on the agenda. A problem had blown up, a problem Sophie would have foreseen — had she been there.

Sophie thought Alex sounded a bit gruff when he took her call, but when she reeled off her story and then asked him to track down Michael James and make a number of security searches, he came around without hesitation. She finished yesterday's call by asking casually, how's Stella doing? He said he had to answer honestly, it wasn't looking good. A problem's come up in the Venezuela program, he said he might have to send Stella down there to sort it out and offered to fill in the detail. Now, on reflection, she probably sounded too casual when she'd replied, 'Later, tell me later. Call you again tomorrow, hey, and please call Marie for me and get her cell phone number, tell her I'll be in touch soon, not quite sure when. Bye. Love you.'

The operator cut in, "Miss Sophie, DC on the line."

Sophie said thanks and smiled as she took the call, "Alex? Hi, you won't believe the day I've had."

"Yeah, tell me."

"I will, but first, did you call Marie?"

"Yes, she asked for money, then she asked if you were back in phone contact, she wants to hear from you on 61 404 297 631. Sounds like she's having a ball."

"Oh, okay, good," Sophie said, "please call her again and let her know that everything is okay, but that I can't call her just yet…don't tell her why, just say there's a few unexpected things come up," then Sophie took fifteen minutes to skim over the day's events.

Alex responded, "Is that a fairy tale, or a nightmare?"

Sophie said, "I'm not sure myself yet," and laughed.

"Don't take things too lightly, Sophie." Alex said, "Just because you're in Magicland, it doesn't mean things can't go haywire."

"Don't worry, I'm not." She said, "Anyway, tell me what MJ found out."

Alex relayed the information that she needed from Michael James and added, "MJ sends his regards and said that the security searches were ongoing, that Rawlinson was a puzzle and that Narguli was a wildcard."

Sophie thanked him and there was an awkward silence. She knew he was waiting for her to ask about her own work, about what had happened in Venezuela, whether or not the problem could wait for her return. She let the pause run too long and said, "I'd better get going, I'll try to call again tomorrow."

"Yes, please do," he said. "And Sophie, from what you've told me, you shouldn't be alone tonight."

She replied, "Alex, I know that, but there's only one person I can be with, and that's Steve."

"Oh! And have you told him about Marie yet? How'd he take it?"

"No, not yet," Sophie swallowed hard, "Umm, I wanted to get to know him a bit better first."

"You're taking your time," Alex said. "I thought that's why you..."

"You wouldn't understand, it's been difficult," Sophie cut in. "I'm going to tell him tonight."

Alex hesitated, then said, "Okay, good luck...and please Sophie, for your own good, share with Steve. Umm, are there twin beds in the rooms?"

"Alex!" She laughed and said, "Of course!" But at the saying of it, something deep inside told her that the final letting go had begun.

Sophie put the receiver down and immediately called the operator back, she gave her another number to call, a number in the region this time.

Steve rushed into the familiar chaos of the Zangbo's reception area and glanced up at the row of clocks: Rome had joined London, it was stopped, but New York and Thimphu both told him it was past six.

Namgay spotted him and waved a letter in the air. "Fax for you, Mr. Steve."

He took it, "Thanks," and walked to the stairs.

Namgay called after him. "Karma came this morning."

Steve stopped in his tracks. "Ohh no! I didn't even think of Karma, what did you tell him?"

"I tell him much trouble come after you. That Mr. Steve stay one more day for meeting."

"Thanks Namgay, you wouldn't believe the day I've had."

Steve opened his door and stooped to pick up a folded note that had been slipped under it. He closed the door, took two long strides to the single bed, and sat heavily. He flicked open the folded piece of paper. It read in handwriting he now recognized,

Steve,
I contacted my office.
I have to speak to you urgently.
I'm in my room.
Sophie

He groaned. "What now?" He put the unread fax down on the desk, went to the bathroom and washed his face. He glanced at the mirror, chose to ignore what he saw looking at him and went back into the room. He sat at the desk, picked up the fax and read.

Tuesday 7th
Steve, I waited until 10pm for your call. The boys have gone to bed, you must be very busy if you can't find ten minutes in the day to phone them.

Anyway, they were glad to get your fax yesterday and to hear that you are well. I hope the problems with your project aren't too serious.

*I'm **very very** unhappy to hear your flights may change. You know that Tristan and I are going to the Wholeness*

*Retreat at Noosa. We planned to leave soon after you got back
here. I don't want to disappoint him.*

*If your flight change means you won't be back by Friday,
I EXPECT you to miss the meeting — it couldn't be that
important.*

Let me know by return fax what you're doing.

Yours pissed-off,

Miranda

Steve glanced at his travel clock, it was approaching eleven
back home, too late to call. He'd missed the boys again. He fell
back on the bed and stared at the ceiling, he was beyond knowing and beyond caring. He had his ticket out, tomorrow he'd
get his passport back and tomorrow night he would go to Paro,
Thursday he would fly to Kathmandu then Delhi. He wouldn't
be home until Sunday morning, it was the best he could do. As
for Miranda's suggestion that he just miss the wrap-up meeting, SHIT, he thought, that shows just how much she understands my business.

He put Miranda out of his mind and picked up Sophie's
cryptic note again. What could she want that was so urgent?
He rolled off the bed, went out his door, walked two yards
down the corridor and knocked on her door.

"Who is it?"

"It's me, Steve."

"Wait a moment."

The door edged open, Sophie peered around. "Thank God
you're here, come in quickly."

Steve slipped in the door. Sophie closed it, then bolted it. He
walked over and sat on one of the beds and looked around the
now familiar room, something was unfamiliar — what was it?
The single beds, the desk and chair and no other furniture, that
was the same. A single light globe still hung from the center of
the room. There was the desk lamp and the candle in its brass
holder. The single cupboard behind the entrance door was still
there, then he noticed it, all Sophie's things were packed and

standing ready to go. Steve's eyes came back to Sophie, she was pacing the floor with Ollie's envelope in her hand.

"Steve, I opened the envelope."

"What? I promised not to look at it."

Sophie stood over him where he sat, she smiled and shook her head, "Do you think I'd let you hand that over without knowing what's in it? And anyway, I didn't promise anything."

Steve stared up at her. "What's in it?"

"Just what Ollie said would be there, photos!"

"Ahh…What sort of photos?"

Sophie moved to the other single bed and sat opposite him. "Photos taken with a fixed camera. The background in each of them is identical. They are taken in a bedroom, over a bed. Ollie's there, and I know now why she didn't want you to look. There's another younger girl, she's perhaps twenty, she looks very uncomfortable with what she's doing. The other girl is perhaps thirty, she's not completely naked. They both look south Asian."

Their eyes met across the small distance between them. Sophie's face was deadly serious. "I knew that landslide was no accident."

The color drained from Steve's face.

Sophie got up and walked to the desk, she sat on it and kicked her heels against each other.

"Steve, I made my call to Washington, then I phoned the South Asia Bank."

"What!" He looked up. "Who'd you call there?"

She ignored him and said, "First the good news, you'll get your passport back tomorrow. They know now that you're not guilty."

"Thank god," Steve said. "So…They know it's Narguli, huh?"

"I don't know that for sure, but I do know that until we know what's going on here, neither of us should be alone. So tonight I'm moving into your room. Tomorrow I'll come to the wrap-up meeting with you. Then, at midday, my trekking group will be back in Thimphu, I'll be okay with them until we all leave on Saturday."

Steve shook his head as though he hadn't heard correctly. "Are you saying our lives are at risk?"

"I'm saying we don't know what's happening, or where Narguli is. I've been told not to risk it."

Steve slumped back on the bed and looked across at Sophie sitting on the desk, she looked great, in command. He felt like a bystander, an extra in a movie she was directing.

She slid off the desk and picked up her shoulder bag, unzipped it and replaced the envelope then turned to him. "I've advised the bank that Ollie's alive."

His mouth dropped open. "What?"

"I've told the bank she's at the monastery."

"Why the hell?"

"It's for her own safety." Sophie stood firm. Her look of total control, her confidence in the matter, left no question about it.

Steve said, "You sure?"

She answered with a slow determined nod. He knew not to take it any further.

"Hey! What level do you work at?" Steve rolled from the bed, "You haven't told me the full story, have you?"

"That's unimportant now. I'm high enough to get help when it's needed. Let's leave it there."

54: Yours desperately

Sophie shut the door to Steve's room behind her and it suddenly felt too small for both of them.

"Which bed are you sleeping in?" she said.

He pointed to the bed against the wall, "That one."

Sophie sat on the edge of her bed, eased off her shoes and swung her feet up, she arranged the pillow against the bedhead and rested back on it. She watched Steve watching her and was suddenly aware of her linen blouse — now, in Steve's room, open one button more than it needed to be. She thought about the last time that they'd shared a room this way, but nineteen years was a long time; too long.

"How did you go at Druk Air?" Sophie asked cautiously as their eyes met across the room. "Did you get another flight?"

He moved over to sit on the edge of his bed, "Yeah, but I've got to go through Kathmandu, then New Delhi."

"When does it leave?"

"Thursday, very early."

"Is it a good connection?"

"It's not as good as direct to Bangkok, I won't get home until Sunday morning."

"Is that a problem?"

A smile of sorts crossed his lips, but she could tell that it didn't mean he was happy. He explained about the fax from Miranda, stood and walked over to the desk and unfolded the single page. "Listen to this," he read aloud, "You know that Tristan and I are going to the Wholeness Retreat at Noosa. We want to leave soon after you get back here and I don't want to disappoint him. If your flight change means you won't be back by Friday, then I expect you to miss the meeting, it couldn't be that important. She signed it, Yours pissed off."

He folded the fax, "You see what I mean?"

Sophie searched for some understanding words; they talked a bit about Ric and Tim. He told Sophie he'd decided to tell the boys what was happening, whether Miranda wanted him to or not. Sophie was about to say, 'kids need to be told the truth, you're doing the right thing, Steve,' but something stopped her, she smiled meekly and nodded.

They looked at each other, Sophie didn't know what to say or do next.

"I guess I'd better answer this," Steve said as he snatched up Miranda's fax again.

"What are you going to say?"

"I don't know. Something will come to me."

Steve pulled out the heavy wooden chair and sat at the desk, his back to Sophie. She watched him write and as she did she thought about her own plans. She had just twenty-four hours left to tell him about Marie. She promised herself that she'd do it at the next opening, as soon as the time was right. Steve sat back and read a few lines to himself, he sighed and put the paper down on the desk.

"Do you want me to read it?" Sophie asked without thinking, and only half-seriously.

Steve didn't turn to look at her, he picked up the page again and held onto it as though it was a key to his heart and his mind. Sophie was ready to say sorry when he turned on his chair. "Sure. Why not?"

He leant over and stretched out his hand. She took the letter and eased back against the bed head. She read.

Tuesday Night,

Dear Miranda,

I'm sorry I didn't call. You wouldn't believe what happened to me today, is still happening. I got called away before nine this morning to an emergency, I didn't get back until after eleven your time. I'll explain to Ric and Tim when I get home.

I did my best with Druk Air, the only flight available is via Kathmandu and Delhi. I won't be home until Sunday morning. There's nothing I can do about it, and there's no way I can miss the wrap-up meeting. It's what I'm here for. It is important. It might even be more important than your Wholeness Retreat — just help me out on this one will you please. I'll pay Tristan for the lost night at the Retreat if you can't cancel it.

Yours desperately,

Steve

After she'd read the letter a couple of times, Sophie looked at him over the top of the page that she was still holding in two hands in front of her. "Yours desperately?" she said frowning.

"Well!" he said and shrugged.

Sophie looked at the letter again. She spoke from behind the page, "I'd remove the last two sentences and just sign off, Steve."

He looked up at her. "I'll do it. But only if I can add, PS: Sophie sends her love."

"*Steve!*" She threw the letter back at him.

The Royalty Room was unusually busy, and noisy, every table was taken. Over dinner, Steve's conversation seemed to purposely veer away from the events of the day. He talked about home, the boys, their dog, Byron Bay, the view that he'd miss when the divorce came through and the boys again. She encouraged him, it filled the void and bought her space. Several times she had the perfect opportunity to begin the lines that she'd rehearsed so many times, but now that they were to share a room for the night, she'd convinced herself it would be fairer on them both if she left it till later, until they were alone.

At a few minutes past eight, the lights flickered, they went out, then came back on again, then the entire town was plunged into darkness. Bijaya said it was a regular enough event and soon had candles alight on every table. Steve and Sophie continued talking, the candle flickering between them. By eight thirty they had eaten well and talked themselves out on all the safe topics. Sophie beat him to sign the chit and they walked back to Steve's room together, she carried the candle, which Steve promised to return to Bijaya in the morning.

As Steve opened the door he said only half seriously, "Not a word of this to Karma, please."

Sophie smiled and said as she followed him inside, "Of course not, Mr. Steve."

Once inside, Sophie settled the candle from the restaurant on the table that sat between the two beds. Steve lit the candle on the desk and the light cast warmly around the room, reflecting on the polished timber floors and walls. Without speaking, Sophie kicked off her shoes, curled herself up on her bed, picked up her novel and opened it to where she'd got to before. She went through the motions of reading, holding her book open so as to catch a flicker of light. Steve sat on his bed and looked at her in the glow of the candle, she was leaning on her left elbow with her chin in her hand.

"Do you read a lot?" Steve asked.

"Yeah, when there's nothing else to do."

Steve unlaced his boots and put them aside. He lay back on his bed with his hands behind his head and stared at the ceiling, candlelight flickered soft and yellow. It was so quiet he could hear his heart beating.

Sophie read the words that she could hardly see on the page in front of her with one eye and the other on Steve watching the ceiling. The silence wasn't uncomfortable, but the small distance between them was: it wasn't enough for two people forced for their own safety to spend the night together, but it was too much for two people who'd been so close.

Finally Steve spoke into the semi-darkness above him. "It feels strange doesn't it, after all that time here we are so close, yet we're really no closer than when we left each other all those years ago."

Sophie slowly closed her book and put it on the bedside table. She sat up on the bed, drew her knees up to her breasts and wrapped her arms around her legs. She didn't respond.

He continued, "I've often thought about that day. It seems hard to believe it was nineteen years ago, you went north to the welcome and love of your family, I went south to the loneliest place on earth."

Sophie put her chin on her knees, she stared at her bare feet and whispered. "You chose it, Steve."

"No," he sighed. "It was chosen for me. You'll never know how much it hurt to have to leave you. It was the hardest day of my life."

"You didn't show it."

"If I could only tell you why I had to leave you that day, you'd understand."

"I pleaded with you then to tell me what had changed," Sophie said on the edge of tears, "would it be so hard to tell me now?"

Even though Sophie wasn't looking at him, she could feel him tense up. The warmth in the room seemed to die and the distance between them was more like three miles, than three feet. He choked as he said into the muted darkness. "I've never told a living soul, not even Miranda."

Sophie hugged her knees and dared not look over at him: whatever had changed that day in San Jose, haunted her then, it had haunted her on and off over nineteen years, and it haunted her now. They'd agreed to go back to California. He'd get a job, she'd finish at Law School, they'd see where their lives and love took them from there. But when he got back from buying the bus tickets, he was a different person. He announced coolly that he was going to Bolivia and handed her a single ticket to Los Angeles. She'd pleaded with him all night to tell her why he'd changed his mind, but as the sun rose on Cahuita that final day, they hadn't slept and he hadn't told her why he was going to walk out of her life, with no promise to come back.

He said quietly. "Sophie."

"Yes," she said without looking up.

"I'm sorry. Sorry for everything. If I'd told you nineteen years ago what I'm going to tell you now, things would have been so different."

Sophie didn't reply, she stayed hunched over her knees and held them tight. Steve lay on his back, his hands still behind his head. The candlelight between them flickered and shadows moved.

"When I left Cahuita to go into San Jose that day, I couldn't have been happier. We were so much in love and for the first time in my life I had a real plan, a purpose for what I was going to do. When I got into town, I thought I'd call in to the American Express office to check our mail, even though we'd been there only a week or so beforehand. There were no letters for us, but the lady there handed me a telegram, it was stamped URGENT. There was a one-line message. STEVE, CALL HOME, REVERSE CHARGES, SOONEST. RON. My blood ran cold. Firstly, what had happened? Secondly, why would my Dad, sign off 'Ron?' I went into the small phone booth in the office and dialed Australia."

Steve's voice started to break up, he reached for the glass of water beside him and drank slowly. "My brother, Bill, answered the phone. He didn't ask how I was, even though we hadn't spoken for well over a year, he just said, 'Hold on a minute.' Then he put Dad on, and he just said 'Ron here' in a voice so distant that I might have been a debt collector. I said, 'Hi Dad, I got your message, everything okay?' He replied, 'No, Steve. We've just heard your father has been in a plane crash. Most probably no one survived.' I couldn't believe what I was hearing. I said, 'What! Dad, I'm speaking to my father?'

His voice came back clear and calm. 'I'm sorry to have to tell you this now, Steve, but I can't live a lie any longer. My brother, your Uncle Cal, was your father. Your mother never wanted me to tell you, she still doesn't, but when the news broke a few days ago it un-silenced the truth. I can't hold it in any longer. Your mother was in love with Cal before he went away to war. By nineteen forty-nine, she'd accepted he wasn't coming back, then she agreed to marry me. I knew I was always her second choice. Cal stayed away for years then turned up just after your brother Bill was born. He left your mother and I with a surprise. That surprise was you, Steve...and I was left to clean up the mess. I've done my best to be fair to you, to be a good stepfather, but now that Cal's gone, it's only fair to *me*, that you know what I've had to suffer. I've carried this weight far too long. Your mother doesn't want to talk to you, she can't face it. She never could. As for me, I'm handing the business over to Bill and I'm leaving. Something I should have done twenty-four years ago.'

'I want you to call me Ron, Steve. Your war-hero dad's just died in a plane crash, on a mountain in Bolivia. They're organizing a search party, but they don't expect any survivors.'

I'll never forget the crazed edge to his voice. Sophie, he told me things that I should never have heard, detail that went beyond his need to unburden himself. He said that he'd walked in on them. That they didn't see him. What Ron told me then was not fit for a son to hear about his own mother.

I'd never met Cal, but I knew he was a war photographer in the Pacific. He settled in Hawaii and then worked as a freelance political correspondent. I remember as a kid if he ever sent a postcard or a letter, it would cause an argument at home. Once Cal sent a postcard from Santiago, Chile. I must have been seven or eight. I brought the postcard inside and handed it to Dad, I was so excited and asked if we could read it together. Even though it was addressed to my mother, he snatched it and then tore it up in front of me. I learnt early on not to ask about Uncle Cal. I'd pretty much forgotten that he even existed, but I guess somewhere deep down, the intrigue of the forbidden, of far-flung places, was still there.

On the bus back to Cahuita that day, I convinced myself that my father was still alive and that he hadn't even been told about me. That I was a kid again with a postcard that no one was going to tear up. That I was going to Bolivia to find him. When I got there I tracked down the plane crash. I learnt that, yes, a Cal Andrews who had entered the country on an Australian passport was one of the listed passengers. It took a week in La Paz to piece the story together. It was an old DC3, and it had crashed at over twenty thousand feet on the southern slopes of Mount Illimani. They sent a search party out and confirmed there were no survivors. They showed me photographs, but I wanted to go and see the plane for myself. I found just to get there would have required a full expedition, I was almost out of money and I felt so alone and so hope-less. The nearest Australian Embassy was in Rio de Janeiro, I thought maybe they could help. I traveled overland through Brazil to Rio. The embassy people were helpful, but there was nothing they could do."

"What!" Sophie said. "Didn't you track him in Hawaii? Did he have a family there?"

"No, I closed the book on that chapter of my life then and there. A few weeks later I was on a flight back to Australia, with no home to go to."

"No home?"

"That's right, no home," Steve said. "While I was in Bolivia, my mother took an overdose. Ron left the afternoon of the funeral, he handed the house keys to my brother Bill and didn't leave a forwarding address. I phoned Bill from the airport in Sydney, that's all he'd tell me, it was more than clear that I wasn't welcome home...that in his mind, I was to blame for all that gone wrong."

Sophie felt her tears wet on her legs, she buried her head. "I'm sorry. Steve, I'm so sorry, I've..."

"Don't be," Steve said, "I've been over and over this story so many times now, it's as though it defines who I am. How I got to be me and why I never felt I belonged anywhere."

Sophie glanced up at the candle burning on the desk and watched the flame hypnotically, she said nothing. Long moments of silence stretched to span a minute or so. The candlelight seemed to dim. Sophie stayed crouched over her knees like a child and said, "I could have helped you. I would have come to Bolivia with you. I would have gone to Australia with you. Why didn't you trust me enough to tell me?"

Steve rolled over and sat on the edge of the bed, he said, "I've asked myself that same question so many times. I guess I felt ashamed." He hesitated. "Your family was so perfect, mine a disgrace. I just couldn't bring myself to tell you. It was easier just to turn my back and pretend I had a mission to accomplish."

"Easier! You closed the book on me too didn't you?"

Steve looked up and tried to smile, "Not completely, I always had you book-marked. I was going to mention on our walk the other day, when you asked what I'd done with the photos I took of you, that there's one hanging on my office wall."

It was as though she hadn't heard him, she said, "I hate what your family did to you. I hate it." Sophie lifted her head, "and I hate what you did to me in Costa Rica." Her face was streaked with tears, her eyes met his, "but I still love the man that did it."

55: Lost in the Last Shangri-La

Steve reached out a hand to her. She looked at it but didn't take it in hers. He whispered the only words that came to mind, "I'm sorry. Sorry for everything. Sorry for you that you met me."

Sophie leaned back against the bed-head and sighed, "Oh, God, I need to unwind. I'm going to run a bath."

Steve lit two candles in the bathroom. He let the tub fill with very hot water. Sophie emptied in the sachet of bath oil that Dechen had given her in Trongsa, just two days ago. She looked at it while the bath filled and read: Wintergreen, Lemongrass, Artemis — A Product of Bhutan.

Steve stood by awkwardly; she let him be unsure, whether to go, or stay. Then she turned to face him in the soft candle-light and whispered, "I want you to undress me, but I don't want you to touch me."

Steve promised. He undid her blouse one button at a time and let it fall. He admired her. She looked at him distantly. He knelt and undid the zipper at the side of her pants, he let them fall. Sophie lifted one foot after the other as he took them off. He stood again. His fingers reached behind her and unclasped her bra. He eased it slowly from her shoulders and it fell to the floor. He bent to kiss her nipples.

"Remember, you promised," she smiled and said, "I'll do the rest myself."

Sophie kept her eyes on him as she lifted one foot, then the other into the bath. Slowly, she lowered herself into the water and felt goodness and warmth all around her. She closed her eyes and laid her head back. She sighed and relaxed into the feeling of the moment.

With her eyes closed, she said, "So…That's why you walked out the other night in Trongsa, when Karma and Dechen started talking about their family?"

Steve hesitated, "Yeah. I couldn't be around you, I knew what was going to happen. They laugh about what I'm ashamed of. It hurts me. As I said, things work in Bhutan that don't work elsewhere."

Sophie considered his answer for a long time. With her eyes closed she cupped water over her face. She opened her eyes wide and said, "Let's see if that's true, if things work here that can't work elsewhere."

She beckoned him to get into the bath and said, "Steve, I can't hate you anymore, so I have to love you. I want to love you."

As he undressed he said he never wanted anything as much as he wanted to love her now.

They sat face to face and slowly rediscovered each other. Then, when neither of them could wait for the other a moment longer, he took her hand and they stood knee deep in the water. They kissed long and slow.

He whispered, "Remember the last time."

"Take me there again," she said.

He led her from the bathroom. Still wet, he lay her on the white sheets on his bed and in a heartbeat her carefully laid plans had been pushed to the deep recesses of her mind.

When finally they thought to sleep, they moved to Sophie's bed. He lay behind her and put his arms around her. He kissed the back of her neck and said, "I never want you to be lonely again."

Sophie replied, "nor you," and hoped that what was missing had been found.

As Sophie woke and the new day came into focus, she was unusually aware of two things. Steve asleep beside her, and how small a single bed was, with two people in it. The events of last night pieced themselves together and became a reality again.

She closed her eyes and tried to recapture the warmth, and the strength she had felt just last night; but the feeling was not all that she wanted it to be. Now that morning had come, there were truths to be told and questions to be asked. Uncomfortable questions.

A month ago when she'd hastily planned her trip, she hadn't planned last night, or she didn't think she had. But deep inside her, somewhere she hadn't explored for a long time, there was peace. Loneliness had left for a while and Steve was still with her now, his strong shoulders, bare under the falling blankets, reassured her. She had lived for the moment, she was in the Land of the Thunder Dragon, and she had no regrets.

Sophie was drifting back to sleep when there was a gentle knock on the door. A voice called softly. "Mr. Steve, urgent fax for you." She opened her eyes, sat up and let the blankets fall. She glared at the gap under the door as if it was an enemy. There was an envelope on the floor, just inside the room. She flicked back the blankets, walked naked to the door and knelt and held the envelope reluctantly in her fingers. She turned to look at Steve who was still in a deep sleep. For a fleeting moment she thought of getting back in beside him, holding him and reliving the night; but a message from the real world was in her hand and she'd made a promise to Marie she had to keep.

Sophie put the envelope on the desk, picked up a nightdress and put it on but didn't button it. She sat on the edge of the empty bed. He was stirring to life, she said, "Steve, there's a fax for you."

He turned over and they looked at each other across the void between the two single beds. They could have joined hands from where he lay, or they could have been strangers. He said, "Happy?"

She answered slowly, her eyes not leaving his. "Yes. Very."

He reached out his hand to her, she took it and held tight: both clinging to the memory of last night, neither wanting the day to begin.

She gestured to the envelope on the desk, "There's a fax for you."

"I don't want it," he sighed. He let go her hand and picked up the envelope. He slit it open with his finger and took out a one-page fax. Sophie watched him as he read it and she saw the expression on his face change. The real world had entered their magic kingdom and there was no way back.

He hit the bed with his open hand. "Shit. That's all I need. Now he's telling me how to bring up my own boys."

Steve handed the fax to Sophie and slumped back heavily on the bed. He covered his eyes with his hands and groaned.

Sophie raised the fax in two hands, she read in neat handwriting.

Byron Bay, Wednesday, 10 a.m.

Steve,

> *We got your fax this morning.*

> *It's lovely to think of you lost there in the Last Shangri-La, how wonderful for you. But somehow, this is all sounding too familiar - too many projects over too many years with too many problems in too many places.*

> *Anyhow, if you want a touch of reality, you might want to know that Ric was inconsolable this morning when he realized you won't be home for his birthday on Saturday.*

> *How many of the boys' birthdays have you missed now? Tristan says that a thirteenth birthday is a big one for boys, they should have their father with them on their thirteenth. He wrote an article on it, it's a 'rite of passage' towards manhood, a step that shouldn't be taken without their father around.*

> *Anyway, Tristan's kindly offered to delay our departure for the retreat. We'll make sure Ric has a great birthday and then leave Sunday as soon as you arrive. So you just take your time. Bhutan obviously needs you more than your own boys do.*

Miranda.

Steve got up, pulled on his shorts and went to the bathroom, he splashed cold water on his face, hoping it would all
go away and leave him alone. He came back into the room and
slumped down next to her, then put his head in his hands.
Sophie moved behind him on her knees and massaged his
shoulders, she whispered, "Please don't let this spoil our day.
It'll be okay."

"Bullshit," Steve said. "How can it be okay with that asshole, Tristan telling me what I should and shouldn't be doing
as a parent. Sure, I'd rather be home Saturday. Shit, why'd everything have to go wrong now?" He pushed Sophie's hands
away and got to his feet.

"Sorry," Steve said. "But you couldn't understand."

She moved from the bed and stood to face him. "And why
not?"

"Because you don't have children, that's why." Steve looked
past her blankly.

Sophie's anger flared, she said with a voice tainted in acid,
"Who said I don't have children?"

"Let's not play games, Sophie, you did."

"I did not."

Steve stared back at her. She stood firm, her hands on her
hips.

"Sophie! You said your husband was too busy for children,
he never wanted kids?"

"That's correct."

"Well, what are you saying?"

"I was saving this for later today, and following on from
what you told me last night this isn't easy, but..." Sophie
spoke slowly, without faltering, "I've got a daughter, Marie.
She turned eighteen on the Fourth of July."

'Eighteen' jabbed at him. Hard. He put his hand on the
wall to steady himself. "Eighteen. A daughter. That means she
was born in..."

Sophie's voice held firm, though inside her emotion was spilling over. "Yes, Steve, she's yours. Ours. And she's never had a father around for her birthdays."

Sophie's words circled him. They cut in slowly, changing his reality with every whirl around his head.

"I, I don't understand. Why didn't you tell me?"

Sophie didn't answer.

He stared at her, wanting answers, unable to speak. She'd waited a long time for this moment. She crossed the room and knelt at her soft-pack. She moved a handful of folded clothing and took out a wallet-sized photo album covered in a bright tapestry cloth.

"Take this and go for a walk," Sophie said and handed Steve the album. "Then we'll talk."

56: Old photographs, new visions

It helped to walk. To avoid thinking about where to go, Steve re-traced his steps of the day before. He walked fast, lunging uphill, toward Tangsangkha Monastery. Children stopped and waved to him, he didn't notice. Dogs barked frantically, he didn't notice them either. A man obsessed: despair hovered over him like a dragonfly on a summer's day.

He muttered madly to himself as he walked. "How could she not tell me? A daughter, eighteen, mine!" He clutched the photograph album in two hands and the higher above Thimphu he got, the faster he walked. The first thing he saw that really registered were the stone steps that led up to Tangsangkha, then the pines opened up and he could see the monastery above him. The steepled roofs glinted in the early morning sunlight. He climbed the ninety-nine steps two at a time, frantically, uncaring; near the top he stumbled and fell. He broke his fall with outstretched hands and the photo album scattered. His face was mere inches from the sharp stone edge of the step above him. He held himself there, not daring to move. He closed his eyes tight and shouted, "NO!" The madness of his voice against the still of the morning was like glass shattering.

As though in a trance, he climbed the remaining stairs and walked into the monastery courtyard overlooking Thimphu. He crossed the ancient stone paving to the far end and spun the prayer wheels as he went. He sat on the stone wall around the outside of the courtyard and dangled his legs over the sixty-foot drop below. Breathing deeply, he tried to focus on something meaningful, something way off in the distance. The Thimphu Chhu was a long shimmering ribbon of silver winding along the valley floor, it was the only thing that moved. It caught his attention and he watched it intently, hypnotically.

Minutes went by, then Steve looked down at the album in his hand and flicked it open. In the first plastic sleeve was an envelope, his name was on it, the address was care of his parent's store in Maitland. On the back was the sender, Maria Vella. Sophie's mother had written to him, and his brother Bill had returned it, **NOT KNOWN AT THIS ADDRESS**. The envelope was slit open, he removed a handwritten letter.

Dear Steven,

I am writing to you now as I am not well, my time is limited. Over three years have passed since Sophie returned from Costa Rica without you, but with your child. You were with us for only a short time, but I have held a very special place in my heart for you. I see you every day in my granddaughter's eyes, and it saddens me to see Marie growing up without her father.

I'm writing to tell you that it was by Sophie's will alone that you were not told about Marie. Her late father and I tried to change her mind, but she was resolute, she would not contact you first; she would wait for you to contact her, she said you'd agreed to that. I admire, but don't agree with Sophie's determination. She has her reasons, I hope one day soon she'll share them with you, and you will try to understand.

You have a beautiful daughter. Sophie loves you deeply and I leave it in God's hands, as to when and how you two will meet again.

Maria Vella.

Steve re-read the letter and tears welled in his eyes. He looked out over the valley and yelled to the four directions, "Bill sent that letter back? The mongrel! He knew how to contact me. Why! Why didn't Sophie tell me anyway? Why?" He looked again at the date on the letter, January 14th, 1982. He was still single then. He could have changed things. Steve stared into the far distance, at the opposite side of the valley where the pine forest clung to the steep sides of the mountain.

And above it, burning its way into the morning sky, the sun was fully up — his last day in Bhutan had begun.

He folded the letter, put it back in the sleeve and turned the page. The first photograph was of himself and Sophie, they were standing outside the stone cottage, his arm was around her. It was taken on her twentieth birthday, he'd never forget that summer, it was the day before they first made love. In the second photo Sophie was alone, she wore her hair short, the way she had in Costa Rica, she was pregnant, near term. He stared at her face in the photograph and saw sheer determination. The next photo was of Sophie holding a day-old baby, she was breast-feeding. In the next, Marie must have been around three years old, her grandmother Maria was with her. Steve looked closely at the girl in the photograph, he saw himself in her. Marie might have been six or seven in the next photograph, she was in Washington, Sophie had her hair tied back and she was wearing a dark business suit. Marie was standing between Sophie and a man in the next one, she was perhaps twelve. That must be Alex, Steve reasoned and immediately resented him. The final photograph was of Marie graduating from senior high, she was standing next to Sophie, an inch or so taller than her mother and just as beautiful. Steve shook his head and tried to clear a confusion of thoughts that were coming at him from all directions. Against the perfect stillness of the early morning he heard the rustle of fabric and faint footsteps behind him. It sounded like a woman's skirt swishing as she walked, he turned slowly expecting to see Sophie.

A man's voice, one he didn't immediately recognize said, "Steven, are you alright?" Steve swung around further to see the lopon, Lama Desi Gampo, crouched down beside him. The lopon's kind face was full of concern. "I saw you sitting here, holding your head, are you alright?"

Steve looked into kind and untroubled eyes, "Lopon, good morning. Yeah I'm okay."

The lopon looked down and saw the open photograph album next to Steve. "This is your family?"

Steve put words to his own confusion. "Well no, not really, they're — yes, maybe they are in some ways."

"You are not sure? This is Sophie, I met her yesterday?"

"You wouldn't understand, lopon. It's all too difficult."

The elderly lama eased himself down beside Steve on the courtyard wall, he spread his flowing robes over his knees and they fell to his sandals. He said, "I might understand."

Steve looked out over the valley, he sighed and turned to the lama beside him. The lopon's face in profile was serene, his dark smooth skin seemed to glow in the early morning light. Steve began, "Sophie is an old friend. A lover. I knew her twenty years ago in America, she still lives there. I met her here by accident, she's with a trekking tour. I have just found out that the girl with her there, is my daughter."

The old lama picked up the photograph album, "She is a very beautiful girl, you're blessed to have such a child as your own."

"Yes lopon, I guess...but I also have a family back in Australia where I live. I have a wife and two boys."

"Then your blessings are rich and many." As the lopon flicked through the pages of photographs he said, "And does Australian wife know about American wife?"

"Sophie is not really my wife, we were never married, and no, my wife in Australia doesn't know."

The lopon shuffled his robes and kicked his feet against the stone wall falling away below them. "Does Sophie know about Australian wife?"

"Yes."

Steve sat by the lopon's side and the stillness and quietness absorbed them both. It was a minute or two before the lopon spoke. "Steven, you mentioned that Sophie is here with a trekking party, that you met her here by chance?"

"Yes at Jakar, we were staying at the same place."

The lopon turned, "Sophie brings these photographs on a trekking tour to Bhutan? And here in the front is an old letter to you?"

Steve's mouth dropped open. His heart raced. He heard himself saying, "She planned this?"

The lopon put his hand on Steve's shoulder. "Yes. First find out why she wanted to meet you this way, then the answers you seek will be as clear as the dawn."

Steve closed the album and held it firmly in his left hand. He thanked the lopon and stood quickly. He turned and strode across the courtyard. He had some questions he wanted answered.

After Steve left, Sophie stared blankly at the back of the door and sensed the emptiness of the room long after his footsteps had disappeared down the stairs. She went to the bathroom, let her nightdress drop to the floor and closed her eyes as hot water splashed on her back. She knew this moment would come, she'd been anticipating how she would manage it right from the day she booked her flight to Bhutan. She'd done it now, Steve would return in a half-hour, or a half-day, it didn't matter: then they would talk about the improbable, or was it the impossible?

Sophie walked into the room naked and stood a long time before the mirror over the desk, then she dressed slowly and looked around. Steve's work diary and travel wallet had been pushed toward the back of the desk. She sat and picked up the diary, felt its weight, then opened it. She flicked through the pages and they brought his life before her: Sri Lanka, Cambodia, Philippines, Indonesia and most recently China. She scanned forward and found what she was looking for, he was planning to visit the World Bank again in early December. He'd be in Washington in two months time.

Sophie replaced the diary and opened Steve's leather bound travel wallet. She knew that Steve had her photograph album in his hands, her life was in it, and it lessened her guilt as she pulled out a photograph. It was a family portrait, in the background was a view of sweeping blue ocean and a lighthouse on a headland. Steve was in an open-necked shirt. Miranda was next to him in a mid-length white dress buttoned to the waist. The boys Ric and Tim were dressed casually, they were tall like their father, good looking country kids with fair hair and brown skin. Sophie stared at the photograph, looked at herself in the mirror behind the desk, then turned to the photograph again: was Miranda what she'd expected? She saw a pretty face, perhaps a beautiful face. Miranda had a fair complexion and blond hair, still long. Steve's had children to two very different women she mused as she replaced the photograph. The dog-eared corner of a newspaper cutting then caught her eye, she carefully took it out and unfolded it. Miranda's face was staring at her again, it was one of her lifestyle articles, it was over a year old. Next to the photograph was the title, 'FINDING THE ME IN US'.

Sophie took the cutting, lay down on her bed and started reading. It was true to the banner that it was under: a sassy style of writing triumphing those that had changed for love. But underlying the bravado, she picked up on a sad story about the unraveling of a marriage. She knew in an instant that she'd never need to meet Miranda to hear the other side of Steve's story. By the time she had finished reading she understood why Steve had cut it out and kept it. It was a prophecy, Miranda's way of forewarning Steve what was about to happen. Was that cruel, taunting or maybe kind? Or was it the only way Miranda could get through to him? Whichever, from what Steve had said a few days back he clearly hadn't read it in time. As Sophie folded the clipping and carefully replaced it in the wallet, she felt mixed emotions; something told her that Steve's marriage breakup would be far harder on him than her own had been on Alex and herself.

Alex and Sophie had worked things out, perhaps the *Washington Post* gossip columnist was right, 'the marriage of convenience had ended in the divorce of convenience'. They were better off living apart; they were better friends living apart. She knew now that neither Steve nor Miranda would understand that; that their breakup would result in different lives moving along different paths, that the only thing that would keep them talking was the boys. That all the good times would be lost.

That thought turned her mind to Marie, and then to Washington and calls that she should make.

57: On neutral territory

Namgay and a couple of the boys that worked in the guest-house were stretched out asleep on the bench seats in the reception area. She looked at the sleeping men and reconsidered her phone calls, then reconsidered again.

Sophie walked over to Namgay and gently shook his shoulder. "I need to make some phone calls."

"Huh," his eyes blinked open. "Who is it?"

"Me, Sophie from Room 203. I need to call Australia, to a cell phone."

"Yes, later."

"No, now."

He checked his watch and groaned, then stretched, sat up and rubbed his eyes. "Ohh, okay ma'am." He rolled out of bed in the gho he'd been sleeping in and stumbled across to the reception desk, he put out his hand for the number.

Sophie put the piece of paper in his hand, and said, "The first one first, thanks."

Namgay grumbled, "So many numbers, ma'am?" He dialed the international operator, gave her Marie's new cell phone number and waited for the phone to ring. Namgay handed her the phone and stumbled back to his bed, Sophie said,

"Hi Darling, it's Mom here."

"Mom, hey, where are you?

"I'm in Thimphu. It's early morning here and I'm in a crowded hotel lobby, I can't speak for long."

"Can't you put the call through to your room?"

"No, there are no phones in the room."

"Really! Hey, what about Steve? What's happening?"

"I've been with him now for the last six days, he needed some help with a problem here."

326

"Six days! Quick tell me, have you told him about *me?*"

"Yes darling I have. He was very excited."

"What'd he say. Tell me, quick."

"I can't talk for long here. I'll call you Saturday when I'm in Bangkok, we'll have a long talk then."

"Well, is Steve there? Can I talk with him now?"

"No, he's gone for a walk."

"Alone? Where?"

"Yes, alone, my suggestion, he needs space right now."

"Oh, is everything okay?"

"Yeah, fine."

"You sure, Mom?"

"Yes darling. I'll have to go. I just wanted to give you a quick call to let you know I've told him."

"Mom, did you also tell him I'm in Byron Bay? That I'm waiting here to meet him?"

"Umm, no, not yet, I'm saving that surprise for later."

"When?"

"Ahh, I haven't worked that out yet…soon, now I'll have to go darling. Is everything alright there?"

"Yes, Mom fine, I've been in touch with Alex. I'd love to talk with dad by phone. Can I call him dad now? Could you call later when he gets back?"

"Marie listen to me, I've still got a few things to sort out, he may not be able to call today. He's got a lot of business problems right now. But I'm sure you'll talk to him soon."

"Oh, gee, okay." Marie's voice lowered a tone or two, "what's your number there, if I want to call you."

"You can't call into this hotel from overseas, darling. This call is through an operator. Now I'll have to go, bye, I love you."

"Why can't you talk more, Mom?"

"The hotel staff are all asleep in the lobby, I'm keeping them awake."

"What? What sort of hotel is it?"

"In a word, quaint...I'll tell you all about it when I call from Bangkok." Sophie glanced over at Namgay snuggled under his rugs again. She didn't have the heart to ask him to make another call, so she added, "Can you do me a favor please darling? I can't call from here again just now, phone Alex and tell him that everything has worked out just fine. That I'll call him Saturday and send my love."

"Oh okay. Bye, Mom. Thanks."

"Bye darling, take care."

Sophie hung up and thanked Namgay who was already snoring. She walked back up the stairs and went into Steve's room. She pulled open the curtains, lay down on her bed and thought back to the conversation she'd had with Alex on Monday night; he'd mentioned something about Venezuela, now she wondered if she still had a job. She knew at least part of the reason that she'd asked Marie to call Alex, was that she really didn't want to know the answer just now. Strangely, what had seemed so important to her a few weeks ago, was now in the back of her mind. What was foremost was change. Was it just Bhutan that had changed her? She picked up the novel that she still hadn't finished and waited for Steve.

He didn't knock on the door, he called out, "Sophie it's Steve, let me in, please."

She tried to judge his frame of mind from the sound of his voice. He didn't sound angry.

When she opened the door, he walked right past her and said, "Thanks." He went to the desk and sat down, the tapestry-covered album was in his hand and he wasn't smiling, he said, "We've got some talking to do."

"Ah ha."

"Why don't you sit on the bed."

"No thanks," Sophie said with her hands clenched behind her back. "I'll stand."

"Our accidental meetings in Thimphu and Jakar, they were no accident, were they?"

"No."

"You planned them, didn't you?"

"Yes."

"Your sprained ankle, missing the trek?"

Sophie just bit her lip and nodded in the affirmative.

"Oh. Okay," Steve stared at her, he'd expected her to be on the defensive. "Tell me how and then tell me why." He added, "please," as an afterthought.

Sophie leaned her back against the wall. "The how was easy. Marie found you first on the internet. She searched Steven Andrews, Civil Engineer, Australia. There you were on the TRANSARCO web site, and a few SAIB and World Bank sites as well."

"You both knew all that?"

"Yes, it's all there, details of your project, everything. I have a good contact at the South Asia Bank, he got through to Dr. Narguli's secretary with a confidential request. She provided the Bank's itinerary for the current supervision mission, yours included. I searched around for a trekking tour that would coincide, found one in New York and booked it in the second week of September."

"You planned this just a few weeks ago? You had my itinerary?"

Sophie nodded confidently but kept her hands firmly clenched behind her back.

He moved forward on his seat, "If you knew all that, you must have known that I come to Washington regularly?"

"Yes, I did."

"Well, why come all this way to meet me?"

"I couldn't wait that long, I'll tell you why later...and I wanted to meet you on neutral territory. Washington would have been far too uncomfortable."

"What?" Steve was almost on the edge of his chair.

"Anyway," she said with just the hint of a smile on her lips, "what better place to meet you than Bhutan. I'd found out that it's cut off from the outside world. It seemed a perfect place for a chance meeting."

"You're unbelievable, Sophie," Steve said. "It's so expensive to come here."

"So! I wanted to visit Bhutan anyway."

"But…I could have seen you on the flight in here."

"I found out you traveled economy, so I traveled business."

Steve didn't need to say a thing, his thoughts were written all over his face.

"I saw you on the airplane. I was hiding behind a newspaper, and when Farley met you and organized our lunch, I knew it was meant to be."

"Huh, so why didn't you tell me then, or in Jakar, we had all that time together?"

"Believe me, I tried…but there was so much else happening."

"Yeah, but I asked you if had children, you said no."

"Steve, I said, Alex and I did not have children…I answered your question honestly."

Steve folded his arms and frowned, "Clever!" he said sarcastically, "so your plan's worked perfectly, hasn't it?"

"No." Sophie hesitated, "not everything has gone to plan."

"Oh, and what hasn't gone to *your* plan?"

"You asked me how, then why. I'll tell you why I came here before I answer that." Sophie took two slow steps to sit on the end of the bed, near the desk. She crossed her legs and held her raised knee with both hands. Steve unfolded his arms and turned on his chair to face her, his hands with an iron grip on his knees.

"Nearly nineteen years ago, I arrived home alone from an adventure that my parents didn't want me to go on. They welcomed me back in November, and on Christmas Eve I told them I was pregnant. Dad was furious but Mom always had a soft spot for you Steve, she said to wait and see, that if you really loved me, you would contact me."

Steve put his head in his hands and groaned.

"The first few years were easy. Mom loved having a baby to look after, Dad softened to the change and I was enjoying being a student again. I didn't forget you, but I tried to. But when Marie was about two, after Dad had died, she started asking about her daddy. It was then that I agreed Mom could write to you, I didn't ask to see her letter at the time. When it was returned unopened, 'Not known at this address,' I swallowed my pride and called the home number you'd given me."

"You called home? When?"

"In February that year, nineteen eighty two, days after Mom's letter was returned."

"And?"

"And, I got your brother, Bill. I can tell you exactly what he said, his words are as sharp in my mind as yesterday."

Steve covered his face with his hands and said, "Not Bill! No!" under his breath.

"Your brother laughed and said to me, 'Christ, not another one he's got up the duff. I don't know where he is now, last I heard he's shacked up with a journalist on the coast somewhere. If you want my advice, forget the bastard. We have.'"

Steve looked up, tears streaked his face, his eyes were a mirror to the pain inside his head and his heart. His fingers dug into his knees, his shoulders shook.

"So I've brought up our daughter alone. I always knew it was inevitable that I'd tell you, but I've put off the inevitable for a very long time."

Steve tried to speak but choked on his first word.

"It hasn't been easy, and I guess looking back on it now, the harder it got the more determined I became that I would never ask for your help."

Steve leant forward. "Why, Sophie, *why?*"

"I've told you why, and when your brother said you were with another woman, that I wasn't the only one you'd 'got up the duff', I needed to put you out of my mind...for my own sake, and for Marie's."

"You believed the lying bastard, he's always hated me, blamed me for everything that was wrong in his life...I wasn't married then, I would have come to you."

"I didn't know that and I had no way of finding you...or, maybe after what Bill said I didn't want to find you. Anyway, let me finish. I've given up everything for Marie, she's been my whole life outside of work. In many ways, my undivided love for her spoiled my marriage. Alex couldn't have been a better stepfather to her, but when Marie was about twelve, she became obsessed with finding and meeting her real father. From then on, everything changed."

Steve put his head in his hands, and sighed, "Oh, god."

"It was tough on me and even tougher on Alex. He'd always said I should tell you about Marie. Just like Mom did."

Sophie unfolded her legs and sat back on the bed. "Up until this year, I've never tried to contact you or even find out where you were, or what you were doing. That's not to say I didn't wonder what had become of you, or that I'd stopped caring for you."

Steve looked up, his eyes more hurt than angry, "If you'd cared, you would have contacted me."

"Steve, let me finish. Marie is a very determined eighteen-year-old now. I've accepted that I can no longer stand in the way of her meeting her father. It's her right."

"And isn't it also *mine*? Wasn't it always?" Steve demanded. "You're the human rights lawyer. You must have asked yourself, 'does Steve have a right to know?'"

Sophie smiled meekly but showed no fear, "I won't deny mixed feelings on that one until recently." She stopped and held his steady gaze, "But remember, Steve, you walked out on me. So I'm not sorry, and I'm not apologizing."

"I think I know you well enough, Sophie." He shook his head slowly, "I wouldn't expect you to."

"Okay. Get angry with me later," Sophie said.

"I will, but first tell me, what's Marie doing now, where's she living? How can I contact her?"

Sophie hesitated, went to stand and then sat again and looked at her knees. "Umm...She's learning to ride a surfboard," Sophie said sheepishly, then she took a folded piece of paper from her pocket and handed it to Steve without making eye contact. "Here's her cell phone number."

Steve took the piece of paper and looked at it carefully, as he did so the color drained from his face and he spat the word, "What!" He looked up, "this is an Australian number?"

Sophie nodded, "Umm, yeah, ahh, she's in Australia."

"Where...in Australia?"

"Ahh...Byron Bay. She's waiting there until her father returns home."

Steve's mouth was moving but the words refused to form properly. He stared at Sophie as though disbelieving, but the piece of paper he held told him it was true.

Sophie took the chance to speak first, "She's staying in a backpackers hostel and working at a hotel on the beach. And don't worry, I have her promise that she won't make contact with your family." Steve was still too stunned to speak so Sophie reeled off the events of the last few weeks; Marie's short stay in Bali, how Marie had forced her hand anyway, how she had no say in it and how she would never have let Marie carry out her threat to meet him first.

It was as though Steve hadn't heard, he said almost to himself, "She was going to turn up at the airport and just walk up to me and introduce herself. I can't believe this. I can't believe she's in Byron Bay."

"I know how you feel," Sophie said, "even now, I find it hard to believe what my own daughter did to me...or rather, our daughter did to us. As I said, it was always inevitable that I'd tell you, just, well, you know what I'm like."

"Yeah, I do. And your mother's letter just confirmed it."

Sophie lowered her eyes to the floor. She had no ready answer, she mumbled, "You could say Marie forced my hand in all this, and in a way, now I'm glad she did."

Steve was in his own world, he hardly heard her, he said, "So now I know why you stormed out of the restaurant last Friday night in Jakar. Why you've never forgiven me for not calling you back."

"It would have changed my life, Steve." Sophie sat forward and faced him square on, "When you called and got Mom, I was away. I went away to think about the news our family physician had given me just days before."

"Look I'm sorry," Steve said and sat with his back pushed straight against the chair. "I should have called again. I called from Panama and left that same day for Colombia. When I got there I just got caught up in my own world of problems."

"And the further south you went, the less you thought of me."

"I told you, I felt ashamed. And I was grieving for a father I didn't even know. That phone call home changed my perception of who I was. I really thought you'd be better off without me."

"You could have let me decide that."

"Yeah, I should have called you," Steve moved forward to face her, "but you should have told me anyway."

Sophie moved to the edge of the bed, her face was just inches from him and an impish smile crossed her lips, "Are you angry with me?" Her will was strong, but her emotion spilt over. Tears welled in her eyes but she dared not wipe them, she'd rehearsed this scenario too many times to let herself down.

"Damn right I'm angry."

Sophie didn't look up, "How angry? Unforgivably?"

Steve shook his head and said, "I can't answer that yet."

"Why not?"

"It depends. What have you told Marie, about me?"

Tears were now making their way down her cheeks, she ignored them. "The truth. I've told her the truth right from her first questions at about age three. I wasn't negative about you, just honest. I used to say to her, that's the way it is for us."

"Did she always know that I didn't know?"

"Yes, of course."

He reached out and put unsteady hands on hers, he said, "And what do you suppose Marie would think about her father now?"

Sophie's face broke into a smile even though tears were running down her cheeks. "She'd love to meet you, and to call you dad."

Steve didn't move, he buried his face in his hands and just sat there. Sophie's gentle sobbing was the only sound in the room. Minutes later he looked up and their eyes met. To begin she couldn't read his state of mind, his face was a blank, his eyes more sad than angry.

"I'm sorry, she whispered, "really sorry, sorry for all of us."

Still Steve didn't move. His mouth was a straight line.

Finally, Sophie broke, she said, "Steve, what are you thinking? Please talk to me."

The faintest of smiles crossed his lips, "I'm thinking about what the lopon said to me this morning. I went back up to the monastery. When I told him about Marie, then about Ric and Tim, he said my blessings are rich and many. You know, I think he's right." Steve moved from his chair and sat next to Sophie on the end of the bed. He put his arm around her and held her tight.

Sophie lay her head on his shoulder and neither of them moved for minutes. Her crying stopped, she looked up at him, "Now you know, the 'how' and the 'why' I'm here."

"There's still one thing that you haven't told me."

"Oh?" Sophie whispered, "What's that?"

"The part of your plan that hasn't worked."

She buried her face into his neck and said through new tears, "I didn't plan on falling in love with you again."

Steve glanced at the travel alarm behind them, it was nearly half past seven. He kicked off his shoes, pulled Sophie down on the bed beside him and said, "There's just enough time to get to know my daughter's mother again."

58: Pride stripped bare

At eight forty-five, Steve and Sophie walked into the Royalty Room restaurant dressed for a business meeting. Bijaya was behind the bar listening to music.

Steve said, "We're running late, can we get tea, coffee and toast quickly?" Bijaya nodded vacantly. Steve wasn't quite sure that it was a yes, but they took a table by the window and sat next to each other.

"Later today," Steve said and touched Sophie's hand. "I want you to tell me more about Marie, and I want a photo of her that I can keep?"

"Yes to both," Sophie said. "Speaking of later today, what have you got planned? Will you call Marie late tonight? Please. She's working an evening shift."

"Yeah, of course, we'll call her together, from Paro. I want you to stay there with me tonight." He hesitated then looked around the empty restaurant, "There's something that I want us both to do before we call her."

"Sounds hard to say no to," Sophie said, "But, I should have lunch with my trekking group, and they're expecting me to be in Thimphu tonight."

"We'll go to Paro after your lunch, and you can come back to Thimphu with Karma tomorrow morning, if you're game?"

"I'm game, it's a date."

Bijaya brought tea, coffee and toast to the table. Over breakfast, Sophie asked about Steve's plan for the afternoon in Paro. When Steve said they were going to climb the Tiger's Nest so that they could tell Marie about it, Sophie thought he was joking. "Tigers live in trees around Paro?" she said playfully. "No," he said, "that would be far too easy, the nest hangs off the side of a mountain."

Karma came into the restaurant at five past nine, and as soon as Steve saw him, his mood changed; it was back to business. Steve offered tea or coffee, Karma declined both with a serious shake of his head.

"Karma, anything happen yesterday?" Steve said.

"No, Mr. Steve. But the lyonpo did ask me to drive to Paro airport."

"Why?"

Karma waited a purposeful moment, "Lyonpo asked me to meet a big Dasho from the bank. One of the directors."

"Who?"

Karma raised his eyebrows and smiled his widest smile. "Mr. Michael, sir. Everyone is talking about him. He's a giant, a huge black giant."

Sophie laughed, Steve didn't. She said, "Karma, you mean he's African American?"

"Don't know, Miss. He didn't say. But he's so tall he could hardly fit into the Landcruiser."

Sophie said, "Michael's six foot seven to be exact."

Steve didn't hear, his mind was already firmly planted in the minister's office. He said as if she worked for him, "Sophie, you've got the envelope, haven't you?"

She just nodded in response.

In the turmoil of the morning he'd all but forgotten about work, but in the Landcruiser on the way to the meeting, a mild panic took over. The thought that the minister was corrupt tormented him. And what about Smyth-Jones, was he part of it too?

As they drove through the main street of Thimphu, images of Ollie and Narguli came into his head. Narguli would be there at the meeting, and as much as Steve didn't consider himself a vindictive man, he could hardly wait to hand over the envelope that would surely destroy one of the few men he detested, and after yesterday, more so for Ollie than himself.

By the time they arrived at the Roads and Transport Compound, the chaos in Steve's mind was written on his face like a confession. He was both looking forward to, and dreading the next hour or so.

⳹

At the minister's offices, Dorji Dukpa showed them to the waiting room. Steve introduced Sophie. Then they sat on bench seats outside the lyonpo's office and waited. Steve asked Sophie for Ollie's envelope. She opened her shoulder bag and handed it across, it felt hot in his hands.

Dorji Dukpa entered the waiting room again, this time with a man who had to bend almost double to get under the low doorway. Karma was right, he was a giant. He was also dressed and groomed immaculately, and in a hand that had thick gold rings on three fingers, he carried a designer briefcase and a conspicuously out-of-place cell phone.

Steve stood, waiting for Dorji to do the introductions, but the man leant over and kissed Sophie on both cheeks. "Sophie, you been calling my office, huh? Your message got through."

She greeted him with a smile, but no reply.

"How's it been working for Alex?" he said.

"Just fine," Sophie said, "he's nowhere near as tough a boss as you were."

The big man laughed. "Huh, you haven't changed one bit," he said.

Sophie gestured toward Steve, "Michael James, I'd like you to meet Steven Andrews. Steve, Michael is a director at the bank, he's in charge of the audit department. Michael, you know who Steve is?"

Steve made a poor attempt to hide his astonishment as they shook hands firmly. Michael James's hand was so big that Steve's felt lost in his grip.

"Michael and I knew each other in Washington," Sophie said. "We worked together." She noted Steve's surprise and added. "Michael was in the State Department before taking up his job at the bank."

The said Mr. James was busily delving into his briefcase, he pulled out a file an inch thick and flicked through it as he towered over the room.

The door to the minister's office opened and an unsmiling Lyonpo Rinchen Dorji appeared. He was dressed in a fine, but plain, gray gho. His orange neck-scarf was a stark reminder of his position. He looked around to see who had arrived, then came into the waiting room and greeted the big man with an outstretched hand.

Michael James introduced Sophie to the minister as an old friend from Washington, and added that Sophie was in Bhutan on a trekking tour. The minister nodded, "Welcome." The cuckoo clock in the minister's office struck half nine Cuckoo! Cuckoo! Sophie and the polished Mr. James both swung around in surprise.

The lyonpo greeted Steve warmly enough, asked about his accident and commented on how well the wound had healed, but his handshake felt somehow insincere. Steve felt the whole mood and feel of the place shift.

The minister led the way into his office. There was a moment of confusion as Steve asked if Sophie could sit in the waiting room. The minister and Michael James balked, they'd already assumed that Sophie would be joining them in the wrap-up meeting. Sophie blushed at Steve's discomfort and followed MJ into the room.

Narguli was already seated and had Steve not known better, he could have been excused for thinking that Narguli was the director, and Michael James his assistant. Immediately, Steve wondered what Narguli had heard of Ollie. Did he know she was alive, or did he think her body was a thousand feet below the road near Trongsa?

As soon as he sat down, Steve put a manila envelope on the table in front of him, it was face up: SOUTH ASIA INFRA-STRUCTURE BANK was printed in the top right hand corner. Only Narguli noticed the gesture. His eyes fixed on the six by eight piece of brown paper and they did not move.

It was clear that Narguli knew Michael James, but how well wasn't so obvious. The minister made no attempt to explain who Sophie was or what she was doing there. Steve could see that Narguli was unsettled by her presence; several times he glanced sideways at Sophie and scratched at his immaculate silver-gray hair.

The minister offered tea; three chilips nodded. Michael James said, "Coffee, black and strong, thanks."

Dorji Dukpa scurried into the room balancing a tray with seven cups. He looked to the minister for direction: who should be served first? The minister gestured toward Michael James as if Dorji should have known. Dorji set a cup and saucer in front of each of them and two on the unoccupied side of the table, he scooped several spoonfuls of instant coffee into Michael James cup and filled it, then poured tea from an elaborate pot while the minister presided over the small talk.

As soon as his cup was filled, Narguli started drinking. Michael James waited for the minister to drink first. Lyonpo Rinchen Dorji was interested in Sophie's trip and her impressions of Bhutan. Sophie did most of the talking over tea. This further unsettled Narguli.

Steve missed the small talk, he was too busy finalizing his strategy. He'd run it over a couple of times in his head and it made sense. If the minister was corrupt, that was Michael James's problem. Steve would focus first on protecting his and TRANSARCO's reputation. Secondly, he'd finish Narguli's career with the bank. This was the part he relished — he owed it to Ollie if nothing else. And speaking of Ollie, Sophie had convinced him to wait and see what unfolded. She said she couldn't put her finger on it, but there was something in Ollie's story that didn't quite add up, that it might be best to wait and see what the others knew first.

The cuckoo struck a quarter of ten, it signaled an end to the tea ceremony and a start to the serious business of the meeting.

"Lady, gentlemen, we don't have a formal agenda for the meeting today," the minister began. "As you know, there have been some extraordinary circumstances preceding this meeting, circumstances that will significantly impact the Two Roads East project."

Narguli grunted nasally, the others spoke their assent in lowered tones.

The minister continued, "We are all relieved that Miss Olivera Ramos is alive and well."

Everyone nodded his or her agreement, Narguli so eagerly that it appeared he alone was responsible for this miracle.

"We're expecting Mr. Smyth-Jones and Dasho Tobgay to join us," the Minister went on, but Steve wasn't listening, he was thinking about photographs that would end a career: vengeance overrode reason, and protocol.

When the minister said, "While we're waiting for the others, could you provide an update on progress, Mr. Andrews?" he was expecting to hear about roadworks.

Steve however, had wound himself up and took it as his cue. He thanked the minister for allowing him to speak, then paused for dramatic effect. With a sweeping gesture of his hand, Steve picked up the manila envelope in front of him and turned to Michael James. "In here are photographs taken by Dr. Narguli."

Narguli cut in, "What? I've never owned a camera in my life. What are you talking about, Andrews?" He turned to Michael James. "Sir, the man is obviously unwell. Do we need to listen to this?"

Michael James opened his mouth to speak. Cuckoo! Cuckoo! Cuckoo! Cuckoo! Cut in over the top of him. He checked his watch for ten o'clock and waited patiently for the bird to retreat, then said, "Continue, Andrews."

"I haven't looked at these photographs," Steve said, and I won't say now where I got them. But Sophie's seen them and I think you'll agree, sir, they raise some serious questions." Steve glanced across at Narguli and smirked.

Michael James's huge hand took hold of the envelope. He opened it and removed six postcard-sized photographs. The room was deathly quiet as the big man leant back in his chair and held the first photo in front of his face. His whole body stiffened as he moved the photo closer. "Good God, Ollie!" He said it to himself, but everyone could hear it.

He turned to the next photograph and his eyes were as wide as saucers. "Anika!" He closed his eyes and shook his head.

Narguli was on the edge of his chair, scarcely breathing. His pallor was near terminal.

With the next photograph Michael James' jaw tightened and the muscles in the side of his huge face bulged. He loosened his tie with one hand and wiped the sweat from his chin with the back of the other. "No! Oh no. *Devi too!*"

An eerie silence descended and hung suspended in the room. Michael James pushed the photographs back into the envelope then turned to the minister and said, "Lyonpo, these explain a few things."

If Narguli had been any closer to the edge of his chair he'd have fallen. His mouth was open but there was no sound, his hands were gesticulating wildly. Michael James handed the envelope to him and Narguli spilled the photographs into his open hand and brought them up close to his face. "That's my room." He said, "They're in my bedroom."

Michael James' face was as rigid as black steel. "This explains the two bank transfers — she paid Anika and Devi ten thousand each for this." He leant across the table and snatched the manila envelope from Narguli's fingers. "Why would Ollie do this? She must hate you beyond loathing, and by Christ, man, I'll find out why!"

Narguli's head fell forward into his hands. His voice broke, he was almost weeping as he said, "She used her key to my apartment. She's set me up. I hardly know Anika, and Devi... that was years ago. I thought Ollie loved me. I thought I had a friend, someone I could trust."

When Narguli's black eyes lifted to face Michael James, his pride was stripped bare. "I thought I could trust, Ollie," he repeated. "I thought I'd found a woman I could trust." He stood slowly and spoke to Michael James as though they were alone in the room. "Excuse me, sir, I'm going back to the hotel."

Steve's was a pyrrhic victory. When he looked up, every head was bent. Even Sophie did not meet his eyes.

59: A Caterpillar did it

The first voice to break the silence was Dorji's. "Dasho Tobgay is here, lyonpo."

The doorway filled with the frame of the police chief wearing a deep red and black tartan gho. He bowed then crossed to the seat left vacant by Narguli, which he filled to overflowing. He spoke to the minister in urgent Dzongkha, then greeted Michael James.

The minister said, "Dasho, you've met Steven Andrews, and this is Sophie Vella. Sophie, this is Dasho Tobgay, he's Chief of Police."

Dasho Tobgay leant over and took Sophie's right hand, held it in both his hands and said, "Miss Sophie." He glanced toward Steve with a frown and nodded once, then turned to the minister and said, "Doctor Narguli go where?"

Michael James answered. "Narguli just lost his girlfriend, he's in mourning — for himself!"

Tobgay considered Michael James' answer, nodded once and slurped at his cup of tea.

"Were we in time?" the minister said.

Tobgay's reply was breathless. "Just!"

Michael James and the minister asked together, "Did she talk?"

"Couldn't stop her. That's why I late." The big Bhutanese laughed. "Mr. Smyth still there talking and listening. There's more listening than talking. He come later maybe."

Tobgay, Michael James and the minister all looked at each other, who should speak first?

"Lyonpo?" James said.

The minister said, "No, please go ahead."

Michael James turned to Sophie. "Yesterday afternoon my office called with your message saying that Ollie was alive and at Tangsangkha Monastery. I informed the minister immediately, and he called Dasho Tobgay, Smyth-Jones and myself to an urgent meeting here. Soon after, Dasho Tobgay and I went up to Tangsangkha. We got there at six, we were too late. Ollie had gone, no one knew where."

Steve and Sophie leaned forward in their seats. Michael James gestured to the police chief to fill in the detail.

Tobgay rearranged his ample stomach inside his gho. "I rush back to office and call all 'round, then I wait. Last night after ten I get call from Phuentsholing. A suspicious-looking monk is trying to cross the border into India. He is a she."

"I can't believe it," Steve blurted.

Michael James turned to Steve. "If Narguli'd done his job, none of this would have happened. Ollie got his trust, then she played him for a sucker. We thought he was involved to begin, but now we know it was just blind stupidity. The sort of incompetence that allows a junior bank officer to single-handedly filter off twenty million dollars in a little over two years."

Steve slunk low in his seat. Sophie just mouthed the word, "Clever!"

"Narguli knows nothing yet," James said. "I'm glad he left though, I might have had to carry him outta here."

The police chief's high-pitched voice cut in over the sounds of James's chuckling. "Miss Ollie tell us everything. She warm Narguli's bed first, then she get him to sign invoices without even looking at them. Narguli suspected nothing, but she worried Mr. Nigel onto something. She think it's time to go, so she fake her own death. She want a few days to get out of Bhutan. It was good job really. With practice she become expert."

Dasho Tobgay laughed at his own joke, but when he saw that the minister didn't even smile, he cleared his throat loudly and continued. "We know it not real accident when driver Jalal say too much to Trongsa Police. Our man there might not look much, but he very smart. Bhutan chess champion. Very good at laying a trap."

Steve and Sophie looked at each other. Steve forced a wan smile.

"Our police chief inspect the landslide with Jalal. He report to me, there is explosion on top road, but it not cause the land to slide. A caterpillar do that."

Tobgay looked around to see who'd got it. He met blank faces all around. His grin turned to a scowl. "Tractor. They push huge boulder from top road with Caterpillar tractor."

"Shit...A planned landslide," Steve said to himself and caught Sophie grinning with a 'told you so' look on her face.

Michael James checked his watch. "Thanks, Dasho Tobgay, well done. I've been watching Ollie for some time now. We had a hunch something was wrong earlier this year. She'd told the bank she came from a fishing village in Cebu, that she'd lived in the Philippines right up until college. In March she was asked to join a mission to the Maldives, to help evaluate a loan to a fish-processing factory. Setting up a fish-marketing cooperative was part of the study. The mission leader chose her on her CV, he thought she'd have a good feel for the topic. After the mission his report said. 'If she's ever seen a live fish before, it was in an aquarium'. I started looking into her background after that. I examined every project that she'd been involved with. Lucky you, Andrews. It's only Two Roads East that she's defrauded."

Lyonpo Rinchen Dorji took command of the meeting again. "We still have one problem, and it's a big one. Money!"

Steve swallowed, one eye on the minister's sword in the corner of the room. Consequences were on his mind again. How would the money be recovered? How would the loan be replenished and when? As the story unfolded the facts fitted together in Steve's head. Ollie had taken just under twenty million, almost all of it was sitting in three bank accounts in Singapore. The names on the accounts were Veejay Industries, Calcutta Pipe Works and Hindustan Corporation — companies registered in Singapore on the one day over two years ago. The owner of each of them was a Ms Olivera Ramos of a dead-end address.

Michael James assured the minister that nearly all the money was recoverable. The accounts were in suspension pending the outcome of their inquiry. He said the only major withdrawals were two bank drafts, both for ten thousand each, one to Ms. Anika Kumar, the other to Ms. Devi Sharma.

Steve felt a lead weight sink lower in his stomach as his mind jumped back to his last night in Trashigang. TRANSARCO's accounts had shown one hundred and eleven invoices from Veejay Industries, the SAIB accounts one hundred and sixteen. He'd picked up a ten million dollar difference and he'd started to check it all again when he got to the Eiger — then Sophie had walked back into his life and, despite his good intentions, he hadn't got back to it. If only he'd had more time he'd have picked it up. But what would he have done anyway?

He hadn't answered his own question when the ten forty-five cuckoo announced the arrival of Mr. Smyth-Jones.

The Englishman entered in a flurry of apologies. "Good morning, chaps," he said, then noticed Sophie and bowed and excused his rudeness as if it were an unforgivable offence. He took a seat at the fourth side of the square around the low table, checked his tie was tight against his collar and straightened his coat.

When offered tea, he replied, "I rather think I've earned it. I've been more counselor than criminal investigator this morning."

"Criminal investigator?" Steve blurted.

Nigel turned to Michael James. "Shall I explain?"

Michael James grinned and said, "Sip your tea, old chap." He looked across the table at Steve. "You might ask Andrews, why we didn't jump as soon as we knew something was wrong? I'll tell you why! When we first started tracking Ollie back in March it took us a couple of months to piece it all together and find the money in Singapore. We knew then how she'd done it, but we didn't know who else was involved. So we let it roll and brought in someone from outside to help, a forensic auditor. Mr. Smyth-Jones has done a number of jobs for the bank since he left Scotland Yard."

"Nigel!" Steve spluttered, "Ex-Scotland Yard?"

"Correct," Michael James added, "Surprised, huh?"

Steve looked as if the whole thing was a conspiracy against him. He shook his head and stared at Nigel to make sure they were talking about the same person.

"Steven, I'm sorry to have led you on," the minister cut in. "When you were here the week before last, we were still unsure whether it was all Ollie's work, or if Narguli and perhaps even your staff were involved."

"But why me? Why take my passport?" Steve said far more loudly than he intended.

"Hey, don't worry, I keep it safe for you," Tobgay joked. "We need Ollie to think we on wrong track. When we looking out for you, she think no one looking out for her."

Nigel just smiled and shrugged. "It's all part of the job, sorry old chap."

Michael James checked his watch. "Briefly, Nigel, what'd she say?"

60: Somewhere betwixt empathy and anger

It was soon clear that even with her head shaved and in monk's robes, Ollie's beguiling ways had challenged Nigel's professional detachment. It was also clear that Nigel's version of 'briefly' and Michael James's were at opposite ends of the spectrum.

Ollie had confirmed everything they already knew, Nigel said. In total Narguli had signed off on an extra fourteen invoices, all of them made out to her three companies in Singapore. The bank paid them without even questioning why most payments went to Calcutta, and a few to Singapore.

"Lyonpo, the bank has made some changes to its Treasury after this," James cut in. Some new checks have been made routine now. It couldn't happen again.

Nigel reached into his coat pocket and put an unlit pipe in his mouth. He sucked at it, then continued. "Ollie was selected to the bank's Young Professional program, not only because she was very bright, but because of the story she told the bank about her background. Her application, including what we now know was a forged birth-certificate, told how she was brought up in a fishing village in the southern Philippines. How her father went from being just another poor fisherman to head of a successful fish marketing cooperative. How he set up and managed income-producing schemes for villagers throughout the Visayas, and how she studied economics with the sole purpose of helping the poor."

Tobgay chuckled, then laughed out loud and slapped his knees. "She help poor alright — poor Ollie."

Michael James scowled at Tobgay then turned to the minister and said sternly, "We've also altered some of our Young Professional recruitment procedures, lyonpo. YPs now go through the same security checks as regular staff."

The minister thanked him and signaled again to Nigel. The police chief was still chuckling to himself.

"Ollie's real story is somewhat...." Nigel stopped then sighed. "Excuse me, won't you, if I've become personally involved. I'm betwixt empathy and anger on this one. Ollie's never been to the Philippines. She lived in Los Angeles as a child. She never knew her father, her mother was a housemaid. When Ollie was twelve, her mother died mysteriously, she was pregnant at the time. Then Ollie went to live with her auntie Doreen, in Las Vegas. Doreen was also a housemaid, one of several to a wealthy family there. Ollie went to a local school and showed some early talent. When she was fifteen, the man of the house said he'd send her to the best private school in Las Vegas, but there'd be a cost; when his wife was away on her frequent business trips, Ollie would take her place in his bed. Auntie Doreen determined that the price was worth paying. Ollie paid it right through school."

The minister looked at the floor and shook his head. Steve knew that the lyonpo's daughter was in senior high in Colorado.

"Her Las Vegas family was big on aquariums," Nigel went on. "When Ollie wasn't studying or attending to the man of the house, she'd spend hours listening to music and just staring at tropical fish. She learnt those fish came from the Visayas, that they're captured with cyanide poisoning, that the poisoning has destroyed hundreds of miles of coral reef."

Nigel turned to the police chief. "It's easier to be poor in some places than others. At private school in Las Vegas, it's not easy to be the daughter of a housekeeper, so Ollie invented a better story for her life. It was a story that never left her. If she'd have got out of here last night, she was going to Singapore, and then she was taking twenty million dollars with her to the Visayas. She said that it was more than enough to look after herself there, and there'd be money left over. She'd start income generating projects for poor fishing families, families whose livelihoods have been ruined by dying coral reefs.

His story finished, Nigel put his pipe in his mouth and sucked at it like a dummy. Every head bent to avoid eye contact. Tobgay looked at his feet and said, "Poor Ollie."

"Ollie gave you some photographs." Nigel said to Steve. "She asked me to make sure they've been delivered."

Michael James cut in. "I've got them and I want to keep them. I want to know why she did it. Why she'd hate Narguli enough to get Devi and Anika involved."

Nigel closed his eyes and squeezed his top lip under his bottom lip. "Certainly, sir. Umm, perhaps you and I could talk privately?"

James frowned, then checked his watch again. "Say it now, man. For God's sake, get on with it."

If James had rebuked him, Nigel missed it. He smiled, "As you wish, sir." He leaned forward, his tie dangled between his knees. "In her first year at the bank, Ollie averaged over eighty hours a week. The harder she worked, the less Narguli did. When it came time for her first annual review, Narguli invited her to his apartment for dinner. That night she was left in no doubt that if she wanted a good report, she'd share his bed."

The minister broke a deep silence. "That's dreadful." Steve looked over at Michael James. His teeth were gritted and every muscle in his huge body seemed tensed.

"She was sick of men using her," Nigel said. "She decided soon after that first night, she'd use Narguli. She didn't try to frame him for the twenty million, she knew the bank would see through that, but she did want revenge. The photos were her way of getting it. Apparently, for the ten thousand Ollie paid Anika, she agreed to tell her story. Narguli had trapped her the same way. And worse still, seven years ago, Devi's first job at the bank was under Narguli. Under him in more ways than one. The three of them hate him so much they'd do anything to see him gone, including posing nude in Narguli's bedroom when he was on mission."

Nigel turned to Michael James. "When Ollie answers for her crimes, she wants to make sure that Narguli answers for his."

No one wanted to be the first to speak. Michael James twisted the three rings on his middle three fingers one at a time, then he adjusted the cufflinks that were expensively prominent under the sleeve of his tailored dark suit. Finally, he cleared his throat and said, "Thank you, Nigel. We'll talk later."

He let a long silence sit there, then shifted his gaze to Steve. "Andrews, your reputation and TRANSARCO's have been damaged by all this."

Steve straightened his shoulders and sat upright. After all he'd been through, surely this would be his moment in the sun. He'd get a written apology from the Bank at the very least. Maybe more.

Michael James didn't say 'sorry'. Instead he outlined the legalities and probable trial process for Ollie and left Steve in no doubt that he'd be fully involved. At TRANSARCO's own cost of course. MJ got to his feet abruptly, his huge hand around his cell phone like he had hold of a snake's neck, "Now, the Lyonpo, Nigel and I are going to find Narguli." The Lyonpo and Nigel also stood. The meeting was finished.

61: *A golden yoke tied with a white silken knot*

Tobgay rested a heavy hand on Steve's shoulder and chirped, birdlike, "Well, Andrews, good meeting, huh. We see you at trial, huh?"

Steve gulped. "Yeah, ah, my passport, Dasho?"

Tobgay rearranged the belt over his copious belly and grinned. He put his fat hand inside his gho and brought out a blue covered passport. Ever the policeman, he opened the front cover to check that he had the right one. With a flourish of his hand he passed it across and said, "On Steve's project, the missing money we find. Here's the passport that he lent me, thanks for being so kind." He burst out laughing, his belly shook and his face went red, then purple. "You good sport, Andrews," he said and put his hand on Steve's shoulder.

The minister thanked Steve and they shook hands. He said what a pleasure it had been to meet Sophie and shook her hand too. As he made ready to leave, Lyonpo Rinchen Dorji turned back to Steve. "TRANSARCO's made the shortlist for the Upper Bumthang Bridge project. I expect you'll lead the bidding, Steve?"

Steve and Sophie stood on the narrow roadway outside. Steve squinted in the bright sunlight and loosened his tie. He undid the top button of his shirt. He was too stunned to speak, too many things had happened too quickly.

Sophie took his hand and squeezed it. "It'll work out."

"Will it?" Steve dropped Sophie's hand and jammed two fists into the pockets of his pants.

They walked in silence toward the compound car park. Then Steve said abruptly, an unmistakable challenge in his voice, "Why didn't you tell me you knew that guy? Did he get you my itinerary?"

"Umm…Yeah!" Sophie turned to him then turned away. "I thought of telling you about Michael when we were in Trongsa, but I didn't know how you'd take it, what you'd think. I was even worried that you'd get suspicious about why I was here."

"Like, I might think you were part of an investigation?" Steve said.

"Maybe, and anyway I knew Michael was only one of four executive directors. I wasn't sure he'd be involved until I called work on Monday night. Believe me, Steve, I wouldn't trick you like that."

"Yeah, okay," Steve said, "but you could have said something."

"I tried to tell you at the restaurant this morning, but you were too preoccupied to listen."

Steve thought back, his mind had been in such a jumble, he could easily have missed it. He said, still with a hint of disbelief, "So, he'd already told you everything he knew?"

"No! When I called him, he'd already left. I got his office, all that they'd tell me was that he was already in Bhutan, and that you weren't guilty. That you'd get your passport back. The only thing I knew that you didn't was the name of the Director that was coming here, and I promised to keep that quiet. Remember, it was Karma that told you he was here."

"Well, what about when he said, 'How's Alex.' That's not your ex-husband, is it? Don't tell me you work with a guy you were married to?"

Sophie stopped while he walked on.

Steve turned, "Well?"

She tilted her head. "Okay, I won't tell you." She walked up next to him. "But when you come to Washington I'll introduce you."

Steve had to grin, but he pushed his hands deeper into his pockets and quickened his pace. Something else rankled. "So, you knew Ollie's story already?"

"Listen!" Sophie grabbed hold of his arm and stopped him, pulling him round to face her. "I said Ollie's story may not be all that it seems, but I'm just as surprised as you are — if that makes you feel better."

"I don't know how I feel."

"Me neither," Sophie said.

"If you hadn't phoned the bank, she might have got across the border into India. They'd never have found her then." He smiled at the irony of it.

Sophie laughed, "I told you I had a good reason for coming here."

⚘

As they walked across the car park they talked about the trial and what might happen to Ollie. Steve feared the worst, but Sophie wasn't so sure. She said, "The police chief mentioned the trial would be here. I read somewhere that the crest of Bhutan's High Court is a golden yoke tied with a white silken knot."

Steve turned. "A silken knot?"

"Yes. A silken knot which can be loosened. Loosened to remind that despite the severity of the crime, sometimes compassion is required."

Steve caught the glint in Sophie's eye. He knew what she was thinking. 'It could only happen in Bhutan!'

With the Landcruiser and Karma in sight, but out of earshot Sophie asked, "So what happens now?"

"I don't know," Steve said. "Let's just go to Paro. I'll forget all about it until tomorrow."

355

"Sure, but after lunch. Remember I want to meet up with my trekking group."

Steve and Sophie both got into the back seat. Karma kept his eyes on the wheel as they drove out of the compound. "Yes sir, where we go?"

Steve got the hint immediately, Karma was his driver, not his chauffeur. "Sorry Karma," Steve said, "let's get Sophie's things from the Zangbo, then you can take her to the River-View Hotel. I'll stay at the Zangbo. I've got to call home and Rawlinson, then I'll pack and check out."

Karma nodded. "And after?"

"We'll go to Paro. We're climbing to the Tiger's Nest this afternoon and staying there tonight."

Farley, at the head of the table, was the first to see her. He called out across the otherwise empty room, "Sophie we're over here, come join us."

Sophie walked across the familiar dragon-patterned carpet and into the RiverView restaurant, which afforded spectacular views over the city and across the mountain range to the north. She grinned again at the irony of it; to begin it had rankled with her that it wasn't called the CityView or the Mountain-View, but now, after a week or so in Bhutan, it seemed perfectly natural to call a restaurant RiverView and not have a river in sight.

They all stood to greet her. She sat next to Farley and he took the liberty of stealing a kiss. For the next hour or so, Sophie was treated to a minute-by-minute account of what she'd missed. The trek had been the most exciting, wonderful, challenging, dramatic thing that any of them had ever done. Anna was beaming at the other end of the table; she'd enjoyed the trek too, unusually so.

After they'd eaten, Anna got up to leave, she had things to do. As soon as she'd gone, Farley said what a great leader Anna was, how she'd forded raging rivers and climbed hills so steep they were more than vertical.

Then Nancy spoke on behalf of the Philadelphians. "And of course we can't forget Farley's contribution. There was hardly a tree or a shrub or a flower he didn't know the name of. You don't know what you missed, dear."

"Hear, hear," Jim said. Then as Farley tried to avoid the limelight, Sophie heard that he'd been offered a part-time job with Mountain Adventures. He'd be accompanying botanical tours to Bhutan, twice a year.

"He'll even get paid for it," Nancy said.

When they were all talked out, the Philadelphians excused themselves. Farley and Sophie sat alone in the large restaurant. He offered her more tea, she declined. More coffee? No thanks.

"Everything all right?" he asked.

"Couldn't be better," she replied.

"Tell me about your week," he said. She smiled and avoided the question. "Why'd you leave Jakar to come back here?" He went on, "Your note to Anna said you came back with Steve?"

She said there wasn't much to tell, it hadn't been anything like as exciting as the trek, but she'd achieved her purpose, she was happy enough.

"And Steve?" Farley asked.

"Leaving tomorrow."

Farley wasn't going to stop there. Did Sophie really think he could be so easily put off the trail? He remarked on how relaxed she looked after the week with Steve, then asked, "Are you seeing him again?"

"Yes."

"Oh, that's great. When?"

"This afternoon." Sophie said.

"Speaking of Steve, I've got a confession to make," Farley said in a hushed tone. He asked her to come closer. "You remember I promised not to tell anyone, about your daughter. Well, I had too much to drink one night on the trek, umm, I accidentally told Anna."

Sophie made sure her face was immediately stern and unforgiving, her eyes piercing.

He stuttered and stumbled, "I didn't realize Cognac was so strong, I've never had spirits before, honestly…I'm so sorry."

She laughed and said, "I'll forgive you…but just this once." And before Farley could ask another question she said, "What about you, Farley. You're a different person."

"Heck, thanks."

"I'll bet Georgie sees the difference."

"Yeah," Farley said, "she might."

"What? She was your reason for coming here. Didn't you want to prove yourself to her?"

Farley pushed back in his chair. "I may not even tell Georgie I've been here."

"Farley! Why?"

Farley smiled, and took his time to reply. "Anna says polygamy might work here, but it wouldn't work for us back in New York."

62: The Tiger's Nest

Steve had made his calls, checked out, paid his bill from a stack of ngultrums, thanked Namgay for all his help and was waiting in the car park when Karma returned. Sophie stayed in the front seat while Steve's luggage was loaded. Namgay and his staff were assembled on the front stairs and there was waving aplenty as the Landcruiser drove slowly out of the Zangbo onto Chorten Lam.

While Karma was busily dodging Tata trucks, buses, cows, children, chatting neighbors standing at roadside and potholes, Steve asked Sophie, "How was Farley?" Sophie began, "You won't believe this," and the tone of her voice lifted steadily as her story of Farley's exploits unfolded. When Farley's epiphany was recounted, even Karma, who'd never met the man, laughed aloud.

Moments later, Sophie grabbed the panic bar as Karma swung wildly off to the side, missing a small tractor and trailer by inches. When they came back onto the narrow strip of blacktop, she turned to Steve. "Did you call home?"

"Yeah, I got through okay. Ric's a good kid. He understands...I think."

"What about Rawlinson" Sophie said. "Did you get him?"

"He was in too much of a hurry to talk." Steve laughed. "He needed to contact his broker and put a HOLD on the SELL order he'd placed for his TRANSARCO stock. Then he was going to a farewell for Martin and Tammy. They're leaving Trashigang later today."

They passed Simthoka Dzong and not another word was spoken. Karma pushed the cassette tape into the player, the sound of waves on the shoreline filled the car. Karma spoke as if in a dream, "Mr. Steve, I'm saving my ngultrums sir, I'll be

'On the Beach' one day. I'll walk with my feet bare in the blue ocean water and feel sand between my toes. I might take all three wives, one day."

The music played and the miles went by. The river valley below them widened and narrowed, the road clung precariously to the steep hillsides and Steve's thoughts turned to the afternoon ahead. Here was his chance to reconnect with what had begun before breakfast. But should he have told Sophie first that the Tiger's Nest was nearly three thousand feet above the valley floor, almost straight up?

As Paro town came into view, Steve and Karma discussed the best place to buy some chocolate, biscuits and cheese, some bottled water. "A few things for the walk," Steve said innocently.

"Karma, in Bhutan, when does a walk become a trek?" Sophie said tongue-in-cheek.

Steve laughed and asked Karma's opinion on how long the walk might take.

"It takes the locals six hours up and back," Karma said.

"Good," Steve replied, "We'll do it in four," and he watched Sophie hold her breath and start turning purple.

When he added, "Anyway there's still a full moon. Even if we walk back in the dark, it'll be fun," Sophie exhaled through pursed lips, and said, "If this is like Central America, where short walks with you became expeditions, I'll..."

Steve put his hand on her shoulder from the back seat, "I'll carry you."

Sophie turned to Karma. "Karma, how did the Tiger's Nest get its name?"

Karma rolled his eyes and nodded his head side to side, he paused. "Dangbo dingbo, a long time ago. The Tiger's Nest, or Taktshang Monastery, was built over three hundred years ago, but the story starts in the eighth century when Guru Rinpoche brought Buddhism to Bhutan. In those days this valley was a trade route between Bhutan and Tibet, but it was also an opening for attack. Tibet and Bhutan fought many wars. On the Guru's third visit here, he flew to Paro on the back of a flying tiger."

Sophie looked out at the broad sweep of valley they were in, "Hmmm."

"But even flying tigers need to rest somewhere. So to be safe from the Tibetans, the tiger perched high on the cliff-side and rested there. Guru Rinpoche meditated in a cave nearby. The monastery is named after the tiger's resting place."

"Do monks still live there?" Sophie asked.

"Yes Miss Sophie, it is the most sacred religious place in Bhutan."

"Are foreigners allowed inside?"

"In tour groups, no," Karma said. "But one chilip…maybe. It all depends on the monks."

The afternoon was perfect for walking. It was sunny but not too hot, there was a light breeze and to begin, the trail was easy. They crossed the river on a footbridge, prayer flags fluttered in the breeze and their pace was relaxed. Once across the river they climbed gently through roughly fenced fields, below them, farmers tilled the land with oxen pulling wooden ploughs.

The narrow trail soon took them from fields to forest. A girl of perhaps seven came downhill toward them, she wore a tattered kira and led a pack-horse by a single strand of rope. They exchanged greetings and Sophie fell into an easy rhythm. Sophie led, Steve was a few feet behind her. The narrow foot-trail followed the point of a steep ridge, Steve said, "You promised to tell me about Marie."

Sophie stopped in the middle of the trail, but didn't turn. "I'm sorry we didn't have time to talk it through this morning."

"Well!" Steve reached out and put his hands around her waist. "Now we've got all day, and I want to hear everything before we call her."

So as Sophie put one foot in front of the other a thousand times or more, she talked. It suited her that Steve couldn't see her face. She began by telling him about her phone call home that morning, how excited Marie had been when she'd learned that they'd met. She told him just how much Marie wanted to meet her father.

"Where to begin?" Sophie said. "She was born in Napa, Mom, and Dad while he was alive, were fantastic and my brothers and their wives were too. She had a happy childhood, lots of cousins around and always someone to cuddle her and take an interest. She lived on the vineyard until she was three. Mom did most of the mothering, I was studying."

They entered a small clearing, a family of four were sitting on the grass taking a late tiffin. Greetings were exchanged as they walked by.

Sophie picked up her story. "After Mom died, Marie and I moved to Washington. She's done all her schooling there. She graduated mid-year and did well, but didn't want to go straight to college. That's when I agreed on the gap year, including the trip to Bali."

Steve asked about her plans, what she might study at college, how long she'd be studying Indonesian. He asked about sports, music, her likes and dislikes, then he said. "Anyone special in her life, a boyfriend?"

"Hey," Sophie chided playfully, "you're starting to sound like the worried father of a teenage girl!"

"Yeah, might be."

"Well relax, she's very independent...she's learnt to look after herself."

"Just like her mother, huh?"

"Maybe, I'm not so..." She stopped above him on the steep trail and turned. He reached up, put his arms around her and pulled her closer. She said, seriously, "I want to tell Marie about us, but what do I say?" She let the moment linger. "Steve, where do *we* go from here?"

"Where else," he said grinning, not wanting to spoil the moment. "To the top."

"No. Be serious."

"I am!" He placed two fingers gently on her lips. "Let's leave the future where it belongs."

She pulled away. Huffed. "I can't, not after..." A stirring of the loving they'd shared was somehow uneasy within her.

"Hey," he said. "I know what's on your mind...believe me, we'll never answer that question here."

She began, "Where then?" But he was already moving.

63: *Two Roads*

The trail tilted sharply upward. Sophie was panting, it was now climbing rather than walking. She was in the lead, she carefully placed each step on the trail, even a stumble would be wasted energy. The trail came around the point of the ridge, then it followed the contour. There was a clearing up ahead, Sophie pointed and gasped, "Let's rest up there, please."

At the clearing, Steve dropped the daypack. Sophie sank onto a patch of grass, he sat beside her. They looked out over the valley and caught their breath.

Steve opened the daypack. "We're making good time."

"Yeah," Sophie said as she panted for breath. "How many feet do we climb from the valley?"

"Ah, Are you sure you want to know?"

"Yes, I've got to convince my legs they can do it."

Steve put his arm around her and pulled her close, "Nearly three thousand."

Sophie leant on his shoulder and sighed, "I should have known better." They shared some chocolate and bottled water and he helped her to stand on aching feet.

Sophie commented on the merging of the broadleaf forest with spruce and hemlock, and noticed mosses and herbs growing in protected areas on the cold ground. Each and every step was an effort and her calf muscles were screaming for her to stop. Steve led, Sophie was right behind him, she dared not let the distance between them grow. Sophie glanced up, she noticed a small monument on the peak of the ridge they were approaching. "A chorten," she pointed up ahead. "That must mark something."

Steve held out his hand and helped her take the last two steps to the chorten. The first thing that hit them when they stopped was the cold. Even though the weakening afternoon sun was still over the valley, the altitude effect was chilling. Steve swung off the daypack and helped Sophie into her jacket before putting on his own. "Hold me," Sophie said as she put her arm around him. He hugged her close, "We're almost there."

The Tiger's Nest was at about the same height as them, but across a sharp valley. To get there they had to descend and climb back up again. The trail was cut into the side of a sheer cliff, it led down precariously, edged around past a small stream falling down from the towering mountain above, then climbed again to the monastery.

They huddled against the cold. Steve said, "Ready?"

Sophie pulled him closer. "Do you think it's safe?"

"Has that ever worried us before?" Steve whispered and kissed her ear. The trail was narrower than it looked at first sight, Steve reached back to take her hand. "Don't look down, just watch your feet."

They edged around and down, each step seeming to take them further away from their destination. They came to the stream, a prayer wheel was being turned by the water flowing past it. The monastery was just up ahead, but the trail was narrower, even more exposed, below them the sheer cliff fell away to nothing. Sophie's eyes were firmly on the monastery, she was going to get there, turning back was not an option. They edged further up the steep trail, hugging back against the sheer wall of the cliff. There were ancient stone steps ahead, the lower temple of the Tiger's Nest was right there above them.

Up close, the impossibility of the place was stark. What had appeared from a distance as one building turned out to be a series of joined, but separate temples. Each temple sat on a narrow ledge, somehow it was all tied into the wall of the mountain. Below was a sheer drop of perhaps four hundred feet. Cloud and mist swirled below them, the late afternoon sun was but a pale reminder of the warmth of the day. They hadn't seen anyone on the trail for two hours and the monastery appeared deserted.

Sophie took hold of his arm. "Let's climb the steps. You said we'd go all the way."

"Okay." He laughed, "You first."

Sophie led and at the third last step, the huge wooden doors began to creak open. A lone monk of perhaps twenty-five peered out through the crack in the door. His smile was welcoming, his robes jostled in the wind. Though the monk said nothing, they felt beckoned to enter. She looked at Steve, her eyes said 'yes'. He took her hand, they climbed the last few steps and walked in through the massive doors. Still the monk said nothing. He closed the doors behind them, they shut with a leaden clunk.

Inside was another set of stairs. At the top they turned around to find they were alone again. An eerie silence seeped from every corner, it hung from every wooden rafter. Ahead was a courtyard paved in moss covered stone. Clouds swirled within the inner recesses of the monastery, a faint chanting could be heard and the smell of butter lamps came and went on the gently moving air.

They crossed the courtyard and entered the inner sanctum of the temple. Sophie heard a noise behind them, she turned in an instant. The young monk was back with them.

"What brings you here?" the monk said with no discernible accent. His robes were rustled by the cold breeze, his shaven head and feet were bare.

Sophie looked to Steve, then back to the monk, she said, "Oh…we're just ordinary tourists…on an extra-ordinary journey."

The monk considered Sophie's reply and looked to Steve.

"That's about it," Steve said and took Sophie's arm, "we're calling our daughter later, we wanted something interesting to tell her about."

The faintest of smiles came then went and the monk said, "On your next extra-ordinary journey, perhaps you will take your daughter with you?" He gestured to one side of the inner temple, "but now, to complete this journey, you must climb the tower. The view from there is forever."

A set of wooden stairs rose steeply then disappeared into a slatted wooden roof far above them. Sophie tested the first stair, it creaked and groaned, but it held. They climbed warily at first, then with confidence. Soft evening light filtered through the void above them, beckoning them. At the top, Steve put his hands either side of a narrow rectangular hole and lifted himself through. He knelt and took Sophie's hand, she climbed through and felt the ancient wisdom of the place like a prayer.

They stood on a weathered wooden platform, above them was a shingled roof. Sophie moved toward a low wooden barrier encircling the deck they were on. She walked to it, sat, and dangled her legs over the edge of the world. Steve sat by her side. An orange sun arched over Tibet. All of Bhutan lay before them, its mystery surrounded them; it was within them, now part of them. Steve put his arm around Sophie and drew her closer. Time stopped. Clouds swirled under them. The only sound was of distant chanting. "Om Mani Padme Hung. Om Mani..."

Sophie rested her head on Steve's shoulder, she said, "I wish a flying tiger would come and take us both away."

"Why?"

"Because tomorrow the real world begins again. Tomorrow, you and I will be back on two different roads."

Steve took her hand in his and said, "Up here there are no roads. Today, anything's possible."

About the Author

Philip Montgomery has travelled extensively for work and leisure across the Himalaya, through China, India and Nepal and in the 1990's he began visiting Bhutan regularly in the pretelevision, internet and mobile phone era. Philip has worked in international development for over twenty years as a technical specialist, project manager, bid writer and negotiator. He lives with his family and a border collie called Monty, in the Southern Highlands, near Sydney, Australia.

www.ingramcontent.com/pod-product-compliance
Lightning Source LLC
Chambersburg PA
CBHW020324180626
46812CB00001B/35

* 9 7 8 0 9 8 7 0 5 1 7 1 4 *